WHAT HAPPENED TO US?

Faith Hogan

HEAD of ZEUS

A catalogue record for this book is available from
the British Library.

ISBN (TPB): 9781838930653
ISBN (E): 9781788548588

Typeset by Siliconchips Services Ltd UK

Printed and bound in Great Britain by
CPI Group (UK) Ltd, Croydon CR0 4YY

MIX
Paper from
responsible sources
FSC® C020471

Head of Zeus Ltd
First Floor East
5–8 Hardwick Street
London EC1R 4RG

WWW.HEADOFZEUS.COM

WHAT HAPPENED TO US?

For the Aria Girls –
Caroline, Sarah, Nikky, Jade, Geo, Sue, Michelle,
Vicky, Hannah and Melanie –
Thank You!

1

Dublin

The first night of winter and it was wet, very wet, and she knew the rain was pouring in drops down her face, could feel them drip, drip, dripping off the end of her nose. She could feel the tears too, hot and stingy in her eyes. Someone had given her a cigarette, miraculously she'd managed to smoke halfway down, but it was soggy and extinguished now, which was no bad thing. She never smoked, why add to her list of failures at this late stage?

At the far end of the lane, something or someone caught her eye, but she must be mistaken, because who in their right mind would be out on an evening like this? Probably a stray cat, attracted by the heat and aromas that emanated from the fans blowing into the frigid night air.

Her thoughts darted back to the kitchen behind her, Kevin, bloody Kevin. Well, she hadn't seen that coming had she? She was still reeling, angry, upset and, yes, she could admit it to herself, broken-hearted. And Valentina? Kevin was in love with Valentina, he'd told her, so it must be true.

She raised the dead cigarette to her lips once more,

hardly noticed that it tasted disgusting. He'd only met her a few months ago, that was when she came to work in the restaurant. The girl, that's all she was, in her mid-twenties at most, but she looked no more than seventeen, had hardly a word of English four months ago. Yet, here Valentina and Kevin had become an item. How did that work? Oh, maybe she knew the answer to that already.

Things had cooled off a long time ago between Carrie and Kevin. She never counted the fact that they didn't have children. No reason, just one of those things, it never happened, she knew that to Kevin it was a relief. They settled onto their path, confident it would lead them to a contented old age. If the road markings she always took for granted were stolen from her, she blocked out her childlessness with the success of the restaurant and a gratitude for the simple things in life. Yet somewhere between moving in together and working sixteen hours a day to get the restaurant up and running, they had lost each other. Funny, but they spent so much time together that they managed to lose their connection. He'd started sleeping in the spare room when her snoring became too loud. He didn't say it was because she had become overweight and the bottle of wine each evening didn't help either. She was fast to point out her sinuses were playing up and what could she do about it? She'd been a little relieved, to tell the truth. He had a habit of leaving hair oil all over the pillows, so she felt like she was wearing half a pot of Brylcreem most days.

It was still a shock though.

It was less than forty-eight hours ago.

They had walked into her office; bold as brass, the pair of them, holding hands.

'There's something I need to tell you, Carrie.' He'd had the good grace to look embarrassed.

'It is only fair, it is only right.' Valentina was contrite, her dusky Colombian voice, throaty and whispering. Did they want her blessing?

'Nothing has happened, but...' Kevin looked down at his hand, joined tight with Valentina's. Well that was a lie straight off.

'Really, nothing has happened?' Carrie looked deep into his eyes, managed to keep the tears from her own. It wasn't hard, she probably should have been angry or distraught, but somehow, she just felt numb.

'No, I mean...' Kevin looked at Valentina, his slack-jawed face was pleading for help.

Carrie had known him long enough to read him like a book. What a pity she hadn't kept her eyes on the pages, she thought.

'Kevin, please.' She wasn't begging him, but the least he owed her was the truth. 'This place, Kevin, all the years, all the days and nights of work... at least be honest with me.'

'We... I didn't want to hurt you. I couldn't... I mean, I can't help it. We're in love, Carrie, and it's a while since I felt this way.'

'I see.' Funny, but having it confirmed did not make it any better. This place, her office, had suddenly felt like none of it was hers anymore. That was just absurd though. It was hers, every bit of it, the restaurant, the five stars, the whole business from start to finish, she had built it up. Kevin might have been the talent, he might have been the toast of the Dublin foodie scene, but she was the brains behind the operation. Kevin was the technical force, but everything else in this business was down to her. She'd picked the building, the art on the walls, she'd organised launches and managed to get the press to feature them. She'd chosen the tablecloths and ordered the wines and she did the hiring and firing. She'd hired Valentina because she came with good references. Of course, she was a stunner, everything about her was glossy, as if she had been dipped in polish; inky black hair, a wide vermillion smile and impossibly white teeth. She slunk about the restaurant, weaving her curves through the tables and flirting throatily with everyone she met. The customers loved a bit of glamour about the place. She was smart too, and from the moment she set foot in the restaurant, Carrie had a feeling that one day, Valentina could be capable of running somewhere every bit as good as 'The Sea Pear', but this was the last thing she had expected.

'Is that all you can say, "*I see*",' Kevin looked like a five-year-old, waiting for a scolding after walking muddy shoes across the kitchen floor.

'Well, it's a shock, obviously.' Carrie had managed to look him in the eye, but she would not cry, not before them. They'd left with light steps and the soft click of the door behind them.

It took two days. It was unreal of course, those two

days; Kevin had not come home. Carrie assumed he was staying with Valentina – where else? Maybe that incongruity had stoppered her rage, because she knew she had every right to be angry with him – with both of them. Instead, by going on as if things were completely normal, showing up for work and still keeping out of each other's way, it felt as though her fury was in a vacuum. Somehow it seemed irrational to cry and scream and wipe the floor with them as she knew they deserved.

They'd gone through their usual routines, arrived at work at the normal time, Carrie spoke with staff and customers with her usual charm, like nothing had changed. Kevin stayed in the safety of the kitchen, immersed in the nuts and bolts of keeping orders moving through to his own exacting standards. Then today, the dam had somehow washed through and as she'd walked through the kitchen, she saw them. It was all very casual. He was checking sauces, Valentina was handing him seasoning and as she placed her hand on his arm, there was just a glance. It was a fleeting look that said so much more than they managed to convey a couple of days earlier when they told her. It was filled with intimacy, charged with chemistry and Carrie could see it was fuelled by alliance. It suddenly struck her, the thing that she managed to ignore for two whole days. It dawned on her, that it was not just that her relationship of over a decade had died a lingering death until it's final cruel severing, that was not what tipped her emotions over in the end. Rather it was realising that Kevin and Valentina were a couple and she was trapped here with the two of them.

She'd run to the back door, flung herself through it. She'd needed air, suddenly, she was stifled with heat, misery and a dreadful tightening in her gut that she knew was something close to emotional claustrophobia. One of the cleaners had been sheltering, smoking a rolled-up cigarette. It could have been a joint for all Carrie knew. He'd tapped open a bruised-looking tin box and handed one across to her, lit it silently with his back crouched over it against the bitter night and left her to it. The door had banged heavily in his wake, and here she'd stood for almost twenty minutes while watery sleet pelted from the heavens.

The evening was beginning to darken, the sky menaced layers of gloomy grey that would not push over until they had blown Dublin inside out. Carrie pushed back her fiery curly hair from her face, the sleet against her cheeks like icy cold slaps that she hoped might snap her out of this nightmare. She tried to imagine that far above the clouds, a blue sky with the sun shining waited to impart some light. She couldn't come near to mustering up the image.

Again, at the far end of the lane, something moved in the dusky shadows, she was sure of it now. Suddenly, she became aware that she was standing sodden and alone in a downpour, looking like an out-of-condition wet T-shirt wannabe. She had to make a choice, go back into the busy kitchen, looking like a drowned rabbit and face Kevin and Valentina or stay here with whoever was lurking about down the lane. The shape was tall, dark, and suddenly a little intimidating.

Carrie quickly pulled the restaurant door, but it was stuck. The cleaner must have let the lock slip in his haste to get away from her. To be fair, she'd probably scared the wits out of him, with her tear-filled eyes and spluttering sobs and now the man – it was definitely a man – was moving towards her. He was dressed in black and he certainly didn't look like the type to be hanging about dark alleys, but then, who knew what he was up to? This was a dead-end alleyway; it led nowhere but to the back doors of businesses. Anyone lurking about down here was either up to no good or making plans to get up to no good.

Anxious and panic-stricken, she turned towards the door, pulled at it furiously, but there was no budging it. Fear tore up through her, threatening to overtake her, she fought the urge to scream, where had the bloody key gone? Carrie began to thump loudly on the door. She wasn't thinking rationally now – she was hardly breathing, never mind thinking. Her logical self was so consumed in just going through the motions these last few days, it meant that she was unusually jittery. It felt as though her natural equilibrium had tilted over, so shadows made her jump, loud noises tripped her up and anything out of the ordinary caused her stomach to turn to a knotty fist. She tried not to picture the stranger advancing at her back in the sleeting rain, with the city a soundless far-off cry.

Carrie filled with fear. Unreasonable as it might be, she just expected the worst on this black night. 'Don't come near me, I'll scream,' she said the words softly, but inside they were already shattering through her brain.

He stopped at the bins, lingered for a moment and she realised, he was looking for something. He turned and, as their eyes locked, she could see he was weary. That realisation didn't exactly foster any sense of civic duty, rather the terror that had filled her up turned to a frantic dread. She banged on the metal door, louder now so it echoed out above the sleet. She closed her eyes, fully expecting the worst. They wouldn't hear her inside. The kitchen was loud and busy and its walls held captive the sound from outside. Kevin was preparing mains for a full house; he wouldn't notice her rattling against the outer door. She laughed, a nervous wretched sound, he didn't notice her when she was standing in front of him these days, not now Valentina was on the scene, it was ludicrous. Madness to think he might come to her rescue now.

It was useless. She turned, accepting her fate. He probably carried a knife; you never knew, after all...

Oh, God, the most terrible thought, all those serial killers, they looked normal, average, even maybe attractive, it was how they lured their victims in. This was the kind of man, tall, handsome, brooding, he could be...

She opened her eyes to see him, just a little distance from her, he was bending down, fiddling on the step near her feet by the pot the staff used for collecting used cigarette ends. He turned abruptly. Something glinted in his hands. She could see the light of it cast up before him, too dull to gleam, but there all the same. She felt weak, but she would not close her eyes again. He stood before her now, taller than her, broader, solemn. In that moment, she thought his face and body were so close, she could smell him. It was a wafting sense of soap, but she felt light-headed and weak with fear and knew she must have imagined it. Then the oddest thing, his eyes, dark and almost shaded in the half-light, creased just a little at the sides. He was smiling at her, holding something before him and smiling. She pulled her eyes from his and looked down. It was a key. He was holding a key; he must have pulled it from beside the pot.

'Here,' his voice was hoarse and heavy, maybe darker than his eyes, but they danced with an emotion she could not name. He handed her the key and stepped back from her, their eyes still locked.

Then, she turned quickly, thrust the key in the lock and pushed the heavy door. Suddenly, she was in the hot kitchen, wafting aromas of beef and fish and pork filling her nostrils. Everyone working busily at their stations. They didn't notice her, standing there, wet, scared and miserable.

Then she realised, she'd never said thank you. She'd never thanked the man. Perhaps she should offer him something, food or at least a cup of tea? She stood for a moment, dripping on the non-slip tiles that Kevin was so obsessed with keeping dry. She watched him now, he moved about the kitchen with the kind of deftness and speed that only shaved past others, while all the time checking over shoulders and seeing to his own tasks. He was immune to the people around him. He worked the restaurant like an intricate dance routine, chopping, slicing, stirring, spinning, weaving, smelling and tasting. It was so unlike Carrie's role and she realised that a moment ago her reaction outside the door had been classic Kevin. Kevin expected nothing from people, he begrudged paying a decent wage to his employees and he assumed that most people he met would take rather than give.

Carrie drew her breath in sharply. She would not become like him now, not just because she was broken-hearted or anxious or... Well, whatever she was – she was holding onto the basic human decency that separated the happy from the empty.

She had to say thanks. Without the key, she would still be there, locked out and forced to walk around the front, in through the crowded restaurant looking a mess. She opened the door quickly, the rush of cold air an instant souvenir of what she'd just escaped. She looked up and down the laneway, stepped outside for just a moment and scanned every crevice along the route. It was snowing now, silent and empty, the only sound a whimpering dog that nosed out from beneath the huge wheelie bin opposite.

'Aw,' she heard the sound escape from where it had lodged at the back of her throat. Carrie dashed across the alley, grabbed the little dog, pulling him out from his abysmal sheltering spot. He nuzzled her neck; they were as wet and miserable as each other, but he was friendless and vulnerable. When she rested her chin on his head, he was soft and silken-haired despite the dirt.

She stood for a moment looking about her in the

hollow darkness. 'Hello, is there anyone there?' She called out to see if the man might step forward again to claim this little dog.

There was no sign of anyone in the alley now, only Carrie standing in the shaft of light and wafting steam at the wedged door. She searched the darkened corners with eyes that stung from salty pathetic tears, but deep down, she knew, he was gone.

It was over a long time before Valentina walked into the restaurant. It was over between him and Carrie, probably for years. The truth was, he needed her and, as Valentina said, that's no basis for a relationship.

God, she was hot. Valentina was the love of his life, simple as that.

'It's just sex, mate.' His friend Jim said when he told him. Marriage and kids had made Jim philosophical about sex – these days he was more interested in football and property prices, or at least that's how it sounded to Kevin.

'It's not just sex, it's…' Kevin couldn't begin to explain to Jim. Jim above all people, with his safe marriage to Sandra and their two perfect children. 'It's the real thing. Valentina is the love of my life, the kind of woman every man wants on his arm.'

'Yeah, but not the kind we marry,' Jim muttered into his pint and Kevin knew it was only because most people settled for what they thought they deserved. Well, the worst was over now. He – or rather they – had told

Carrie. It wasn't even as bad as he'd expected, actually, she'd taken it rather well. He'd been steeling himself for weeks, if he was honest. It wasn't cowardice, so much as picking his moment. In the end, Valentina picked it for them and he knew it was for the best. No more sneaking around – the stress of all that, while no doubt it had added a risky excitement to the sex – he knew, he'd probably have a heart attack if he kept it up for much longer. Kevin just didn't have that additional layer to him that subterfuge required, although, he was flattered that Valentina assumed he might and that all this was standard for a man about town like himself.

'Pure and simple, I said it to you years ago. You and Carrie, too young to settle into all that happy families.' But of course, there was no family, just a partnership that never made it to a marriage. Sometimes, Kevin wondered why they hadn't married – perhaps Carrie had been waiting for him to ask? Of course, she must have known, after all these years, Kevin would never get around to asking. If they were to marry, it would be down to Carrie to organise it – and, of course, she never had.

'It wasn't just that,' Kevin said. He wanted to tell Jim that he'd pursued Valentina, had seduced her and set about staking his claim on the future that was assembling before him. Although, the truth was, they'd fallen into their relationship one night when Valentina had teased him into opening a bottle of red after everyone had left and they'd made ravenous love against the stairs in the restaurant. Red wine always made Kevin tipsy; he just didn't have the constitution for it. Even now, it was like a dream to Kevin. He was seducing this beautiful woman and he wasn't entirely sure how he'd managed it, but he could no more halt than the world would stop spinning.

'No, there was no family, but the restaurant that was your baby. It was hers too.' Jim shook his head, considered his pint of beer. 'I suppose you've thought about what will happen with that?'

'With the restaurant?' Kevin had thought about it, but not in any concrete way. First he'd had to tell Carrie, now that bit was over, they could make plans, decide what to do for the best.

'I can't see her walking away from it, and to be fair, you'd be mad to let her.'

'How do you mean?' Kevin was a little affronted.

'Mate, I've known you both a long time, remember, we go back to first-year catering college together. Without Carrie, you'd be like all those other guys. True, you have talent, but let's face it, Carrie is the brains behind the operation.'

'Hold on, Jim. It's my food people come for.'

'Yes, and they also go to the Shelbourne for food and to McDonald's. They go to your restaurant for the experience and that's everything from the food to the people-watching, to the comfy chairs and even just to have Carrie look after them.'

'Valentina is very good with the customers.' Kevin might have been insulted if anyone else had said those things, but with Jim, well, he was probably telling the truth.

'She may well be, but she's not Carrie.'

'God, no, she's definitely not Carrie.' Kevin smiled, remembering the way Valentina affected him. She did things slowly, spoke slowly, ate slowly. God, but she took off her clothes slowly. Each and every item hitting the ground, and his pulse began to beat rapidly just thinking about it.

'Stop it, you're torturing yourself.' Jim could read his thoughts almost as well as Carrie could. 'Actually, when I think about it, a Colombian hottie, you're bloody torturing me as well.' They sat for a while, looking at the giant TV over the bar, neither of them really following the game, both lost in thoughts of their own. 'You'll have to sort something with Carrie, mate.'

'I suppose.'

'There's no suppose about it. It's a right mess. There's the house, the business and then all the other stuff that's going to get tangled up in the crossfire.'

'What other stuff?' Kevin didn't want to hear this, probably it was to be expected, but why couldn't Jim just be happy for him, well, ideally, if he could be a little jealous too – it wasn't much to ask, was it?

'Have you forgotten Melissa and Ben's wedding?'

'Oh, Christ.' Kevin had completely forgotten Melissa and Ben's wedding. It was all planned, and as best friends of the bride and groom, Kevin and Carrie were asked to be maid of honour and best man. 'That'll be a bloody nightmare.'

'Ah well, fun and games,' Jim said, draining his pint. He nodded to the barman. 'Must be off, back to the old ball and chain,' he looked at his watch, 'getting late for you too, Romeo.' He slapped Kevin hard on the back. He took up his newspaper and headed into the night winds; leaving Kevin for another half-hour before he was due at the restaurant for the evening rush.

It was a mess. It was a right bloody mess, but he had no choice. He and Carrie were finished. He was in love with Valentina now and there was no going back. Not even for The Sea Pear.

God, The Sea Pear. They'd named the restaurant together. Had they been in love then? He thought they were, but it was nothing like with Valentina. Now, it seemed their restaurant would outlive whatever had drawn them together all those years ago. A favourite celebrity haunt, Carrie had furnished it with a mixture of classic modern cleanliness accented with the occasional antique worn down to just the right degree of easy charm. They had opened up when Dublin was crawling towards some kind of financial stability. While other haunts were closing their doors, The Sea Pear whispered a note of optimism amongst the set who never really felt the economic crash. They managed to get a pretty premises on Finch Street, close enough to Temple Bar for ambience, but far enough away to distance itself from the madding crowd. The building itself was perfect, set back from the neighbours on either side, it had a grandeur about it far beyond its size. With three small steps rising to its fanlight door and original carriage lamps either side, Carrie had made the most of the original facade without swamping it out with decorations it didn't need. Instead she kept things simple, the red brick was washed down each spring and, when the weather allowed, she set up bistro tables on the patch of grass outside. Since the city began to turn towards booming times again, the properties around them became packed with professional offices. These days, they were surrounded by financial services, solicitors and advertising companies who closed their doors at five each evening, even if their employees did not go home until much later. All but the shabby pub across the road had filled with young and wealthy customers only happy to wine and dine in one of the city's top eateries. Yes, The Sea Pear was a great success all right. They'd have to sort it out.

He would tell Carrie tonight that perhaps tomorrow, if it suited, he'd pop round to pick up some clothes. He needed clothes and he needed to clear a few things out of the house. The house was in both their names. He hadn't told Valentina that. He wasn't sure why, but he had a feeling it could cause a row and it was enough to be in the bad books with Carrie for now.

And Jim was right, he hadn't thought about Ben and Melissa either. He'd been in primary school with Ben. There was no way he could miss out on his wedding. They'd gone on holidays together, their first foreign trips as a couple were with Melissa and Ben. Perhaps Carrie wouldn't want to go? That would be great; Kevin was getting a warm feeling thinking about it. Carrie probably wouldn't want to go. They were holding it in one of the most splendid locations. Coole Castle had four hundred years of history and a pastry chef who could whip up desserts that were lighter than clouds, just west of Sligo town. Valentina would love it. Carrie had booked them a room for two nights, yonks ago. Well, there was no way she'd want to go now and no point letting the booking go to waste, right?

Right.

Kevin got up from his stool. Cleared his throat, half coughing to draw attention to the fact that he was leaving, he pulled his jacket from the hook on the wall beside him. The barman at the far end of the counter didn't notice he was finished. Kevin tried to grab his attention. He liked to feel he had the gratitude of the staff for spending time in their establishment. When there was no salute, he stuffed his arms into his jacket and headed out into the icy evening air.

Maybe Carrie would be happy to keep the house and pull out of The Sea Pear. Maybe. She hadn't said a word either way yet, so Kevin knew he might be able to talk her round. He could always talk Carrie round.

Jane Marchant wasn't sure, as she looked out of her sitting room window, if there was a movement in the street outside or not. It was dark, but the light dusting of sleet brightened the city and the streetlights – tall mock-Georgian beamers – cast their glow so there were no shadows. It wasn't the lighting that was the problem, Jane was sure of that, nor was it her view and there was absolutely nothing wrong with her eyesight. No, the problem on nights like these, and most days too if she was honest, lay somewhere altogether deeper.

Once, when she was younger, they'd have blamed her nerves – they were probably right. Things hadn't been the same since that awful night fifteen years ago, when she had lost her soulmate. Jane shivered, she was not cold, but it didn't do any good to think of things that upset her at this hour of the night. She turned from the window, pinching the heavy velveteen curtains in a hard bunch at their centre. She could stand there all night, if she let herself; it was a rabbit's hole lined with insecurity and carpeted with fear. She'd only just managed to get out of it once, and she was not going there again.

On the mantle, the carriage clock struck out midnight. She sighed, over halfway to daylight; it was what she'd always thought. The clock reminded her of Manus. It was a gift from his mother on their wedding day. Jane loved that clock, it was probably the most precious thing Theresa Marchant had had to her name. A family heirloom, really, brought over from France after the Great War, by her brother. It was a measure of the family. The only thing Theresa had had of any great value and she gave it freely to her daughter-in-law. Jane knew she'd been lucky, Manus had taken after his mother and their lives together had been happy and content, until that awful night.

The clock struck its final chime, a soft peal that echoed from so many years before. She wiped her eyes, sentimental old fool, it was all she was, but since there was no one to see, it probably didn't matter very much, she told herself.

Jane made her way down through the bar one last time

before she went to bed. She did this every night, walked through the old building in near darkness, checking doors, rattling locks, securing everything as if it might make some difference. Sometimes she stood, listening to the silence and let the many satisfied years roll past her. And they had been content, she and Manus here in The Marchant Inn. It had been a joyful home and a thriving business, once. They'd been happily married and run this bar together. She never imagined he'd leave her so unexpectedly, so violently, fifteen years ago. These days, she lived between two rooms and opened the bar up in the afternoons, and only then for a few hours, to pretend to herself at least that she was still in business. Of course, the smart young people who worked on Finch Street now rarely darkened her door, but the old regulars turned up to drink bottled beer or tea and share stories of times that would never come again.

There was a time when she wondered if they'd had a family, how things might have turned out differently. It made no difference now, one miscarriage and a botched-up job of setting her straight wasn't something they could do much about afterwards. Manus had just been happy she'd survived. When she'd realised the truth of it, Jane sank into such a darkened place she feared she'd never find the path back home again. So now she refused to think of how things might have been. She'd learned a long time ago that thinking like that didn't make things better and so she buried that sadness long before Manus had been interred in that too large plot beside his mother. The main thing was not to think too often how much she looked forward to joining them in their peaceful place.

The cold floor beneath her feet made her shiver; drawing her from those gloomy thoughts once more. At her neck, she wore a pendant. They'd given it to her a few years earlier, a lovely woman who called on people like herself, old people, vulnerable people, who were mostly forgotten about in this speeding city. The pendant had an alarm button attached to it and although she'd only used it once – and then by accident – it gave her a kind of refuge, as if she carried some bit of courage about her neck.

Jane stood at the door for a moment; across the road, that fancy restaurant was just closing up for the night. The lights dimming and then extinguished, there was the sound of an alarm, cutting across the silence of the empty street and then that pretty waitress standing on the path outside. The girl, foreign, by the looks of her, wore an impatience about her like a shawl, as though she couldn't get away quickly enough. Jane had seen her hanging about on her smoking break and she sucked ferociously on her cigarettes with the same irritation. Next, him, the owner – he was a right sour piece, not like his partner. No, Jane never liked the look of him at all, and from the carry-on she'd seen with that foreign girl, her instincts had been right from the start. Jane wondered if she should mention something next time Carrie called across for a cup of tea. *Knowing what to do for the best*; that was the problem. Her mother-in-law would have advised, the least said, the soonest mended.

Carrie dropped in to see Jane every so often, not enough to interfere, but she'd taped her mobile number to the wall beside the phone, just in case. Not like that man of hers, he'd never so much as set foot across the threshold of the bar. Now, there was a man who'd landed on his feet, even if he'd never know it. Jane watched as he fiddled with the lock, balancing under his arm a bag that surely held the day's takings. He grumbled and then gave the door a push, checking to see all was locked up safely. There was something strangely final about seeing just the two of them walk home for the evening. It was unusual that Carrie was not there, but then, everyone deserved a night off.

She sighed and turned from the door back into the empty bar, its memorabilia a persistent reminder of happier times that seemed to fade a little more gently away from her with each passing moment. Photographs of Manus lined the walls all about her, but it was funny, these days, they made her feel as if he was further away from her than ever.

'Goodnight, my sweet,' she said as she climbed the narrow stairs that led up to the flat above. It had been her home for over fifty years. She knew every inch of this old place, the creaking floorboards, the rattling panes of glass and the verbose piping that complained in the otherwise silent night. Perhaps her mind was full of memories or maybe just a lingering uneasiness about that foreign girl across the road, but Jane managed somehow to stumble on that final, slightly higher stair. She heard the soft thud, thud of her body, light and fragile, hitting off each carpeted step. It was with a sickening crunch that she reached the cold floor and it seemed as though she'd been tumbling for an age.

She wasn't sure how long she lay there, but when she woke, her body shivered, cold and sore, there was no picking herself up. She was old enough, and maybe just about wise enough, to know she didn't have the strength. Instead, she fidgeted about until she found the alarm pendant that had lodged beneath her. Freeing it with an almighty tug, she pressed her thumb down hard, praying that tonight someone would come to her rescue.

Luke Gibson wasn't sure what brought his father to this place. True enough, they'd gravitated back to Dublin often over the years, but it wasn't as if they had family here or any kind of stake in the city. Truthfully, he should probably just buy a sensible little house somewhere quiet, settle there and count his blessings. He could understand his father's wanderlust was beginning to abate. But Ballyglen? A nursing home? Really, it was like giving up and Conn Gibson had never been a man to give up.

It was almost two o'clock in the morning and Luke couldn't sleep. He pulled on his jeans, shook himself into the big wax jacket that hung on his bedroom door. He slunk out of the bed and breakfast; it was hard to resist walking on newly fallen snow and the little dog still played on his mind. He was like Luke, no different, drifting, maybe searching. He turned the corner and came back to the street where he'd seen him last. Certain he'd disappeared down a lane, Luke had followed him, but he'd only ended up half scaring some poor woman to death. He smiled now as he remembered the surprised look on her face when he handed her the key that was glinting so close to her feet. Still, there was no sign of the little dog and in weather like this... well, he didn't like to think of the small chap out and about in the snow.

Outside the old pub, an ambulance throbbed blue light about the buildings and the melting slush. Luke stood in that uncomfortable place between watcher and voyeur. In the end, he walked past, just catching sight of an old woman being wheeled helplessly from her home. Her eyes were dark and penetrated him with the kind of fear that held him up. He considered walking over, to see if there was anything he could do for the old dear, but of course, what did he know of her or she of him? They were strangers, nameless and unconnected in a city of anonymity. Instead, he stood for a moment, did something he hadn't done in years – he offered up a prayer that he might see her again, well and soon.

The sound of the paramedics, securing their patient and getting ready to set off for the nearest emergency ward made Luke shiver. Finally, the younger, burlier of the two, locked up the pub, standing back for a moment, perhaps checking that all the lights inside were switched off. He rattled the door with an irrevocability that made Luke wonder if they thought she might not be coming back. Strangely, that notion filled him with unreasonable loneliness that made him pull his collar closer and decide that tomorrow he was going to drop into that pub and enquire how the old lady was.

2

Carrie tucked the little dog beneath her jacket and left the restaurant early. Kevin would surely manage without her for one night. After all, he had Valentina now. Either way, Andrew was happy to hold the fort for her once he saw the state of her when she called him up to tell him she was going home. Andrew was more than any employee could ever be, they had become friends, in spite of Kevin's barely masked homophobia.

Carrie was cold and miserable and empty. Her bones felt as if the sleet of earlier had cut deep wedges in them and she would never feel warm again. Normally she had a glass or two of wine when she finished up for the day. Usually, she was wrecked, the restaurant business was gruelling, torture on the feet and by the end of a twelve-hour shift her brain was either too hyped up to rest or too tired to sleep. Tonight, she felt she could do with something warmer. She looked at the shelf filled with bottles of wine and various spirits and reached for a bottle of brandy. This would warm her up.

Taking the first sip, she caught her reflection in the kitchen window. Did she really want to be one of those women who came home gasping for a drink each evening? If she was going to live alone, what would she turn into if she sat down with a bottle of wine every night? There could be no pretence now that she was sharing it with Kevin. Truthfully, he hardly touched the stuff anyway. She turned the glass into the sink, watched as the bronze contents flowed down the drain. The bottle of wine every other night had contributed to her expanded waistband and to her chronic sinus infection, she could admit that to herself at least. Perhaps without it, she might not have been such a fulsome snorer.

She washed out the glass, left it on the draining board, placed the bottle back on the shelf – she was better than that. She was going to be better than that, she decided, and turned towards the little dog at her feet. He was a tricoloured smooth-haired crossbreed. Carrie couldn't decide what his parents were, but she'd hazard a guess that there was a mix of springer spaniel and hound somewhere in his lineage.

'Teddy?' she had checked his collar earlier and now he looked at her with a keen interest as though he couldn't quite figure out how she might know his name. What had she been thinking bringing home a stray mutt? But she couldn't leave him out in that weather. He could freeze to death by the morning if he didn't find shelter. 'Just one night,' she told him softly as she rubbed his filthy ears. Food and heat were what he needed most and he seemed glad to take her conversation with him as a bonus.

She opened the fridge. Considering the meals she served up to customers each evening, her own stock was meagre. There were a few portions of lasagne in the freezer and she figured that they may as well go to her unexpected canine guest.

He lapped up the lasagne and seemed satisfied to let her wash the dirt from him in the bath filled with warm sudsy water. Then he settled contentedly on a fluffy bath sheet under the radiator.

'Well, it's just you and me tonight, Teddy,' she whispered, when he nuzzled into her later. It was funny, but she'd used generous fistfuls of Kevin's expensive shampoo and conditioner on him, and yet, to her mind, the fragrance sat much easier on this little fellow. She'd worry about finding his owner tomorrow, she promised herself. There weren't any contact details on his collar, just a name, and Carrie wondered if perhaps he belonged to the man in the alley earlier.

Later, after she settled the little dog for the night, she dropped her clothes to the floor, while she selected the fluffiest pjs and thermal socks she could find. For a moment she lingered before the rails and shelves filled with Kevin's clothes. A lesser woman might take a pair of scissors to them, she told herself, but the truth was, she was too tired to think of revenge. Suddenly even picking up the clothes she wore earlier seemed like it might be too much. So, she left them where they landed, knew that if she wasn't suffering from a broken heart, they would be put away as she always did. Instead, she folded herself into the king-size bed they'd bought together. Would he want to take this with him? For Valentina? They hadn't thought of any of those things. She'd bet it hadn't even entered Kevin's head. They spent years gathering up the things that people work for. A home, a successful business, they had been the inevitable milestones along the way; tying them together, as firmly as any ring, or so she believed. Kevin's clothes in the wardrobe, she had bought almost every item, apart from a few errant scarves, gifts from his sister, his mother, her mother.

God. She couldn't face telling them yet. At least, she wouldn't have to tell Kevin's mother. Maureen Mulvey would be Kevin's worry now and that at least made her smile as she lay in bed. For tonight, she'd just close her eyes.

A slight whimper and the sound of a tail thumping on the carpet outside her door made her smile. Teddy.

'Okay, you,' she said opening the door softly, 'you can sleep on the floor, but one sound and you're back in the kitchen,' she ran her hand across his curled-up body. He settled himself just outside her bed on the deep shag rug that Kevin always hated. Soon, he was sleeping gently, his breath an easy accompaniment to her own, so Carrie realised she was drifting towards sleep with the hint of a contented smile on her lips. She reached out, turned off the alarm so she could sleep right through. The next day was Sunday and that's what normal people did, wasn't it? They slept late on Sundays.

Carrie woke at five, perhaps it was the niggling worry that Teddy might need to relieve himself. She herded him downstairs and out for a quick round of the garden, although he was not keen. He moved slowly and grumbled like an old man at the disruption of his beauty sleep.

Would Kevin be sleeping late with Valentina? He must be staying with her now. Kevin couldn't go out and buy himself a pair of socks without Carrie. He would need someone to slip into that role. Carrie couldn't imagine Valentina hitting the men's underwear section any time soon. It struck her that Kevin hadn't really thought about this at all. He couldn't survive without Carrie; he needed her. The problem was, she suddenly realised with the clarity of that sheeting snow against her window, he didn't want her anymore. He just didn't want her.

There was light outside when she woke next, that sort of sterilised whiteness that always comes with snow and made her feel as if, in some way, her life had been untainted and made purer. The notion was in itself an odd if satisfying surprise. It was a dull insipid bright, but still much better than the heavy leaden look of the day before. On the other hand, she knew, with her sleep-filled eyes, it may just be very late. It was after eleven in the morning, as late as she could remember getting up for years. Normally, on a Sunday morning, she got up early and headed for Mass with Kevin's mother. She'd completely forgotten that today. She did the journey more for Kevin than for his mother. Maureen Mulvey had a way of getting them all to jump to her command. Carrie didn't even like Mass. She wasn't sure she believed in any God anymore; maybe less today than any other Sunday. She hadn't thought about it before, but she picked up Maureen every Sunday morning, while Kevin slept late. She drove her the short distance from Maureen's semi and parked where she was told and then trudged to the same seat each week. At least, Maureen had stopped giving her digs about 'living in sin' with Kevin. Maureen had all the benefits of a daughter-in-law, without having to part with her son.

Carrie lay in her bed looking up at the ceiling. It needed a good painting; a crack ran right down the middle, as though it separated the two sides of the bed beneath it. This house was ninety years old. The crack in the plaster over her head was nothing to worry about; perhaps it had been trying to tell her something all along.

Reaching out for her phone, there were five missed calls, four of them from Maureen, the fifth Carrie didn't recognise, so she let it slip. She wondered idly, if perhaps some poor neighbour was roped in to take Maureen in the end. She presumed Kevin had not contacted his mother nor had he brought her to Mass. She wasn't surprised, he would put off telling his mother. He would put off telling everyone. Kevin hated any kind of conflict. He'd miss that too; Carrie had removed as many of those stressful situations from him as she could. Not this time. She pulled her phone closer to her and flew off a text to Kevin.

Better explain to your mother why she has no lift to
Mass anymore – unless Valentina will oblige.

She'd hesitated about putting an x on the end. Kevin would know she was only being bitchy, she wasn't a kiss-kiss sort of woman. She was good old Carrie, get things done, keep things moving along. On the drive, outside her door, she had a BMW. It was a compromise. She'd have preferred a Volkswagen, they were meant to be so reliable, but Kevin insisted that they needed to look the part of successful business people. With the sort of customers they had coming in, having a twelve-year-old crock outside the door just wasn't going to cut it. There it was, in a nutshell, the difference between them. Valentina would probably give her false eyelashes for a Beamer. Carrie assumed Valentina's eyelashes were false, after all no one gets the eyes, the legs, the teeth, the boobs and the lashes – not unless they're a Victoria's Secret model.

So what would she do with her day? Now that she didn't have to sort out Kevin's mother, Sunday seemed to stretch ahead like a jail term. She couldn't think like that, she knew she couldn't afford to. She had two choices, either she could sit here, stare at Teddy and hope Kevin came to his senses, wait and die a lonely spinster or... Well, she wasn't sure there was an alternative, but she wasn't going to be sitting here waiting for Kevin bloody Mulvey to come round.

Teddy slept soundly until Carrie threw the quilt back on the bed. It was as if he'd marked time with her, loyally waiting by her bed. She opened the back door and he scooted out immediately, prancing over the icy whiteness as he nosed about the potted plants she'd dotted around the little patio. Carrie enjoyed watching him, diverted for a short while from a slowly gripping desperation, as the life she thought was hers slipped from her.

After a quick bite, Carrie cleared away her breakfast and she set the kitchen to rights. 'Well then, Teddy, what are we going to do about you today?' she asked him and he tilted his head as though she might have the answer already. The poor little thing, she really would have to figure out what to do with him.

Apart from the refuges and the pound, she wasn't sure where else she could check on a Sunday and once she'd made a couple of calls to clear her conscience, she was glad to be headed towards the nearest pet shop to pick up food and a decent lead and chew bones for him. She enjoyed that, spoiling him. It was a little like shopping for Kevin, but she felt it was much more deeply appreciated, then she drove into town and headed for The Sea Pear. She wasn't sure why; she knew it would be empty now. Perhaps she could see how last night had gone from the state of the place and from the till receipts.

She pulled up on the empty street at the front. Normally, on weekdays, you couldn't move on Finch Street, but Sundays saw the place deserted and she'd often come here, just to update her blog and have a quiet cup of coffee on a Sunday afternoon, after dropping off Maureen.

She wasn't in the mood for opening the blog today. Not, she realised that anyone would notice. It was just a hobby, somewhere to share recipes and tips and chat with her friends from college who were spread across the world now. Her only true follower was her friend Anna who had no interest in cooking or kitchen hygiene. Anna was her best friend; they'd stuck together since primary school. They were, as her mother liked to say, 'chalk and cheese'. Anna was arty, flighty and insuppressibly flirty.

She was an ice cool blonde with a precarious acting career and an even more precarious approach to her domestic life. She lived like a student and blew between jobs and men like other women did nail varnish shades. She liked the idea of supporting Carrie in her one occupation outside of 'Operation Kevin', as she termed the rest of Carrie's life.

Carrie walked through the restaurant with Teddy at her heel, picking up cutlery and checking that it shined. In the kitchen, she switched on the kettle for a cup of instant coffee. Carrie never bothered with the machine. It was far too much effort for the same results, as far as she was concerned. The kitchen was clean; it looked and smelled as if Kevin had gone through his usual night-time routine. He was obsessive about clean-up. Probably, he'd have a fit if he knew she had brought a dog in here.

The back door caught her eye, for a moment. She thought about coming through it the evening before, standing there, no one had noticed her. She had walked through the kitchen, the dog in her arms, up the back stairs to her office, before picking up her coat and tidying herself up as much as she could then dashed to her car without so much as one person lifting a head to greet her. Only Andrew, whom she had summoned, had regarded Teddy with interest.

Now, she walked to the door, thinking about the man who had given her the key. It felt like a dream today. He seemed unreal, as if she imagined those dark eyes in the rain. She pulled across the latch and threw back the door, the smell of last night's refuse pinching her senses. What on earth had he been doing in the alley at the back of the restaurant? Perhaps he lived locally. Although Carrie was fairly sure she knew most of the people who lived around here. There was a guest house, just around the back of the block; maybe he was staying there?

She turned to go back in, she would have a coffee and then decide what to do with the dog and the long day stretching out ahead. Then, at the top of the road, she saw him. She was sure, it was him. Standing, undecided as to whether he should come towards her or not. She waved at him, a small movement of her hand; caught her breath while she waited. Then, there it was. He waved, as self-consciously as she had, back at her and then he moved off. Carrie popped back into the kitchen, propelled by she was not sure what. She ran to the front of the restaurant, the dog at her heels. He was almost three doors down by the time she got out onto the street.

'Hello,' she called after him and her voice sounded strange and disconnected on the empty street. 'Hello,' she shouted again, but still he kept on walking away from her. She left the restaurant behind her, the keys held firmly in her hand, the little dog enjoying the excitement of running about her. Then, she was beside him and suddenly, she realised she didn't know what she wanted to say. 'Hello,' she said a little breathlessly, she was never an athlete, even before the toll of her daily bottle of wine had led her into the darker end of the doctor's BMI chart.

'Hello,' he said automatically, looking at her as though she'd just lost the run of herself, but much too polite not to greet her. Then he smiled, when they both realised the awkwardness of the situation.

'I wanted to thank you, for yesterday. I never said… and then, when I went to look for you, well, you were gone and I thought…' He was looking at her blankly and she realised perhaps he didn't recognise her. 'Thank you.' She held out a hand to shake with him.

'You're welcome. I'm sorry if I scared you,' he said and looked down at the dog at her feet. 'Well hello, you.' He bent down and patted his head. 'I was looking for him, last night when you…' He stood then, smiling at Carrie.

'Ah, that answers a lot of questions,' she said. 'He's yours so?'

'Not exactly…' The man smiled, 'I thought he was a stray…' He looked up and down the street, his eyes drifting across the pub opposite. 'I was going to pop into the pub over there for coffee, but it seems to be closed.'

'Oh dear, The Marchant Inn only opens when Jane feels like it and even then, you can't be sure of opening hours. But, funny you should mention coffee…' Carrie found herself smiling at the man now. 'I'm Carrie by the way,' she said. 'I – or rather we, myself and my… partner, we own The Sea Pear.' She nodded back towards the restaurant.

'Nice to meet you,' they shook hands again and Carrie couldn't remember if they'd already been introduced, because there was something so familiar about him. 'I'm Luke Gibson.'

'Come on, come with me,' she said and then she was leading him back towards The Sea Pear before she had time to think about it. 'The least I can do is make you a coffee to say thanks.' She brought him through the restaurant, into the kitchen, the little dog yapping happily beside them. 'So, you and Teddy?' she nodded towards Teddy when she had made two coffees for them.

'Yes, I've just been kind of looking out for him,' and he smiled again. 'I've noticed him around the streets these last few days. So, I've been making sure he had something to eat, you know…'

'Well, that's strange, because I'd surely have noticed him before if he was hanging about.'

'He looks like he could belong to someone elderly, but then sometimes…' He shook his head. 'The old lady over in the pub, he wouldn't be hers, would he?'

'Mrs Marchant?' Carrie's eyes drifted towards the little dog who sat now watching them both with interest, as if he might at any point contribute to their conversation. 'No, she's all on her own over there. Mind you, if she was a dog a person, he'd be lovely company.' There was a thought; she'd never considered suggesting a dog to take the loneliness for Jane out of The Marchant Inn. 'I might pop across later and see if she'd like to take him in for now.'

'You haven't heard?' he said, sipping his coffee.

'Heard?' Carrie began to laugh, but it was a nervous sound, there was no mistaking the tone of his voice.

He sighed. 'She was taken away in an ambulance late last night, it looked serious. It was why I intended to pop over there for coffee today, just to see if she was all right.'

'Oh, no, my phone, there was a missed call…' She

rummaged in her bag, fished the phone out from what seemed like the very depths. 'Thank goodness I didn't delete the number.' She dialled it and waited as it hummed and beeped until various admin staff could put her through to a ward nurse. 'I'm her next of kin,' it was a white lie, but she made a face at Luke to share the guilt of it.

'Your aunt?' the nurse said on the other end of the line and Carrie had an unfortunate feeling that the woman was wrinkling her nose, judging her for not being by Jane Marchant's side when she was needed most.

'Yes, that's right.'

'Well, she's here on the main ward. She's been badly bruised and knocked about. At her age, falling is never good and falling down stairs, well, it can be...' her words tapered off. 'But, she's been lucky, no broken bones, although, as you can imagine, she's very shaken – upset and extremely nervous in herself.' The nurse lowered her voice then, as if she was about to share some vital confidence, 'To tell you the truth, she could do with people around her – that would probably mend her quicker than any medication we can give her here.'

'Right, thanks for that,' Carrie said and she ended the call. She looked across at the man opposite her. 'She's in St Teresa's, just a few streets away. I'll have to go there now.' Then she looked down at the little dog. 'What to do with you? That's the question.'

'Oh, no. I can see where this is going.' Luke smiled. 'I can't have a dog, not all the time. I travel too much and anyway...'

'Anyway?'

'Well, I'm not a dog person, not really.'

Carrie didn't believe him. She figured he was as much a dog person as she was. She'd never been able to keep a dog in the same house as Kevin. He was allergic to everything and dog or cat hairs would have brought him out in a rash.

'Well, anyway, I don't know how long I'm going to be in Dublin for, I'm really just passing through. I'm staying in the little bed and breakfast, just around the corner – they're not going to let me keep a dog there.'

'Ah, well, that's a shame,' Carrie said and when she met his eyes, she realised that the words could mean any number of things. 'About having a dog, I mean.' Then she looked at the dog, 'It really is a shame, because, I can't possibly keep him either.' She shook her head, but of course, she wasn't going to just throw the poor little thing out.

'I'm sure you can't. Perhaps it will only be for a night or two. No doubt his owner will come forward soon enough, there's a good chance that they're worried sick about him already.' He held her eye for a moment too long. The grandfather clock that stood in the restaurant chimed loud through the open door.

Carrie checked her watch and sighed. The old clock was still, after all her tinkering, running almost eight minutes fast.

Luke got up from the table, moved his cup towards the sink.

'Oh, you don't have to do that,' she said needlessly.

'Here,' he said, digging deep into the wax jacket. 'Just hold onto Teddy for a day or two,' he pulled out a card. 'Here's my number, if you give him a bed for a few nights, I'm sure we'll have him back with his family before you know it.'

Carrie didn't remember agreeing to take the dog in, but she followed Luke to the door of the restaurant and let him out into the street. She watched him walk towards the corner, checking his watch and pulling out his phone. Carrie smiled, perhaps just a little thankful to have an excuse to hold onto Teddy for a short while. It was funny but, somehow, this little dog made her world feel better than it had in a long time.

Jane knew it was slightly irrational to look about at all the other old ladies on the ward and feel that she didn't belong among them. They probably all felt the very same, or at least the ones who still had their wits about them. The nurses were lovely, if harried, but they were still kind.

'Your niece called, I'm sure she'll be here soon, Janet,' one of the younger ones promised her softly, as though she was placating a child. Jane didn't have the stamina to correct either her name or the fact that she didn't have a niece – she didn't have a soul in the world to call her own, not for the last fifteen years.

'That's nice,' Jane managed to nod, she might have embellished the notion and made a true lie of it, but she had a sense that the nurse wouldn't remember or notice if she had a visitor or not.

'Better off here,' said the old lady in the bed next to her. She had a locker overflowing with grapes that threatened to choke her and enough fizzy drinks to put her in danger of full-blown diabetes if she ever got to the end of them. At her back, there was a line of get-well cards, all of them pronouncing her role as granny, mother or friend. Jane felt bereft by comparison. 'Who wants to be out there with the snow building up at your front door? That's what I say, here we are, sure you wouldn't get this service in the Ritz!'

Jane was just patting down her hair when a familiar face appeared at the foot of her bed. 'Oh, hello,' she said rather awkwardly and she could see from the expression on Carrie's face that she felt every bit as uneasy being here.

'How are you?' the look of concern in Carrie's eyes was unmistakable and it managed to create a wave of something warm and unexpected within Jane.

'That your niece?' asked the matriarch in the next bed.

'That's right,' Carrie said, smiling across at the other woman before she took a seat and sat close to Jane. Then she lowered her voice and explained that she'd never have known Jane was here if it wasn't for some random man in the street.

'I saw him,' Jane said softly. 'Last night, he was standing at the restaurant and there was something about him...'

'It seems you made quite the impression on him too,' Carrie laughed. 'He was going to drop into the pub today to find out how you were,' she said. 'It was an eventful night for all of us,' Carrie told her about meeting Luke and bringing home Teddy. 'So, for now at least, I have a house guest, but if you're interested in some company...' Carrie smiled kindly and Jane thought there was a new warmth to her when she talked about the little dog. Now, she wondered if Carrie ever knew what it meant to have a partner who really cared about you. She shook the thought away, of course, she did, after all, didn't she have Kevin.

'That's nice.' Jane murmured, but her eyes began to fill with tears. 'I'm sorry, it's just... probably shock – you know, last night it was all a bit...'

'It's okay. You're going to be fine; everything is going to be all right.' Carrie moved closer and took her hand. The action seemed so natural that Jane hardly thought about it, but it was nice. Strange to think the last hand she'd held had been Manus's, his grasp had always been firm and gentle all at once. Whereas, Carrie's was filled with a concerned warmth – it was comforting, in some unfamiliar way.

'I just...' How could she say that she didn't give a damn for the bruises or the scratches, all those pains were nothing compared to the ache of loneliness that filled her every moment and had become like a searing pain that forged through her now. Then she looked at Carrie, a young woman with life ahead of her, she was successful and happy and capable of doing anything she wanted in the world. 'I suppose, it's the thought of going back there,' she whispered when the tears had run out. 'I lay there, thinking that perhaps no one would come.' Then, her biggest sadness, on a shuddering empty breath, 'That there was nobody *to* come.'

'Hush, now, don't upset yourself.' Carrie wrapped her arms around her. She held her like that for an age and Jane didn't hear the nice nurse come along and pull the curtains about her cubicle or the gentle snores of the woman in the bed next to her. 'You're not on your own, not really, not any more than the rest of us.'

Staying with Valentina wasn't the same as being at home. Sure, the sex was great, but her flat was small and then there was the question of the other people who came and went at all hours of the day and night.

Kevin was no longer twenty, even if his girlfriend was – living like a student no longer suited him. Not that it ever had. Back in the day, he chose to stay at home with his mother. Why move into some grotty, germ-infested set, when you could stay in your own bed, with your favourite dinners on the table every night and your chef's uniform washed and starched to perfection. It just didn't make sense to move out.

'Emm, have you thought of moving?' He was trying to be tactful.

'Why would I move, I can afford theese place? Eetees the best I can get in Dublin.' She looked perplexed, as though he was suggesting she might downsize.

'Well, that was when you came first, but now, well, you're settled now, not just a student anymore. You have your little job at the restaurant and...'

'Yeees, and I have a very wealthy boyfriend who might pay my rent, non?' She raised an eyebrow.

'Well, we'll see, I mean, it's early days, isn't it?'

'Eef you are staying here, they will expect you to pay too,' she said as she brushed out her long dark hair. God, but even when she brushed her hair, she managed to make it look as though it was some sort of erotic foreplay.

'Right, well, I don't mind paying my way. I'll throw fifty in for the electric, will I?' He pulled a note from his wallet. 'And here,' he handed her another fifty, 'maybe we should treat ourselves to new sheets, so long as we're here, yeah?'

She looked at him blankly, and for a moment, he thought she may not ever have gone out to buy sheets before. Who knew what they slept on back in the old country.

'Well, I must be off,' he kissed the top of her head, lingered for a moment; she really was the best-looking girl he'd ever laid eyes on, never mind actually dated. 'You take your time coming in tonight. I appreciate all the extra responsibility you took on last night, and I'm sure Carrie will be back to herself this evening.' Actually, he wasn't sure. He didn't want to think how she was feeling, this was a bolt from the blue. But, Carrie was a trooper, she was the strong one, he'd always said it.

'No problem. I enjoyed eet. You know I love the restaurant as much as you do.'

'Well, last night you proved that you're good at it anyway,' Kevin had enjoyed watching her from the safety of the kitchen.

Simo and Reda were having what Kevin presumed was

breakfast on the dirty leather couch as he left the flat. He didn't ask them what they were eating, but it smelled of yesterday's fish heavily spiced with cayenne, turmeric and garlic.

'Good morning, lads,' he said cheerfully, attempting to cover his fear. Valentina had told him they were her cousins. Kevin thought they looked like a different species, never mind actually being related. Still he had a feeling that they were watching him. One wrong move and he'd be put in his place.

'You call this good?' Simo said, jabbing his thumb towards the window. 'They are saying on the news that this month there will be one snowstorm after another.'

'Your country stopped for the Beast from the East last winter; already it looks worse this year.' Reda spit his words in Kevin's direction.

'It's when July blows in and there's been no let-up, that's when we Irish start complaining.' Kevin said, keeping his smile fastened tight.

'That is why you let everyone and anyone in to your country, no? You are hoping we will all leave Colombia and you will emigrate there for the good weather.' He guffawed, and Kevin spotted a long tattoo than ran down his neck, it seemed to slither right across his chest.

Kevin shivered; he was not used to men like Simo and Reda. They came to Ireland to find work, any work. They ended up delivering free newspapers and advertising door to door. They were the kind of men who knew how to take care of themselves; their dark skin bulged with muscles Kevin would never possess. Their eyes moved quickly, their bodies cut lithe sharp movements and when they spoke to each other, they hardly halted for breath. Their English was impressive too. They'd hardly a word between them a few weeks ago and now they said things and Kevin thought he could hear the Liffey in their voices.

'You ever theenk about getting security at your place, Keveen?' Reda asked slowly, concentrating on each word.

'We have security, when we need it,' Kevin said automatically. 'Why?' It just occurred to him, were they going into the business of racketeering?

'It ees just, we were thinking of starting our own business, something small, something we know more about than...'

'Oh, I see,' Kevin said, although he wasn't sure he did. 'Well, good for you,' he said and grabbed his coat. He didn't want to hear about their business plans. He didn't want to be part of them and he certainly didn't want to be backing them financially. 'Well, must be off,' he said and his voice sounded a pitch too high for the cheerfulness he was aiming at.

'Maybe we tell you about it the next time you call...'

'Of course, of course,' Kevin said and he fled, carrying his jacket over his arm, even though there was a blizzard blowing through the narrow Dublin back streets. He had parked his car four streets away, now he cursed under his breath, but better get soaked than have it vandalised or stolen in this dodgy area. Still, Kevin hated this weather, he gripped the railings as he passed by streets, always felt like a ninny, but he hated the notion of the wind catching him off guard. He sighed with relief when eventually he sat into his expensive car.

He wasn't due at the restaurant for another hour or two and he had no intention of showing up there until he had to. The last thing he wanted was to run into Carrie. He hated fights, hated any sort of confrontation. Carrie didn't like them either, he was sure of that. She went out of her way to avoid any fuss. Maybe that was the problem; they were in some ways too alike. There was no passion between them anymore. They made great business partners, no doubting that, The Sea Pear was making them a lot of money. And they could continue to work together, why not? Lots of couples did, surely. He could think of lots of couples like...

He leaned his head against the window of his car while he waited for the lights to change at the end of a very long, slow-moving snake of traffic. God, but sometimes Dublin was the pits.

Sonny and Cher? There was a couple he could give as an example. She even went to his funeral, didn't she? Ike and Tina – he was getting good at this.

He just had to figure out what they needed to do next in the divvying out of their lives together. There was so much to sort out. So much, that he hadn't even thought of before they broke the news to Carrie. He knew now, maybe he knew it then, but it was all very fast. True, he was in love with Valentina, but maybe he should have thought through how he wanted things to fall, once they declared their love publicly. He hadn't even told his mother yet. God, he was dreading that, even more than sorting out everything with Carrie.

He took the coward's route and turned his Mercedes towards Dundrum. His sister Penny worked in one of the smarter men's shops in the shopping centre there.

'Penny,' for once she answered her mobile on the first ring, 'I need a favour,' he shouted into the phone, flicking his indicator to take him out of the city centre.

'I bet you do,' Penny said. She sounded like she did when he was fourteen and she caught him leaving school early so he wouldn't have to face up to Bullet Delaney, his biggest tormenter in the school. 'Mum knows.'

'What? What does Mum know?' He could feel his blood pressure drop down through the accelerator.

'She knows something is up. Carrie never collected her for Mass and she's been ringing her ever since, and not so much as a dickey bird. That's not like Carrie.'

'I can't believe she didn't collect her.' He'd seen Carrie's text, but there hadn't been a word from his mother, so he convinced himself that maybe Carrie had collected her anyway, this one last time, and the text was an attempt at niggling him.

'So, she's not down with the bubonic?' Penny's voice was calm, no kids in the vicinity. She must be on a break at the shop.

'Emm, no. She's not sick, exactly,' he couldn't believe that Carrie had let his mother down. Just like that. It was as though she meant nothing to her, and after all these years, really.

'Well, is she, or isn't she?'

'What?'

'Sick, oh, for God's sake, Kevin, keep up. How's Carrie?'

'I'm not sure.'

'How can you not be sure; don't you live with the woman?'

'Well, not exactly, not anymore.' The words brought a certain reality into the car, one that he wasn't entirely sure he wanted to face. The world, suddenly, seemed a little scary without Carrie bringing his mother to Mass. What else would she renege on?

'Oh, Kevin, she threw you out?' Penny paused to let this sink in. 'What did you do?'

'How do you mean, what did I do?'

'Well, for her to throw you out of your own house?'

'I didn't do anything,' he knew he sounded indignant, but really the very thought of anyone throwing Kevin Mulvey out of anywhere – it was preposterous.

'Well, the rotten old cow. I always said she was a hard piece. Listen to me now, Kevin, you have to go back there. You don't want her taking the house out from under you. I know you bought when the prices were low, but it's worth an absolute fortune now. You won't pick up anywhere for even double what you paid for that place.'

That was true. 'Penny, I can't talk about this now. There's too much to sort out. I need to get clothes; can you help me?'

'Clothes?'

'Yes, are you turning into a bloody echo? I need socks and underwear, a couple of tops and jeans. Can you choose some clothes for me and I'll pick them up in half an hour?'

'Of course, but, Kevin...' Penny stopped talking. She was on commission. As far as Penny was concerned, you couldn't have too many clothes. She'd kit him out and he'd look well. The prices would be top dollar, but at this stage, Kevin felt like he'd pay anything just to get everything sorted. He couldn't face going back to the house today.

3

Carrie eyed her stocky frame critically in the mirror. She had washed her hair and attempted to brush it out straight, but of course, as always, it disobediently fell back into a mass of curls. In the end, she pinned it up in a messy bun and pulled a few tendrils free, in case she needed to hide behind them. She had just spent an hour crying about the way things had turned out, so she hoped there were no more tears left. Her shift in the restaurant started in less than forty-five minutes. The last thing she wanted was a replay of the previous evening. She may be an emotional wreck; it didn't mean that all sense of herself had to be obviously lost.

She pulled out an emerald wrap dress she'd bought in New York a few years earlier. It was made of the softest wool and always garnered a compliment when she wore it. It worked quite well with patent heels and her black lacy bolero. She needed a splash of Manhattan in her life now. The wrap top managed to hold in her ample boobs. The skirt though narrow didn't make as much of her peasant thighs as some clinging skirts did. It was the best she could do, and she wasn't sure who she was trying to impress anyway, she could never match Valentina for looks.

'Right, Teddy, how do I look?' she quizzed the little dog when she went back into the kitchen. He looked at her curiously, she was not sure if she passed the appearance test, but she had a feeling he saw something in her that went deeper than her figure. She bent down and scratched his head gently. He seemed content to slumber in the same spot in her kitchen, so she left him there.

She was dreading going into The Sea Pear. There, she'd said it. How long had she felt like that? She shook her head, not long, probably only since Kevin made his announcement. God, it was almost a full fifteen minutes since she gave him a thought. Now the dread filled her again. There was no point going through the thoughts that were cramming her mind: *What was she supposed to do now? What was Kevin going to do? Was he going to shack up permanently with Valentina?* Carrie couldn't allow her mind to go there, not yet. For now, she had to get through working in the same building as the pair of them. For now, that would be as much as she would demand of herself.

The restaurant felt warm and fresh when she arrived. It wasn't four hours since she walked through here with Teddy and Luke. Yet, knowing that Kevin was going to be here now, the place felt different. As though its familiarity was jarring with what it should be. She hadn't been at work since yesterday evening, when she'd run out of here distraught. No one had checked up on her and the business had not come crashing down without her.

Actually, the place looked fine. Everything was exactly as it should be.

The smell, familiar, trailing before her was Kevin – a mixture of Calvin Klein and hair products to make his wiry hair appear sleek. They had not spoken, not really, since he had trotted out of her office with Valentina at his side. Oh, they'd exchanged orders from the kitchen to the front of house. They'd worked around each other in careful silence for almost two days, until finally the hollowness inside her had given way last night. He, she knew, was much more cowardly than she. Had she always known that? Was he actually spineless? She thought about it for a moment, then she threw her shoulders back, her ample chest out and marched into the kitchen. She was not afraid. Broken, but not afraid.

'I can't believe you left my mother high and dry.' Kevin's voice reached a pitch she hadn't heard in years.

'*How are you Carrie? How are you doing? I was worried about you?*' Carrie said the words sarcastically; after all, they were what she imagined she would say to him if things were reversed.

'Of course, I was worried about you, we both were, but…' He ran his long fingers through his thick hair and she noticed it seemed greyer now than it was before. Could he have aged overnight or was it really so long since she'd actually properly looked at him? 'But still, what was I supposed to do, drag you back to work. Valentina said you probably needed some time to get your head around things. We managed fine, by the way,' he nodded towards the restaurant.

'Really,' Carrie said and she let the hurt of him talking to Valentina about her slide sideward on her consciousness. She couldn't think about all the times they'd probably spoken about her these last few weeks or maybe months. 'Well, good news for both of you. But I'm back now, so...'

'Well, of course,' Kevin bit his lip, a nervous habit he had worked hard to kick in college. 'And...'

'Yes?' she said. Had he thought about the restaurant, had he thought about the house? She'd bet Valentina had thought of it.

'Well, it's just...' He was too weak to move things forward and for that, perhaps, she was glad; she had enough to cope with for now.

'You'll need to tell your mother, Kevin. From now on you're going to be bringing her to Mass every Sunday.' She grabbed an apple from the top of a newly delivered box and took a satisfying bite. God, but she'd love to be a fly on the wall when he told Maureen Mulvey about Valentina.

Working in the restaurant that evening was hard. There was no point lying to herself. Carrie sidestepped Valentina when she could, but they couldn't avoid each other. Perhaps she could ask some of their friends to give Valentina work in their restaurant. Jim McGrath ran a little bistro on the north side; she'd make a bomb there in tips. She could suggest it to Kevin, maybe, in a few weeks, when they had time to cool down, all of them.

That was the funny thing though; they were all very cool about this. She hadn't lost her temper, she hadn't screamed or shouted, or thrown plates. Today at least, she didn't want to hit him or hurt him in any way and maybe, that meant something. Maybe it meant something more than she'd have realised if this hadn't happened. Oh, she was hurt. She was hurt beyond description, the kind of pain that goes deep into the core of you. Even when she thought she'd cried herself out, she felt a new current of grief rise within her, bringing waves of tears to her eyes that there was no stopping. Poor Teddy had leant against her leg, lapped up the tears and occasionally rested his head on her lap, as if to offer her his own brand of sympathy. It was a funny thing; there was something in the dog that made her feel he actually got her pain, he, by his very wish to console her, somehow made things better. She was so glad to have him in the house with her.

She looked up at the clock, almost ten p.m. She walked to the door. Across the road, The Marchant Inn was in darkness and its emptiness thrashed like a wave of lonesomeness through Carrie. She thought of Jane, so fragile and alone in the hospital. Through all those tears, Carrie had made a promise of sorts, even if she hadn't put it into words – she was going to look out for Jane from now on. Somehow, she was going to help that lonely woman get back to a life that meant something. She sighed, perhaps it would do her good to think about someone else for a while and take her mind off Kevin and Valentina.

Sunday night was always quiet, very few bookings this evening and generally, everyone was seated by nine or half past and they managed to clear out by twelve. She was looking forward to getting out of here now. Funny, but she'd never felt like that before.

Carrie slipped upstairs to her office and turned on the computer. She logged into her Facebook account to catch up with what was happening with people she knew who were flung all over the world these days. For one more time, she could pretend that everything was normal. Then she'd call Anna and tomorrow she'd go and see her mother.

'I have been thinking Keveen, thees place, you are right, it ees not good for us,' Valentina pouted at him the following day.

'Of course it's not, we should be…' he wasn't sure what to say next. Did he want to set up home with Valentina? Of course he did, he'd be mad not to, wouldn't he? 'We should look for somewhere to live, properly, a nice place, just the two of us.' He'd had enough of Reda and Simo.

'Yes, just the two of us. We should go hunting houses, ees that what you call it?'

'House hunting, of course,' he hated the idea of having to find somewhere, but equally, having seen how Valentina was content to live, he wasn't sure he entirely trusted her judgement around the bigger issues in life. 'Er, what kind of place would you like?' It was worth asking.

'Oh, I don't know, not too big. But somewhere nice, maybe close to the restaurant?'

'Well, that all sounds very sensible.' He was trying to rack his brains for houses in the outlying areas of

Dublin, 'Perhaps the Liberties?' It was a reasonable area, certainly not posh or glamorous, but it was safe and very affordable.

'Oh, no, Kevin, that is just grotty and we would want to be in a safer part of the city, especially for parking your car, non?' she shrugged, threw her eyes up towards heaven and snorted a feminine little sound that made him smile. 'Maybe, I go looking, I pick something nice and then you decide? Non?'

'Well, there's no harm looking, I suppose.' Kevin wasn't sure. Carrie took care of all the domestic issues for him and before Carrie his mother had made sure that life was just tickety-boo. His mother. He would have to talk to her. He would not be telling his mother about Valentina. Wasn't she always saying she had a delicate constitution? What good was there in giving her too many shocks at once? He'd managed to avoid Penny, by the grace of God, she'd rung up his purchases in advance, so all he had to do was swipe his Mastercard while she talked to some smart young buyer they'd foisted on her from head office. Maureen Mulvey, his mother, would not be so easily distracted. He would bring flowers. Flowers were always good for women of a certain age.

'Kevin, you know I hate flowers. I've been allergic for years,' she sniffed as she put them in a vase and left them in the front porch for all the neighbours to admire. 'Anyway, I don't need flowers from you, all I ask is a lift to Mass on Sundays and an occasional phone call during the week.' She was still miffed at having missed Mass. Honestly, sometimes women could be so unforgiving.

'Yes, Mum, about Mass.'

'What about Mass?' she whipped around, far faster than he thought possible for a woman of her age.

'Well,' Kevin moved towards the kitchen, 'Carrie, didn't collect you?'

'You're not telling me something I don't know. She didn't even have the decency to ring. Not so much as an apology and me sitting here in my Sunday best and no Mass. I mean, if she'd said. If she'd had the manners to ring and let me know. Well then, maybe I could have gone with the Brownes next door, or even a taxi.'

'Yes, Mother, the thing is…' this wasn't easy, he knew it wouldn't be. 'Well, we're not actually, I mean, she's not actually my…' God, he was making a complete bags of it.

'Kevin, for goodness' sake, out with it,' his mother spat angrily in his direction.

'That is to say, we're not actually…' he chewed his lip, could feel a salty rise in his gums, he had to say it. 'We're not together anymore. We're finished, I mean, she's not my girlfriend anymore.'

'She's not your girlfriend?' His mother shook her head. 'Really, Kevin, that's ridiculous. You're not fifteen anymore, either of you. You don't just go breaking up with your girlfriend when you're forty-something and you're living together with a business. It's the other way you're meant to be going. Booking the day, I should be buying a new hat.' The news was sinking in; she fell into the reclining chair Carrie had bought her a few Christmases earlier. It was deep and plush and the most comfortable chair she could find in Dublin. It was from them both, of course, but his mother always called it Kevin's chair. She placed a hand, smaller and older than he remembered, on the arm and held it tightly. 'No, Kevin, you have to do something. You've been living together...' she shook her head, 'in *sin*.'

'Mum, it's not like that nowadays.'

'Sin is sin. It doesn't matter if you're about to walk across the Red Sea or boarding a spaceship. In the Lord's eyes, a man and a woman, living together like that... Well, it's just not right.'

'People don't actually see it like that these days; it's not how things work now.'

'Well, how things work now isn't always the right way round.' She went silent for a moment, digesting perhaps the reality of her newly single son, or some greater question about the lost morality of a whole generation. 'So?' She met his eyes and there was no looking away.

'So?' He wasn't sure what she wanted him to say. Did she want him to tell her that he would go and try to win Carrie back or was there some more awkward question settling on her lips.

'So, did you ask her to marry you?' She nodded, perhaps believing that all would be well if he popped the magic question.

'No. It's not like that, Mum. Getting married doesn't fix things. For some people it only adds more complications.'

'Of course, we wouldn't want to complicate it by doing the right thing, now would we?'

'Oh, Mum.' He slumped down opposite her at the table. He didn't like this. He was normally the apple of his mother's eye. Sometimes, even with all the giving out and the sarky remarks, he used to think she liked the idea of him not having married Carrie. It was no secret – Maureen Mulvey believed the woman good enough for her son had yet to be created. Carrie was as good as they could manage, although perhaps not good enough to marry. 'Mum, I didn't ask her to marry me because I'm not in love with her anymore.'

'What kind of a reason is that?' She looked completely perplexed.

'I think it's a very valid reason. And, maybe, if you asked Carrie, she might feel the same way.' Well, he reasoned, she might very well feel the same way now that she knew he was playing away with Valentina.

'Young people, I don't know.' She sighed. 'Do you think I was "in love" with your father every day of our lives? Don't you think for one minute that any marriage is all roses and light, because it's not. No, but it's the determination to stick with it, that's what gets you to the end.' She was tapping her fingers on the armrests, as though playing out a complex piece of music and Kevin had a horrible feeling it was moving towards a crescendo.

'Well, it's important to me, Mother.' He kept his voice low; he couldn't manage to meet her eye. He was willing himself not to let Valentina's name slip into the brewing disapproval between them.

'And what about the restaurant? What about that lovely little house you bought together? What about all the years? You've taken that girl's best years from her; do you know that? Have you thought about that, Kevin?'

'It's not like that,' of course he hadn't thought about that. He'd fallen in love with Valentina and she was dark and dusky and beautiful. She did things to him that had nothing to do with best years or The Sea Pear or the smart little detached house that he'd bought with Carrie when prices were low and they had money flowing in. 'Carrie never mentioned kids or marriage or any of that. She wanted what I wanted, she wanted the restaurant and to be a success. We've achieved a lot together, but things change.'

'It wasn't up to Carrie to mention marriage or kids,' Maureen Mulvey sighed, and in that lament, Kevin caught a whole lifetime of discontent blown into the kitchen. A whole raft of frustration and disillusionment fell heavily on his shoulders. Suffocating silence cloyed about them, but there was nothing to say. To Kevin's mind, his mother's ideas were outmoded – best years indeed.

Later, on his drive back into the city, he would find the words he needed to say. He'd given Carrie as much and, to his mind, more than she'd given him. The truth was, they slept in separate beds, in separate rooms and that had suited Carrie every bit as much as it had suited him. They had stopped being a couple and fallen into something platonic long before Valentina had arrived. Carrie might have encouraged him to sleep in the spare room because she had a sinus infection, but she'd never suggested he return when medication cleared it up.

It seemed to Kevin that the only thing holding them together was the restaurant.

Luke hated the nursing home. It wasn't that there was anything wrong with it exactly, but it was that overriding feeling, that everyone here was standing in line. They were all in a waiting room and nobody particularly wanted to be first called. It was unfortunate that the place backed onto a graveyard. The original building started out as a convent, the graveyard had long been decommissioned, the nuns buried elsewhere and two lines of small black crosses now weaved evenly along a narrow path. It was cruel too, to think that even the people here made him feel just a little anxious. Would his father become just like the old man who wandered the corridors always searching for Emily?

'Dad, are you ready?' Two months ago, Luke would have said that his father was probably the fittest man here, if not the youngest. But it seemed over the last few weeks his father had very quickly fallen into old age, as though he'd taken a giant leap and bypassed several years where he might have just slowed down more gradually. Still, he had a mop of strong snow-white hair that truculently misbehaved when it grew a little too long. Like Luke, Conn Gibson had spent most of his life travelling. He had pulled his only son to the four corners of the world in the name of research and archaeology. There was no doubt he had lived a full and interesting life, but the downside was that when it came to retire, nowhere really felt quite like home. He had chosen Ballyglen, over other equally available options, but lately, Luke wondered if even Conn was beginning to realise he'd chosen in haste.

'Always ready, you know me,' Conn quipped. Still, he kept a compass by his bed and a penknife in his pocket. 'Where are we off to today?' and it seemed to Luke that there was fatigue that hung about his father and it went far beyond his years, to something deeper that couldn't be papered over for much longer.

'I don't know, where do you fancy?'

'Well, they put up dinner here at five,' Conn looked at his watch, but they both knew that it would take more years than he had left to become a man who worried about mealtimes or regular hours.

'Should we skip out of here and make dinner my treat?' Luke offered and they made their way out of Ballyglen without a backwards glance.

It was always the same, they took the battered jeep that Conn had held onto for years and drove out to the Phoenix Park. If they were lucky, they would watch as a herd of deer made their way across their paths. In this weather, it was hard to knock half an hour out of Conn's favourite bench, but sitting there, watching their icy breaths on the afternoon air, somehow settled Luke. It wasn't what they spoke of, so much as knowing that they didn't need to say a word; their companionship was complete already. Luke sensed that his father had hit some kind of divide in his life. Conn Gibson wore hesitancy like a buttoned-up coat, sometimes sunk deep within it and hardly saying a word when they sat here together. At other times, it was as if it stifled him and he was restless, wanting to be gone without any clear destination. There was an undercurrent of decisions to make and, at this moment, he was just treading water, unsure which path to take. Perhaps this unease had some contagious quality, because far from wanting to get back to the real world, Luke was feeling more each day that he too was being faced with a choice, not to go, or where to go, but rather that he might stay. Very often, they just sat contemplating so many things, comfortably and silently.

'Colder today,' he said gently after they had watched a stag course through the open plain, his hoof marks cutting deep into the untouched snow. Behind him, the herd followed, a mixture of reluctant keeping up and playful sauntering. 'There's a nice place to eat, near where I'm staying, if you fancy something warm,' Luke offered.

'As long as we don't have to meet your awful Mrs Peril.' Conn chuckled. Luke's landlady had a way of enquiring just a little too earnestly after everyone's affairs.

'No fear.'

They made their way back to the jeep.

The Sea Pear was quiet, only just opened for the evening trade. It was Luke's first time to eat here, and somehow it didn't seem quite as welcoming without Carrie. Instead, a dusky Colombian showed them to their seats and flirted with them both as though she might make off with their wallets as soon as they turned their backs. Still, the food was good and on their way out the door, his father noticed the pub opposite.

'God, that brings me back,' he sighed.

'What's that?' Luke asked.

'Nothing, just – The Marchant Inn – there was a pub in London of the same name, must be sixty years ago now.' He shook his head sadly. 'That's the problem when you get old, Luke, too many memories not enough time to think of them all and then some of them jump at you like The Marchant Inn, and it's so long ago they're almost like they belong to someone else.'

'Hmm,' Luke said and it struck him then that there was something about the place, as though it was drawing him. He decided he would ask Carrie about it again the next time he ran into her.

4

'You should tell Kevin to stick it, Carrie, seriously, cut your losses and make a run for it,' Anna was topping up her glass of Chianti.

'Mum said the same and then some,' Carrie had cried for real when she went to her mother's house. It had taken as much courage to be able to come clean with everyone that mattered as it had to face the truth herself. 'Melissa wants me to dig my heels in, take half of everything and start fresh over in Scotland,' Carrie exhaled noisily; Glasgow seemed like just the new start she needed.

'Would you?' Anna stopped pouring wine into her glass. 'Glasgow,' she tried the word for size on her lips. In Ireland, in deepest November, when falling snow turned to sleet and then to slush on the city streets, anywhere at all seemed like a good idea, even if it turned out to be every bit as wet and cold as Dublin.

'It was just a suggestion,' Carrie smiled, she'd considered it for all of two minutes. But she knew that would be running away and she wasn't going to be the one to run away. 'Why would I? Anna, it dawned on me, why should I be the one to leave? And anyway, by the time I'd sold the house and got the business sorted, perhaps all the tension would have died down and then I might be really sorry.'

'So, you're going to soldier on?' Anna sat opposite her friend, tucked her long legs beneath her on her second-hand couch. Carrie loved Anna's flat, always had. It was like visiting a friendly aunt – the place had its own identity. It was filled with market and pawnshop finds, always messy. The scent of beeswax and old books and Chanel No. 5 held a comforting medley. It played out against a backdrop of some of their happiest times spent together righting the world with tea and wine and cake. Teddy just seemed to blend into the place, taking up a deep cushion on a ratty ottoman that Anna had promised to dump years earlier. 'Keep going in there to face Kevin and his dolly bird.'

'I don't think I have a choice, not really, not yet.' Carrie had mulled over it for the whole week, she thought about little else, at least thinking about her future kept her mind out of the present. 'I'd be mad to do anything rash. I'm giving it six months. Then, if I feel I want a change, I can tell Kevin I want out. By then I'll have a better idea of what I actually want.' At least, that was what she hoped.

'Can you really go in there and face them every day?' Anna shook her lovely steely blonde hair. They both knew Anna would have walked away long ago.

'I'm hoping it'll get easier.' Carrie smiled and felt again the stab of something rise in her chest. She knew that being here, with Anna, she could easily begin to cry once more.

'Well, you should think about at least taking a holiday? It seems like a long time since you went anywhere and it's not as if they can't cope, from the sounds of things. Surely they can take the Christmas party bookings and you can dive into it when you get back?'

'A holiday?' Carrie hadn't taken a holiday in so long. Not really. She'd been to Italy for a weekend a few years earlier, but that was for Penny's wedding. Spending three days and nights with Maureen Mulvey hardly counted as a holiday in anyone's book.

'Yes, people do, all the time. They just book a flight and disappear; you have a passport, haven't you? Lots of people just book a hotel and they sit by the pool, getting slowly sloshed while reading a trashy novel. You should, it would do you good.'

'I suppose I could...' Carrie closed her eyes for a moment, could imagine the sun on her skin, the smell of somewhere exotic. 'Perhaps, I will.'

'God, I'd love to go on holiday,' Anna said. Anna was always flitting off somewhere, 'Not that I'm not grateful.' She had landed her first part in years. It wasn't a big part, but it was *The Mousetrap* and it was in the Olympia Theatre, so that much alone was enough to keep her in Dublin for the next six weeks. 'You should go on your own. I've always met nice... people,' they both knew she meant men, 'when I've travelled alone.'

'Honestly, Anna, I'm fine without meeting anyone, nice or otherwise.'

'Still, imagine turning up at The Sea Pear with your hot new Latino lover,' Anna smiled, but Carrie had a feeling that Kevin would hardly notice, not if Valentina was anywhere near.

Carrie caught a taxi home late that night. The driver was Romanian and as dog crazy as she could have hoped for – Teddy lay on the floor, but it was better than walking. She could have stayed with Anna. Normally, when they had too much to drink, she hopped into the large creaky double bed and fell into a stupor beside her childhood friend. Then, in the morning, Anna made tea for both of them and they nursed their sore heads over whatever Carrie could rustle together from the scant contents of the fridge.

Carrie wasn't sure why she needed to get home so urgently. She didn't think Kevin would be there, locks changed with her bags packed in the garden. It wasn't anything like that. But, she just needed to be home.

She went straight to the narrow dresser she kept in the kitchen. It was filled with bills and bank statements and somewhere, at the back of many pieces of paper that spelled out their financial lives together, she found her passport.

Of course, she could book a holiday. A week in the sun, somewhere she'd never been before. Somewhere warm, exotic and anonymous. She looked at the passport in her hand, another two years left on it. The possible destinations were endless. This time of year, she could head for Mexico or Dubai or somewhere even more exotic, like St Lucia or Antigua. She stood for a moment, the passport in her hand as visions of all of these places floated about in her mind. Then she looked down at Teddy, his brown glassy eyes staring up at her with a growing adoration and reality set in. She knew – some deep part of her knew – that she couldn't do it. For one thing, it would be running away and for another, how could she just leave this little fella?

She opened her eyes, looked around her kitchen. It wasn't big, it wasn't an impressive space where Kevin could whip up extravagant meals for them. It was a small galley with a round table that seated four, but rarely did. Mostly it was a place where she ate breakfast – tea and toast with too much butter and jam. It was her kitchen. Here, every item meant something to her, from the cracked pottery vase at the window, to the salvaged tiles beneath her feet. This was her home and, deep within her, she knew she had made one important decision. She was staying put, in this house at least. Even if she wasn't sure about The Sea Pear or anything else in life, she was sure about that. This little house that smelled of yesterday's toast and needed a good clear-out, this was her home and she was not leaving it.

When she fell asleep, it was fast and deep and she woke in the morning with a sense of some calm. Two decisions were made.

She rang Kevin as soon as she got up. On the mobile, he answered, his voice filled with a deep sleep, she felt he had no right to.

'Yeah,' he said and Carrie imagined Valentina's arm snaking across his pale chest as he spoke.

'I'm taking a holiday Kevin. I need to sort things out. I won't be at the restaurant for the next week, at least.'

'Oh. Okay.' Suddenly the sleep had fallen from his voice, torpedoed as much from her call as from its contents. She never took time off and she knew Kevin well enough to know that it would bother him. It would upset him that she was not in the restaurant. It would irritate him that she had somewhere else to be. It would rankle that she had not consulted him; even now it would peeve him. And perhaps it would annoy Valentina too, once the gloss dulled on having the restaurant to herself for a few days.

'I'm entitled to a holiday, I'm taking it to...' and then Carrie smiled thinking of the next few days and how this conversation would play around in his head. 'Well, never mind what I'm doing, that's really no concern of yours now, is it?' and she hung up the phone.

Then it dawned on her. What on earth would she do with herself for a whole week?

She would clear Kevin Mulvey out of her home; that was what she would do. She would clear him out in every way she could.

At ten o'clock, she rang the bank and made an appointment for the following day. There were practical things that needed to be done and Carrie was nothing if not practical. She looked down at Teddy, ruffled his suede soft ears, 'And then, we must see how we're going to manage to sort you out.' His eyes appealed to her in their own silent way, beseeching her to do the right thing by him. The least she could do now was get Teddy chipped, then she could see about adopting him if no one came looking for him.

First though, she would visit Jane and her heart felt even lighter, because that was eminently more enjoyable than what had once been her daily penance of dropping into Maureen Mulvey.

'Eet is a surprise,' Valentina was saying as she dragged him through morning shoppers, crossing O'Connell Bridge at speed. 'I am so happy, with eet. I hope you will like eet too.' This was their first to view together. 'Eet is not cheap, but eet is...' she waved her lovely tapered hands in the air in a theatrical way and he knew he could not say no to her.

She was right, it was not cheap. It was astro-bloody-nomical.

'Eet is expensive for a reason. Over there,' Valentina pointed along the balcony, 'you see, over there, you are looking into the studio where U2 record their albums and there, you see...' She was so excited, it would have been adorable if she didn't expect him to sign a lease that was going to cost as much as buying on the Champs Elysées.

'Okay, Valentina I get it, there's boy bands, and rockers and lots of wealthy people living here, but I'm just a chef. I'm not in Coldplay or the Rolling Stones, you know.'

'You are keeding,' she smiled. God how he loved the way she pronounced her i's making her smile in the middle of sentences when really she was quite perplexed. 'You own the most successful restaurant in Dublin. These people they would kneel to get a table on a busy night. You told me thees, yourself, you remember.'

He did remember, of course he remembered. He may have mentioned this more than once, in the beginning, when he was trying to impress her and the tall tales didn't seem like they could do any harm.

'Okay, so this is what you really want, is it?' To be fair, it wasn't huge, there was only one bedroom, but the living room was vast, the agent kept calling it the studio. It was built to impress. The kitchen was tiny and the bathroom was just about big enough to stand in between shower, toilet and sink. It was all about the balcony; the view was impressive. He could imagine them, sitting out there, drinking champagne, perhaps making love... 'We'll take it.' He said the words firmly, what was he resisting for? He could afford it. He was just used to not thinking about these things. Carrie dealt with the mortgage; she dealt with everything. The lease was only for a year, while the owner was out of town, so it wasn't as if he was tying himself to it forever, and it came furnished. So, in the space of an hour, they had found somewhere to live, together, stylishly and, dear God, he couldn't help himself, but very expensively.

'You can move in immediately,' the agent was telling Valentina.

'That ees good, eesn't it Keveen?'

She turned to him now, her dark eyes held so much promise and he couldn't help but think how lucky he was to have this whole new, easy life opening up before him. Still, in the back of his mind, the call from Carrie unsettled him. What was she up to? Carrie never took time off. What would she do with a whole week? It wasn't like Carrie to be so… secretive. The thought made him feel cold, then he caught Valentina's eye and smiled at her. What was he thinking of Carrie for? After all, he'd gotten what he wanted, he had the lovely Valentina here before him.

The next few days ran into each other too quickly, it seemed to Kevin. The restaurant was crazy busy. He and Valentina moved into the new apartment. There wasn't a spare minute to catch his breath until Wednesday afternoon when he met up with Jim for their weekly catch-up. Jim was halfway through his pint when Kevin arrived.

'Starting early?' he eyed the half-drunk pint of Guinness.

'Running late?' Jim countered, they both knew that Kevin hated people being late. *He*, he would tell people proudly, was never late.

'I didn't realise there was a clock on me?' Kevin sat grumpily on the high stool and nodded towards the barman at the far end of the counter. 'Same,' he looked to Jim and nodded towards the barman.

'So, how's paradise?' Jim asked drily, keeping his eyes on a rugby match playing silently on a screen over the bar.

'Don't start,' Kevin needed a pint. He remembered his father coming in late on Friday nights. He had 'needed a pint', too. He needed, Kevin realised later, to meet up with a woman who worked at the reception in his garage. Thelma Jones was a plump middle-aged woman. She looked nothing like the vixen Kevin imagined someone having an affair should be. She'd turned up at every family event, cheesecake or lemon drizzle cake in hand. She smiled kindly at his mother, while unbeknownst to all of them she had cheerfully carried on with his father for over two decades. Thelma Jones, he hadn't thought of her in years. And this, this was nothing like that sordid affair. For one thing, Valentina was nothing like old Thelma, with her cheap mackintosh coats that strained against her ample bosom and behind.

'So, the word is out, anyway,' Jim peered at him now, as though inspecting some laboratory experiment.

'What's that?' it had to be important to distract Jim from the rugby.

'Sandra said that Carrie told Anna who told everyone. Women, what are they like?' Jim shook his head, smiling benignly.

'What did Sandra say?' Kevin had to know, this was the bit he was dreading after all. It was why he put off telling his mother, why he didn't want to hang about for Penny. It was why, if he was honest with himself, he hadn't really told anyone, apart from Jim, and really, blokes don't count for something like this.

'What do you think she said?' Jim shook his head. He nodded thanks to the barman and straightened his pint carefully on the beer mat before him. There was no beer mat for Kevin and it didn't look like one would be forthcoming. Did the barman know too? 'Come on, Kevin, you know the score. Sandra and Anna and Carrie, they've been friends for years. It'll have spread like wildfire.'

'What did she say?' He repeated.

'What didn't she say you mean?'

'Carrie?'

'No, Sandra. Don't be a dope. Carrie wouldn't say anything bad about you, not really. She's hurt, according to Sandra. But Anna? Now that's a horse of a different colour. She has plenty to say, but nothing you wouldn't be expecting.'

'Like what?' Part of Kevin didn't want to know, in fact even now, he felt his collar tighten uncomfortably about his neck. He hated the idea of not being perfect. He hated the idea of what they might be saying about him and how it might be drawn out to look like something it wasn't.

'Look. Nothing that isn't the truth as far as they see it, mate. Nothing to worry about. Maybe you won't be fooling them as much as you have before, but we're still mates, aren't we?'

'Yes, but what's that supposed to mean?'

'Well, I've seen through you for years. I've always known that you were a selfish bastard. It hasn't changed our friendship, though, has it?'

'Thanks for that, mate.' Kevin shook his head. He needed to know what they thought of him. No, he needed to know that they weren't going to see him as he'd seen his father all those years ago. He needed to know that he could still be Kevin. Sound, successful, hard-working Kevin. He couldn't bear it if they thought... What? He didn't want to think about it anymore. He returned to his pint. His eyes drawn involuntarily to the rugby. He hated rugby. The silence between them, which in the past Kevin never noticed, seemed to stretch awkwardly, intensely now. Jim must have felt it too; he turned towards Kevin.

'Don't be too hard on yourself, mate. These things happen. So? Sandra and Anna will bitch about you being an ungrateful, disloyal sod with no backbone for a while. They'll get over it. Carrie will move on. She'll meet someone else.'

'I can't really see Carrie meeting anyone, can you?' Carrie was far too... boring. She was like Kevin really. Only she was curvier. To Kevin's mind, Carrie was unlikely to become desirable anytime soon, because she was too fond of Kevin's cream sauces.

'You never know, mate. Look at you.' Jim nodded towards his pint, as though confirming it all in his mind. 'These things blow over. In time, you'll get the restaurant sorted and the house and you'll both move on. You and Valentina will become as boring as me and Sandra or you and Carrie. And then, who knows?'

'Who knows what?'

'Well, they may want to spend time in the same room as you again.' Jim chuckled as he drew deep into his fresh pint. 'Anyway, what do you care? You have Valentina, you're madly in lust with her and you still have Carrie taking care of business. The best of both worlds, I'd say.'

Naturally, Kevin did care. He cared very much that they should think badly of him. He could blame it on his middle-class upbringing. He could hold his mother responsible for her pious affliction sprinkled liberally about their home. It was nothing short of a miracle that his father managed to survive it for as long as he did. For Kevin it meant that he had to be the best he could be, in every way. Some might call him weak. Kevin liked to think of himself not so much as an outward people-pleaser but more as a lover of stability. Why rock the boat? Why not present the parts of yourself that others would like best? When there were battles, Carrie took those on. She fought with the landlord when they had one, to make sure they got the best deal on the rent. She took on the council when they wanted to increase their rates. Carrie sorted out disgruntled staff, unhappy customers and, back in the day, when things were tight, suppliers who had to wait another week for payment. Kevin reasoned, these tasks were not in his skill set.

Now, with Sandra and Anna and all of their other friends, Kevin wanted to set them straight. He wanted to let them know that... He wasn't sure what he could do to let them know that he was still good old Kevin. Suddenly the landscape had changed, the ground beneath him felt uneven and rocky and he wasn't sure there was anything he could do that didn't make him look like he was a disloyal git. At least, he didn't have to face Carrie this evening. That was something; the breathing space would be good for all of them.

Luke wasn't sure if he'd talked Carrie into it, or if she'd invited him along, but there was something right about going to the hospital with her to visit Jane Marchant. Strangely, it seemed to Luke that the hospital was a better destination than the nursing home. At least people were moving about in the corridors with purpose. They may not get well, but at least they would go home. That was unfair, he knew that plenty of people in Ballyglen were very happy to be living there – the thing that hung about Luke was the feeling in his gut that it just wasn't the right place for his father to be.

'I remember seeing you,' Jane Marchant smiled once Carrie had made the introductions. 'That night, you were on the street, opposite, I thought for a moment...' Large tears rested in the corner of her eyes. 'But it was dark and I was probably in shock, but you looked for all the world like my Manus, standing there. He was tall and dark too, broad-shouldered, very good-looking. God he took on all the worries, he made me feel so safe. Oh, he was such a fine man when I met him.' She smiled now, the memory taking her to a happier place, so when she dried her tears, Luke could see that, once, she must have been very pretty.

'I wasn't sure if I should go and offer to help, they seemed to have taken good care of you, but when Carrie said she was coming to visit you...' He had brought along a small bunch of flowers, bright and gay, full of cheer, a measure of optimism for her neat locker. Their startling colours held tenaciously against the insipidness of the surroundings.

'Ah, yes, the ambulance men were lovely, they tried calling,' she nodded across at Carrie, 'but of course, I knew they wouldn't get her, sure, anyone would be worn out with the long days you put in over there.'

'Well, not this week.'

'No?'

'No, I'm making changes and this week I'm on holiday with a whole seven days to spend sorting out some things that have probably needed sorting for a long time.'

'That's good, you deserve a break, you really do work awfully hard,' Jane said.

'Do you want me to go into the pub, water plants, check that everything is unplugged and all of those sorts of things?'

'Would you? I don't suppose there's a whole lot of post, but certainly, it'd be good to know that everything is safe and sound for when I have to go back.'

'You sound as if it's the last thing you want?' Luke chuckled.

'Oh, well…' Jane shook her head sadly. 'It's actually been quite nice here, you know, a bit of company…' She looked at the bed opposite and a plump woman propped up on pillows. She was surrounded by a gaggle of visiting grandchildren; all tucking heartily into sweets and grapes.

'Still, it'll be nice to get back to your own corner, a bit a peace and quiet and all that,' the woman opposite her shouted from amidst the din of her visiting relatives.

'Yes, and I'll visit you every day, and you'll have your regulars, I'm sure they're really missing popping in for a pint or a cup of tea,' Carrie said softly.

'Oh, I'm afraid since Manus died, I don't have what you'd call a roaring trade anymore, just a few of the locals who drop in for a catch-up as much as anything else. I'm sure some of them will probably be relieved to see the doors closed.' She laughed at this, and Luke figured he couldn't imagine someone so frail taking care of herself, never mind looking after a pub on her own.

'It seems like a lot, to get back to straight away,' he murmured.

'Well, they're saying I'll be here for a few more days anyway. I think they're erring on the side of caution in case I slip on an icy path and the fact that I'm living on my own. Perhaps they're afraid that I'll go hitting the brandy bottle and fall over again.' She smiled and Luke realised she must have been good fun when she was fit and healthy.

'Well, I can get the heating on and get the fridge filled before you come back,' Carrie said. She dug into her bag and pulled out a bundle of magazines and a large bottle of mineral water; which she left on the locker. 'It'll be lovely to have you back, and you'll see, it'll be great to be home.' Carrie smiled at her and even Luke knew she was doing her best to make everything right.

5

Six large black bags. Six plastic refuse bags and counting.
They were lined up in the hallway. She'd placed
almost all his clothes, folded carefully, in the bags while
Teddy watched intently, perhaps knowing that in some
way this ritual was marking out something momentous
in Carrie's life. She hadn't included his socks. Kevin loved
his socks, always suffered from cold feet; his long bony
toes went a peculiar shade of blue-purple-orange when
he was cold. So, Carrie bought his socks specially, from a
woman who lived deep in Connemara – the other side of
the country. She shook her head now thinking of her own
stupidity. She paid handsomely to have them knitted and
then lined in cotton. He wore them winter, spring and
autumn. Replacing them would entail a special trip across
the country, very cold feet and a gnarly temperament
until he got there. Carrie made quite the ceremony out
of laundering them and then taking them along to the
nearby Simon office to donate to the homeless people.
It was an act of generosity, she reasoned. It gave her far
more satisfaction than she had any right to. She made
up for it by taking extra care of what she did pack for

him. She carefully folded each shirt. Would he notice? Probably not. Each bag filled with shoes at the bottom, jackets next and so on until the lighter items sat on top.

Six bags and she had not even looked at their CD collection or the other bits and pieces they had accumulated over the years. He could have the CDs. She wouldn't be listening to them anymore. The same went for photographs, albums and anything that would bring memories flooding back. She would have to ask him, but she had a feeling he would not want them either.

She called a cab when she managed to pack up the last of the black bags. She paid the driver extra to deliver the lot to the restaurant. They would arrive before opening time and she gave him directions to leave them with either Kevin or Andrew.

Andrew. She should ring him, at least let him know that she was fine. Andrew was more than an employee. He'd been with them since they started. Carrie made sure they kept him by paying him well and looking after him when he needed it. He had become a friend, well, Carrie's friend anyway. Kevin was much too homophobic to make any real connection with Andrew. When she rang him, she told him about Teddy.

'Carrie, perhaps you should just leave him at the dog shelter, before you get too attached,' he said gently.

'I won't get attached, but he's nice company for now,' Carrie said and she loved that Andrew understood that you could become so fond of an animal so quickly. 'Will you keep an ear out, see if anyone is missing him about the area?'

'Of course I will, but you know, he might have just been dumped here. He could be from the other side of the city for all anyone knows.'

'Luke says that he has a feeling that he's been well looked after, perhaps he belongs to someone elderly.'

'Luke?'

'Luke Gibson… he's half the reason I've got Teddy here, he's keeping an eye out to see if anyone is missing him.'

'I see,' Andrew said thoughtfully. 'Will you be all right?' Andrew kept his voice light, but Carrie heard the concern in his words.

'I'll be fine. I need to take a little time. You just make sure I have a restaurant to come back to, okay?'

'Sure thing, boss.' He said the words in a Boston accent, thick and nasally and they both laughed at it. 'You know, it's his loss. Valentina, well, she's not all she cracks herself up to be?'

'So her boobs aren't real, is that what you're telling me?' Carrie joked.

'No, they probably are, but boobs and butts, well they tend to lose their pertness. A kind heart never does.'

'No, but Mother Teresa had a kind heart, and I don't think she had a legion of suitors knocking down her door.'

'You know what I mean,' Andrew's voice was low, as if someone was close by. 'Mind yourself, okay?'

'Sure thing, boss.' And they both laughed at her disastrous attempt at a Boston accent.

★

The clear-out took a solid two days, but it was worth it. Carrie cried when she came across mementos that brought happier memories flooding back. She would be lying if she didn't admit that she was still angry, still wanted to kick against the unfairness of it all. But she was practical enough to know when she was beaten. She couldn't compete with Valentina and when she thought about them together, she wasn't sure she wanted to. Sometimes, when she was really still, she remembered that things with Kevin had already fizzled away long before she suggested he sleep in the spare room. Honestly, maybe she could have tried to ignite more of a spark, but she had come to the stage where mothering had taken over and attraction had long since rushed out the door. When Carrie sat down at her kitchen table at the end of it, she felt somehow the whole house had been exorcised of Kevin and it was, unexpectedly, a good feeling.

The bank had been very happy to help her buy him out of the mortgage. It wasn't a huge amount, but it was enough for him to start somewhere else with the wind on his back. And that was what she would tell him. This house, regardless of anything else, this house was non-negotiable. The loan would be sorted within a few days. Once she had the relevant documents from the bank and their solicitor drawn up she'd get Kevin to sign away any right he had to it. She was being reasonable and fair about it. It was hardly her fault that the property market had changed so drastically in the last five years. Anyway, she couldn't see Valentina living somewhere like this.

She looked about her little kitchen. 'Perhaps we should

repaint?' she whispered to Teddy who was lying at her feet.

The following morning she woke, her head pounding with an overwhelming dose of cabin fever. Teddy looked as if he might be feeling it too and he dropped his lead before her while she lazily picked up the letters from inside the front door. 'You really are very good for me,' she nuzzled his warm neck. There was no danger that she could cut herself off with Teddy around. Melissa rang her before she had a chance to boil the kettle.

'Hi stranger, have you forgotten I'm flying in today?' Melissa was already at the airport, but that realisation was only dawning on Carrie. After all, she'd marked it on the calendar weeks ago. Funny, this was the first time in years she hadn't moved the page forward. Now a golden retriever sitting in tawny autumn leaves glared at her from the spent page on the cork notice board.

'Oh my God, is it today? I can't believe it, oh, Melissa, I'm so sorry.' Carrie said the sentence as though it was one word. She never forgot things like this.

'Don't worry, it's a first.' Melissa laughed lightly into the phone. Life was good, she was marrying Ben in a couple of weeks and then they would go on living their organised lives in Glasgow. 'Listen, why don't I take a taxi to yours, drop my bag off and then we'll hit the shops. You sound like you had a late night.'

'I did.' It was all Carrie could manage. How could she have forgotten about Melissa? How could she have forgotten about their wedding? And, God, what was she going to say to her in less than an hour? This was meant to be one of the happiest times in her friend's life. Getting dresses organised for the day of her dreams. They'd booked a castle, down the country. The whole place would be filled with their friends for a three-day celebration in the Christmas holidays and... Oh, God. She and Kevin were going to be best man and maid of honour. She'd have to tell Melissa everything – well, a version of everything at any rate. She'd have to tell her this morning – wouldn't she? She'd have to bow out, after all, Kevin was friends with Ben long before Carrie and Melissa had ever met, in the post-break-up divvying out of alliances, surely this one belonged rightly, if regrettably, with Kevin.

Carrie ran upstairs. She pulled off her pyjamas and stood under the shower, blasting hot water down on her for as long as she could take it, until she felt too weak to stand for much longer. Then she ran a towel roughly across her body, half a thought running through her. Why should she be the one to break this news to Melissa? After all, Kevin and Ben were friends since primary school. Had Kevin actually told anyone?

She sprayed deodorant liberally about her whole body, perhaps, hoping to keep the fumes of melancholy tight within her pores. She didn't want Melissa to think she'd completely lost it. She still had her pride, she would not let herself down over Kevin Mulvey and certainly not over Valentina. She sat on the bed, thinking about the wedding. Could they just do it? Could they go through a whole weekend and pretend everything was perfect for Melissa and Ben?

No. No. No.

That would be so wrong, and anyway, they'd see clear through Kevin, wouldn't they? A niggling feeling crashed through her, falling somewhere at the bottom of her empty stomach. Would Valentina stand by and let Kevin and Carrie go off to a fancy castle for three whole days for the sake of two people she'd never met?

No.

There had to be another way.

Carrie pulled out a pair of jeans and a top. She eyed the knee boots at the bottom of her wardrobe. An unfortunate choice for her short legs and thick calves, they too should be taken to the Simon community. Instead, she pulled out a pair of black Chelsea boots and headed to the toaster.

It was as she was spreading marmalade across her third slice of bread that she knew. Melissa's wedding could be perfect; it was in Carrie's power to make sure it was perfect. The problem was not Kevin, it was in fact her. Kevin could still be best man and bring along Valentina as his date. He would not be staying in the room she'd booked months ago. He could book a bed and breakfast down the road.

And today, they were going shopping, for a dress that didn't exist. Carrie's figure would dictate that outcome. She knew when Melissa asked, it would have to be a dressmaker job for her and, even then, ample bosoms, jelly bellies and wide thighs did not go well with satin fabric. Yes. That was it. By the time Melissa arrived, her plan was shaped fully. It was only a little bit devious. She would pull out, do the honourable thing, when they couldn't find a dress to suit.

'So,' Jim was saying towards the TV screen, it was football today, some European match; it seemed to Kevin endless how many sports his friend followed. 'That's a turn-up for the books.'

'What's that?' It had been a long week. A week in which his life had tumbled over once more unexpectedly when a dozen bags arrived at the restaurant. It was silly really, of course it was inevitable, the mechanics of splitting up and moving on, but still... his clothes. All neatly folded, delivered by a taxi driver who seemed to know far too much for Kevin's comfort. There had been no socks, Kevin figured the driver had taken them. He was too annoyed to even bother chasing them up. Instead, he ordered more. They would take two weeks to arrive. Bugger. 'What's a turn-up for the books?' Suddenly he didn't like the way Jim was watching him.

'Didn't you hear?' Jim shook his head, as though he was talking to a child. 'Carrie's only got a date for Ben's wedding.'

'She can't have,' Kevin had a feeling Jim was having him on. How could Carrie have a date? For heaven's sake, she never went anywhere to meet people. And anyway, it was Carrie – who would Carrie have a date with? 'Where did you hear that?'

'Oh, Sandra was full of it. Carrie told Melissa about

you two breaking up. She said if she wanted she could choose someone else as maid of honour, that's so typical Carrie, isn't it?'

'How's that?'

'Well, putting other people first,' Jim looked across at Kevin for a moment, he sighed, as though there was no point explaining. 'Well, never mind. Anyway, she said that it didn't much matter. She could still do it, but would it be all right if she brought along a friend.'

'She probably means Anna,' Kevin felt better at that, as though the world was where he expected it to be.

'No, mate. It's not Anna.' Jim smiled now; a patronising flicker of his lips. 'She'll be having the room she booked for both of you, double bed and all. His name is…' Jim scratched his head for a minute. 'Oh, I can't remember what his name is now. Sandra never said a word to me, of course. Then Melissa lets it all spill. Never could hold her water, that one. Women, eh?' He shook his head, perplexed.

'So?' Kevin gulped down his pint. This was a lot to take in. It was the last thing he'd expected. What did she mean, going off and meeting someone like this? Someone he didn't even know? At least with him, well, it wasn't as though they didn't know Valentina. In many ways, Carrie had vetted her for him. If she was good enough to work in the restaurant after Carrie interviewed her, she had to have at least a brain in her head and something about her. No. Kevin knew Carrie better than anyone. There was some mistake. There was no way she had met up with some bloke in the space of a couple of weeks. But then, he thought about her clearing out all his stuff. Was she making way for someone else? No. He sipped his pint thoughtfully. He managed to ignore the superior twitch about Jim's lips. No, it was all some mistake. Carrie hadn't met anyone, it was just absurd. Carrie would be at home now, stuffing herself with Belgian chocolate and guzzling her way through a bottle of Pinot noir. He knew her so well. The very idea was preposterous.

Still, an uneasy feeling settled in Kevin's lower gut. It mingled with the Guinness making him feel a little nauseous. He made his way back to The Sea Pear. It was strangely liberating having both Andrew and Carrie gone for the evening. It turned out Andrew had booked the evening off weeks earlier. Valentina was well able to manage the front of house. It wasn't as if they were going to be madly busy. Kevin walked through the restaurant. He felt taller, more in command of his little empire without Carrie there to correct him or shunt him back into the kitchen out of her way. He had thought often in the last few days, what would happen to the restaurant? More so than the house, The Sea Pear was the most important thing they shared. Carrie couldn't keep working here. She wouldn't want to keep facing him and Valentina every day, would she? He should make her an offer, he thought, leaning against the old dresser that Carrie had picked up in a salvage yard when they were starting out.

Outside, he spotted a tall man, loitering for a second, then crossing over towards the old pub on the other side. He watched the man for a minute, he had taken his phone out and was talking while he crossed the street.

Obviously worked out, he decided. The man had broad shoulders and was well proportioned; he looked like one of those men who thought climbing a mountain might be a fun activity. Truthfully, he was the kind of man who made Kevin feel even smaller than he should. Funny, but up against someone who seemed so utterly normal, Kevin shrank into the sulking teenager he'd been years ago. The man turned then, caught his eye and raised his hand, as if there was some connection between them that Kevin didn't understand. Those lively green eyes seemed to take him in and assess him in one look. Kevin had a feeling the man instantly got his measure and it fell somewhere below what he had expected.

Across the road then, Kevin spotted Valentina. She was sashaying towards the man with a sense of purpose to her steps. Kevin loved watching the effect she had on other men, but the reaction of this man deflated him, he hardly noticed the Colombian beauty. Instead, he walked towards the kerb when a familiar BMW pulled up. He bent down and opened the driver's door with a gallantry that irritated Kevin. Somehow, it was all wrong, standing here, in the restaurant watching Carrie with this stranger, as though he was watching a giant screen in the movies, with familiar actors taking on unexpected roles.

Kevin stepped closer, he couldn't quite believe what he saw next. Carrie reached into her pocket and drew out the keys of The Marchant Inn, letting both herself and the stranger through the front door without a backward glance at the open-mouthed Valentina. Kevin felt a swell of something close to jealousy as he heard the door close firmly behind them.

'Who is he?' Kevin asked Valentina when she arrived in the door, bringing a blast of cold Dublin air with her.

'Heem, he eez...' she cast her eyes about trying to find the right word, 'oh, I don't know, he eez a nobody,' she said then, peeling off her new expensive coat.

'Hmph.' Kevin had long since developed the capacity to communicate a variety of negative emotions with a single sound and a shrug of his shoulders. Valentina didn't yet understand them. Her automatic embrace curbed his words before they were spent between them.

Jane hadn't forgotten that last night, or so many nights beforehand when she'd spent hours sitting on her own, listening to the sounds of the night and nursing her worst fears so even if they were realised, it would probably be a relief in the end. She knew that she couldn't expect Carrie or Luke to call on her every day. For one thing, she wasn't even sure if Luke planned to stay in Dublin. It seemed to Jane he had a restless soul and Carrie admitted late one evening that she actually knew very little about him. Rather, it seemed they had been drawn together by the little dog she talked of with such affection. Over the last few days, Luke had taken to calling in to visit her on his own and each of these visits brightened up her days no end. It was on these quiet visits, when the woman beside her either mercifully slept or was surrounded by too many relations to eavesdrop, that he managed to get the real reason she didn't want to go back to the pub out of her.

'It was fifteen years ago now,' she'd said softly and reached automatically to the side of her head, still she remembered the stitches and the searing pain that seemed to linger on far longer than it was reasonable to believe was medically possible. 'It was my fault, completely,' she drew in her breath, but each time she thought about that night, it became ragged and uneven.

'I don't believe that we can be absolutely sure that anything is ever our fault...' he'd said gently.

'Manus had gone to a tournament and I was closing up the bar for the night. I must have forgotten to lock the door. He came home after midnight, through the bar, he stumbled across a robbery – it wasn't even as if there was that much worth taking, to be honest.' She shook her head, 'When the police came, I couldn't tell them what was missing, that's how unimportant it was, but Manus was a boxer, he'd fought all his life and trained the best and, well... you can imagine...' She shuddered when she remembered the injuries they'd inflicted on him. 'You see, he would have fought fair, but they had a crowbar, they'd come prepared, probably to open a safe or locks or whatever...'

'It must have been terrible, I can see why you'd feel nervous.'

'It's nerves now, but then... really, I didn't feel anything at all. It was grief, of course, the worst kind.' She'd wiped a tear from her eye, roughly, as though it had no right to sit there anymore, she'd cried enough already. 'We were...' she stopped for a moment, then whispered, 'soul mates.' She'd smiled then, a brave watery smile, 'Now I know, I was just lucky to have him for as long as I did. The trouble is, when you lose someone like that no matter what the circumstances, you're never quite the same again.'

'You were brave to stay on, by yourself,' he said gently.

'There was nothing brave about it, I just did what I did. Leaving The Marchant Inn would have been like closing a door on the life we had together and I could never do that. I was probably in shock for years, to be honest, but you don't think like that at the time.' She shook her head, it felt good to tell Luke this, perhaps because she hadn't spoken about it in so long, only replayed it all over and over in her memory, so it felt like now she was sharing the load. 'Do you know what the worst part was, when I thought about it later?'

'No,' he said and again she saw something of Manus in him, as if he was here, right beside her at that moment. 'Tell me, if it makes you feel better.'

'He never made a sound, they beat and battered him and he took it all in silence so I wouldn't come downstairs. He died on the bar floor and I didn't know when he took his last breath – I think that's been one of the worst things to live with. To think that maybe, if he'd called out, I could have been there with him at the end.' She wiped away a gentle tear from her cheek.

'I'm so sorry,' he breathed at last. 'And that's why you're not looking forward to going back, I can understand it now.'

'No, that's not it. No, that sadness will always be with me, it wouldn't matter if I was living in The Marchant Inn or set myself up in a condo in Malibu.' She laughed at the very idea of it. 'No, the reason I don't want to go back is because I'm afraid. I've been scared in my own home for years. I dread when Finch Street empties out at the end of each day and I check the locks about fifty times after I close up.'

'You could always move?'

'I suppose I could,' she said then, looking across the ward. She sat in silence for a little while, contemplating all the reasons why she couldn't move and she wondered if there were really all that many. 'The thing is, I'm not so sure why I can't move, but I think the only thing that's kept me there is that I felt Manus wanted me to stay for just a little while longer.'

'Well, you know, mad and all as it seems, perhaps he was right, maybe you did need to stay for a little while longer.' Luke Gibson smiled at her then and it suddenly felt as if something she couldn't put a finger on had slipped into place. A warm feeling enveloped her and she just about recognised it as assurance, things might just come right at this late stage.

6

What was she thinking? Melissa's plane had hardly taken off the runway when she realised the enormity of her words to reassure her friend. How was she going to meet a mysterious man before Melissa's wedding and manage to be all loved up with him enough to get him to come down to the back end of the country with her? Carrie wasn't even sure she wanted to meet someone new – certainly, if she did, she couldn't imagine drumming up the kind of intimacy that being surrounded by her friends would involve. For now, Teddy was as much as she wanted, he had all the perks of Kevin, she could mother and smother him, without having to launder the smelly socks. She tried to calm herself down, thought about the various scenarios. Relationships finish, this she knew better than anyone now. She could just as easily unknot herself from this imaginary face-saver before Melissa's big day as she had entangled herself.

Carrie was racing up O'Connell Street. She was late, thanks to missing her bus because she was gabbing to her mother. It was not as though they had anything new to say to each other. That was unkind, once more the guilt of her mother, getting older and not seeing enough of her, stabbed at her. She was just concerned. Pamela Nolan was an active woman and, in many ways, Carrie knew she had no right to feel guilty about not seeing her more often. Her mother was far too busy to be entertaining Carrie or anyone else on a daily basis. That didn't mean she wouldn't give Kevin a piece of her mind if she got her hands on him. The first thing she'd offered was a place for Carrie to stay. They both knew Carrie wouldn't take her up on the offer. It would have annoyed Pamela if her daughter just walked away from everything she'd worked so hard for.

Carrie stopped at the top of O'Connell Street. She waited for her opportunity to cross once the heavy traffic obeyed the red light that seemed far too slow to show. Just as the lights began to change, her attention snapped towards the exuberant cheering of a group of visiting rugby enthusiasts that stopped on the kerb beside her. She smiled at one of the women tagging along behind them, knowing in some way that feeling that they were alike. The woman was decked out in team colours, but wearing full make-up and neat shoes. She looked bored out of her mind and as if she'd much prefer to be hitting Grafton Street than milling about listening to stories about passes, tries and throws. Carrie didn't envy the woman one bit and actually smiled, thinking of the imaginary boyfriend that she'd invented in a hot flush of nervousness – what had she been thinking?

For a short time, telling Melissa that she had met someone else salvaged some of her self-respect. Yes, it was rash, but it had felt good. It was immature; she admonished herself now. Since when did she need a man to make her feel good about herself? It had got her out of a spot. If only Melissa hadn't bought the dress. In the end, that was what tipped things over. Carrie was a size sixteen, with short arms and legs and she believed she had a back that had more rings than a mature oak – she was not built for silk or any kind of shiny fabric normally associated with weddings. Melissa would want everything perfect and that would be Carrie's get-out-of-jail clause. She had imagined the scenario perfectly in her mind beforehand. Hours spent trying on dress after dress and nothing within a donkey's roar of looking passable, never mind elegant.

And then, Melissa had produced the most divine chiffon and velvet creation in a midnight blue. It was, Carrie had to admit, perfect.

'It found me,' Melissa had said, delighted with it. 'Don't tell, but I picked it up in the market.'

'Second-hand?'

'Well, sort of. It's made by a local Pakistani woman, she makes a lot more traditional stuff, usually, but she made this for her daughter's graduation. It's quite demure, but compared to what her father wanted her to wear, well, I suppose it's the meeting of two worlds.' Melissa held up the hem. 'The stitching is amazing, look.'

'It's really beautiful,' Carrie had said and it was, she only sounded doubtful because of Kevin and Valentina.

'Well, come on, try it on. I'm taking a chance, but I've met the daughter and your shapes are really similar, so...'

It fitted as if it was made for Carrie. There wasn't a seam snagging or an unsightly stretch across her round torso, even the length was perfect. What could she say, it was a fait accompli, meant to be. And then she started to think, maybe it was up to Kevin to back out? After all, she had done nothing wrong. Valentina wouldn't want to meet a busload of their shared friends, Carrie could see her being bored out of her tree within five minutes of arriving. Did he really think he was taking Valentina to share *her* four-poster bed in the lovely room *she* had booked months ago? No, he probably didn't, because Kevin, it seemed to her, hadn't thought about a lot of things lately.

Carrie was almost out of breath by the time she reached the restaurant. Andrew was waiting for her, looking at his watch. He was used to her being a fashionable five minutes late.

'Come on, they'll have given away our table,' He said, but he was smiling at her. Andrew, truly was a friend. He'd invited her here weeks ago; before the Valentina debacle, and she'd completely forgotten about it until he rang her the previous evening. It was impossible to get a table at Clair's Kitchen, or at least that was what they'd heard. Andrew had managed to get an invite from the manager. It turned out they were in the same book club and he'd rescued her cat from the jaws of a particularly nasty Labradoodle one evening. He had told her it was nothing, but it had taken three stitches and tetanus shots to put him right. The cat was fine, apart from a residual nervousness that meant he no longer left her apartment for more than a three-minute toilet break.

'Hi Clair,' Andrew greeted his friend with a kiss on either cheek and, for a moment, Carrie wondered how much he had to patrol himself while working at the restaurant. In his normal working day, he seemed almost gender-neutral, while here – Carrie took in everything about him – he was a very typical gay man. Everything about his appearance and his gestures, and he seemed right within himself.

When they were sitting comfortably, in the oversized kitchen chairs she said it to him.

'Ah, you know how Kevin is?' He smiled and batted away her interest, and the unsaid words between them meant more than they might have a few weeks earlier. 'Clair is delighted you're here by the way, she loves The Sea Pear.'

'I don't remember meeting her before,' Carrie said, although Clair was the kind of woman who could easily blend into so many other customers.

'Well, she remembers you. She said that the way you looked after customers was an inspiration to her when she started this place.'

'Stop it, she did not say that.' Carrie looked at him, it was embarrassing, but he raised his eyebrows and she knew he was telling the truth.

The meal was superb, every morsel cooked to perfection and Carrie enjoyed being out with Andrew. He was good company. She realised, that for as long as they had known each other, they'd never actually spent time like this together before. They shared a mutual respect and friendship based on their working relationship. When it came to The Sea Pear, Carrie knew she could walk away and that all would be well so long as Andrew was there.

'How's the blog going these days?' he asked her as they tucked into dessert.

'Oh, I haven't looked at it, not since...'

'You should.' He held his fork mid-air. 'I've been thinking about it. Look at us, here tonight. You should start including reviews, places like this that most people up and down the country only hear about in the gossip pages. You could let them see what it's like. If the review was favourable, you might even get the chef to share a recipe. Who knows? It would be fun, something to take your mind off Kevin and Valentina.' It seemed strange to hear their names tagged together so easily. It made it more real, not just a figment of her imagination. Of course, it was all real, and maybe it was no harm to be reminded of it.

'Oh, I don't know, I mean, it's not like anyone actually follows it, apart from my family and a few friends.'

'Well, maybe that's the problem, maybe you need to pick a topic that pulls people in. Seriously, what have you got to lose? You could be sitting on a gold mine, or at least a whole lot of fun.'

'I don't know, I...'

'Come on, just do a post on this restaurant, and see how it goes, then after that, well...'

'No one will read it, I was thinking of taking it down anyway.'

'Do this one, as payment for your dinner, what do you say?'

'You're not paying for it anyway,' she laughed at him; he was so earnest as if a silly blog could change her life. All it was, all it had been so far, was a running commentary on her dull life and no one was really interested. It was oddly depressing when she thought about it. After all, did she want to spend her spare time looking at a computer screen?

'Come on, can you think of anything better than spending your downtime in places like this?' It was like he could read her mind. 'Seriously, just one and then we'll see if it doesn't lead to something better.'

So she agreed, but only because with Clair's Kitchen she could easily give it five stars and it deserved every one.

It was late when they left the restaurant, ambling down O'Connell Street and heading for the last buses of the evening.

'Tonight was great, thanks Andrew,' Carrie said as they stood at neighbouring stops.

'It was good, you needed it, you can't spend every night sitting in with a dog at your feet, no matter how adored he makes you feel.' He smiled at her thoughtfully.

'Oh, Andrew, you know me so well.'

'I'm not sure about that, I always wondered what you were doing with Kevin.' He moved closer to her now, lowered his voice. 'I mean, I hope you don't mind me saying this, but he's a bit of a prat.'

'Funny, but at the moment, I completely agree.'

'He's good at what he does, I can see that, but really, Carrie, the restaurant, even Clair said it. *You are* The Sea

Pear. In the morning, you could bring in another chef and things would go on, but if you left…'

'Oh, Andrew, if I wasn't there, you'd run things as smoothly and efficiently, probably even more so…'

'Carrie, the truth is, if you weren't there, I'd have been working for Clair a long time ago.' He shook his head smiling. 'But I'm glad you're taking time off, you deserve it and I'm happy to do the best I can until you get back.'

She looked at him now, realising that she'd never quite understood how much his support meant to her. 'Thanks for, you know…' She wasn't sure she could put words on it, but she had a feeling he knew she was thanking him for so much more than a lovely dinner.

'It will all work out, you'll see.' His bus pulled up and the crowd around him began to move him forward towards the open door. As he was getting on, he turned towards her, 'I'll be checking your blog tomorrow, you have to get cracking now.' He shook his head and she watched as he showed his commuter pass to the ambivalent driver. Then he was gone, into the night, and soon her own bus arrived and she found that somehow she was filled with an uncertain feeling that she was too scared to name as hope, but it was strong and pleasant and she luxuriated in it anyway.

Kevin had to admit, apartment living suited him. From here, he could see right across the city. The good parts – the parts that had been revitalised during the Celtic Tiger years. His view took in the Aviva stadium, the Canal and far off on the horizon he could see the Dublin Mountains. Valentina loved it. She left the apartment each day dolled up to the nines. She really was the kind of woman he'd always dreamed of having on his arm.

Sometimes, he thought back to when he was at school. Never the popular one, not even the clever one. He'd passed a dozen years and, mostly, he felt invisible compared to so many others. This was his time. He was living the dream. He was living in the swankiest address in the city, surrounded by the most successful people of the moment. He owned the best restaurant in town and he had Valentina. He'd like to see any of those boys who had laughed at him all those years ago now.

He sat on his balcony, a cup of the finest espresso in the city in his hand and thought about how well life had turned out for him. Then, out of the side of his eye, he saw Valentina. Her heels echoed on the shiny marble-effect stone of the courtyard below. She was carrying bags with labels from the most expensive shops in Dublin. He had to hand it to her, she knew how to spend. From here, he admired her elegant walk. He loved the way she moved slowly, cat-like, her curves gathering pace at a fraction of a second behind those confident steps. She didn't notice him, here in the shadow, and a shiver of desire shot through him as he thought of how she'd coaxed him into wakefulness hours earlier.

On the still air of the deserted plaza he heard her phone ring out. It sounded out a tinny melody that parodied some song that probably travelled from Colombia, though badly. Valentina reached her hand into the oversized bag on her shoulder. One move, smooth and assured. She was the antithesis of Carrie. Carrie spent half her life emptying her handbag to find things that were invariably somewhere else. Valentina had the kind of sophistication that if Carrie lived to be a hundred and ten, she'd still never manage.

Kevin squinted now, the sun Arctic bright, bouncing stinging rays off Valentina's dark hair and gold bangles. She stood for a moment attending intently to the words in her ear. Kevin wondered who she was listening to. Then, he heard her strong accented voice ring out. She was speaking in her own language. Her voice lilted and her tongue rolled easily around the heavy consonants. Then, she threw her head back and laughed that deliciously dirty laugh and it sounded as though she might be sharing a joke that was far too crude for such a bright day.

Kevin stepped a little closer to the edge of the balcony then, trying to hear her voice, she was nodding and running her hand through that luxuriant hair. Her voice was low and gravelly. He could just catch it on the wind, the kind of tone she used when they were together, an intimate sound that drifted lazily upwards. She looked then, towards the apartment, catching him off guard. He wanted to step back, but he knew he was too late. Suddenly he felt as though he'd been caught spying on her, as though he was a crass voyeur. Their eyes locked for a moment, an unspoken word passing between them, as though they'd both been caught in some illicit act. Then she waved at him and it felt as if he was standing in the sun again.

*

A parent's infidelity, it made you insecure, that's what Carrie said anyway. Kevin couldn't see it. He hadn't been insecure with Carrie. Had he? Maybe a little, in the beginning, but these last few years? No, they'd settled into something too comfortable for him to doubt her. He knew she'd never leave him. He knew that she'd always be there for him no matter what. His father had not managed to crush his ability to have a relationship without fear of being rejected.

His father's affair. Funny, but up until recently, he hadn't given it a second thought. Even saying it now, sounded a little strange. His sister took it badly, at the time. Penny had always been a daddy's girl and these days it seemed, to him at least, she used this as a kind of absolution, so the responsibility of their mother had fallen on his shoulders now that Carrie was no longer around. His mother? Who knew what Maureen Mulvey thought – certainly, Kevin wasn't going to try second-guessing her now. He rang a taxi company earlier in the week. Sorted out a driver for Sunday mornings; Kevin had no intention of stepping into Carrie's shoes and turning up every Sunday for a Mass that meant nothing to him. It was going to cost, but it was worth it. It meant he didn't have to face her, answer any more questions, not until he was ready at least. This would all blow over. He was sure of it. His mother had never really liked Carrie anyway. Oh, she pretended to, but Carrie knew it and Penny knew it too. She almost said something when he rang her to organise the taxi. He could feel it, over the silences between them on the call. She was biting her tongue.

'It's just really busy, Mother,' he'd picked his words carefully. She worried about him working too hard. Worried he might have another 'little turn', as she called it, but that had been years ago, before he met Carrie. He'd been a fretting, spotty kid with a mother who liked to mollycoddle him. It was hardly surprising that his nervousness spiralled into anxiety that needed medication in the end to bring him back to par. Maureen still reminded him of that time when she saw his colour rise or heard that edgy tension tighten up his voice.

'I hope that Carrie is doing her share, not leaving it all to you,' she said, but then, perhaps he caught something else.

'You know Carrie, she'd work until she drops, mother.' He had to hand it to Carrie, she really did work hard and maybe she deserved a break away from The Sea Pear for now. He didn't tell his mother she was on holiday for a week. It would open up too many enquiries, questions he didn't want to answer.

'It's still your restaurant, Kevin, you make sure she knows it. You've worked just as hard for it and it wouldn't be much of a restaurant without you.' Her voice was severe, but he could hear the brittleness of age behind her words. She was right, of course, Kevin knew that. The Sea Pear was a success because people came back for the food. 'I know everyone thinks that Carrie is the be-all and end-all of that place, but if you were serving up half-cooked food she wouldn't be a lot of help to you then.'

'Oh, Mother,' Kevin said, but Valentina was pressing him on the subject of the restaurant too.

'You have to sort it out, Keveen. You have to let her know who ees the boss. I can take care of the front of house for you and Andrew is there too, for now; he knows everyone. He could show me who is who, until I get the hang of eet.'

'I can't just dump Carrie and then sack her,' Kevin tried to laugh condescendingly, but he lost his breath and managed to sound as though he might be crying. 'This isn't Colombia, Valentina, we have employment laws here. I can't just get rid of her.'

'Huh, in Colombia, we would not sack her. I would just take her out and sell her on to some old farmer looking for help in the fields.' She laughed at this and Kevin hoped she was joking. 'She would make good money, she has the thighs for eet.' Valentina rarely talked of Colombia. Kevin had a sense that her life there had not been easy. He had a feeling that her journey to Ireland had cost more than her fare. These days, he didn't ask her any more about the family she had left behind, fearing that he may be overrun with Colombian relatives if he enquired too often. The last thing he wanted was a rush of relatives like Simo and Reda applying for visas to study English and descending on him with loud voices, throaty laughs and expensive habits.

'We have to be careful how we treat her, if we break any employment laws, she can sue the pants off us. It will cost me a lot of money.' He had long since mentioned to Valentina that the restaurant was his. It seemed like a small lie at the time. It was a way of making him feel and look like the big man and it seemed harmless enough then. Now he regretted it. Now, it seemed all Valentina talked about was getting Carrie out the door of The Sea Pear. She had ambitions to run the restaurant in her place. He supposed it was admirable. He supposed he should be glad. After all, she was at least earning her keep. Well, sort of. God, but she knew how to spend money.

He peeked into the shopping bags she left at the foot of the bed. How could anyone pay so much money for shoes? He picked up a pair of plain black patent heels, red soles beneath them. God, but she looked good in heels. He held them close to his face, just for a moment. He should probably feel bad about the lie. A lie like that would eat Carrie up. But then, he reasoned, where did that get Carrie in life?

'It's really nice of you to offer to come in and freshen the place up for Jane,' Carrie said as the little dog sniffed happily about the new territory. Teddy was enjoying the years of scents laid down by shoes that trod across the bar long before Carrie or Luke had ever stepped inside the front door.

'I'm happy to do it for her, she's a lovely lady,' Luke said, looking about the bar. There was no doubt the whole place could do with a good overhaul, not even paint, but soap and water, good old-fashioned elbow grease could really make a huge impact on it.

'You're right, of course you're right,' Carrie agreed with him when he said it to her.

'I think that if I just gave this place a good going-over, maybe cleaned out the chimneys, shined up the brasses. If we have the place looking and smelling like it's welcoming her back, it would be good for her.'

'And you don't have anywhere else to be?' she asked and, of course, he realised, she meant a job, a wife or a family or the many other commitments that most men of his age had.

'Nope, I'm free as a bird.' He smiled at her then, enjoyed the perplexed look in her eyes, matching it with a challenge. Perhaps he wanted her to ask him the obvious questions, but then, she hadn't told him about Kevin Mulvey. Jane had told him all he needed to know. They were in partnership together, but Carrie was the brains and the heart of the business – they were an odd couple, Luke thought when he saw Kevin on Finch Street. But then, who was he to figure out someone else's relationship. He was hardly an expert when it came to love and marriage, was he? 'How about if I get cleaning and you supply the coffee?' he said good-humouredly. 'It doesn't have to be the posh stuff you serve over in The Sea Pear, instant will do fine.'

'I suppose, if you're taking out the mops and buckets, it's the least I can do.' She looked inside the counter, filled the kettle and dropped spoons of coffee into two cups.

Luke settled himself at the bar, watching her for a moment. 'It suits you,' he said then.

'Oh?' she smiled at him.

'This place, I could imagine you working in a big old-fashioned pub, I'd say it's steeped in history.'

'You like history?'

'You could say that,' he laughed, then shook his head, 'I suppose I should come clean, shouldn't I?'

'Should you?' Carrie didn't lift her eyes from the old-fashioned kettle, although there was nothing much to see.

'Well, a man, living in a bed and breakfast, all day long with nothing to do, it's… intriguing, surely?'

'No, not really.' She smiled then. 'Well, I did wonder…'

'I'm between jobs.' Teddy settled on the floor beside him, leant against his legs with the familiarity of a child who expects only ease.

'And when you're working, what is it you do exactly?'

'Exactly, it's hard to say. The last few years I've bummed around the world working on historical digs…'

'So, you're an archaeologist?'

'You make it sound like it's the last thing I should be,' he laughed now, it was hard not to crease his face into a smile when he was talking to Carrie. 'I know it doesn't seem like the most fascinating work, but I'm a historian, I've written a few books, worked in universities, all that jazz.'

'So would I have read anything…?'

'It depends, do you usually borrow from university libraries?'

'Emm no, but I like vintage markets.' They both laughed at that.

'Good enough, I suppose,' he said. 'I came back to

Dublin a few weeks ago, one job finished and there wasn't anything special calling to me. My father lives in a nursing home here – Ballyglen – so it's a chance to knock about with him, until after Christmas anyway, then I'll definitely have to go back to work.'

'We're both kind of in the same boat, so...' Carrie said, pouring boiling water into the two cups.

'How's that?'

'Well, we're neither of us exactly teenagers and we're both thinking about where we are in life.'

'I would have thought you were well sorted, you seem so... together.'

'Sometimes all that glitters and all that...' There was a mismatched air between her eyes and her voice that she quickly covered over with a shriek of excitement, 'Well, would you look at that?' she pointed to an old photograph on the wall next to the bar. 'Isn't he the spit of you in that photograph?' she said.

'Oh, my God.' Luke stood before the photograph. It was the strangest thing. He stood for a moment taking it in, it was as if he was looking at his twin brother – only there were more than three decades between them.

Perhaps it was their way of rendering release, a sort of clearing of the spiritual slate as well as the physical one before patients were sent home. The chaplain spoke in stops and starts, stumbling over his consonants and elongating his vowels. Uncomfortable around the conversational furniture of dying and conscience, he shuffled quietly from one patient to the next, offering what he could of well-worn quotes and derelict prayers. He was a man perhaps more suited to his crossword and allotment than sharing confidences with old women who expected answers rather than platitudes.

We've heard all the psalms you're likely to spring on us already, Jane wanted to tell him, but, of course, politeness kept her opinions fastened tight so they only played behind her eyes. The woman beside her snored loudly, a rocketing crescendo that never failed to halt as soon as he had left the ward. She had no time for silly men; she told Jane one afternoon, she'd much prefer to save her energy and her attention for the children and grandchildren who would descend upon her as soon as visiting time arrived.

Jane looked across at the woman next to her. She was right of course, but what of Jane who had no one coming after her? Neither herself, nor Manus had a relation left between them, or at least none that they knew of. And, there it was again, that notion that going back to The Marchant Inn was so futile, what on earth was she keeping it open for? Albeit half-heartedly, but there was no one coming behind her to thank her for the effort.

Jane sighed, considered closing her eyes, but too late, the chaplain spotted her. He smiled a thin line of constant abbreviation – as though a full smile might require a quote so great it would be the breaking of him. He was moving away from a woman who had arrived just the night before, a moaning, tiny form in the far corner and something in her pathetic shape castigated Jane for being so ungrateful. She had her health, or enough of it to leave here at least and she had visitors, two people who had thought enough of her to come and sit and talk to her for hours at a time.

'Our Lord works in mysterious ways,' seemed to be the chaplains' favourite quote. He'd spun it out half a dozen times in this ward already. It was Jane's last day; tomorrow she would return to The Marchant Inn and the solitude of living with only ghosts for company. She was surprised when Mr Donoghue, the chaplain, dropped into the seat beside her and wondered, for a moment, if perhaps he knew it was his last opportunity to toss another canticle at her.

'But what of the rest of us?' she ventured mildly.

'The rest of us?' he asked, pushing his glasses up higher on his nose.

'Well, people like myself, the non-believers, those of us who are just too tired waiting for his mysterious ways to make a difference to us?' Jane had grown up with the nuns, the daughter of a woman who didn't have the courage to keep her at a time when it was easier to leave your child behind and make a new life somewhere else. It meant that she had no family, or none that she was ever able to find at least. It also meant that she knew by heart every psalm the chaplain could think to throw at her, and if she tried, she didn't doubt she could dredge up some he'd never even heard of for herself.

'Well, aren't we the ones in most need of faith?' he said easily and she thought that wasn't much of a help really, expecting him to say that the darkest hour came before the dawn or some other such nonsense. 'Be strong and take heart, all you who hope,' he muttered, then his eyes rested on her for a long moment. 'You're not as alone as you think,' he said softly before moving on to the next ward. Oddly, his words brought Jane some comfort and she lay quietly on her pillow, letting them wash over her for some time. Perhaps, he was right. After all, either Carrie or Luke had visited her each day since she'd arrived here. Maybe, she was not alone after all.

7

Carrie was making her way back from the bank, a hundred things running through her mind when Anna rang her. Anna nearly had a fit when she told her. Of course, she couldn't tell her face to face, even Carrie wasn't that brave.

'You what?'

'I know, I know, I know, it was a stupid thing to say.' She knew it at the time. What in God's name had possessed her? But it was Melissa and she couldn't upset Melissa for the world. Telling her that she'd met someone new seemed the only way to convince her that she was absolutely fine with Kevin being best man while she was maid of honour at their wedding.

'Well, she'll be pretty upset if she finds out you lied to her,' Anna said, still spluttering, it had to be Chardonnay, Carrie decided. Only Chardonnay made her friend splutter.

'No. I've thought about it. I'll make it a hot torrid affair, it won't last any longer than a week or two and then I'll dump him, because...'

'Well, you'll probably have worn him out by then.

Look at the state of Kevin after all and we all know what a stud he was when you met him.' Sometimes Anna could be downright cruel or too funny for words.

'Stop it.' Carrie giggled in spite of herself. 'Anyway, that's how I'm playing it, so, for heaven's sake, don't let me down if you run into any of them.'

'Sure thing.' Anna sipped whatever had almost caused her to gasp earlier. 'It's a pity Andrew is gay, isn't it?'

'Yeah, I suppose it is. He'd have been lovely for Valentina.' They both giggled at that, neither of them could imagine Andrew having anything to do with someone as obvious as Valentina. 'Anyway, how's *The Mousetrap*?'

'Actually, it's doing really well. It looks like we could be running for an extra month and they're talking of a tour.'

'Oh, Anna, I'm delighted.'

'Don't get too excited, now, nothing's set in stone, and it's not as though I'm a main player, so even if it does tour…'

'Of course, you'll be on the tour. It's time your luck turned, this is it, I'm sure of it.' Neither of them said that they'd been waiting for Anna's luck to turn for almost twenty years. No one could accuse them of pessimism.

'Anyway, the reason I rang you. I have a meal for two at the Otter's Lodge for Friday, do you fancy coming along?'

'Has Andrew been talking to you?'

'No, why?'

'No reason. I'd love to come with you and I'll tell you

all about Andrew's plan for me when I get there.' Carrie hung up the phone quickly, before Anna could wheedle any details out of her about the blog. Carrie managed to put a piece together on her night out with Andrew. She was quite proud of it and even though it was only posted a few hours already she'd garnered a dozen comments.

Kevin woke up in a bad mood. He wasn't sure why. He looked across at Valentina, her soft dark hair resting in a shiny coil across her shoulders. Even asleep, she was beautiful. No, Kevin wasn't pissed off with Valentina, how could he be? The next thing that popped into his mind was The Sea Pear, but no, everything was ticking over nicely there. He rolled over onto his back and lay looking up at the pristine white ceiling and, for a moment, he thought, heaven must be like this. Except, in heaven, people were happy, weren't they? But Kevin was happy, of course he was, to suggest anything less was just preposterous. He had a beautiful woman lying next to him, he was living in a fabulous apartment and he had a thriving business. If it was six weeks earlier, well then, maybe...

Six weeks earlier, things had come to a head with Valentina. She was sick of feeling as if he was ashamed of her. The excitement of a secret affair was wearing thin and she was tired of playing second fiddle to Carrie, as she saw it. She gave him an ultimatum. One of the worst she could give, in his opinion.

'If you don't tell her, I weel.' She'd roared in that

passionate way she had. He still thought it was so cute, if a little scary. He wondered if some day it would irritate him.

'I will, my darling, I will. It's all about timing. Carrie will be heartbroken.'

'She should have thought about that when she wasn't keeping her man happy,' she'd said and drew him closer, pulling open his shirt to reveal his pasty white chest. Of course, when Kevin was with Valentina, she made him feel like a god. Maybe in some ways, to her, that's what he was.

'Don't kid yourself, mate,' Jim said when he'd first told him about Valentina. 'She sees a full wallet and an easy catch who is lusting for a trophy girlfriend. I mean, seriously, what do you even have to say to each other?'

'We have lots in common,' Kevin had drained his pint at that, it was true. There was never a lull in conversation. Valentina found everything he had to say interesting and amusing. Perhaps it was the age difference, or the cultural difference. Where Carrie would have told him to bugger off and stop annoying her, Valentina could sit for hours gazing into his eyes.

And that was it, wasn't it? That was niggling at him, just a bit. The notion that Valentina had taken charge. It was on Valentina's terms that he had ended things with Carrie. They were living in Valentina's apartment – her choice, even if he did pay the lease. Mostly, when he wasn't at work, he was here alone. Valentina always seemed to be off somewhere. Either she was going into college or the library or meeting up with her college mates. Kevin wasn't keen on college kids, he couldn't imagine what Valentina could have in common with a bunch of yobs in bad clothes with collectivist ideals and breadline budgets. He'd met some of them once. They were all foreign, older as it turned out than he had expected. Like Valentina, it seemed to him, college was just a way in, a stepping stone to a work visa, these people were unskilled labourers, not doctors or lawyers or academic bright lights in the making. It was a couple of weeks ago now, she brought him into the Buttery bar in Trinity. Their little group sat unevenly in the hallowed surroundings, out of place among the budding intellects. They were an unusual bunch to see Valentina ensconced in. They were a tribe of bouncy-haired, bearded and booted pseudo-intellectuals; they just irritated Kevin. Valentina seemed to be as relaxed among them as she was in the restaurant or with Simo and Reda in the flat. That was the great thing about Valentina. She wafted from one group to another, and wherever she went, she brought glamour and that radiant beauty which made conversations stop when she entered a room.

No, he wasn't angry at Valentina.

He was angry at Carrie. He was angry because she was going to Ben and Melissa's wedding without so much as consulting him. He was angry, because, he had been looking forward to the luxury of a castle hotel for a couple of nights with Valentina. He was looking forward to turning up there and showing her off. He was looking forward to watching Jim and Ben and all those other losers who'd settled in life. He couldn't flaunt Valentina about with Carrie there, even he knew that would be callous.

As for the idea of Carrie bringing some new lover? Hah! He'd believe it when he saw it. It had to be some huge mistake. There was no way Carrie had hooked up with some guy already. Of course, she'd taken the week off – she'd never actually volunteered where she'd been. Jim had really set him off suggesting that perhaps she'd met this bloke while they were still together. But that was just Jim, trying to wind him up again. He wasn't jealous, he was sure of that, wasn't he? He was just a bit... He sighed, trying to pick out the right word – perturbed, that'd be it. He was perturbed.

'You are dreaming?' Valentina shifted herself a little so she was facing him.

'No, wideawake,' he said.

'You haven't forgotten that we have the party tonight?'

'No. No, of course not.' That was it. That was what had woken him in such a foul mood. Valentina had managed to get them invited to a party in the penthouse at the opposite end of the building. Kevin had met the couple, Raleigh and Dean, in the elevator. He seemed pompous and she had more plastic in her face than Barbie. When she smiled, it seemed to Kevin that she leered at him. 'I'll just have to make sure the restaurant is okay and then I'm good to go.' He tried to sound upbeat, it wouldn't have fooled Carrie, but then with Carrie, he just wouldn't have bothered turning up.

'The party starts at nine, so you weel have to be back

here and changed in time. Keveen, I don't want to be late. They seem very nice and it is our first time to meet all of the neighbours.' She slid from the covers, with hardly a movement of the bed or sheets, and slinked into the bathroom for her usual morning half-hour shower. Carrie would be horrified, *think of the climate*. He was quite sure that the last thing on Valentina's mind was global warming.

'So,' he asked her when she came into the kitchen later. He had made coffee and toast for both of them. It was much too cold to eat on the balcony, they would have to save that for warmer months. 'What does a man wear to a party in a penthouse?'

'Well, not your chef's uniform, that's for sure,' she said, snatching his toast from him. That irritated the hell out of him, he'd just buttered it so all the bread was evenly spread and then placed the marmalade on top, having taken out all the bits. Then he'd cut off all the crusts so the marmalade fell down the sides. It was a work of art, and she bit into it like she was eating gruel and then discarded it after one bite. 'You weel look good no matter what you wear, after all you weel have the best-looking girl in the room on your arm.' It was true, of course, but Valentina said it with such conviction that for a moment it sounded mean. Normally, Kevin would have made fun of her and said that, likewise, she'd have the wealthiest man in the room, but this time, that wouldn't be true.

★

When Andrew poked his head about the office door, Carrie had a feeling that something was up.

'Well, maybe it's nothing and perhaps you have a simple explanation,' he looked ruffled.

'Go on, whatever it is, it can't be that bad,' Carrie said, pushing her chair back from her desk. It was her first day back, really, she had every excuse to hide among the accounts for the whole day if she felt like it.

'Someone has emptied the tips jar,' he said, flatly dropping to the seat before her. 'All the notes and I'd say there was about a hundred euros in it, because we hadn't emptied it in almost three weeks, it's just the coins at the bottom left over.'

'Andrew, that's terrible. Are you sure one of the others didn't just empty it to count it up?'

'I'm pretty sure and... there's something else.'

'Go on.'

'Well, I noticed the jar last night, put it on my mental to-do list, you know, and so I'm pretty sure that...'

'It's an inside job?' To be fair, it was unlikely that a customer would get the chance to drop their hand into the tips bowl. 'Oh, God, perhaps we can replace the cash from the takings, I'll talk to Kevin.'

'It's not just that, Carrie.' Andrew studied the floor intently, his face burned pink, then he brought his eyes up to meet hers. 'You see, here's the thing, there were only four people who could have taken it – me, you, Kevin and...'

'Valentina?' Carrie whispered hoarsely. She was the only unknown quantity among them, really.

'You see, if you mention it to Kevin, the last person he'll suspect is Valentina and the first person he'll want to blame is...'

'Oh, Andrew, you've been here for years, I couldn't have kept this place going without you, especially these last few weeks.' She shook her head, pulled out her wallet and took out two fifty-euro notes. 'Here, put those into it for now, if anyone asks, we'll say we took change out and replaced it from the till. Will you ask one of the other girls to split up the jar between all of you this evening? Anymore, we keep our eyes open, yes?'

'Of course, I think we'll be on our guard from here on.' He shook his head sadly, it was the first time they'd ever had a problem like this in The Sea Pear. 'Maybe I'm wrong, you know, about Valentina.'

'God, Andrew, for all our sakes, I do hope so.'

The nurses couldn't be nicer, they'd organised for a lovely young woman to come and talk to her about going home. Jane had been a little unsure, after all, she wasn't crazy, just a little nervous.

'It's okay, I'm not the one they send for the crazy people,' Justine, a South African woman, shook her hand and explained that, as a social worker, it was her job to make sure that Jane was able to take care of herself when they sent her home from hospital. 'Have you thought about moving into somewhere with people of your own age?' she asked gently. 'You know, lots of people about, you'd be surprised what a difference it can make.' She smiled, 'You'll find that a lot of younger people, in their sixties even, are choosing to downsize, live closer to their families, but they don't want to be… too close.'

'You mean a burden?' Jane shook her head. 'Don't worry, I won't be that. I don't have any children or grandchildren to burden.'

'But you have regular visitors?' Justine bent forward a little, taking her large folder up as though she might capture some of Jane's life within its pages.

'A neighbour and a… friend,' Jane said easily, because when she thought about Luke Gibson, that was, unexpectedly, what he was becoming. He visited her each day on his way to visit his own father. He always brought along something small, a bar of chocolate, a newspaper, fresh flowers, something she could claim as her own beside the overflowing locker of the woman in the next bed.

'Well, think about it, at least,' Justine took some brochures from her large bag, propped them up on the locker, blocking Jane's view of the lovely freesias Luke had brought the day before.

'I'll certainly do that,' Jane said and she meant it, because even now the thought of going back to The Marchant Inn and closing her door on a deserted Finch Street each night filled her with a kind of panic that she knew would only grow.

Raleigh and Dean were even more sickening in their home than they were in the elevator. Dean had made his money in property, during the bust, capitalised on the wrecked economy and now he was happy to crow about it. 'People can't be sensitive about it anymore, for God's sake, it's life. You win some, you lose some, right Kenneth?' he slapped Kevin on the back, hard, so his Martini almost choked him. Dean didn't notice and continued to talk about himself making grand gestures so there could be no doubt just how wealthy he was.

Raleigh whipped Valentina across the room as quickly as they arrived. Soon she was deep in conversation with a group of women who looked like they might be twice her age. Somewhere between the bankruptcy and eviction stories, Kevin lost sight of her. He assumed she disappeared into the kitchen. Eventually, when he got a chance, he went in search of her.

Dean and Raleigh's apartment was five times the size of their place. The living room alone was like an airport hangar. It was a medley of muted greys, walnut and glass. A wall of windows looked out into the Dublin night sky and Kevin had to admit it was as impressive as he'd ever seen. He walked slowly through each of the rooms, a sprawling sitting room, then a study, then some kind of long corridor that was probably meant to be an exhibition space. Eventually, he came to the kitchen. Outside he could hear Valentina's delighted shrieks. It sounded like a completely different party to the sedate one that was taking place in the main lounge. Here a moody rhythm sounded out. Inside was the low hum of a group deep in conversation, punctuated by occasional raucous laughter and Valentina's sporadic shriek of delight?

He stood for a few minutes, deliberating. He knew, on some level, that he would be further out of his depth in there than he had been earlier. This was where the beautiful people were hanging out. This was the glamorous Dublin where everyone was successful, beautiful and rich. In Kevin's experience, there had always been a great divide. He'd never been one of the cool crowd. He'd never been a party animal, and even with his success, he was not part of the in-crowd like some of the other big restaurateurs around the city.

That was part of the reason he and Carrie worked so well. Carrie would trundle through that room oblivious to who was cool and who was not. Carrie never measured people like this, so these events never fazed her. She just took people as she found them and, miraculously, they seemed to do the same with her. Carrie could navigate this room fearlessly. With Carrie by his side, he would have been fine. He could have stood beside her, laughed at whatever jokes were told and they'd make a steady beeline from one end of the party to the other. She'd insist on meeting everyone, and then they'd go home to their boring but safe existence far from anyone who intimidated Kevin.

'Come on, darling, they won't bite,' a blonde girl he'd seen earlier arriving with the lead singer of a boy band pushed past him. She opened the door so he had no choice but to enter in the middle of a group of people half his age and twice as confident. The kitchen was suddenly very bright and Kevin took a second to adjust to the group before him. No sign of Valentina, that was all that registered at first. He stood uncomfortably on the outer reaches of a number of conversations for what seemed like forever, but he had nothing to say to these people. Then, after what felt like forever, Valentina emerged from what he assumed was the pantry. It was the first time he'd ever seen her look dishevelled and something gnawed at him that he'd missed a step, somehow, in coming here.

'Ah, Keveen, meet my new friends,' she was almost singing. Her voice had reached such a high pitch, he thought she might top soprano notes. Then he realised, there was something different about her. He looked at the ruggedly handsome young man with her and he wondered if he'd ever know half of what went on in that pantry. One thing he knew for sure, they'd taken something and if it wasn't cocaine, then Kevin was even more naïve than he felt.

Luke found an ancient set of chimney brushes in a small lean-to in the backyard of The Marchant Inn. Teddy scampered happily about his legs, delighted to spend time with Luke while Carrie went to work in The Sea Pear. Luke had never actually cleaned a chimney before, but he figured that the principle was simple, so long as he made sure that he contained the mess that was surely likely to follow once he started. What he hadn't expected was how tired his arms would become. The Marchant Inn, like all of the other buildings along here, was three storeys tall. Luckily, there seemed to be an endless number of attachments to the brushes, but that just meant more work.

Eventually, with much clearing and more groaning, he managed to see light at the end of the flue. To be sure, he walked outside the pub, to the far side of the road, and there, sure enough, the end of the brushes had popped into the grey Dublin air at the top of the chimney. After all the hard work, Luke filled with a giddy sense of elation – he shook his head as he walked back into the pub. It seemed silly that such a menial task could make him so happy. Then again, he had a feeling that it wasn't the actual cleaning of the chimney that counted; it was the idea that it would make some kind of real difference to Jane Marchant when she returned here. A fire in the grate, what could be more welcoming than that?

He set about clearing up the mess of soot and ancient birds' nests that had gathered in a pile in the grate. A low, warning growl from Teddy broke into his thoughts and Luke turned to see two unsavoury-looking characters watching him from the doorway.

'You are closed?' the stockier of the pair said through thin lips, surveying the bar with narrowed eyes.

'Yes, I'm afraid we're closed for another few days, we're doing a bit of an overhaul.' Luke stood up and moved away from the grate. 'Can I help you?' he enquired, although, he couldn't see them standing at the bar shooting the breeze with Jane.

'No, we thought we might have a proposition for the owner, she is not about, is she?'

'Emm, no, she's away on holidays actually, can I help?'

Luke moved towards them, they were each built like Sherman tanks, angular and hard, and their eyes darted about the pub, as though they were on a reconnaissance job and filing every corner to memory.

'Ah, and you? You are here also?' the greasier of the two poked his head forward as though it might soften his words.

'Yes. I'm always about the place,' Luke lied. Up close, he was taller than the two of them, but they had a street meanness to them and he had no doubt, that in the wrong place or at the wrong time, even he'd be intimidated by them. 'Your proposition… you're…'

'Oh, we are security consultants, we are visiting all of the businesses in the area, we are…' he showed his teeth in what was meant to be smile.

'You're not Irish?' Luke moved a little closer to them, but they wouldn't meet his eyes.

'We are Colombian,' the stockier one drew out the word lazily. 'But we are here so long, it feels like we are more Irish than the Irish,' he laughed, an empty barrelling sound that was more cruel than jovial. 'We are all legal, if that is what you're wondering, our business is legit.' There was an undercurrent of menace and it reeked not just from his words, but from his pores.

'Well, if you want to leave a card…' Luke walked to the door, opened it for them pointedly, 'but, as I say, we're not open at the moment, and since I'm always about, I think we're pretty much good.' He knew there would be no card, there would be no names for these men, but he would remember their faces and the street tattoo that ran along the second man's neck and down towards his chest, and he'd be keeping an eye out for them. When they left, he closed the door and pulled the bolt, yes, he could see why Jane might be nervous here on her own all right.

8

'You seem very happy with yourself,' Anna said.
They were drinking mojitos in a small Mexican
bar before going for dinner.

'Do I?' Carrie wasn't aware if she was happy or sad.
But now that she thought of it, she wasn't exactly pining
for Kevin these last few days. 'Maybe it's this red-hot
Latin lover I've got on the side?'

'Stop it,' Anna snorted. 'You're going to have to come
clean, you know that?'

'Do I though? Really?' Carrie laughed. 'I'm so
enjoying Kevin walking around me like he's on eggshells.
I'll tell you, it's really taken the condescending look off
his face.'

'Yeah, from that point of view, it's no harm, but how
are you going to magic some hunk for the wedding at
Christmas?'

'That's the tricky bit, all right,' Carrie wagged her
finger. She hadn't the slightest hope she could get some
good-looking man to pretend to be her boyfriend for a
whole weekend. 'To be honest,' she said, the reality hitting
home, 'it feels a bit sad. Like something kids do, but I

have to say, I've enjoyed pulling back a bit of my self-esteem in front of Romeo and Juliet in the restaurant.'

'I'd be all for keeping it going, but you never know, there might be some decent and real human being out there just dying to go to the wedding with you.'

'Oh, there is.' Carrie shook her head. 'My mother!' It was true, Pamela had offered to accompany her to the wedding, but they both knew it would be a strain for her not to tell Kevin exactly what she thought of him. Neither of them mentioned the dint in her self-respect if she turned up with her mother as her plus-one.

'So why the smile?' Anna sipped her drink.

'I don't know, I suppose that I'm not unhappy, I feel...' What was this feeling that she had? 'I don't know, I feel like there's something better waiting for me, does that sound a bit mad?'

'No, it sounds like you're returning to your normal enthusiastic self.' Anna had always been a strange mix of pragmatism and joyfulness. It did not take a lot to make her smile, on the other hand, she never expected things to turn out well. 'So, do you see a tall dark stranger in your crystal ball?'

'No. Definitely not. I'm not sure I want to get into another relationship. I'm quite enjoying having the house to myself. I'm enjoying not having to be organising someone and making all my plans around them.' It was true. She was in no rush to jump back into a relationship for the sake of it. Now that she was over the shock, and apart from the sense of betrayal, there had been a number of times when she'd actually thought to herself, *Isn't this nice!* as she sat curled up on the couch with Teddy and a box set of her own choosing. She had no doubt that she'd feel exactly the same emotion on Sunday mornings for a long time to come when she remembered that she no longer had to take Maureen Mulvey to Mass. 'Anyway, as it turns out, I do have a couple of tall dark men in my life!'

'You can't count the electrician or the door-to-door salesmen as being in your life, Carrie.' Anna smiled.

'Actually I'm not. Last week I was out to dinner with one of them...' Carrie made a face, *so there.*

'You can't count gay friends either.'

'That's not fair. Just because there's no sex...' They both laughed. 'Andrew is great company, seriously, it's like being out with you or Mum and he looks quite good on the arm too, I think.' This was the moment, Carrie knew, when she should have mentioned Luke Gibson and perhaps she would have, but there wasn't a lot to mention. What could she say? That she'd met a man who seemed to be kind and sweet, intelligent, and if you thought about how much he was spending in the bed and breakfast – obviously solvent. On the other hand, even though they'd spent quite a bit of time together, she knew very little about him other than the fact that he'd been a rolling stone for most of his life and if he had gathered any moss he wasn't telling. Nor, she suspected, did he want to gather any at this point. It was funny though, because for all that, he made her feel connected? Luke seemed to be everything Kevin wasn't, except she had a feeling that if she fell for him her heart could be in a much worse condition when he surely rejected her. Still, Carrie thought about him more than she should, probably, but perhaps that was just because now she didn't have to think about Kevin anymore and maybe, that wasn't such a bad thing.

The restaurant was fabulous, sitting on the bank of the tiny river Dodder; low windows allowed a view of just the river, and high waters obscured the mossy walls that probably reeked a bit in warm weather. Otter's Lodge was just the right mix of casual chic, so new and old blended as though they were puzzle pieces cut from the same picture and tastefully reassembled. As they tucked into starters, Carrie could hear the words forming in her mind that she would use to describe the Crab Benedict.

'So, it's taking off?' Anna asked between delicious mouthfuls.

'I don't know. I mean, the first review got a lot of positive comments, but then everyone's talking about Clair's at the moment, aren't they?' It was true. The day after her review appeared a young British royal stopped by for lunch. 'I was just lucky to have hopped on the back of the zeitgeist.'

'There's nothing lucky about it. It was a great review. Take the praise when it comes your way, Carrie. That's always been your problem, you know. Even with The Sea Pear – you let Kevin believe that he's the star of the show, when it would have just been like every other place that went down the plughole during the recession if it wasn't for you.' Anna was getting cross.

'Oh, come on, don't be like that. The Sea Pear is a partnership. But this, the blog, if it takes off, okay, I'll take full credit. Never mind the visiting princess, okay?'

'Deal.' Anna smiled, she'd always been a bit protective, but it was a good thing, Carrie knew that.

'Does he know?'

'Who?' Carrie sipped some water; the food here really was delicious.

'Kevin, does he know that you're doing reviews now?'

'I'm not *doing reviews now*. I'm just...' What was she just? Would she be doing reviews all over the city? Could she? She had a feeling she'd absolutely love it, but she couldn't keep dragging Andrew and Anna out every second week. They had lives too, after all. 'Why? What has it got to do with Kevin?'

'Well have you?'

'No. He never looked at the blog, he was never interested, so why would he be bothered now?'

'I don't know.' She opened her eyes wide, 'Perhaps he'd see it as a conflict of interest?' She smiled, no doubt enjoying what Kevin's reaction might be.

'Probably. If he knew, he'd want me to give them all nil points! Like in the Eurovision. He used to say it in the French accent. For days afterwards he'd drive me mad with his "*deux points and dix points*." God, there are a good many things I will not miss.' That was so true.

'Wait until it takes off,' Anna said, playing the possible scenarios to their last glorious conclusion in her overactive imagination. 'When you're flying all over the world. Reviewing, like some of those big gastro boys, one week New York, the next it's Kuala Lumpur, tea at the Savoy, dinner at the Ritz...' Anna's eyes glazed.

'I think you're mixing me up with someone who actually knows what they're doing,' Carrie said drily. 'Although, I'd love to do more of them. I'd love to be putting up one a week, but I've made a promise to myself – I'm not giving bad reviews. That'd be devastating for people.'

'So you're going to lie?' Anna jumped onto the high ground with the speed of one who rarely gets the chance to speak from that lofty position.

'No. I'm not going to lie. But I'm not going to include the bad ones.'

'Will you tell them?'

'I don't know, I haven't thought that far ahead yet. I think, when and if it happens, I'll try and put myself in their shoes and I'll decide then.'

'Good move,' Anna said stoically. 'Although I'd say Kevin would disagree, he'd want you to only put up the bad ones.'

'Oh, and don't I know it.' Carrie picked up her glass and toasted Anna. It was hard not to feel there were things to look forward to with Anna at her side.

Kevin couldn't figure why, but he had a feeling things were not working out quite as well as he expected they would. He spent most of the morning convincing himself that was just stupid.

He checked on Valentina at about eleven. She was out

of it. Snoring, delicately, it had to be said, but snoring away. She'd been doing that all night. She claimed it was the shellfish. She shouldn't touch them, had a mild allergy. Kevin had a nasty suspicion that whatever she'd taken at the party had done more than make her laugh like a hyena all evening. She'd been horribly ill when they got back, retched so loudly Kevin felt his insides churn alarmingly. Thankfully, she managed to make it to the bathroom. He hated vomit. He couldn't look at it. Thank God they had cleaning staff at the restaurant. In the early days, Carrie took care of all that... Carrie. He thought about her for all of five seconds. There was a nagging guilt if he lingered on her for much longer.

'Only natural, mate,' Jim said that evening as they sat nursing pints in McDaid's. Jim had clocked off for the day, while Kevin was just about to start his shift in the restaurant. 'Haven't been round there yet, see how she's doing?'

'Emm, well no. I didn't like to...' he was going to say intrude, but they both knew he was a coward and that was the only reason.

'The way I hear it, she's probably relieved to see the back of you.'

He had a feeling that Jim was trying to annoy him. 'Well, I'm happy for her.' His words were automatic, there was no real feeling in them. Kevin still couldn't imagine Carrie with anyone else. Not Carrie. Now, if it was a French poodle, an Afghan hound or an Abyssinian cat, then maybe, but actually dating someone. No, the more he thought about it, he'd believe it when he saw it. He mentioned it to Jim.

'You managed to pull a hot Colombian. If you'd asked any of us who was more likely to do the leaving we'd all have said Carrie.' Jim snorted into his pint.

'Hmm.' Kevin might have been insulted, but even now, he couldn't believe Valentina had been interested in him. He wouldn't tell Jim about the party. Well, he might mention the party, but he wouldn't say a word about the cocaine, or Valentina, or how he'd felt as if he'd stepped on a different planet. That was the truth of it, he could see it now, sitting here with Jim. This place, McDaid's, it was the kind of place that suited him. They'd come here for years, twice or three times a week. It was close to The Sea Pear and just around the corner from the catering company Jim had set up a couple of years earlier. It wasn't just that he'd felt uncomfortable at the party, he never liked that kind of thing. With Carrie, he'd cry out of it when he could, and if he couldn't, they'd stick together. Carrie was a great woman to talk to everyone, work the room and then get out as fast as they could decently manage. It was obvious that he wouldn't have that kind of support from Valentina, at least not yet. But it was early days, and, Kevin reasoned, in a few years' time, it probably wouldn't be her scene either.

'How's the restaurant going, by the way?' Jim's eyes darted from the TV screen to Kevin, for just an instant. 'Cosy, is it?' he smirked.

'I don't know what you mean?' Kevin said and focussed on a match that was playing somewhere the sun was shining. But even Kevin was not so obtuse that he didn't feel the atmosphere in The Sea Pear. It vaulted before him, like a battle line, troops were falling into trenches either side and it seemed that his ground forces consisted of just two – himself and Valentina.

'Well, it can't be easy, not for any of you, but especially not for Carrie.'

'Carrie's fine.' Bloody typical of Jim to weigh in on Carrie's side, Kevin thought, but of course, he wasn't surprised, Jim had always preferred Carrie to him anyway.

'Yeah, sure she is.' Jim shook his head. 'It's not going to be doing you any good either, mate. After all, you can't expect Valentina to be playing second fiddle to Carrie forever. You need to get it sorted, if that's what you want.'

'I know all this, Jim, can we talk about something else, okay?' So they sat in silence, until Jim drained his pint.

'Night, Mick,' he nodded towards the barman who looked positively disappointed that he was leaving.

'See you Tuesday,' Mick said.

'Must be getting back to the wife and mortgage,' Jim said, but there was a trace of contentment dug deep into his cynicism that Kevin had never noticed before.

The problem with Jim, as Kevin saw it, was that he was stuck. He couldn't see beyond what he had in his own house. The other big problem with him was that, like Carrie, Jim could read him like a book. Kevin wasn't sure he wanted to be read like a book anymore. He liked that Valentina couldn't see right through him.

He decided he would put Carrie out of his mind as he

headed for work. Damn Jim anyway, with all that talk of Carrie, it seemed as if somehow she managed to invade his mind even as he should have been bragging about how great things were now that he'd moved on. Valentina was working harder than ever, perhaps trying to prove herself. Kevin had a feeling that now they were officially an item, she felt a little more proprietarily about The Sea Pear. It wasn't a bad thing, as he saw it. It took the swagger out of Andrew's walk, for one thing. Carrie was starting to take more time off too. That made things easier for everyone. She was still working all week, but now she was just clocking in her forty hours, she was there when she needed to be, not like before, not all the time. When she was on shift with Valentina, if things were quiet, she left them to it and retreated to her office upstairs. God alone knew what she was at up there, cooking the books or perhaps playing on the computer with that blog thing. His mobile phone pulled him out of his thoughts.

'Hi Penny,' he said automatically. His sister rarely rang him unless she needed something.

'Kevin, thank God you answered. It's Mum, she fell earlier. I'm only after finding her.'

'Is she okay?' He could hear a note of panic in Penny's voice, but then she was married to an Italian, and she'd always been a bit of a diva before that.

'For heaven's sake, of course she's not okay, Kevin. She's an old woman, living on her own. We're at the hospital, you're going to have to come. When did you last drop in on her, Kevin?'

'Ah, it was, let me see now.' Of course, he hadn't

gone near his mother. He'd visited that once, then he'd organised a taxi and hoped that by the next time they saw each other there'd be no more talk of Carrie.

'Seriously, haven't you been to see her at all. At least when Carrie was around I knew she was being dropped in on. Really, Kevin, you're worse than useless.' Penny cut him off before he had a chance to defend himself. The thing was, she had a point.

Kevin hated hospitals. They were full of sick people and, to Kevin at least, they always seemed so hazardous. There were alarms, constant floor-washing and he could smell day-old stewed beef as he passed the stairwell. There were far too many people rushing about, really; he often wondered how anyone survived the place.

They'd put his mother in a six-bedded ward. Kevin muttered about health insurance and private rooms and the nurse gave him a withering look that only just compared to the daggers Penny gave him when he sat at his mother's side.

'Ah, Kevin,' she said, but her voice sounded reedy, too thin, like her best china that they never used and he always suspected wouldn't survive a scalding, never mind a good scrubbing. 'Can you believe it? I fell in my front door? I feel such an old fool.'

'Don't say that, Mum, it could happen to anyone,' Penny soothed her.

'It's that step, isn't it?' Kevin said. 'We could get someone to come and put in a ramp, if you'd like.'

'Oh, Kevin, if it was that easy.' His mother shook her head sadly. 'You're just both so busy and now with Carrie gone... I...' a small tear rolled down his mother's cheek.

'Carrie used to pop in every other day with milk and bread and anything Mum needed. It was on her way to work, you see,' Penny said archly.

'I didn't know, did I?' Kevin could feel his hackles rise.

'Today, I was out of butter. I asked along the road, but there was no one.' She sniffled again and Kevin felt cruel for imagining she was actually enjoying this. 'I set off with my bag. It took a while, I've slowed down a lot, you see.'

'Oh, Mum.' Penny looked as if someone had shaken the spirit from her.

'And I don't mind that, I mean, that's to be expected, after all, you can't go on forever. I made it back to my own front door, I was a little puffed out, but nothing that a nice cup of tea wouldn't set to rights and then bang. Before I knew it, I was on the ground.'

'The doctors are running tests, don't worry, Mum,' Penny soothed.

'Oh, tests. There's no medicine for old age. I suppose, you'll want to put me into one of those homes now, no good to anyone anymore.' Maureen Mulvey started to cry again as though her heart might break.

'Mum, we'd never *put* you anywhere,' Kevin said, his voice strong and sure. His mother needed him to be strong now. 'There's no need for that kind of talk.' He sighed deeply. 'All it is,' he looked across at Penny, 'it just means that we have to drop by every day. And sure, Penny, that's no hardship, is it?' She wasn't wiggling out of this.

'Well, it would appear that it is for some people,' Penny shot at him. 'Really, Kevin, you're the one that's free and easy and you haven't so much as checked that your mother is alive in weeks.' She was fuming and he had a feeling that she was only saying words that their mother was biting down.

'I'm sorry, it's just been very busy.' He smiled now at his mother, older and more fragile than he'd ever seen her before. 'What with work and moving...'

'You've moved?' his mother suddenly seemed to get some of her old fire back. 'You've moved house and you never told your own mother?'

'Well, I...' he squirmed uncomfortably in the seat, caught the satisfied look on Penny's face.

'And what about that lovely little house you had with Carrie, that's gone too, I suppose,' his mother had always, not too quietly, fantasised about her grandchildren growing up there. 'Did she throw you out?'

'No, Mother, I wanted to leave. It seemed only fair, since we...' Kevin bit his lip.

'We?' Penny was in like a vulture. 'Who's we?' She already knew, he could tell, but then lots of people knew. All of their friends knew and Penny wasn't exactly a recluse.

'I...' God, this was even harder than he thought. 'I've met someone.'

'Holy mother of the divine.' His mother blessed herself

piously. 'As if it wasn't bad enough, deserted by my own family, and now this...' she shook her head sadly.

'It's not what you think.' Kevin said.

'And she was so good to you,' his mother lamented the loss of Carrie, then softly, as though it just dawned on her, 'she was good to me too, not that I ever...'

'Did you meet her before or after you had finished up with Carrie?' Penny was never one to hang about. Kevin cursed her under his breath. Maybe if he'd come clean with her from the beginning she might have covered for him.

'I've known her for a while. But, if you're asking me...' he couldn't lie, could he? Silence was his best option, then inspiration struck. 'Carrie has met someone too,' he said, quickly, perhaps a little high-pitched.

'Are you trying to give me a heart attack as well as letting me fade away by neglect?' His mother gasped. 'Who on earth did Carrie "meet"? And more importantly, what kind of a woman did you meet up with that would have you moving out of your perfectly comfortable home, away from a girl like Carrie who was so kind and solicitous of your mother?'

'It's not like that.'

'Well, I'd very much like to hear what it is like,' his mother said impatiently, waving away a nurse who arrived with a vase for the tragic flowers Kevin had picked up in the shop downstairs. 'Close those curtains, Penny,' His mother elbowed her way higher in the bed. She may want them to think she was at death's door, but there was no way the other patients were getting an earful of her son's uncommon domestic arrangements.

*

The brochures were the first thing Luke spotted when he arrived to visit Jane that day. 'Ballyglen?' he said, nodding towards the open brochure on the bed. 'My dad lives there, although...' he didn't finish off the sentence. He wished that his father had not settled into Ballyglen and seemed, with it, to have given up on living the full life that Luke believed still stretched out before him. Luke didn't want that to happen to Jane as well.

He didn't tell Jane that he'd worked so hard to make the pub feel as though it was welcoming her back. He didn't say that something niggled him about the place, as if it felt lonely without her. It was a little peculiar, even in his own head, but he felt there was something about the place that resonated with him. Perhaps it was those faded photographs that hung on the wall and oddly resembled his father and indeed himself. The Marchant Inn could be home to him, if he'd ever known what a home was, or if he gave it half a chance.

'Does he like it?' Jane asked and he had a feeling that, unlike his father, she might actually listen to his opinion and so he trod far more carefully than he might have otherwise done.

'You'd have to ask him that, it's... not the same as living in your own house, but I suppose...' Luke faltered. 'Anyway, that's a decision for another day,' he said, because maybe he could see that Jane might actually enjoy being surrounded by other people, especially when he thought of her alone in that big empty building with people like those two yobs who'd dropped in on him.

'Hmm,' she said, gathering up the brochures and placing them in a neat bundle on top of her bag. 'Well, as you say, we'll see...' and she fingered the collar of her cardigan, pulling it around her in a habit Luke had quickly picked out as nervous.

'My landlady says she knows you,' he said lightly. 'Mrs Peril.'

'Of course, Winnie, she's been running that bed and breakfast for as long as I can remember.' Jane shook her head. 'I haven't seen her in an age; her family must be all doing for themselves now.'

'Well, she told me that she has a son on every continent except the one she's living in.' He couldn't help feeling that there was a bitterness to Mrs Peril's words as she'd pronounced this curious fact. 'Mind you, the more time I spend in her company, the more I can understand why they'd want to put a bit of space in between them,' he said conspiratorially. 'She's an awful woman for giving out. If it's not the weather, it's the price of things. I can't help but think that she probably gives out about her guests too,' he said then, shaking his head.

'Probably, but once you realise it's just her way...' Jane smiled wisely. Perhaps it was good to know some things didn't change. 'What will you do for Christmas, does she keep guests over the holiday?'

'I don't know, to be honest, I never thought to ask,' he mused, because, really, he hadn't given much thought to Christmas, it hadn't particularly featured in his plans, usually it came and went. He made his way to whatever city his father was living in and they cooked steaks, watched TV and either caught up with each other over a few beers or caught up with sleep to hijack the jet lag that was an inevitable part of living from a suitcase. 'I suppose I'll have to ask.'

'You should, while there's still time to make some kind of a plan.' She looked at him then, thoughtful for a moment. 'You know, if you needed a room, well, you've seen what my spare rooms are like, they haven't been slept in, not in years, but...'

'That's really kind of you, but I couldn't do that, really, it just wouldn't be...' He didn't finish off the sentence, because in some ways he felt no matter what the conditions of the rooms, he'd rather stay with Jane than Mrs Peril any day. The only thing stopping him was the idea that it might feel as if he was taking advantage of her loneliness. He was almost certain that when he moved on, the loneliness might be sharper than it was already, because there would be one more voice to miss. 'Do you know?' he said then, leaning towards her, 'that's the best offer I've had in years,' and he winked at her. They both laughed so much, the woman in the bed opposite looked across at them suspiciously as though she'd just missed an important joke and she was not one bit pleased about it.

9

It was as she was tidying away her laptop, having written up her blog post, that she came across a bundle of receipts and Kevin's credit card. She couldn't help herself. The receipts alone were overwhelming. It was all there, detailed in black and white – and almost red too by the looks of things. The deposit on his apartment was more than they earned each year in wages. He was paying a fortune on the lease for his swanky new love nest, but she could have guessed that anyway. Panoramic views in Dublin don't come cheap. It was the other spending. Jewellery from Grafton Street, designer shoes and bags from the Dundrum shopping centre, clothes from shops that Carrie wouldn't be brave enough to enter, never mind brandish her credit card in. He was spending a fortune on Valentina. For a minute, she wondered if he realised, but of course, this was Kevin. Kevin had all but receipted his confirmation money and kept a close eye on every penny since. He must be worth a fortune, Carrie reckoned now. When they were together, everything was paid from her account, from the mortgage to the weekly shopping for his mother. She had always assumed he never thought of those practical things, and they were a couple anyway. Well, he was certainly paying the bills now. She folded them all up together, left them on a worktop where, hopefully, Kevin would be first to see them, then she left the kitchen and headed back upstairs until she heard him switch on the radio when he arrived in for the evening shift.

'We need to talk,' she said to his back. He was busy pulling food from the cool cupboard for prepping by one of the junior chefs later.

'We do,' he said calmly, 'but is this really the place?'

'I think it is. At least while we're here alone. I don't want you coming back to the house, Kevin. Don't take that the wrong way, but... I need the space.'

'Yes, so I hear.'

'What's that supposed to mean?'

'Oh, I think you know exactly what it means,' he said, his voice was low. Kevin didn't 'do' angry, not that he had any right to be, anyway.

'Well, whatever it means, I'm going to rise above it. We need to be practical, Kevin. You have moved on with your life and I know that it hasn't been very long, but we both know you're not coming back.'

'You say that as if I don't have a choice?' He turned to look at her now, his expression one of mild bewilderment.

'Well you've made your bed and it's one you seem to be more than content to lie in.' It would do no good now having a blazing row, and anyway, Carrie wasn't sure she had a blazing row in her, fighting with Kevin had always been like going ten rounds with a wet tea cloth. She'd cried plenty already, shouting at Kevin wasn't actually going to make her feel better. There was only one thing that would do that. 'I want the house, Kevin. I haven't decided about this place yet, but I want to buy you out of the mortgage.' She dropped to the high stool that Kevin had always objected to but Carrie insisted on because somehow it gave the kitchen a homelier feel. 'Will you do that for me, let me have that one thing,' she didn't add that she felt he'd taken her dignity, he'd taken her future and, perhaps, her opportunity to have what every girl dreams of. Carrie was under no illusions. She'd given Kevin the best of her twenties and her thirties too. They'd ploughed their time into building up the restaurant when other women were setting about selecting bridesmaids and getting married. 'Please, Kevin, you know Valentina wouldn't be happy there, it's not like you'll ever settle down somewhere like that and it's my home.'

'I've never had any real attachment to the place, you know that, Carrie. I'm more concerned about The Sea Pear.' He stood opposite her and for a moment she wondered if perhaps he didn't regret not conceding to a second kitchen stool. 'I think we should prioritise the restaurant, I think...'

'I can't think about that until I know my home is secure.' She had the forms for the bank and the solicitor upstairs, he could sign them now and she knew it wouldn't mean a thing to him. 'You've set up a new home, I know that...' she nodded towards the bundle of statements and receipts. 'I have no interest in the kind of high-society life you want, Kevin, all I want is my own little house, it is all I ever wanted.'

'Okay, okay.' Kevin looked past her, the front door of the restaurant opening signalled the arrival of some of the staff, early for their shift. 'Okay, but I don't want to talk about it in front of anyone here.'

'Fine,' Carrie said, knowing that Kevin would die of mortification rather than have people know the ins and outs of his domestic arrangements. 'I have the forms in my bag; perhaps before Valentina comes in you'll come up to my office and sign them?'

'Yeah, sure,' he said, moving away quickly at the sound of voices in the restaurant outside.

And, so it was done. Carrie left the restaurant that night, feeling, if not elated, certainly secure in the knowledge that she'd sorted out the mortgage at the value they purchased rather than the newly inflated prices of the current property market. It was only fair after all, when she looked back on their time in the house, she had paid the mortgage and selected every piece of furniture they had. Kevin knew it too, and so long as they kept Valentina out of things, it should all be fair and square.

It seemed to Luke that his father had become a smaller man since he'd come to live at Ballyglen. It wasn't a gradual shrinking, as he'd seen in other men of his age, this was something more than just losing two inches off his six foot frame. It was beyond simply the bend that made his back a little more crooked than before, or the fact that these days he leant forward to hear more clearly. Conn Gibson had shrunk in a way that was much more profound and, for that, Luke found it hard to put a finger on where that change had started or how he might put some kind of stop to it.

'But you never got chest infections,' he said when he saw his father propped up in bed wearing an oxygen mask.

'No. But I'm not as young as I used to be, am I?' he said sadly and those familiar green eyes seemed heavy with more words than he could convey.

'And you've seen a doctor? I mean, they didn't just pop this thing on you and decide that...'

'Yes, I've seen the doctor. They're very good here, I know you forget that I'm not forty-five anymore but, Luke, this is just a chest infection.'

'Well, I want to see the doctor.' Luke stood up; even to himself, he knew, he filled the little room.

'No. I absolutely forbid it,' his father pulled the mask from his face. 'I mean, really, when did you turn into such an old woman. It's a chest infection, if it makes you feel any better I'll put on some clothes and we'll go out somewhere together, but you're not going to take up their precious time here when I know they have to attend to really sick people.'

'Okay, I'll take your word for it, but really, Dad...' Luke dropped into the chair beside his father's bed. 'These places, I've said it a million times, they make people old before their time.'

'Come on, tell me about The Marchant Inn and your

latest run-in with the local Colombian mafia, or were you just taking on the ironing today?' Conn Gibson smiled and perhaps it hid the concern in his eyes. He wanted to see Luke getting on with his life, taking up a new university post, getting back out on a dig, forgetting about his old man and letting him age in peace.

'Ah, I'm afraid I might have scared off the Colombians,' Luke smiled easily, but he had the strangest feeling that he'd missed something important in their shared banter.

'Wasn't Castro from Cuba?' his mother said as they were driving back to her house.

'Indeed he was, Mother, but Valentina is from Colombia.'

'Well, Cuba, Columbia, it's hardly Ballybrack, is it? Can this creature even speak English?'

'Mother, her name is Valentina and she's a very smart lady. She's university-educated.' That was true, in that she was taking language classes in a room in Trinity College. It turned out that Valentina had enrolled in English language classes only as a way of securing a work visa.

'Poof, they are all doing eet, Keveen,' Valentina had said when he finally realised that she wasn't studying to be a doctor, lawyer or engineer.

'So, why is she working as a waitress?'

'We all had to start somewhere, Mum.' He could feel a headache beginning to throb at the back of his eyes. The doctor had made the right decision telling his mother she was fit to go home. She was lucky. She fractured her wrist; it could have been much worse. By the time he did his rounds, she'd all but moved in with Penny – though she soon changed her mind at the thoughts of screaming children and an Italian husband who liked to sing opera at seven in the morning. She had just about fixed herself into Kevin's new apartment when the doctor told her she was fit to go back to her normal life. Although he'd cast a severe look in Penny's direction, when he suggested that she'd need to be checked up on every day.

'Well, more in her line to start in Colombia and finish there too,' Maureen Mulvey sighed loudly and Kevin thought he could actually *hear* her raise her eyes to heaven. He was being patient, but this was unfamiliar territory. Normally, his mother vented her dislike and enduring hostility to Carrie, while Kevin remained her golden boy. Now, without the foil of Carrie, it was Kevin's turn to get the brunt of his mother's critical charm. To be fair, Carrie never rose to the bait. In all the years that Maureen Mulvey had commented, sighed, rolled her eyes or insulted her, never once had Carrie said a bad word about his mother. Kevin had a feeling his mother knew this too. He had a feeling that it annoyed her, probably far more than any other part of their relationship did; even more than the secretly held belief that Carrie was at least half-responsible for the success of The Sea Pear. The truth was, that as far as Kevin could see, behind all the barbs, Maureen Mulvey had developed a grudging respect for Carrie. He hadn't realised that until recently, but it was quite apparent now that not only was there respect, Maureen had actually become fond of Carrie.

In the car park, Penny devised a roster of sorts for keeping an eye on their mother. Kevin was doing mornings, except Sundays. Neither of them could face Sunday Mass, an hour of droning sermon and then another hour standing by while Maureen crowed to all her old biddy friends about the general superiority of her brood. Penny would check in on their mother in the evenings.

'I suppose we can't expect Carrie to help out?' Penny said and Kevin thought for a minute she might be actually serious.

'No. We can't expect Carrie to help out,' Kevin said flatly.

'And Valentina?'

'Well, if we're scouting about, how's Nanni fixed for weekends?' Kevin knew it was low. Nanni had as much time for his mother-in-law as she had for him. To be fair, he was probably afraid of her. His own mother was one of those women who was born to be a granny. She had silvery white hair, eyes that were creased by smiling more than frowning and a warm heart that didn't judge or criticise. Kevin thought his own mother could take a leaf out of her book.

So they agreed to take responsibility for their mother and rather than feeling relieved that she was well enough to go home, they both felt disgruntled that suddenly their days had shrunk by at least an hour. Kevin didn't exactly regret that Carrie was no longer in his life to carry on as she had before, but he certainly knew he wouldn't be asking Valentina to take over any time soon.

*

Honestly, Kevin felt a little relieved to be out of the mortgage with Carrie. He wasn't keen to buy, certainly not that pokey little semi that Carrie was so fond of. It reminded him too much of where he grew up. The last thing he wanted was to feel he was turning into his father. Carrie had only talked him into it because it was such a bargain. Still, even with the rising cost of Dublin housing and the obvious difference in what they'd paid for it, he didn't like the place. It was little more than a two-up, two-down, surrounded by hipster neighbours who no doubt would have to leave as soon as their squawking kids arrived on the scene. Carrie had spent ages doing the place up. She seemed to actually enjoy doing manual labour like tiling and painting and potting up summer plants for window boxes that would die anyway. So, he hummed and hawed for almost a week, but then, he signed the place over. No doubt an accountant would tell him he was a fool. If they sold the place now they'd make an obscene profit on the buying price.

As much as Carrie loved the place, Kevin disliked it. He'd lived there because it was convenient, easy. He loved the anodyne emptiness of the apartment. There wasn't a distressed pine board in sight and it was unlikely that Valentina would begin to collect pottery or cultivate an interest in fairy lights, solar panels or indoor plants – ever.

Of course, in other ways the apartment was not as convenient. It was not as easy as living with Carrie. In his new home, he was expected to take care of all the bills. He knew this without it being explicitly agreed. Already, a pattern had been established. Kevin paid and Valentina spent. Valentina did not buy things like milk or coffee. No. She believed in buying her coffee fresh from the perennially empty coffee shop that leaked the heavy aroma of an expensive Colombian bean onto the courtyard beneath his balcony. It wafted up towards him while he made do with the jar of instant from his sparse kitchen.

When Simo and Reda visited, they too had to make do with instant coffee. Kevin tugged his collar from his neck, thinking of the frequency of their visits. He didn't like them 'popping in'. He didn't like them sitting on his lovely corner sofa, whiling away the afternoon with Valentina while Kevin felt obliged to either leave or make do with perching on an uncomfortable chrome and leather high stool that vaguely resembled a deckchair.

'How come they're always here?' he asked Valentina after one of their marathon visits.

'They are my cousins, Keveen, of course, they must come and see me. You would prefer that they veeseet the restaurant?' She sighed in that way she had of making him feel as if there was a gulf between them that was vaster than the ocean and it was caused by his stupidity. 'Of course, they would love to come to The Sea Pear, they would love to eat your expensive foods, perhaps even...' It was wearing a bit thin, so Valentina didn't mention it anymore. Kevin was not going to be feeding her cousins for free at his restaurant; there were perfectly good supermarkets all over the city with deli counters if they didn't feel like cooking for themselves. 'No, they're better to come here.' Kevin knew what was coming next, Simo had hinted often enough already. He didn't need security, not the kind that Simo was offering anyway.

Sometimes, Kevin left them to it. They spoke mostly in Colombian anyway, so it wasn't like he was missing much.

Occasionally, Kevin thought he was just being stupid. After all, what had Simo and Reda ever actually done to him? True, they didn't like him, but the feeling was mutual. Perhaps he'd started to dislike them first. He reasoned, that they had every right to be jealous of him, but secretly, he knew that they made him feel aware of his own stuffiness. They made him feel like an old man, compared to their evident vigour and robustness. Ultimately, they made him feel like *his* old man – and that was the one thing Kevin never wanted to be.

'You can't get away from it mate,' Jim said one evening when Kevin had been turfed out of the apartment. 'What you've done to Carrie is no different. Those Colombian boyos, they're just keeping an eye out for Valentina, in case you throw her over for some young one from...' Jim scratched his head. They both knew the idea was ridiculous. Already, Kevin was punching far above his weight. 'Well, you see blokes, don't you? Internet Brides, that's what they're called,' he said it into his pint. 'Internet Brides,' he said thoughtfully, as if confirming it for himself at least.

'Valentina is nothing like an Internet bride,' Kevin

spluttered, spraying Guinness across the bar counter. 'For your own sake, don't ever say anything like that again,' Kevin wasn't so sure who'd do Jim more harm, Valentina or her cousins, if she thought anyone saw her as something cheap and for sale.

'No, well...' It was hardly an apology, but Jim's mouth had turned upwards, so perhaps he'd reaped what he'd hoped for. 'What I mean is, you have form. After all, you've cast a perfectly good woman aside, just to take up with someone else, whose charms are more obvious, granted, but it's doubtful she's really a patch on Carrie. To anyone's money, that's a bit like the situation with your dad.'

'There's a big difference between me and my father. He kept up the pretence for years, he never had the gumption to come home and tell my mother.'

'Yeah, well, fair's fair, Kevin. There wouldn't be too many people who'd be jumping at the idea of confronting your mother.'

'True enough.' Kevin had to concede. He was happier at that. It made him feel a little more confident to think that the two Colombians might see him as a player, better that than an easy mug from whom they might score protection money. 'I've signed over the house to Carrie.'

'What the...' Now it was Jim who gulped down a mouthful of Guinness before it splattered the bar. 'You what?'

'She wanted it. I think she'll let me have The Sea Pear,' Kevin looked up at the TV over the bar. That wasn't what she said, exactly, but Kevin had a good feeling about it.

'She's lost the drive for The Sea Pear. The place, with me there and Valentina, it's like she's not so bothered anymore. She spends most of her time up in that office, fiddling with her computer.'

'But the house, Kevin?' Jim was still spluttering. 'Do you know how much it's worth?'

'She's giving me half of what's paid on the mortgage, which is fair, actually, it's probably more than fair, she's paid it mostly over the years anyway. It's better than her wanting to drag it out and sell it. You know the way estate agents and solicitors can smell out a good fee.' He hadn't seen the figures yet, but he'd signed the papers in good faith. The last thing he wanted was to have Valentina being part of that too. He knew, whatever chance he had of holding onto some peace, he had to keep Valentina out of things. 'To be honest, it was always more hers than mine, Jim.'

'Maybe, but...' Jim drank from his pint, swallowed with it whatever words he was about to say. 'Yeah. You probably did the right thing there, mate. Save yourself a lot of aggro.' All the same, he shook his head as if he couldn't believe Kevin could be so stupid.

10

Already, Carrie had managed to make Sunday mornings her own. Teddy snored contentedly on the floor beside her bed and she slept until she knew her body had picked up the slack of all those early Masses. Still it seemed like a decadent luxury to wake without an alarm. Last Sunday, she and Teddy wandered to the corner shop and then she sat reading the papers while she drank tea from a pot that had once belonged to Maureen Mulvey. Teddy sat at her feet, chewing happily on a bone rescued from the restaurant stockpot the night before. Sometimes she would look at the teapot and wonder how the old witch was getting on, truth be told, she still worried about her occasionally. Kevin mentioned that she'd fallen and injured her wrist and Carrie had felt the automatic pull to go and visit the old girl.

'Don't you bloody dare,' Anna warned and, of course, she was right. Maureen Mulvey had disliked Carrie since the first day they met. She'd spent years griping and sniping at her, but the truth was, Carrie could see right through her. She was a lonely and bitter old woman who didn't know how to handle what life had thrown her. She was her own worst enemy. Carrie settled on a bunch of flowers, she ordered specially, all old-fashioned country garden blooms: sweet williams, foxglove, hollyhocks, peonies and carnations. On the card, she wrote a simple message with her best wishes and thought, perhaps one day, she'd go to visit, but not yet. Definitely, not yet.

Instead, she made an appointment with the hairdressers, it was time to overhaul her tired hair, maybe get a pampering facial too. Perhaps she was motivated when she saw the fortune Valentina spent on herself. Since the *splitsville* diet had kicked in, or perhaps it was just not having any wine each night, or maybe just the extra walking that Teddy put her way, Carrie knew she'd lost weight. Her clothes were looser, a lot looser, and she had places to go these days. Turning up in the swankiest of restaurants looking like she'd ridden backwards on a motorbike just didn't cut it anymore. She deserved a little indulging, now that she was not spending all her time indulging others. For the first time in years, she wanted to look as well as she felt and she was happy to invest in looking good.

'A penny for them,' Luke murmured one afternoon as he sat in the visitors' room with Jane. He'd been watching her for a while, lost in thought as she looked out across the snow covered grounds where two children scrambled happily about while their father occasionally bent down and picked one or the other up and swung them high over his head much to their delight. There was a lingering discrepancy in her expression, as if she might have been sad, but it was pushed out by something unfamiliar.

'Oh, I'm not sure they're even worth that now,' she smiled easily as she said the words and nodded towards the family beyond the glass. Glazing prevented the shrieks and laughter that must be filling the air outside from penetrating the aseptic buzzing silence of the day room.

'You never know, they might be,' he chided.

'To tell you the truth, I'm lost so far in dreams and memories, I'm not sure what I'm thinking about.' She nodded towards the action outside, 'there was a time when seeing children like that and knowing that I'd never have a family of my own would have made me sad. I'd almost forgotten that, the awful heaviness that I carried about with me for years, even Manus felt it.'

'You couldn't have children?'

'We almost did, but then... Manus would have been a great father,' she broke off wistfully.

'I'm sure that you'd have made a smashing mum too.' Luke squeezed her hand gently.

'Well, it isn't everything, is it?'

'No, I suppose it's not.' Luke said. He'd never given it much thought, marriage, kids all that. They didn't really fit with moving from dig to dig.

'What about you?' Jane asked, almost reading his thoughts.

'Me?' he laughed. 'Oh, I'm just a confirmed old bachelor, a drifter in some ways, I suppose.'

'You might want to settle though, some day?' She looked at him now, something far more behind her eyes than she'd ever put into words, probably. 'Don't leave it too late, will you? Don't leave it until you're thinking that there's nowhere else for you, or nobody who...'

'Hey, you're making it sound as if...' he moved closer to her, put his arm around her shoulders.

'If I tell you something, you won't laugh, will you?' She looked up at him now and he felt as if his heart might melt, such was the fragility to her.

'Of course not.' He said evenly.

'Year's ago, oh, dear, so many years ago now.' She shook her head. 'I would dream about my children, what they would be like, how they'd turn out – you know, fantasize, daydream, silly sort of stuff...' her cheeks reddened, a bashful pink striding across them, but she took a deep breath. 'Well... if I'd had a son, in my mind, he'd have turned out just like you.' Jane pulled away from his embrace, for just a moment, smiled at him in a way that made him feel as though some kind of magnet between them had just squeezed a little higher. This growing bond between them was... well, it wasn't like anything he'd ever felt before. He pulled her close to him again, his arms about her, as if *she* was the child and he kissed the top of her head softly.

'That's probably the nicest thing anyone has said to me in the longest time.' He said and he wiped a small tear before it ran down his cheek and into her soft grey hair. He thought of his own mother, curiously absent for so many years. Yes, he would have loved a mother like Jane Marchant, a woman who got him on so many levels and asked for nothing in return. They sat like that for a few moments, until Jane heard Carrie's voice in the corridor outside, greeting nurses with her usual upbeat friendliness.

'Well, what's going on here?' Carrie smiled when she put her head around the door. There was an unopened bag of fruit on the table and a stash of newspapers Luke had brought along, as if she'd ever get through the mountain of daily gifts he had already placed on the locker beside her bed.

'We're just watching the world go by,' Luke said as he sat back in his chair. Outside, one of the children had fallen and now there was a flurry about picking him up, setting him straight on the snow again. 'Families...'

'Ah, yes,' Carrie said and he wondered if she felt as Jane had all those years ago. She would make a terrific mother too. He could imagine her with a brood of children, doling out more love than lectures from a busy house in Dublin's deepest suburbia. He pulled himself up from his wandering thoughts. Too easily, he found himself slipping into this imaginary life, which of course was madness – he was hardly settling down material. 'Children,' she said happily, 'they're just the tonic to put a smile on your face on an overcast day like today.' She turned to watch as the two kids outside began to pelt each other with watery snowballs. There was no sadness about Carrie, no sense of loss or desperation about her. If anything she was quite the opposite, actually, today, she looked better, brighter and happier than he'd ever seen her before – there was something different about her. Perhaps it was her hair?

He smiled at her now, he had a feeling it was something much more profound.

'Well,' Carrie's mother was positively glowing. 'I can't remember when you looked so well.' She kissed her daughter's cheeks, relieved perhaps, because they both knew that the break-up with Kevin could have gone either way. She was excited about the success of the blog too. 'I think it's a splendid idea. Count me in. Any night – except Wednesdays and Fridays – we're having extra bridge practice.' She looked around the bar. They were just having lunch, but her mother liked to make an occasion of it, so she always got her hair done. Today, Carrie had made an extra effort too. 'Oh, and for the next few weeks I won't be around for weekends either.' She smiled at the waitress. 'I'm doing a yoga retreat.' She leant across the table and picked a stray rib from Carrie's shoulder. 'With the bowling ladies. Did I mention that we're starting a book club? That's on Monday nights.' For a long time, Carrie had considered that she and her mother had their social lives the wrong way round. Her mother, living off the pension her father had paid into for many years, was making up for years at home with all sorts of activities filling her retirement.

'You don't have very many nights free so?' Carrie laughed. It was good to see her mother happy. She looked well, with her newly 'done' hair. It was shorter, blonder and sleeker than before. Still, it framed her softening features and added the glamour that had turned many heads back in the day.

'No, I suppose I don't. But still, Carrie, I'm glad that you're doing this blog with the restaurants. Apart from anything else, it gives you something to focus on.'

'I'm doing fine, Mum. Really, much better than I thought I would be.' Truthfully, that was down to a number of different things. It was down to the reviewing and the blog, of course, but there were other things too. Like the fact that she'd managed to clear Kevin out of her home and she was enjoying having the place to herself with only Teddy to think about and he was a much more appreciative housemate. She wouldn't miss Maureen Mulvey half as much as Maureen would miss her, she knew that for sure. And as for Kevin and Valentina – mostly, when she was thinking straight, she thought they were welcome to each other. She could see him for what he was. She had for a long time.

'What about the wedding in Sligo? Have you decided yet?'

'Didn't I tell you I have a new mystery man?' Carrie laughed at the idea of this. 'The word is out that I have a hot foreign lover hidden away, just waiting to unleash him down the country.'

'And, have you?'

'Of course not. But if all comes to all, I can always arrive on my own and say he had to go back to wherever he doesn't come from, very urgently.' It was exactly what she was planning on doing. For now, she was enjoying watching Kevin try to circumvent any talk of new relationships.

Perhaps he only half believed the nonsense that Jim had been primed to feed into him when they went for their weekly pint, but that didn't matter to Carrie. Only half believing was a damn lot better than having Kevin looking at her with smugness or, worse, pity. 'In the meantime, I'm having the nice suite in the castle. Apparently, there's a four-poster bed and views across the gardens. Kevin and Valentina are going to have to make do with whatever is left over in bed and breakfast accommodation in a town that's going to be chock-full of wedding-goers in off season. It's going to be pretty dismal.' Carrie laughed. 'At this stage, I'd say, he'd be safer bringing a tent.'

'Well, you know, I'm always up for staying in a castle and I'd promise not to snore or put my cold feet on yours,' her mother said, running her finger down the wine list. 'Anyway, by then, who knows, you may have already met the man of your dreams.'

'Oh, Mum, I hardly think so.' Carrie shook her head. 'I can't see them beating down the door for me, can you?'

'Actually, I couldn't imagine anyone breaking the door down to get Kevin, but there you go.'

'I always told you he had hidden depths.' They both giggled at that.

'Have you thought about Internet dating? Lorna Kennedy does it and she's been out on lots of dates.'

'Is she still a nymphomaniac?' Carrie decided on the monkfish.

'She was never a nymphomaniac; really, Carrie, I wish you wouldn't call her that. She's just a bit more open-minded than the rest of us.'

'I bet she's had some very satisfied dates, though.'

'I'm not commenting.' Her mother's smile said it all. 'Do you know, I think I was about your age, when I completely went off having sex with your father?'

'Too much information, Mum.'

'Well, it's the menopause, though, I mean, there was no HRT for me.'

'Good God, Mum, I'm not ancient and there's no sign of that yet.'

'Yes, well, it's different when you're married.' The waiter poured a taste of house white and Pamela sipped it, smiling her appreciation before her glass was filled. 'There's more of a reason to go off it when you're married.'

'So, I'm off on Wednesday night and I've a booking at Chez Rouge,' Carrie said abruptly. The only way to avoid hearing about any more of her mother's love life was to change the subject. 'I was hoping you'd come.' Her mother wouldn't miss out on her bridge night if she was on the pains of death. 'But...'

'Well, I do have bridge,' she said, looking about the bar and waving across at someone Carrie did not recognise. 'You know, that's exactly where you could use the Internet dating? How popular would you be, bringing them to the best restaurants in town, and it'd really spice up your reviews. You could post them on the dating site as well as your own.' Pamela found this hilarious.

'Thanks Mum.' When she was like this, there really was no talking to her.

They ate their meal, catching up on the little bits of gossip that would otherwise slip between them.

'I'll bet you're glad to be off the hook with Maureen Mulvey,' her mother said it as if she had mentally counted the benefits to the ending of Carrie's relationship with Kevin.

'Well...' Carrie had always been careful not to talk too much about Kevin's mother, mainly because she'd have been hard-pressed to find five good things to say about the woman. 'She's really not as bad as you all make out...' Carrie felt her voice peter off, knew she had no real belief in the words.

'She is too, and then some. I met her coming out of Mass last Sunday...'

'Hold on, you were at Mass?'

'No. I wasn't at Mass, she was, but I was on my way to the Lady President's Day at the golf club when I met her. She was getting into a taxi outside the church.'

'Ahh. That sounds more like it.'

'Didn't you always take her to Mass?' Pamela had laughed her socks off at that one many times over the years.

'For my sins.'

'She was certainly sheepish last Sunday when I met her. Neither Kevin nor Penny have seen fit to step into the role of dutiful Mass goer.'

'I really couldn't blame them, Mum. It's one of the best things about my weekends now. Sometimes, I just lie in bed and imagine the church bells ringing out.' Still, Carrie couldn't help feeling just a little bit sorry for Maureen Mulvey. The woman really could be the devil incarnate, but even she didn't deserve the self-centred children she'd ended up with.

'Well, she's still there. She could hardly meet my eyes, but I was very civil. Well, there's no point, is there?' Pamela smiled. 'Do you think she knows?'

'About Valentina? No, I wouldn't think so, he's as spineless now as ever.'

'Yes, but Valentina doesn't sound like she'll let him off the hook too easily.'

'No, Mum. There's no way,' Carrie whispered and for a moment, she felt like she'd been betrayed again. How could Kevin replace her so fully, so completely, so quickly? It made it all a thousand times worse and she knew again that she still had a long way to go to get over it all. No matter how sorry she might feel for Maureen Mulvey, there was still too much hurt there to get drawn in and used all over again.

There was no point arguing, but Jane had a feeling that all the surprises in the world would not change how she felt about going back to The Marchant Inn.

'Seriously, he's put a lot of work into it,' Carrie said, 'at least humour him.' She shook her head and Jane wondered exactly what kind of work could take the anxiousness from her stomach every time she thought about spending another night alone in the pub. Only the bundle of brochures buried deep in her bag felt like they might be the answer to this rising fear in her. 'He's come in here every day for the last week, honestly, I'd never have imagined the place could feel so...' Carrie pulled up on the path outside.

'Right, well, I suppose, I have to go somewhere,' Jane sighed, although there was no missing the shine of the stained glass or the gleam of the brasses on the freshly painted front door.

She didn't expect much, but when she stepped into the pub, rather than everything feeling smaller, greyer, less than she imagined, it actually felt better. There was an enveloping warmth that welcomed her as soon as she stepped through the front door. The oak of the bar counter gleamed with a fresh stain of varnish, the glasses shone, even the ceiling had brightened with the benefit of a good washing. But it was at either end of the bar, a roaring fire lit in each of the Victorian grates, which seemed to make the biggest difference. The little dog Carrie had told her so much about lay curled up before one, as if he had always been here and raised his head lazily to greet her, before laying it easily against the fender once more. At the counter, Manus's friends, a half a dozen of them, her only regulars, sat waiting for her and at the end of the row was Luke, smiling proudly.

'Oh, dear,' she said as she felt tears sting behind her eyes. She was not sure if they were tears of joy or some other emotion she could not put a name on.

'Cup of tea?' Luke asked and he made his way behind the counter where one of her familiar mugs stood bleached squeaky clean beside the kettle.

She settled onto one of the freshly scrubbed stools, looking about the bar so she could take in the changes.

'You've transformed it,' she said eventually to Luke. 'I mean, it's as if you've brought the whole place back to life.' She wiped the tears from her eyes, but they were tears of pleasure now. She'd never expected anyone to do so much for her, even to have this lovely welcoming committee organised for her arrival. 'I'm just...' And of course, what she wanted to say was 'speechless', but again her emotions got the better of her.

It was probably one of the nicest afternoons she had spent in years. But what is it they say? All good things must come to an end. Once everyone started to leave, she felt that terrible weight of loneliness and fear descending on her again, so when she closed the front door she knew she'd be checking the bolts a dozen times as the evening wore on. She was sorry that Luke had not taken up her offer to stay in the spare room, but she could understand his reluctance, after all, he was a free agent. What would he want to be surrounded by her memories for? So she didn't ask him again, instead she hoped that maybe the excitement of the day might be enough to send her into a deep and undisturbed peaceful sleep.

Quietly, they were all just a little relieved when Carrie suggested they meet up in The Sea Pear for the hen night get-together. Melissa was hardly a party animal – of all their friends, she was probably the most reserved. The idea of a drunken trawl with straw willies or wearing L-plates over skimpy outfits was her idea of hell rather than a good time. They had agreed the date months ago, Kevin would prepare the food, but they would close the restaurant and bring in music for the night. It would be a girls' only night, with Melissa's friends and family filling up a long table that Carrie and Andrew had arranged down the centre of the dining room.

'This is so lovely,' Melissa said when she arrived. Carrie had pulled out all the stops. She'd taken down the Christmas lights and found every photograph she had of Melissa, then had them blow up as large as she could manage and pinned them along the walls so it was a gallery of happy, smiling images for her friend. 'You really shouldn't have gone to all this trouble.'

'Well, Kevin had something to do with it all too...' Carrie nodded back towards the kitchen where Kevin had prepared a five-course meal for everyone. 'It's all hands on deck back there now, but he'll come out and say hello later.'

'I can't quite believe how civilised you're being about it all,' Melissa confided.

'Oh dear God, you've faded away,' Melissa's mother stood stock-still at the door, taking in Carrie, but her eyes were shining with approval.

'Hardly, but...'

'You look amazing, don't mind Mammy,' Melissa said, putting her arms around her mother's shoulder and guiding her towards the top of the table. 'Although, if you keep going like this, we might have to get that dress altered,' she smiled at Carrie, admiring her. 'Honestly, you're transformed, new hair, new figure... new man. A good old overhaul seems to have a lot going for it.'

'Don't tell Kevin,' Carrie leaned in conspiratorially, 'but Teddy has as much to do with how I'm looking and feeling as anything or anyone else these days.' They all laughed at that, but it was probably nearer the truth than any of them might imagine.

'Is the Colombian concubine here?' Anna drawled.

'Stop it, you have to behave yourself now,' Melissa said. 'Is she though?' They were all dying to catch a glimpse of Valentina. It was understandable; they'd heard so much, mainly from Kevin, through Ben and Jim, but in the beginning, when she was too raw to help herself, Carrie had vented too and now she wondered what they really expected her to be like.

'No, I'm afraid not, she's taken the night off, I think maybe it would be just a bit too much for her...' Carrie smiled. The truth was, she'd rostered Valentina off, the last thing she wanted was to waste a night with her friends talking about Kevin's new woman. She could think of nothing worse than watching Valentina sashay about the restaurant while her friends tried to make all the right noises about imperfections that clearly, to Carrie's eyes at least, simply were not there.

'Well, I suppose it would have been a bit uncomfortable for her,' Melissa said, then she smiled. 'Of course, she'll have to face us some time.'

'Is Kevin bringing her to the wedding then?' Carrie asked. He was hardly the most socially commanding man, hurtling through the uncomfortable introductions would be enough to make anyone cringe, never mind Kevin.

'Well, I think so. There's been no definite word either way,' Melissa said.

'He'll need to get his skates on,' Anna said, already a little worse for wear thanks to the cocktails Andrew was concocting from the drinks cabinet. 'Has he got a room booked, do you think or is he…' she hiccupped, 'maybe they'll sleep in the car.' Everyone giggled at this notion, there was no one less likely to sleep in the car than Kevin – or at least that's what most people would think, until they met Valentina.

'Well, they won't be staying in the hotel,' Melissa said, bending down to pass a length of beef steak to Teddy who was moving diligently around the table to maximise his chances of securing treats. 'I've had a bugger of a job trying to get a double room for one of the girls from work, and even then I have a feeling they'll be essentially sleeping in a broom cupboard.'

'Oh, God, who brought that thing in to my restaurant,' Kevin snarled at Teddy when he arrived in the dining room after desserts had been served up. The whole restaurant burst into immediate hysterical laughter.

'Oh, Kevin, you really are too funny,' Anna said when the laughter had finally subsided and Kevin made his way back to the kitchen with enough praise to just about overcome being the brunt of a joke he didn't understand.

It was all about the language school these days, apparently.

'Eeeh, I weel not be paying them another cent.' Valentina had arrived home in foul humour, one afternoon. 'Keveen, what do you think?' she asked, though clearly she wasn't interested. 'Five thousand euros, that ees what they are looking for. Poof I tell them, they can steek their classes, my Engleeshees good enough. I'm making good enough teeps already, but not enough to pay that kind of money.' And she clattered about the bedroom, kicking her sky-scraper heels towards the opposite wall and flopping onto the bed.

'But, Valentina, don't you have to attend.' Kevin hovered at the door, as once he might have done with his mother. 'I mean, isn't it part of the deal that if you're working here, you're only meant to be supporting your classes?' He'd heard Simo give out about it often enough. They had found a loophole. An opportunity, which for people like Reda and Simo, meant they'd milk it to the last. Somehow, his lovely Valentina had been pulled into it too, but perhaps she didn't realise exactly what her being here meant. 'I mean, without being a student, you can't actually work. I'm not even so sure that you can stay in Ireland, not without the student identity papers, and if you're not attending...' he smiled at her, but there was no happiness in his smile, it was meant to be conciliatory. 'Perhaps you could find a different school?'

'No, Keveen. Don't you see?' She sat up on the bed, her lovely soft curls falling to her shoulders. 'They are jealous, they see me arriving in to classes each day. I am doing well. And the teacher, he has – how you say it, he is wanting to take me to...' she nodded towards the bed behind her. God, the way she said it, it was so throaty, so worldly, he felt himself tremor with longing for her. He tried to concentrate on what she was saying, but it was useless, so in the end he just nodded at her.

'Well, he can't just...' suddenly it dawned on him what she was saying. Some letch ogling his girl, or maybe worse. 'I'll go in there tomorrow and talk to his boss, this is Ireland, he can't come onto you like that. It's not professional, it's not...' But of course, then he realised, it wasn't very different to the business owner coming onto his immigrant waitress, really, was it?

'Eet is all a mess. I am not that kind of woman. So, you see, Keveen, if you are serious about me, there really is only one thing for us to do.'

'Oh,' he said stupidly. He'd completely lost track of the conversation. Was he giving her the five thousand euros or finding her a different language class? He definitely didn't fancy forking out five grand. Already, his new life with Valentina was costing him a fortune, and it wasn't just the flat. It was everything about how Valentina thought they should be living. 'Well, I'm not paying out any more money to a swindler like that guy,' he said, warming to the feeling of standing up to some bully who'd tried to have his way with his girlfriend.

'So...'

'Well, if there's another option...' Surely there was some way round paying what amounted to extortion.

'I've just said, there's another option, Keveen, I thought you were listening to me,' she cast her beautiful dark eyes towards the ceiling.

'Of course I was, Valentina,' he moved towards her, wondering if she was feeling as energetic as he was. 'Let's go for it,' he said, sitting beside her on the bed.

'Really?' She threw her arms about him and he

wondered briefly what he'd agreed to, assuming it was a different language school.

Whatever it was, it was well worth it. He'd never experienced such enthusiastic love-making in his life. If this is what talking big did for you, Kevin decided, he should have started a long time ago.

The next few days seemed to float by. They were easy, loving days with Valentina bringing him breakfast in bed – cremated toast and coffee from the shop downstairs. Kevin told himself it was the thought that counted. He sipped the coffee and tried not to think of the stiff prices the Colombian called John Paul charged for a little banter and the intensely aromatic coffee that made Kevin feel light-headed for hours after he drank it. When Valentina was like this, it seemed to Kevin he was as happy as he could be. Her fiery temper quelled, she was content to lounge about the apartment in the expensive silky underwear she seemed so fond of buying. At the restaurant, there was a new confidence to her. Andrew grumbled, but he brushed along with her on nights when they had to work together. Only the arrival of Carrie seemed to thwart her growing self-assurance.

Valentina no longer attended the language school, instead she regaled him with the story of how she told the tutor where he could stick his classes. It took almost a week before Kevin connected this buoyant mood with the conversation about the language class. Valentina spelled out what it meant not just for him, but for Carrie too, and Kevin knew that whether he had planned it or not, his bed was well and truly made now.

11

He was a little bit sorry about Carrie. He supposed that it probably had hurt, the way Valentina had just blurted it out. At the time, he hadn't really thought about it. The announcement had been like a bolt of lightning, hitting him somewhere in his conscious mind, but afterwards, he wondered if it had sliced through his shoulder blades. It was vicious, but he wasn't sure which of them it had been aimed at. He had upset Valentina earlier that day, it was silly really. A pair of shoes – but they cost almost a thousand euros. He didn't even know what they looked like, but he had the evidence on his credit card.

'How in God's name can you spend a thousand euros on a pair of shoes?' It was too much, Valentina had to know that. He couldn't sustain that level of spending. He took his credit card, cut it in half. 'I'm cancelling it, at the bank, just so you know.' He'd been tempted to just cancel it. Let her come home red-faced from having it refused, but the truth was he was afraid. Valentina was a passionate woman. With her passion came a certain volatility, which on the one hand made him giddy with a deep longing and admiration – he'd never be able to muster the kind of strength that she had. Unfortunately, it also brought out his more cowardly nature. He would not cross Valentina when she was in a fit of temper. He saw her reach for one of the large kitchen knives and make ribbons of a scatter cushion that tripped her up one morning. Still, he knew, in spite of her temper, he would not trade her. Having a beautiful woman like Valentina on his arm made him feel as if he was somehow a bit better than the next man.

Maybe that was why he was looking forward to Ben and Melissa's wedding. Yes, he was a little nervous – he knew that, mostly, their friends would take Carrie's side. They would think he'd been a cad, but he wanted them to see. He wanted them to know that Kevin Mulvey could do better. Ben had rung him last week.

'I don't expect it, mate, being best man, it's a lot to ask. You know, people may not be very...' He was letting him step down, he could ask Jim to be best man, but Melissa was set on having Carrie.

'How can you be getting married?' Carrie heard herself say, then she clamped her hand before her lips. Kevin had to know, even with his limited well of understanding the emotions of others, that this was a cataclysmic blow. Then she saw something in his expression, his wordlessness, his posture – this was not planned.

Carrie knew, instinctively; he was as stunned as she was. Stunned, that was the only word she could use.

Not the word most people would want to describe their forthcoming marriage or plans to embark on a long and happy life together. Shock. It registered in his eyes and it knocked Carrie's heart so it felt like a beat deep within her was missed and its irregularity would forever more mark the passing of something momentous in her life. She had to breathe. She just had to stand there, in her lovely restaurant and breathe; for now, that was all she could do.

It was absurd, really; here they were, the three of them, standing over Kevin's Christmas dessert menu. Carrie thought her biggest challenge today would be facing down the mint and orange truffles. She would do well not to succumb to the charms of Kevin's treacle pudding. She'd lost weight. Carrie didn't know in ounces and pounds, she wasn't exactly a devotee of the weighing scales, but her clothes were very loose. She felt quite proud, knowing that the last few weeks, she could have gone either way. Under the circumstances, she told herself, the heartbreak diet, well, it was the first diet she'd ever stuck to – actually the first she'd ever tried or perhaps more accurately, that she'd had thrust upon her. However much she'd like to tuck into a slice of chocolate fudge cake, news of Kevin's impending nuptials managed to completely wipe out her appetite.

'Yes, we are getting married and we weell have lovely babies,' Valentina leant in close to Kevin and he had the good grace to at least look uncomfortable. 'Eetees, in the end, what everyone wants.' It felt like her eyes cut daggers in Carrie's soul and later she'd wonder how she managed to stay so calm.

'Oh, I see,' Carrie managed as bravely as she could, but she wanted to run away and cry. How could they both be so cruel?

'I, we...' Kevin hadn't the words. He'd never had them for Carrie either. They'd never spoken about marriage. In the early days, Carrie assumed it was one of those things they'd get around to. There was a time – going to her friends' weddings every other weekend for two or three summers running – that she'd wished for more. Then that voice that she'd cultivated many years earlier spoke sternly to her of priorities and what Kevin wanted and perhaps the fear of rocking the boat so much it would send him scuttling back to his mother. God, but she'd been a terrible fool. She watched him now, his mouth open, the words hanging somewhere on the air between them, but this time she stopped herself from making it easy for him.

'Yes?' she said and if her heart wasn't breaking again, she might have relished his utter discomfort. She stood, watching him squirm, waiting. He looked tragic, his shoulders slumped in resignation, hardly the vision of a freshly engaged fella – that observation settled on Carrie somewhere and she knew she could examine it later, but for now she had to remain poised.

'Well, now it's not exactly...' he looked at Valentina who raised an eyebrow, and in that moment, something clicked. Valentina was like Maureen. He was marrying his mother – was this what he always wanted? Maureen Mulvey was a bully. She had bullied her son, her daughter and probably her husband. Carrie knew it was unkind to think it, but many times she felt she understood why Kevin's father had an affair that lasted twenty-odd years. She could see too, if he was like Kevin, how he never had the gumption to leave her. Spineless, both of them – in the end, perhaps they would all end up with precisely what they deserved.

'Oh, well, I suppose, all that's left now is to wish you both well,' Carrie said, keeping her voice as steady and even as possible. She cut him off, she didn't need to hear any more. She would not give either of them the satisfaction of seeing her upset. She looked at the desserts before her; her sweet tooth abandoned her. 'Honestly, Kevin,' she cast a hand over the beautifully presented desserts, 'they're grand. Perhaps a little last year, but they'll be fine.'

She walked off towards the restaurant; her legs felt frail, as if her whole body suddenly turned to a substance too heavy to carry. She needed to get away from Kevin and Valentina for now. Perhaps it would get easier with a little time.

In the kitchen, she imagined Kevin and Valentina whispering and perhaps giggling at the bombshell they had just exploded. Perhaps they didn't talk or think about her at all, probably Kevin didn't much at least. Valentina though, she was the kind of woman whose pleasures in life increased in correlation to the depths of misery of those around her. Had she always known this of Valentina? No, she'd just hired her because she was bright, pretty and Carrie had a gut feeling that she'd be charming with the customers. Well, she was right on all three fronts. Carrie hadn't banked on her setting her hat at Kevin. He was after all, just Kevin, probably the most boring man in Ireland – that was the moniker Anna gave him all those years ago. She'd started using it again now. Anna was right, Kevin could be the most boring man in Ireland, but he had been Carrie's and she had loved him. Now, with Valentina it seemed like he was anything but boring. He was living in one of the swankiest buildings in Dublin and hanging about with the fast set. Carrie wondered what on earth Kevin would have to say to those people.

Carrie took another deep breath and Luke Gibson came to mind. It was funny, she had a feeling he would calm her. He had a sense of peace about him, he was easy to get along with, but then she nudged herself back to reality. There was so much about Luke that she didn't know. Self-preservation, that's what she had to think about now. Luke Gibson was the kind of man that could make you lose yourself completely if you let it happen, this much Carrie was certain of. Kevin and Valentina had hurt her, but she was fine. She still had her mother, friends, a home and an income. She had her blog. It was coming along nicely. She had posted her seventh review earlier. Her sixth was published all over the place. After it, one of the daily papers contacted her; they wanted to meet her. Adrienne, a busy-sounding woman whose voice lilted with a sense of fun that was beyond her control for professional phone calls wanted to buy her lunch. She would think about that tonight. She would think about the fact that she had things to look forward to.

At that, the kitchen door swung open and Valentina breezed through it. Although her generous red lips smiled to reveal a glimpse of the whitest teeth, Carrie caught something in her expression that made her stop. She thought of those missing tips again, they still hadn't got to the bottom of that mystery. Carrie had a feeling there was a nasty side to Valentina and, perhaps, she was exactly what Kevin Mulvey deserved.

A million things flooded Luke's brain, and yet, as he tossed and turned in bed, he wasn't sure which of them to blame for his wakefulness. It was no good. He swung his legs out of the bed, planted his feet on the floor, he would go for a walk, otherwise he would end up lying here until breakfast time. There was a time he would blame his restlessness on his upbringing, but he had a feeling that particular kind of restlessness had grown still. Tonight, it was more like a niggling feeling, as though there was something he needed to check.

He took his key from the door and dropped it in his pocket, making his way down the street steps two at a time. His feet brought him towards The Marchant Inn. Finch Street held the eerie silence of a tomb. Apart from Jane, tucked in bed over the pub, all of the buildings along here were deserted at this time. There was something about it. There was a feeling of desolation that went beyond the stillness; it was an echoing loneliness that stretched into infinite isolation.

He walked halfway along the street, stood outside The

Sea Pear. It, like everywhere else, was locked up for the night. He thought about Carrie and her partner Kevin, there was something very odd going on there all right. Then he shrugged, what did he know?

Overhead, the night sky was a funnel of grey clouds, racing against the full moon. He wasn't sure how long he stood in that spot, thinking of his father first and then Carrie. When Jane wandered into his thoughts, his eyes drifted across to The Marchant Inn. Even here, in the darkness, he knew, there was an unmistakable freshness after all the work he'd done on the place for her. He still wasn't sure why he'd taken it on. He shrugged when Carrie asked him, mumbled something about having time on his hands and needing something to do, but it was more than that. It was the historian in him, he knew, there was a story to uncover in that place. It was there as surely as one of those civilisations he'd worked on in Greece or Bolivia. It was deep in the fabric of the place and he had a feeling that it resonated with him for a reason. Even now, something about the place was pulling him nearer.

He looked up to the first-floor window; saw the frail outline of Jane watching him from the upstairs rooms. In all of the days he'd spent in the bar, he'd never gone upstairs. It seemed like too much of an intrusion and, anyway, everything he needed had been at his fingertips in the bar or the yard. He watched her now, wondering if he should wave up at her, perhaps him even being here scared her more. He felt in his pocket, if he had his mobile on him he would ring her, tell her not to worry, it was only him, out for a late-night walk, but he'd left it at the bed and breakfast. So, instead of waving, he pulled his collar tighter about his neck and made his way back to his bed, with an uneasy feeling hanging about his shoulders. It seemed he hadn't made things any better for Jane Marchant, he had a feeling she was still checking the locks at all hours of the night.

Surely, he thought to himself, there must be some way of making things better for her.

Kevin's father had just settled, he'd always felt that. Tim Mulvey had settled for Maureen although he knew there was more out there. Penny told him that Tim had known Thelma Jones long before he met their mother, but it was Maureen he married. Well, Kevin wasn't settling. Carrie was the first girl he ever dated, not that he'd tell Jim that.

'Well, good for you,' Jim said when Kevin shared the news of him getting engaged, but his voice held a funny mixture of amusement and derision.

'You don't sound surprised?' Kevin managed.

'No, I suppose I'm not really. From what you've said about her, I suppose Valentina is just that kind of girl…'

'The kind I don't want to let slip through my fingers?'

'I suppose.' Jim ordered a second pint.

'What?'

'I didn't say a word.'

'No, but you're thinking it.' Kevin hated it when Jim was silent and smug. 'Why aren't you surprised about me getting married?'

'Oh, well, I am a little surprised at you getting married, just not at Valentina.' He sat back on the stool. 'I mean, we both know you were never in any great rush to the altar before this, right?'

'I wasn't against it, exactly. It just never happened, that's all.' Kevin hated that he felt he had to defend himself. It was true though, if Carrie had wanted to get hitched, he'd have had no problem with that, so long as she organised it.

'So, if she'd asked, you'd have said yes.' Jim shook his head. 'God, you're such an ass, Kevin. Honestly, have you no backbone at all, man?'

'I'm doing it now, amn't I?' Kevin said, he certainly wasn't going to tell Jim how it had all come about. He wouldn't tell anyone that he didn't even remember proposing. His only recollection was that he was saving five grand and then Valentina had made love to him in a way that still sent shivers through him when he thought about it.

'So you are,' Jim said smoothly. 'Good luck with getting a best man, mate.' He shook his head.

'But I thought...' Of course, Jim probably wouldn't even be at his wedding. They both knew he'd always preferred Carrie to him. The two men met up twice a week, but if Carrie were here, they'd hardly speak two words. The truth was, all of his friends were Carrie's friends first and last. He may keep up the pretence of having a wide circle, but when it would come to his wedding to Valentina, he knew he'd be lucky now if his mother showed up.

'Don't worry, can't you always run off to Colombia and marry there?' Jim was actually serious and, for one awful minute, it struck Kevin that this was really happening. Mostly, since that terrible scene in the restaurant, he managed to block it out. Valentina arriving back to the apartment each day with armfuls of wedding magazines was something he managed if not to ignore, certainly convince himself that it was something remote and unreal.

'Maybe we'll just do that,' Kevin said grumpily. Of course, the reason for his dark mood was not Jim. True, Jim added to it, but the real reason was that Valentina had taken him to look at rings earlier that day. She had the energy of an Olympian when it came to shopping and she did not suffer amateurs charitably. It seemed to Kevin they visited every jeweller in Dublin and still she did not find *The One*. Kevin saw it as a reprieve. He would need the cash from his share of the house sooner than he realised if Valentina's ring tastes were anything to go by. In the recession, you could buy a small house in the suburbs for the prices of some of them. He shook his head at the thought and returned to the conversation. 'Ye'll be sorry then, when I'm sitting back in the sun surrounded by...' Kevin wasn't sure what he'd be surrounded by. He knew nothing of Colombia.

'Drug barons and missionaries?' Jim snorted.

'No, actually, I was going to say good food and the arms of a beautiful woman.'

'Like I said, best of luck to you, mate.'

'Thanks for that, *mate*,' Kevin spat.

'Seriously, Kevin, what do you expect? You've just met Valentina and you're getting married? You're rubbing Carrie's nose in it every day of the week and, let's be honest, you hardly know Valentina.'

'I know her enough to know she's the one.' He sounded like a schoolboy hung up on the cool girl, which perhaps wasn't that far from the truth.

'Sure.' Jim sighed. 'Look, for what it's worth, I'm wishing you well, but you know how I feel about Carrie. She may not be a supermodel compared to the nubile Valentina, but she's gold, Kevin. I don't care what you have with Valentina, she can't hold a candle to Carrie and it's as simple as that.' He shook his head. 'All those years ago, when you two started going out, there were loads of us who fancied Carrie like mad. Half the college couldn't figure what she saw in you and even if we're all a little older now, she's still one of the best-looking women around. She just has something that you don't get every day and if you think you can match that with Valentina, well, the best of luck to you. Just don't be surprised if you end up looking over your shoulder someday.'

'Right,' Kevin said and he downed half his pint. He'd never seen Carrie like that or imagined anyone else did either. He looked across at Jim, wondered if he'd been in McDaid's for long, perhaps he was suffering from blood pressure or stress? 'Well, I must be off,' Kevin said to no one in particular, because he had a feeling that he wouldn't be missed much anyway.

★

He had things to do before going into the restaurant. First off, he had to pick up a prescription for his mother. He'd never done errands like this when Carrie was around.

'It's a sprained wrist for heaven's sake,' Kevin said when Maureen had called him over to open a particularly stubborn pot of jam.

'Well, I'm not as young as I used to be,' Maureen had sniffed and then recited her usual mantra. 'Carrie wouldn't have complained.'

It was three o'clock in the morning when she'd called Kevin again. This time, she couldn't lock her back door.

'I can't sleep with it open,' she'd whined. 'Do you want some scoundrel to break in and do God alone knows what kind of unspeakable things to me? Rob me blind? Or perhaps leave me for dead?'

'Technically, Mother, they won't be breaking in, if you've left your door open.'

'Are you coming or do I have to ring the police? If Carrie were here...' she'd lamented.

So Kevin had called round for the third time that day and locked her back door. She also made him check every window twice, and close the gate four houses down because she could 'hear it creaking in the wind.' Then, he made her hot chocolate and buttered up two slices of toast, which she ate in bed while he watched (in case she might choke in the night) and washed the dishes before he left. The whole trip had robbed almost two hours from his night's sleep. 'When you get to my age,' her voice was thin, 'you get used to not sleeping much. I suppose soon enough I'll be going on the long sleep...

and then you won't have to be worrying about checking the locks on this place.' She had been talking about her looming demise for twenty years, but apart from her sprained wrist, there wasn't a lot wrong with her.

The following morning Kevin had contacted the locksmiths and was happy to pay them to check every lock and replace any that seemed to be past their best working order.

Every week it was something. Every day that had meant to be a drop-in, just in the mornings, was turning out to be so much more. When Carrie had called in, she seemed to sort out his mother within fifteen minutes. She kept the fridge stocked, the medicine cabinet replenished and magically Maureen got to appointments or Mass without either Penny or Kevin being any the wiser. Still, he knew he could not ask Valentina to take on visiting his mother.

'Why not, she's not going to college now, is she?' Penny had asked one day between visits.

'No, but she's working here and...' he didn't mention that they were meant to be getting married to Penny. He still hadn't found the right time, perhaps he couldn't face another conversation like he had with Jim. 'Anyway, they just wouldn't get along. They're too...' Was he about to say – alike? No. Valentina was absolutely nothing like his mother. He was sure of that. He was completely one hundred per cent sure. Wasn't he?

The night seemed to go on forever, and yet, when the grey skies of the morning penetrated through the faded curtains, Jane tried to convince herself that maybe the next night would be better. She decided on a boiled egg for breakfast and smiled to herself grudgingly. It was how she'd managed to stay on here since Manus died. Convincing herself each morning that things would get better. She should ring Carrie. In the early hours of the morning, when she spotted that man watching The Marchant Inn from across the road, she'd made a firm decision then. Or at least, it had seemed firm at the time. She would ring Carrie and ask if she'd take her out to see some of those retirement homes in the brochures from the hospital. She topped her egg neatly; it was, she'd always believed, an art form, to get an egg just right. This morning she had managed it and that seemed like a good enough reason to put off lifting the phone and asking for help.

Carrie arrived just as she was about to clear away her breakfast dishes, Teddy at her heels. He bounded towards Jane and stopped short gently at her chair, resting his head affectionately on her knees.

'You're a one,' she said tenderly, patting his head and admiring his new collar. 'And you're looking particularly smart today.'

'New collar and a bath,' Carrie smiled adoringly at Teddy, 'I just thought, better to have my phone number on him, just in case.' The dog was becoming Carrie's more each day, they belonged together; a blind man could see that.

'Well, he's yours now,' Jane sighed.

'No, I'm afraid there's a bit more red tape yet,' Carrie

bent down and rubbed his back fondly, he repaid her with a look of complete adoration, then she tucked the front door key carefully in her pocket.

Jane sighed, an easy contentment descending on her. She had a feeling it was in part the effect Teddy had on all of them, but it was lovely to think someone else had a key to her front door too. Almost reassuring, as if it was some small measure of how their relationship had grown.

'Well, be honest, how did you sleep?' Carrie asked and she plonked herself before the still warm teapot, resting her cold fingers on its fat body.

'Honestly?' Jane smiled, no one liked a complainer, then she looked across at Carrie, really looked at her, and suddenly she saw something that she had missed these last few weeks. 'What is it? What's happened?'

'Happened?' Carrie shook her head and smiled, but this time she wasn't fooling Jane.

'Yes, Carrie, I know something is up, I can see it in your face.' It was true, the rounded cheeks, the constantly smiling eyes and mouth had been drained of their essence, as if someone had come along and rattled the spirit from her. Instead, there was a new quality to her, something Jane couldn't put her finger on, but it was a kind of strength, an independence. How had she not noticed this change in her over the last few weeks? 'You've even lost weight,' she said, placing her hands gently over her friend's and she listened while the whole sorry story of Kevin and Valentina poured out of Carrie. Carrie told her everything; from that awful night when they told her they were a couple, right up to the announcement of their wedding. 'I can't believe you've kept this bottled up all this time.' Jane shook her head sadly.

'Well, I haven't really. I mean, it hasn't been a secret exactly, our friends know and I've told my mother, obviously, but there just didn't seem to be a good time to say anything. God knows, you've had enough on your plate, and besides, it's not as if you really ever knew Kevin.'

'I suppose that's true,' Jane agreed and she managed not to say that even so, she'd never much liked the look of him anyway. 'Is it too early to talk about all those fish in the sea or missed buses or…'

'It's too late, more like.' Carrie laughed, 'I think I'm a bit long in the tooth to be going out with my fishing net at this stage, and as for the buses, I'll stick to my car, thanks all the same.'

'Well, I will say that you deserve to be treated much better than he's managed, and if it's okay with you, I'd also say that in my day, we believed it was better to be alone than in bad company.' She shook her head.

'Well, it looks like I've cleared out all the bad company now.' Carrie laughed. 'Come on, let's get this pub opened for business,' she said gently and they made their way downstairs to see Luke sitting in front of a blazing fire that he had just set for the day.

'You two look very pleased with yourselves,' he said when they stood beside him and Jane thought she noticed a flicker of admiration in his eyes for Carrie. Now that, she thought, would be a perfect match.

12

Carrie felt like a bitch for the way she spoke to Kevin. Ordering coffee as if he was her skivvy wasn't something that she'd ever done before. Not so much to Valentina, but she had a sense that if Valentina had half a chance, she would bully her, here in her own restaurant. It had happened in a flash. Carrie saw something in the way Valentina was speaking to Kevin. It was the body language. She was threatening him. Everything about her seemed in a split second to have become unfamiliar, suddenly, it was easy to see where the balance of power lay. Carrie would have ordered her coffee from Valentina, but she wouldn't trust her not to spit in it when she was out of sight.

'I'm not your waiter,' Kevin said as he dropped the coffee on the desk before her. She noticed though he'd managed to put it on a saucer and add one of her favourite biscuits on the side.

'I never said you were, but I wanted to talk to you in private.' That was true. 'I've got something for you.' She reached into the drawer she normally kept locked and pulled out a large envelope. 'It's your share of the mortgage to date. It's all signed and sealed and you can deposit it in your bank account today if you'd like.' She reached in to the envelope and handed him the cheque. 'It might be handy when it comes to paying for the wedding; I hear castles don't come cheap.' She smiled at him; this was easier than she thought.

'We won't be getting married in a castle, Carrie.' His voice was short, she assumed he was still angry with her for ordering him about.

'I have a feeling you might be. Valentina has her heart set on something like one of her boy band friends had.' It was true. Valentina had been gushing about it with one of the part-time waitresses – as much to rub Carrie's nose in it as to share any information with the other girl. Carrie had given up on the idea of Valentina finding work elsewhere; it was obvious that the only place Valentina wanted was The Sea Pear. Sometimes, she wondered, if Valentina got what she wanted – would it be enough? She suspected not. As the days passed, it was becoming more glaringly obvious to Carrie that Kevin had fallen for a woman who would never be happy with what she had, a bit like Maureen Mulvey, actually.

'Thanks for this, Carrie.' He glanced at the cheque.

'It's all fair and square, the bank have set out the details here.' She tapped the larger envelope she still held. 'I've opened new accounts and taken my name off the old ones. We'd have had to do it anyway, at some point. You can just keep all the account numbers and your pass codes if you want. The joint credit card is cancelled and I paid it off, your half from the mortgage proceeds.'

'That's very decent of you.' He looked relieved. They both knew he'd never have got around to sorting out the financial entanglement of their joint accounts. The last thing Carrie wanted now was to see statements with details of what Kevin was spending on Valentina. Cutting all the ties she could was for the best, for her and for him.

'And of course, there's this place.' Part of Carrie wanted to run away from The Sea Pear and never set eyes on it again, but she knew that was crazy. They had worked hard to build the place up, it was as much her success as it was his. She remembered only too well how much they had to work in the beginning – the last few weeks had drained her of the kind of energy she'd need for that. She needed time and part of her wondered if she'd want to set up another restaurant. Start-ups took money too, lots of money, and her savings had taken a big hit with buying Kevin out. No, Anna was right; she had all the time in the world to decide on what she wanted to do next. 'But it's early days, right?'

'Right, I suppose so.' Kevin stuffed the cheque inside his chef's uniform.

'So,' she said, slipping the envelope across the desk. 'It's a nice clean break.'

'Carrie,' his voice sounded thick and emotive, 'thanks for all this. Thanks for sorting everything out, you know me, I'd never have got around to it.'

'I know, Kevin. You're welcome, but I did it for me as much as for you. Maybe we both need to move on now.' Her smile was genuine when she met his eyes and she wondered if the sentiment that clouded his was embarrassment or guilt, or perhaps something else that she couldn't quite place.

'I wonder... that is, would you mind if I...' he held the envelope out from him for a second. 'That is, our apartment it's very...' He was searching for words that wouldn't come.

'Yes?' She had a feeling he didn't want Valentina to know about the cheque, did he want to hide his bank details as well?

'Well it's just, there's nowhere really to put things in the apartment, people in and out of it all the time. Would you mind keeping these here, in a drawer, for now?'

'Sure, but you know I lock it when I'm not here?'

'Really?'

'Yes, really.' Carrie had a feeling someone had been snooping about. She was sure it wasn't Kevin. He didn't think she was mysterious enough to have secrets from him, but she suspected it might be Valentina. 'My laptop and stuff... I just thought it's better...' This was her opportunity to mention the tips jar and the missing money. She should say it now, but there was a defeated look about Kevin and she knew she couldn't put another pressure on him at this time. This one, like so many other things in their relationship, she would have to burden alone, for now, or at least until she got to the bottom of it.

'Sure, of course I'll just put these in the car, so,' he said, backing away from her and knocking into the filing cabinet as he went.

It was liberating, tying up the loose ends of her relationship with Kevin. Funny, but she went through extremes. Sometimes, it hit her like a water cannon, startling her, blowing her out, emptying her with the force of it. This morning, she'd cried. She'd sobbed like a baby for almost an hour, and now, seeing him, sorting out the mundane stuff of their lives together, she knew she wasn't crying for the love lost. If she was truthful, the love between them had died many years before. They suffocated it, beneath the earthiness of her mothering and his neediness. It had drowned in the gushing waters of her solicitude and his detachment. Had there been romance once? It was very short-lived, if it had ever truly existed between them. At twenty-two years of age, Kevin had been her first real boyfriend. The first boy interested in more than just the fact that she had the biggest boobs in school. Penny told her later, years later, she was his first girlfriend. It was naïve. To settle for someone because they appeared to be happy settling for you couldn't lead to any kind of real contentment, could it?

She watched Kevin outside the restaurant. He slipped the envelope in the boot of his car and she wondered exactly what he had settled for. Did he realise what he had given up? Or was he, like she, just a little relieved to be out of it?

Carrie sighed, she was tired after a busy evening. Trade was good and there was no opportunity to leave the tables all evening. Valentina had slunk from table to table, smiling and twirling her hair as she took orders. She was a tremendous flirt, one of those women who teases and charms every man she comes across. With the women, she was pleasant and efficient; there could be no complaints about her. By eleven, Carrie had had enough. She offered to let Valentina go early, but the girl scowled at her and flounced off towards the kitchen. The dining area was put to rights quickly, and after the last customers left, Carrie made herself a hot cup of tea and headed towards the office. It was funny, but now, every time she passed the staff tips jar, she scanned it, a new habit that made her uncomfortable, jarring on her nerves so she never fully relaxed in The Sea Pear anymore.

She sat for a while, thinking of the day gone by. It had been a long day, but it was a good day. The house belonged to her now. No question. It was done. She took a deep breath and engaged with the sense of ease it brought to her, knowing that her home was safe and waiting for her at the end of the day.

She cashed up the night's takings, carefully adding all up as she did every other night and then dropped the night safe bag down to Kevin in the kitchen before heading home contented and happier in herself than she'd felt in a long time.

It was nice to be asked, there was no doubt about that, but Jane was just about managing to finish a boiled egg for her breakfast, dinner in a posh restaurant would be just wasted on her. Apart from which, even the effort of having to doll herself up and get to the place just seemed like it would be too much for her at present. 'Still, I want all the details, every single morsel you put in your mouth,' she told Carrie. 'It's the most glamour I've rubbed against in years,' she laughed then.

'Oh, dear, well, in that case, you really do need to get out more.' Carrie laughed too. 'It's just dinner and then back to sit at a computer trying to put it all into words that might just about give people some idea of what it's like.

'But still, I think Luke would really enjoy it. It can't be very nice, hanging about the bed and breakfast in the evenings, I'm not even so sure that Mrs Peril can cook much more than rashers and sausages.' Jane shook her head. Surely, if there was ever a chance of romance between those two, sending them out to dinner together was their best shot?

'Well, he's hardly fading away, whatever she's feeding him,' Carrie laughed, but she agreed to ask him along with her all the same.

'So, Valentina wants Carrie gone, is that it?' Jim shook his head and made a sound that was somewhere between a sigh and an *I told you so*.

'What?' Kevin looked into his pint. Sometimes he wondered why he even came here and met with Jim. It seemed that increasingly their friendship was turning into that of confessor and priest and Jim wasn't exactly an understanding priest. 'There's no reason why they can't work together, in the future, when things settle.' Kevin hated how his voice petered out. He hated more that maybe things might never settle. Sometimes he wished things could go back to how they were. Not that he wanted to give up Valentina, but if it could be as it was before they told Carrie – he was happiest then.

'Mate, there's no way they're ever going to be buddies,' Jim said with a finality that marked the end of the conversation.

'But...' There was so much more Kevin needed to say. He'd built up such plans, such dreams for his future with Valentina.

'The only but is if Carrie decides she wants out. And is that what you really want?'

'I'd manage. We'd manage without her, you know Valentina is very capable.' He looked at Jim; there was something else. 'What, what have you heard?'

'Nothing. Nothing really. It's just that blog she writes, it's going really well. Sandra says she's had some offers to write in one of the papers.'

'Write about what?' It was news to Kevin, Carrie hadn't mentioned a word to him. But then, since she'd handed over the cheque for the house, he'd hardly seen her all week. She seemed to be either flitting in or out, or else spending her time in the office away from the restaurant. Kevin had assumed she didn't want to work shifts with Valentina.

'Have you no idea?' Jim swallowed a quarter of his pint, as if gearing up for a long story. 'She's been reviewing restaurants all round Dublin. She's doing all the best ones and giving them great reviews.'

'She's what?' Kevin felt the blood flow from his head

to his toes, an odd sensation that brought him back to childhood when he fainted regularly. Low in iron. That was his mother's pronouncement at first, and when it persisted into his teenage years, she referred to him as a sensitive soul. 'Like a food critic? When did this start? How the...'

'Hold on. It's not a secret. She's running it off that blog she started a couple of years ago. It still looks the same, only now she's writing about all the top restaurants around Dublin.'

'And if she gives one a bad review? What happens then?'

'Ah, that's the most brilliant part. She's only posting the good ones... they're lining up to be on it. Anyone not included feels they've been snubbed.'

'And The Sea Pear?'

'Well, mate, she can't very well do her own place, now can she?'

'But...' For once, Kevin didn't know what to say. This couldn't be happening. How could Carrie be a restaurant critic and he didn't know about it? Suddenly Kevin didn't want to be here, he wanted to be back in his old world, safe and secure where everything was easy and he knew exactly where he was with everyone.

'I don't see what the problem is, really, Kevin, no one else has suggested for a minute that there might be a conflict of interest.' Carrie was tired; talking to Kevin just drained her these days, as though some invisible fatigue emanating from him was contagious. Honestly, where did Kevin Mulvey get off trying to tell her what she could and couldn't do? 'If you were going to say anything, you might say, *well done Carrie*, that might be more appropriate, don't you think?'

'Well, of course, well done,' he said tightly, 'but I mean, you might have at least told me.'

'Why?'

'Why?' he echoed.

'Yes, why exactly should I be telling you anything, Kevin? We're business partners now, that's all. And as such, so long as I do my work, so long as this place keeps moving in the right direction, really, I can't see that I have any other attachment to you or reason to tell you what is clearly not your business.'

'Well, even in passing conversation, you might have mentioned…' his words petered off.

'Passing conversation? Kevin, we don't *do* passing conversation. I have to summon you to my office if I want a private word with you.'

'So, what's this offer you've had, or is that a secret too?'

'No, it's not a secret, I told Anna and the girls about it.' The truth was, when the editor of Ireland's bestselling newspaper, asked her to write a regular weekly column, she'd been over the moon. The first person she'd been about to tell was Kevin – old habits die hard. Then she remembered he was with Valentina now and she wondered how long would it be like this? How many times would she forget that the whole world had changed and she was on her own in her little house with her little dog? 'I'll be doing a regular column, really it'll just about cover my expenses and they'll pay for dinner for two in a fancy restaurant once or twice a week.'

'For two?' He raised an eyebrow.

'Well, dinner always tastes better if you have good company. Anyway, it just looks more normal than a woman dining alone.' The truth was, half the time she did go on her own, there just wasn't anyone to bring, with Anna's play getting an extended run and her mother's busy social diary. On her own, it wasn't fun at all. Her last two posts had left her feeling like an outsider. At least Luke had said he'd come along next time. She was looking forward to that, even if she had a feeling, he was just coming for the food. What did she think she was playing at? And then the call came offering her a small payment for the reviews. She signed up with the paper for three months, then after that they would renegotiate, but she had a feeling she'd have had quite enough of it by then.

'I can't believe he'd be so precious about the blog.' Anna was still cross, but her temper was diluted while scouring the charity shops for accessories for the wedding.

'How *is* the reviewing going, by the way?' she suddenly brightened. 'For a woman that's eating out every week, you're positively fading away.' She winked at Carrie. Of course, she saw the whole reviewing business as an opportunity to socialise, perhaps to meet a new man. 'After all, you've got to think of yourself now.'

'Oh, yes,' Carrie said drily, 'because, before, Kevin was doing such a good job of looking after my every need.' They both laughed at that. In many ways, things had never been easier for Carrie. She no longer had to organise Kevin's every waking hour and she was pleasantly surprised at how much more time and energy she had as a result. Not having to look after Maureen too gave her time to spend with the much nicer Jane Marchant and for that alone she'd have traded her toenails.

'So, no dates?' Anna inclined her head, but her attention was on a display of chiffon scarves behind Carrie.

'Honestly, Anna,' Carrie pulled down a light green and silver pashmina and held it out to her friend. 'Where would I get the time or the inclination?' She had no desire to find someone to replace Kevin. She had enough people in her life to care about and who she knew genuinely cared for her. In fact, these last few days, she couldn't help but feel relieved to have severed her personal connections with the Mulvey family; in truth, they were just hard work. When Carrie thought about her relationships with each of them, it seemed, from this vantage point, that it had been all give on her part and take on theirs.

'Okay, I suppose it's early days.' Anna draped the fabric across her shoulders and peered at her face in a small mirror more suited to checking her make-up than her outfit. 'What do you think?'

'It suits you,' Carrie said, and it did. The colour made her skin more translucent and brought out the light green of her eyes. The silver strands running through it caught the light and it seemed to shimmer as Anna moved about. Everything about it made her look striking.

'Hm. But will it go with my dress?'

'It doesn't matter. You're taking it anyway, it's too nice on you to leave it behind, and what is it anyway, a fiver?' Carrie took the pashmina and rolled it up loosely to avoid creasing the material. 'My gift to you,' she said and she winked.

'Pity we didn't head into Tiffany's,' Anna said, laughing. 'Okay, so where are we? We both have shoes, dresses and bags,' she was counting the items off her fingers as they waited to pay for the pashmina.

'We're definitely done. I'm shopped out.' It was true. Carrie wasn't a big shopper and she was blessed with a friend who could spend hours on a vintage stall but was virtually allergic to high street shops. She looked at her watch. 'Actually, I need to be heading home soon. I have to get to work and it's a long night ahead.'

'Not dining with the stars tonight so?'

'Not tonight, later this week though.'

'Oh, very posh, I'm sure, while I'll be dining on Pot Noodles no doubt in the green room between acts,' Anna laughed, but they both knew it was where she was happiest, sitting on the floor, surrounded by the greasepaint with the footlights waiting for her.

'Yes, it is rather, but I'm not paying, remember.' Carrie smiled. She was looking forward to being spoiled in one of the top restaurants in the country.

'And you're going on your own?' Anna inclined her head in the same way she would have done when they were four years old and she was enquiring about Carrie's Barbie pencil case.

'Well, why wouldn't I go on my own?'

'You're not answering the question, Carrie.' Anna smiled. 'Why don't you ask that historian to go with you?' She whispered the words, but they were outside now, surrounded by passers-by who had no interest in Carrie's non-existent love life. 'Or am I behind the times and you've already asked him?' She threw her head back and laughed. 'You coy old thing, and here was me feeling sorry for you. I was thinking, poor you, all alone. Well, that'll teach me.' She was grinning from ear to ear now.

'No, Anna, it's not what you think.' Carrie had lowered her voice too, 'I mean, for all I've seen of him, I really don't know very much about him.'

'Oh, no. You think he's married, is that it?' Excitement glittered in her eyes. Anna had had a string of affairs with married men.

'I don't know if he is.' And there it was, in a nutshell, all she knew of Luke Gibson she could probably fit on the back of a postage stamp, but at the same time, she liked him.

'I've been on dates with men like that, let me tell you, it's true what they say, they never leave their wives.' She shook her head, but they both knew that Anna had never been the settling down type anyway.

'No, Anna, it's nothing like that, he's really a very private man...'

'Okay, let's just think about this, he seems to be nice and genuine and at a total loose end. He's taking the old dear across the road under his wing and he's staying in a city centre bed and breakfast. I'd say he'd be chuffed to go along to some of the best restaurants in Dublin with you.' She shook her head, as though it was a no-brainer. 'And who knows... dum, dum, di dum,' she started to hum the wedding march.

'You're wrong, we're just friends.' Carrie meant it, but there was an odd niggling feeling somewhere near her heart and she wondered if maybe she was a little fond of Luke. She knew it would be ridiculous, so she looked her friend in the eye. 'Really, he's got his own life going on, he's not looking for a complication and neither am I. I'm very fond of him, but there is nothing between us, nor will there ever be.'

13

'We're really going upmarket with this stuff,' Andrew said when Carrie got back to the restaurant. He was unpacking a delivery of wines before the restaurant opened for the evening.

'No. Just the usual order,' Carrie replied, stepping around him so she could select some music for the evening.

'Not half. You've ordered double the amount and not just the house plonk. Some of this stuff costs a couple of hundred a bottle. Did you get a deal on it?'

'No, I just—' Carrie bent down and picked up one of the bottles. It was their usual supplier, but every bottle was from a reserve stock, some of the names she recognised, but only from wine guides. 'Oh, no. Andrew, there must be some mistake. I never ordered this.'

'I think you did.' He searched around the floor and passed her up the order docket. 'I checked it, before I took it in. The boxes didn't look right, so...'

'Seriously, I never ordered all this. I wouldn't.' Carrie knew, even at a glance, there was no way. Still, everything was checked off, the docket a photocopy of the original was ticked and dated. She ran her finger down the order, gasping when she roughly totted up the cost of the lot. 'Oh, no.' There at the bottom, sure enough, was her signature. Frazzled and hurried, part of her thought she could remember the day she put in the order. It was just after Kevin told her about Valentina. She'd buried the pain, deep inside, determined not to cry or show any sign of weakness in front of either of them. Well, she thought now, so much for that. Her stiff upper lip had probably cost them thousands. 'I'll ring them, perhaps they'll take them back...'

'Too late. They're COD, remember. Kevin has already given them a cheque and he's livid.'

'Christ.' Kevin never liked dealing with the accounts; he rarely dealt with suppliers and never for anything they used in the dining room. 'He'll be a bundle of fun in the kitchen this evening.' She knew she'd have to go and say something to him, explain it had been her mistake. Perhaps, if she played it down, he might think it was what they always paid out on a delivery. Who was she kidding? It was ten times what she normally paid for wine supplies. 'Tell you what, leave those. We'll just bring them in the boxes up to the office and I'll see if I can't fix this some other way, okay?'

'Sure thing, boss. I have one opened and stacked already though, sorry.' They took the remaining boxes up to her office and stacked them in three neat piles along the wall.

She tried ringing a girl she knew in accounts and managed to swap forty crates, leaving her with just two.

It meant that they'd have four times more wine than they needed in the restaurant, but that wasn't exactly the end of the world.

'I did wonder,' Sheila said as she worked out the details.

'Oh, things are a bit mad here, I just wasn't thinking straight.'

'No, I have the docket here, the original. Oh, dear, it's in a different pen. You did your usual order in a black pen and then added the extras in a light blue biro. It just looks odd. Maybe you didn't order it at all?' Sheila's voice was low.

'You're saying someone might be playing silly beggars with the orders?'

'Well, it's a quick way to make a few quid. And anyone passing on the reserves will make a heck of a lot more from them than they will from your ordinary Merlots or Pinot noirs.'

'Thanks Sheila, I'll keep it in mind.' She sat for a moment, thinking. She would have to tell Kevin, this was all wrong, someone had ordered that wine. 'Sheila, any chance I could get a colour copy of that order slip?' This was something that couldn't be swept under the carpet like the tips jar.

'Of course, Carrie, I'll organise it for you today,' Sheila sounded thoughtful. 'You really do need to get to the bottom of this, what with the Christmas party season upon us, it's going to be easy if someone is...' she let the words hang on the air between them.

'Well, let's just hope that it's down to an honest mistake, eh?' Carrie said a little unevenly, she wasn't fooling anyone, not even herself this time. Somehow, even here, in her little office, it felt as if she'd been moved about. It wasn't the first time over the last few weeks that she had a sense that someone had been here, poking about.

Well, she thought, that does it, tomorrow, she'd buy a new basket for Teddy and he could stay here while she worked downstairs. He'd be more than happy to snooze away a few hours, and if he seemed bored, she could always bring up a meaty bone from the kitchen. Even settling on the idea made her feel better.

'Penny, what are you doing here?' Carrie couldn't remember the last time Penny had dropped into the restaurant.

'Mission of mercy, Mum needs Kevin and he's not answering his phone, so I said I'd pop in on my way to pick up the kids.' She looked distractedly about the restaurant.

'We haven't seen you for a while,' Carrie said, 'how are you?'

'Oh, I'm good. Busy, you know, with Mum and all.'

'Yes, Kevin mentioned she fell. All hands on deck so, I suppose.'

'You can sing that one.' Penny looked at her for a moment, perhaps remembering. 'Oh, Carrie, I'm sorry. I haven't seen you since you and Kevin...'

'Oh, that's a while ago now.' She didn't want to dwell on it, didn't want Penny to think she was counting. 'Life goes on, you know.'

'Of course. Mum was raging, as you can imagine.'

'Was that because she has no one to bring her to Mass, or has she finally seen through darling Kevin?' Carrie didn't want to sound mean, but the truth was she felt no compunction now to be anything other than honest, and it was strangely liberating. She'd never much liked Maureen or Penny, they were both too self-consumed for her liking and Maureen always made her feel that she would never be good enough for Kevin.

'Fair enough.' Penny smiled, a cool movement of her well made-up lips. 'In the beginning she was mad with Kevin. She gave him the whole *"you took the best years of that girl's life"* lecture. Now, she's gotten over that, I think she realises it didn't work anyway. No, she just misses you dropping in to see her. She was genuinely fond of you, Carrie.'

'Really, she had a funny way of showing it.' But Carrie knew that in spite of herself, Maureen Mulvey had warmed to her, well, thawed at least. Carrie had been the only one to visit daily. She took her to Mass, made sure she had her tablets and the one hundred and one other things that Carrie did for her. 'Maybe, in a funny way, I miss her too.' It was true, sort of.

'You could always visit... you know, just pop in occasionally.' Penny was as subtle as a woodcutter's axe.

'No, Penny, not now. I'm afraid that's up to Kevin and Valentina now.' Carrie might have put up with a lot over the years, but she certainly wasn't going back to be used by Penny and Kevin anymore.

'Valentina?' Penny craned her neck around the restaurant. 'We haven't actually met *her* yet. Is she here?'

'I'm afraid you're out of luck.'

'Pity. From what I can gather he's fallen for her, hook, line and sinker,' Penny said tactlessly.

'Indeed.' Carrie turned on her heels. She had work to do and while she didn't mind making small talk to be polite, she certainly didn't need to have Penny as a bosom buddy now. 'Anyway, Kevin is in the kitchen, why don't you just go through?' Carrie returned to double-checking the night's bookings. These last few weeks in the run-up to Christmas, they were booked solid every night with office parties and Christmas celebrations. It would be a gruelling few weeks ahead, but it was no different to any other year, Carrie reminded herself.

'Right, right, I will so,' Penny said and headed towards the kitchen, obviously thrown by Carrie's new reserve.

Carrie smiled, it was nice not to have to pretend with Penny anymore. She wondered idly why Kevin hadn't brought Valentina to meet his mother, but maybe she already knew the answer to that one. Oh, how she'd love to be a fly on the wall when those two met up.

It wasn't like Carrie to muck up the orders. In all the time Kevin had known her she'd never made a crazy mistake like that before. He'd been fuming when he had to find the cheque book and hand over five thousand euros, but he managed to keep a lid on his temper, at least long enough so that he paid the man. Then he'd strutted back to the kitchen, looking more chilled than he felt and he took his anger out on the fresh fish filleting that he normally left for one of the junior chefs. He decided he'd have it out with her, when she came back from wherever she'd skived off to.

'Have you seen what she has ordered, she eez gone crazy, spending all of our money like that...' Valentina breezed into the kitchen and stood over Kevin. He hated it when she did that, especially when he was busy.

'What's that?'

'Carrie, she has ordered far too much expensive wines, she weell be the finish of this place. I don't know how you have managed to keep this restaurant going with her spending the money like she ees a crazy woman...' She was leaning over Kevin now, the strong smell of her sweet perfume, expensive and suffocating.

'What do you mean?'

'Well, she ees ordering these wines, but we never get these wines, the other orders, I have seen them. I have seen her pay for them. They are never all of that. They are never half of that.'

'Yes. I suppose it does seem expensive.'

'Poof. She is trying to reep you off. She times eet so you pay for the wines, she dreenks them then, I suppose?' Valentina threw out her hands in the air, as though in praise of some greater power. 'Oh, only the best for Carrie, isn't that right?'

'Well now...' It was true, Carrie did enjoy a glass of wine, but she never drank here, not in the restaurant. She drank at home, in front of a box set with chocolates and crisps for company. Only, she didn't need chocolate anymore, did she? She had the hot foreign boyfriend now. Kevin's imagination began to work overtime. He wondered what they did together, exactly. He had a feeling she met him here, did she entertain him when the restaurant was closed. Did they sit here, in his kitchen, eating the food he'd prepared and drinking the wine he paid for? He'd have assumed she'd bring him home, to the little house they'd shared. Kevin thought about that house now and, not for the first time, he missed it. He missed the familiar smell of coffee and toast first thing in the morning. He missed the soft velvet sofa that Carrie picked up in a market that Kevin wouldn't go near. He missed the super-strong hot shower that her cousin had rigged for them before he left for Canada. He missed going home in the evenings and falling into his own sofa without Simo and Reda making him feel like he was crashing their party. The truth was, he realised now, as he gutted a large salmon, he spent most of his time at the new apartment, either cleaning up their mess or sitting out on the balcony in freezing temperatures, convincing himself that he was a lucky bastard to be living with such a view. 'You might think that, but Carrie doesn't drink at home anymore,' it was the truth, she may not have broadcast it but Kevin reasoned it was told for all the right reasons. 'Carrie told me herself, she hasn't had a glass of wine in weeks.' Valentina was spoiling for a fight and he had a feeling she'd like to be in the audience, watching him and Carrie tear strips off each other.

'Huh, so she says, I'm not sure I would believe anything Carrie has to say.' She shook her hair out. 'Never trust a fat woman, Keveen, not around food or wine.'

'Well, now I wouldn't exactly call Carrie fat…'

'You wouldn't…' Valentina's voice dropped like a stone in icy water. 'And what would you call her…'

'I…' God, but now was the time for someone to walk in so they could change the subject, but of course, they didn't. 'I'm just saying, she hasn't eaten us out of business yet and I don't suppose she's going to start now.'

'Well, the only theeng I can say to that is you are a very naïve man, Keveen. She is scorned, she has lost her man to a beautiful younger woman and she has spent your money like eet ees going out of style. Now, you tell me that there isn't something funny about that.' She drew one of the sharp knives from the block and stabbed it into the chopping board so it stuck hard. 'No, you cannot say there is anything funny about that, can you?'

'I'll check it out, but I'm sure there's a logical reason for it. Knowing Carrie, she probably got a good deal on them or maybe she's doing a deal with one of the other restaurants for a bigger discount.' Though, he knew, if she was, she'd have certainly mentioned it to him, or at least that's what the old Carrie would have done.

Hoffa's Restaurant was where Michelle Obama had lunch when she visited Dublin quietly to meet up with the elders and speak in Trinity College. The owners claimed that its walls were among the oldest still standing in Dublin and proudly featured them with carefully placed lighting and tasteful prints of Viking and Norman structures from around the city. If the restaurant were famous for anything more than its heritage, it was its warm welcome. All over the Internet, patrons were tripping over themselves to gush about the service, the atmosphere and the ambience. Tonight, it was especially nice, with Christmas decorations tastefully adding a sense of seasonal cheer. Each table had a small but elaborate centrepiece handmade with fresh cinnamon sticks, holly, ivy and a sprig of mistletoe – it really was quite charming.

'You never mentioned we'd be coming somewhere so nice,' Luke said when they were shown to a comfortable booth table.

'Oh, really? Well, next time I'll bring you for a Big Mac.' She smiled at him as she scanned through the menu.

'Well, you were right. I needed the suit,' he didn't seem to realise it, but he turned heads as they walked into Hoffa's.

'It looks good on you,' Carrie didn't add that with his brooding good looks, he could be a movie star, the suit polished him off. It probably wasn't expensive but it fitted him perfectly, she couldn't help but think of Kevin by comparison. No matter how much she'd ever paid for a suit for him, he always managed to look like a sack of potatoes poured into it, while Luke looked like it was tailored to him exactly.

'It's nice here, nice to get out for a change,' he said then.

'Yes, it's good. I've been doing these reviews for a few weeks now and really enjoying them, but I've done a few on my own and it's not nearly as much fun. The problem is, I'm running out of people to bring,' she broke off then, afraid that she might give him the impression that she was somehow desperate.

'I can see how that could happen,' he said gently. 'I mean, we're at an age, aren't we? Everyone has mostly paired off and settled into the kind of lives that don't really afford dining out midweek, not unless it's a bit of an occasion.'

'Yes, well, it certainly is nice to have a friend along to enjoy it too,' she said easily, slipping off the scarf she'd worn about her shoulders. 'And bringing you along is the least I can do to say thank you for all you've done for Jane,' she smiled then. He really had pulled out all the stops, first cleaning the place up and now bringing it back to life with Christmas decorations, even a tree he'd managed to pick up in the local market for a song because it was too big to fit anywhere else.

'Oh, that, it was nothing. I'm fond of her, you know, there's something about her, it's rare for me to connect to...' Luke murmured, meeting her eyes for a lingering moment. 'Well, you know I'm a bit of a wanderer...' His eyes were compelling.

'Well, you're certainly a hit with Jane. I'd say you've definitely made a lifelong connection there.'

'Lifelong? Gosh, I'm not even sure how long I'll be here for.' He said and she caught something in his voice that didn't quite sit with the man she thought she was coming to know.

'Oh?'

'Well, it seems like I've never had less to keep me in a place.' He shook his head and smiled at what she hoped was the look of interest as opposed to nosiness in her expression. 'What I mean is, I don't have any real work lined up. I haven't even tried to touch base with the universities. I'm living in a bed and breakfast. I'm driving my father's van and even my father seems to be just waiting for me to move on.'

'Don't you get on?' She bit the words back, but perhaps it was the ambience or maybe Luke Gibson was finally ready to talk.

'It's not that, we've always been close. My mum, well, she was never really around, so it's always been just the two of us. Dad spent his life travelling the world with me and a backpack, this is really the first time I've seen him settled and it's kind of…'

'*Unsettling*?' She smiled at him, but she could understand it. Let's face it, she knew as well as anyone what it was to be thrown sideways by life's curveballs.

'I suppose. He's not an old man, but it's like he's made this decision to give up. No particular reason; just piled his life savings in a corner and booked himself into a place that feels to me like he's waiting to die.' He shook his head sadly. 'Sorry, we're meant to be having fun.'

'No, please, it's always good to hear what other people are worrying about, it makes me feel like more of a lightweight.'

'Well, you seem to be very well set up.'

'You think?' she laughed at him, made a face, 'I'm afraid I'm not quite as close to having the perfect life as I once thought I was.'

'I don't know…' A smile played about his lips. 'Owning

a restaurant and your own home, having friends, being in a committed relationship, you even have the dog to round things off... it seems to me like you have what most people would consider the "full package"?'

'I'm not complaining, but...' she lowered her voice, 'I might as well tell you, because it's hardly a secret, but I'm probably going through my own mini life crisis, reassessing things, you know...'

'And there's been a catalyst?'

'You could say that. I'd call a Colombian waitress half my age gearing up to marry my long-term partner a bit of a spur, all right.' She laughed now. 'Don't mind me, I'm just a typical cliché I suppose. Anyway, I'm coming to the stage where I'm seeing that it might all be for the best.'

'I'm sorry,' he said softly. 'I didn't realise, I thought you were... as good as married.' Here, in the intimacy of this space, just a table between them, it felt like his eyes were drawing her in further. They were captivating, so everything and everyone else in the restaurant might be a million miles away from them. Somewhere, perhaps only a table away, the crash of glass hitting the floor cut into the loaded silence between them. It was like waking up from a dream and Carrie let her breath go – she hadn't realised she'd been holding it. She inhaled and closed her eyes for a second, willing herself back to normality. For a moment, she wasn't sure what had passed between them, but she had a feeling it was a lot more than she had bargained for.

'No, my worries are small, I'm sorry about your dad; it's good to hang on though, until you're happy about where he's at.' They were interrupted by the arrival of the waiter. 'So?' Carrie smiled warmly at Luke. 'Starters?'

They managed to get through the meal enjoying each other's company. Luke talked about his job with such passion it was obvious how much it meant to him. He explained, he felt grateful to be part of a discipline that not only uncovered the past but also instructed on the future. Carrie told him about how she had fallen into reviewing as much by accident as by design and the prospects that seemed to be unexpectedly opening up for her.

It was a lovely meal and not just because the food was even better than she expected. 'They say this is the friendliest restaurant in Dublin,' she said as their coffee arrived.

'I think they're right. It has character too, there's something gracious in its humility though, not like some of the other old buildings around here.'

'Ah well, these walls were built before we had notions of grandeur. Trinity College and Leinster House? They're all much newer buildings, built by people who were conscious of their colonial reputation.' Carrie had researched the restaurant for her review.

'You've been doing your homework, but you don't need to impress me, the company *has* been great, Carrie.' His voice was low and she had a feeling that the words conveyed more than just a flippant compliment.

'Well, thank you, Luke. I've really enjoyed it too. Thanks for coming with me.' She meant it. She was getting tired of going to restaurants alone and then writing up her blog post. She was genuinely pleased to have Luke for company and delighted when he told her he'd come along any night she found herself without a plus-one.

'Well, you know, it's the least I could do.' He was being facetious, his expression stern and then he broke into a huge smile. 'I can't believe you get paid to go to dinner. It is a really nice job.' He whispered the words, 'You're very lucky. Only, I don't understand, now why you don't…'

'Leave The Sea Pear?'

'Well, yes. I think you could easily find work anywhere in Dublin, Carrie.'

'It's more complicated than that, I'm afraid.'

'Carrie, I have seen complicated, believe me. This,' he waved his hand across the table, 'this is a good kind of complication.'

'Yes, I suppose it is.' And at this moment, she couldn't help but think there really was no choice, why would she want to go back and work in The Sea Pear when she was so clearly just in the way there.

'Can you tell me why it's complicated?' His voice was gentle.

She took a deep breath. 'Kevin and I started The Sea Pear together and I suppose that over the years my dreams and his got all tied up with one another, so somewhere along the line… I don't know, it was like I lost sight of what I was working towards and then…' Carrie looked about the restaurant. It was full of people who seemed to have normal uncomplicated lives, but what did she know? 'When Kevin said we were finished, that he was leaving me for Valentina, it felt as if he'd pulled the ground from under me.'

'I can understand that. You needed time.'

'Yes, I needed time. I needed so much more, but I hoped, if I sorted out the things that were important to me, like my home, the rest would kind of fall into place.' She shrugged her shoulders.

'And is it? Falling into place?'

'I'm not sure. This, here…' she smiled at Luke, 'blogging and reviewing, it's been great. I think I needed something to focus on, you know? Maybe if things had remained the same with Kevin, I'd never have tried my hand at it, so I think that's been good…'

'And The Sea Pear?'

'That's the hard bit.' Carrie bit her lip, she was still figuring it out for herself, perhaps talking about it would help. 'I… there was a time when I loved The Sea Pear. There are things about it that I still love, but I have a feeling that I don't belong there anymore. Things change.' She shrugged. Funny, but she'd never thought of The Sea Pear as a crutch to get her through the emptiness that had become part of living with Kevin. Now, realising it was very liberating, but scary too, and a range of emotions she hadn't expected began to play somewhere in her chest. 'I don't enjoy The Sea Pear anymore, not like I used to. I'm not sure if that's because it's downright miserable having to look at fabulous Valentina each night, or Kevin who acts so smug, he's like the cat that got the cream.' She shook her head. 'The thing is, I'm not sure if I felt a bit… bored of it before Kevin dropped his bombshell.' She didn't cry, Carrie was aware that among all the reactions forcing their way to the top of her throat, sadness was not one of them. 'The more I think of it now, perhaps we were both just going through the motions of living, getting through each day and, certainly, compared to now, I'm not sure there was a lot of joy in any of it.' She smiled at Luke. It was true, these last few weeks had been tumultuous, they'd been exhausting, just in terms of the range of emotions she'd experienced, but they'd been exhilarating too. 'I suppose what I'm thinking is that if I can see light at the end of the tunnel without Kevin, perhaps without The Sea Pear...' She felt a sense of dawning optimism and it was coming not from Luke or from anyone outside of her, it was coming from deep within her. 'Perhaps I would be much happier somewhere else? Perhaps I'm missing out on great opportunities by being tied to it?'

'Perhaps.' Luke was watching her. 'I think you have a lot to think about, Carrie.' His smile broke wide across his face and creased all the way up to his eyes. He moved towards her, brushed her lips gently with his, they lingered there, barely touching each other, and yet the embrace felt so much more intimate than anything she could remember. Then he moved back, perhaps embarrassed because, certainly, Carrie felt a huge upwelling of deep attraction flicker between them in that one intimate moment. 'I think you're right,' he said, eyeing her with a worldliness that threw her for a moment, so she really wasn't sure what that kiss had meant. 'There are good things waiting for you, if you give them a chance.'

★

Jane woke with the certain knowledge that something, some noise, had disturbed her sleep. For a long, drawn-out second, she lay perfectly still. It was a bang, the sound of a door being shut too quickly, perhaps the crashing of a load against the pavement. But it was outside and she released a relieved breath before pulling herself up in the bed, enough to check the travel clock. Voices, angry, shouting, but muffled by the wind wheezing through the emptiness of the street below. If she turned on a light now, it would surely draw attention to her, so she stretched her legs into the cold bedroom air and gingerly stepped towards the window in the dark.

Gently, as if they might hear her very breath, she pulled back the heavy damask curtain, and squinted to make out the figures below. There were two men, working against each other to bring boxes from the restaurant. Although it was dark and she couldn't say why, she thought she recognised them and when they marched back in the front door she felt sure they must have a legitimate reason for being there. After all, burglars break in through windows, don't they? She watched until they loaded up the final box and drove calmly away into the night, making sure to switch off lights and lock up everything before they left.

14

It was late when Kevin got home, it was his new thing, driving about before he returned to the apartment. It took hours to unwind and somehow, the apartment made him feel empty, an outsider – perhaps it was all too new to relax in. There was a time when he never closed up the restaurant, Carrie was always the last to leave, and it had been their routine since they opened the place. Kevin left when the kitchen was shining like a new pin, Carrie waited until the last customer left and the dining room was tidied for the following day. That had changed since he told her about Valentina. These days, it seemed Carrie couldn't get out of the place quick enough, with that nuisance dog at her heels.

That dog was another thing that annoyed Kevin. He suspected Carrie only brought him to work to annoy him. He hated dogs, had always maintained an allergy to keep any notions of one coming into the house at bay. And that bloody mutt didn't even like him, he could see it in his eyes, he actually bayed at Valentina. Some judge of character he was; Kevin hoped he was a better guard dog.

He wasn't sure if the new routine was good or bad. After all, if Carrie was here, digging her heels in at every turn, that would be a real nightmare for him and for Valentina. Jim was right; any other woman would have made his life hell. She was well within her rights to take the business apart if she wanted to. She could demand her share and leave them to it and with the benefit of a few weeks' thinking time, he wasn't sure if The Sea Pear would survive without Carrie. The thought was numbing. The wine order debacle was just another example of why Kevin couldn't manage the restaurant. Even thinking about sorting out that kind of mess inflicted a soft sheen of sweat across the nape of his neck. No matter what had happened, he just wanted it sorted, and sorted in a way that didn't impact on his stress levels. He hadn't even asked Carrie about it since, couldn't face the details being poured out between them.

He flicked off the low background music that Valentina had left playing in the apartment. Normally, he didn't notice what was playing on the sound system, but this was a mix of contemporary music, perhaps some people might call it soulful? He preferred the gentle piano pieces that Carrie favoured. What if she decided to leave? What if she was offered a job doing the reviews full time? Would she choose The Sea Pear over the allure of something different? Surely she would choose the option that meant she didn't have to face the ruins of a relationship and Valentina each day.

Valentina. The name played like a sigh in his mind. She made him feel exhausted and it wasn't because they made love all night. These days, he hardly noticed that she was beautiful. This last week had been one long argument between them and he wasn't even sure why. It seemed that no matter what he did, he couldn't get things right.

His mother was an added pressure. It felt sometimes like he just about touched the pillow at night before he was off again the following day to sort out her shopping and her various medical appointments. With Maureen Mulvey, you had to tread carefully. She was not, as his father had told him many years earlier, the kind of woman who forgave easily or accepted anything less than exactly what she wanted. Even then, by the time she got what she wanted, invariably it had lost its allure.

His father. He thought about his father a lot these last few weeks. They never spoke about him, he and his mother. Well, that wasn't true. Sometimes she mentioned him, but they never *really* talked about him, not with any sense that he had been a part of their lives. Penny talked about him though. It seemed to Kevin that since he had announced the changes in his relationships, Penny talked about him more than ever, and when she did, her words were warm, her expression softened.

'You never really got him, did you, Kevin?'

'I think we were as close as any father and son,' he found himself saying defensively, when she called in one day to drop off their mother's prescription. 'After all, he wasn't exactly the most honest man, in the end.'

'Oh, that. You've just let that take over from all the other stuff. Don't you remember, when we were younger, he was the one who brought you fishing?'

'I hated fishing.'

'Oh, come on. You loved going fishing with Dad. He even let you throw them back in, if you didn't want to…' Penny had turned vegetarian at thirteen, *a phase,* their mother called it. Now, she was involved in every animal rights organisation going. 'And he was the one who made all your school costumes.'

'Don't remind me. I nearly broke my neck learning to walk on stilts.' Kevin had managed a weak smile at that. But it was true, his dad had been the one to bring any fun there was into their home. Suddenly, he was flooded with happy images of his childhood and mostly those were times spent with his dad. 'Mum always said it was why he had taken up with…' even now, he hated mentioning her name.

'Yeah, well, if I was married to Mum, maybe I'd make a run for it too,' Penny had said, hoicking up her over-sized handbag. 'Anyway, you're hardly in any position to talk.'

'What's that supposed to mean?'

'Well, dumping Carrie – the woman who set you up in this place. Kevin, she all but spoon-fed you your breakfast and look at you now.'

'There's nothing wrong with me now.'

'Seriously, Kevin, you've lost weight. You look dreadful; honestly, you've aged about a decade since you split up from her.'

'Well, it's been difficult, what with Mum and everything.'

'Yeah. Well, I'm sure Dad said the same when he first left Thelma for Mum.'

'How do you mean?'

'Seriously, Kevin, do you not see this?' Penny had begun to laugh her annoying nasally laugh that they'd all secretly hoped she'd grow out of one day. 'Thelma Jones is a lovely woman. I know you've never given her a chance, but she's a genuinely lovely woman.'

'Do you still see her?'

'All the time. She lives just down the road from Dad's old garage.'

'Does Mum know?'

'Kevin, I'm not that dense. Mum would have a conniption if she knew I visited Thelma.'

'So, why do you visit her?' He didn't add that it seemed so odd to be visiting their father's mistress while visiting their own mother seemed to be such a chore to her.

'I visit her because I like her and because Dad loved her. I think he made a mistake. I think he loved her and needed her very much, but his head was turned by Mum,' Penny finally pulled her phone from the bottom of her bag. 'Hard to believe, but I think he fell for Mum, hook, line and sinker, because you have to admit that before life took hold of her and she became so bitter, she was quite beautiful.'

'She was.' He'd always thought that life had been cruel to their mother. It had turned her lovely mouth down, her eyes hard and her face creased with resentment. 'Certainly, from the looks of Thelma, she was never a beauty.'

'No, but maybe she was beautiful in her own way. That kind of beauty men don't always appreciate, not until it's too late, Kevin.' She'd held his eye for a fraction too long and he wondered if she was trying to tell him something. 'Anyway, we know Mum never made him happy, and no matter how hard he tried, he never seemed to be able to make her happy either. I think, if things were different, they'd have divorced, but, back then, well, people, our sort of people, didn't do that,' she said and, of course, she was right. Even now Maureen Mulvey was a great woman for talking about the mortal sins and the grievous sins. She could rhyme off everyone else's sins for miles around. The last thing she wanted was a scandal of the sort that would have come with separation or divorce. 'The truth is, if Dad had divorced Mum, they'd have been the talk of the town and he'd never have done anything to hurt us, Kevin.'

'Do you think that, if things were different, they could have been happy together?'

'What do you mean?'

'Mum and Dad – if he'd done something differently, I don't know, been more successful or maybe made more of her, that they might have had a shot? It must have been hard for Mum, having another woman in the background all that time.' Kevin wasn't sure if he was thinking about his parents or trying to figure out his relationship with Valentina.

'That's the thing, Kevin. Mum won. Mum won Dad over from Thelma. She breezed in and he fell for her. Thelma knew there was no point in hanging about. She headed off to the States for nearly a decade. She walked away, but it still wasn't enough for Mum. Don't you see?

Some people – you can't make them happy, because it's just not in them. For Mum, I'm not sure she ever had the capacity to be happy with what she had, she only wanted what she couldn't have.'

'But she came back? Thelma, she came back here, worked in the garage with him, that wasn't exactly going to help Mum and Dad have the happiest marriage going.'

'He begged her to come back. He was on the point of doing something really... not good.' Penny had put her phone on the worktop before her, giving Kevin her undivided attention, as if he was a toddler she had to impress with vital information. 'Kevin, Mum almost drove Dad over the edge. He thought about committing suicide.'

'But we never saw...' Kevin wanted her to stop talking now. He wanted to silence all those things he'd managed to bury over the years. It was enough to pretend they'd never happened with his mother, he didn't want to dredge it all up again with Penny.

'I know. He was the best Dad, like I said.' She shook her head and Kevin felt like they had grown up in completely different worlds. 'He was desperately unhappy. Trapped, and the best and worst of it was he had us. So, there was no leaving, but he couldn't find anything with Mum to keep him.'

'And she... Thelma, told you all this?' Kevin knew his voice dripped with sarcasm, but it was all too much to believe. He knew his Dad and he knew that when he'd died and they'd learned about the relationship with Thelma everything seemed to skew. Maureen had, in her own way, rewritten everything about their earlier lives to accommodate the man he seemed to be in light of his relationship with Thelma. Thelma had caused far too much pain for any of them to waste their time thinking about her now.

'She has letters from him. Letters he wrote to her when she was in America. He begged her to come back Kevin. He begged her because she was the love of his life. He just didn't realise it until it was too late.' She took up her phone and checked her messages. 'Anyway, take from that what you will. I'm not preaching, but I have to get to work. Will you drop off Mum's laundry this evening?' she pointed to a refuse bag on the floor at her feet. 'I have to pick up the kids and then head into work.' She was gathering up her bag and her phone and being the Penny he knew. He felt for a second that was much better than this stranger who knew far more than she should about things that really had nothing to do with them anymore.

It was almost three o'clock in the morning when Kevin finally switched off the lights in the apartment and put away thoughts of his parents and Valentina, and yes, he could admit it here in the silence, Carrie.

Carrie woke early to the sound of traffic stopped on the road outside. Council workers were pulling up wires or pipes and it seemed as though the background engine noise of start and stop had punctuated her sleep for most of the night. She wasn't hungry, the meal the evening before still made her feel satisfied, but she decided to get up and go for a walk with Teddy. It would do them both good to get some exercise and fresh air.

Afterwards, there didn't seem much point in hanging around the house for a few hours so she made her way to the restaurant intending to write up her review of Hoffa's. It would be a great review. The restaurant deserved five stars, if she was rating it. She stood firm with the paper about the rating system though, she wasn't giving stars, just an opinion, and then there could be no falling out. The food had been prepared to perfection, the décor charming and the staff solicitous without intruding. Had that been what made the night special, she wondered as she slipped her key into the front door of The Sea Pear. For some reason, remembering the evening before with Luke made her smile, then she gave herself a swift mental prod, it was time to get a grip, they were friends, that was all. He had not asked her on a date; and even if they had almost kissed, the moment passed and, at the end of it, Carrie really wasn't sure if the chemistry between them wasn't all one-sided anyway. Luke had said it himself; he didn't know how long he'd be in Dublin for. He had no plans to settle here or anywhere else for that matter. But still… she couldn't help but feel that maybe…

Teddy's growl pulled her from her thoughts and back to the present. He strained on his lead, drawing her away from the restaurant. She assumed he just didn't want to end his walk yet. Perhaps he thought he was going to spend all day in the basket she'd placed in her office. The funny thing was, he didn't stay there all the time anyway. She'd seen him, several times, walk cheekily out the door and wait for a break in the traffic before heading across to The Marchant Inn to stretch out before one of the fires over there. Of course, the fact that Jane kept a jar of treats for him beneath the bar probably added to the allure of the place too. He really had managed to carve his way into everyone's heart. Well, almost everyone's heart. 'Come on, you, we can drop over to visit Jane in a little while.' She didn't notice the hair on his back stand taller as he walked reluctantly in the door behind her.

She spotted the wine cabinet first. Funny, she thought. She carried on past the maelstrom of linens and aprons, discarded as though scrambled by a child at play, and the overturned glasses and a chair smashed against the wall. But it was the wine rack that woke her from her daydream. Every expensive bottle that Andrew had stored only days earlier was gone. They'd broken the lock, an antique flimsy set-up that was more for display than any security reasons. Carrie stood for a moment, trying to figure out what she was looking at, then standing back from it, she took in the whole scene. Her beautiful dining room ransacked, it was thoroughly gone through, pulled apart and for what?

As she stood there, a slight shiver beginning to take over her body, she knew the only thing of real value missing was that expensive wine. They never left the takings here overnight and, these days most of their business was transacted through cards anyway. She felt herself backing away from the wine cabinet, moving as if propelled by something other than her own will. Fear dug deep into her bones, what if they were still here?

Whoever did this, what if they were lurking, somewhere in the kitchen or in her office? She still could not move any faster but found herself suddenly at the front door. The police. She had to call someone.

She looked across at The Marchant Inn. She wanted to run there, perhaps Luke would be there to make her feel what? Safe? It wasn't a feeling she'd ever had with anyone before; she shook the thought from her mind. She stood for a moment, stupidly on the pavement outside The Sea Pear, Teddy at her side, trying to figure it all out. Then the most outrageous notion floated into her panicked mind, Kevin Mulvey had never made her feel safe. Not ever.

She had her phone in her pocket. It was all she brought with her. The keys were still inside and she wasn't sure if she'd locked the door or not, but she couldn't think about that now. 'Yes. Hello. Is that the police?' She waited until they put her through. 'Hello. I want to report a break in.' Her words had a remote quality to them as though someone else was speaking. Carrie rattled off the details in the same monotone voice and waited for two young police officers to arrive. It was the police who called Kevin. She *had* locked the keys inside, senselessly, blindly panicked, and when they went to look for the spare, it was no longer where they'd always left it.

'Well, we know how they got in anyhow,' the older officer said, but if he thought they deserved to be broken into for being irresponsible enough to leave a key outside the back door, he managed to remain kind and considerate to Carrie.

'I'd forgotten it was even there,' Kevin said, looking

at Carrie, but then she'd always taken care of keys and alarms and all that side of things. Today, in the midst of all this, Carrie could see how much he had aged. Had that only happened in the last few weeks? Or had they both been getting gradually older without noticing? 'Anyway, I have my keys here now, so...'

The younger officer took the keys from him. 'Better if we just stay here, for now.' He looked at Carrie. 'They'll send out a team to dust for prints and see what else they can find.' He smiled at her, perhaps hoping to calm her a little. Carrie wasn't sure how long they waited for the forensics team to arrive. Then, gingerly, it seemed to Carrie, they entered The Sea Pear and sat at the window table, answering what sounded like the same questions a thousand times over.

'The only thing of any value really was the wine.' Carrie looked at Kevin. They'd allowed him to walk through to the kitchen, but apart from leaving the cold store open and causing a lot of food wastage, really there wasn't a lot to take aside from pots, pans and kitchen knives.

'The wine was really expensive, do you have many people who pay that much for a bottle of wine,' a stony-faced detective asked her later. He introduced himself as Coleman and it was hard to say if it was a first name or surname.

'No. That's the thing. We, I mean, *I* ordered the wine by mistake. Normally, our house wine, well, it's decent but nowhere near the same value. I was hoping to swap them and I managed to get most of them returned the same day, but we were stuck with the box that had been opened. I thought the worst thing that could happen was it would age in the wine rack – you know, maybe even appreciate,' her laugh was high-pitched and nervous, but the fear of earlier was slowly beginning to subside.

'You're in shock,' Kevin said and he put his arm around her a little self-consciously. It felt wrong to Carrie, so she shrugged him away. 'Will I get you something, tea, brandy, I'm sure something warm might settle your nerves.'

'No. I'm fine,' she said, her eyes taking in the street outside. 'The thing is, not many people would have known about the mistake in the wine order.' She felt empty and low saying it.

'Can you tell us who would have known?' the detective didn't take his eyes off his notebook.

'Well, there was me and Kevin, Valentina, the guy who delivered the order and a girl, Sheila, I rang the accounts department who helped me sort out the order so we didn't have to keep it all. And of course, Andrew.'

'Who's Andrew?' the detective looked up from his notebook.

'Andrew is our head waiter... he's a bit...' Kevin said.

'He's lovely,' Carrie cut in. 'He's as honest as you'll meet and he's been here for as long as we have almost. Kevin doesn't like him because he's gay,' Carrie said bluntly and watched as the detective raised an eyebrow, perhaps sensing the tension between them.

'Well, I'll need to talk to him anyway, and if you could get me contact details for the suppliers?'

'Of course. I'm as sure of Andrew as I am of myself, Detective,' Carrie said firmly.

None of them said it, but she knew they were all thinking – inside job, for sure.

'Well, we have to do our job. I'll be talking to everyone here, not just this Andrew bloke,' he said, looking at Kevin. 'When are the others due to come to work today?'

'Here.' Carrie handed him the roster.

'You can't open tonight, but we'll get out of your hair as quickly as we can. For now, I'd like you not to contact anyone on this list, just let them come in as usual and we'll question them here. Is that understood?' he looked again at Kevin, as if sensing something was amiss. Although, for the life of her, Carrie couldn't fathom what Kevin might have to hide. She knew that there was as much chance of Kevin having pulled the place apart as there was of her, probably less, because he lacked any real imagination and he hardly had the courage to face his mother, never mind take a chance on prison.

'Unbelievable, mate, un-bloody-believable.' Jim had the decency to stretch out the last word, maybe he was as shocked as Kevin was. Kevin hoped he had managed to hide it from Carrie. He'd never seen her so vulnerable. It was like he was seeing a side to her he'd never seen before. A side that made him want to reach out and take care of her. Funny, but for those few hours, it felt like everything they knew about each other had been turned on its head. He felt, for the first time in his life, like the strong one. Like the kind of man you could depend on.

Like the kind of man he always thought his father was, until he found out about Thelma.

'Well, that was my day,' Kevin said, sipping his second pint of the evening, feeling it going to his head a little too much, but knowing it was probably just the shock of the burglary settling on him. 'It looks like whoever did it knew the lie of the land. They knew that we kept a spare key in the side alley. They knew that the wine was expensive and worth taking and any other damage that was done was only to mess things up.' Kevin shook his head, it all added up to something that made him very uneasy. He knew that the feeling in the pit of his stomach had more to do with what he hadn't said than the clear hard facts of the day gone by. It had to do with Simo and Reda – rubbing their hands together to tell him he needed security now – and it had to do with the notion that his restaurant had been broken into by someone who knew they had a delivery of very expensive wine.

'How's Carrie, must be a nasty shock, arriving in to that.'

Jim had texted Sandra as soon as he heard, doubtless there'd be a gang of women calling to make sure Carrie was all right now. Still it felt wrong, just letting her drive off home without him. Kevin had stood outside The Sea Pear for a moment, watching her car disappearing into the evening traffic. Funny, but a few weeks ago, she would have been okay and he wouldn't have thought to ask. Now, today, she seemed smaller, more delicate than he remembered. Perhaps she had lost weight, or maybe it was just that he hadn't seen her without her work clothes and make-up on for so many weeks. She seemed to be younger, fragile, perhaps more feminine... there was definitely something changed about her. He mentioned it to Jim.

'It's this new bloke. Maybe he's doing things differently, Kevin.'

'Ha ha, Jim, you're quite the comedian.' But somehow, Kevin felt it was all wrong.

'Maybe she's just happy,' Jim said, nodding at the barman. 'Apart from today obviously.'

'Maybe she is,' Kevin said and for some reason he thought back to the conversation he had with Penny, about his parents and Thelma Jones. He had a feeling Penny told him that for a reason, but he was damned if he could fathom it.

'So, all of her fancy wines have been stolen. Eetees the good job for her. Thees would not have happened if she didn't get these pricey theengs.' Valentina was painting her toenails, holding a file between her teeth, elongating her e's now so they had become irritating to Kevin's ears. 'I said it so many times, Simo and Reda, they would have made sure no one came near The Sea Pear.'

'You know, it's not just my decision. I think Carrie told you too.' He was cooking an omelette for them. There really was nothing else in the kitchen and there was no going back into The Sea Pear until the following day.

'We should go out,' Valentina said. 'Other people go out all the time and here we are cooking eggs, poof. In

Colombia, eggs are poor people food, Keveen.' A smear of red varnish burned across the leather sofa and Kevin dived for it with a cloth as though putting out a fire. 'Keveen, you have to start taking me to nice places, other couples, they go dancing and drinking. You. You meet some old guy in a pub every other evening. And me, where do I go? Why do I even make an effort? For The Sea Pear?'

'Oh, Valentina, I'm not in the mood to go out tonight. Don't you see, it's been a horrible day?' Kevin tossed the omelette without really thinking and pulled cutlery from the drawer. It was so tempting to argue with her. How could she know what his day was like? She hadn't spent the day with a detective that looked like he ate flint for breakfast. She hadn't been the one to walk into The Sea Pear and find a life's work trampled on. She wasn't thinking that someone who knew them had broken in to their restaurant and robbed them.

'Oh, poor Keveen.' Her voice dripped with disdain. 'But what about me? I have been cooped up here all day.'

'I'm sorry if your day was crappy too, Valentina. Maybe we could just eat our dinner and chill in front of the TV.' He'd like that. He'd like to sit in front of something comforting and familiar, maybe the soaps, and just lose himself for a few hours, especially if he had the sofa to himself. No Simo and Reda were like balm on his rattled nerves. 'Come on, we can open a nice bottle of wine and just relax.'

'Oh, Keveen, you are so boring. I never thought it would be like thees, I thought it would be…' She tossed her lovely long dark hair over her shoulder. 'I thought eet would be fun. That we would have more than just work and fried eggs.'

Her eyes darkened, but Kevin wasn't expecting the wrath of temper that bayed behind them. She looked about her frantically and then pitched the bottle she held in her hand with venom. The nail varnish scudded towards him, narrowly missing his head. He bent to pick it up, but it had shattered into dark red pieces across the beautiful marble floor.

'I am going out. You can stay here and seet like an old man with your television all night.' She grabbed her leather jacket off the chair and headed for the door, but Kevin didn't look up. He was too busy trying to clean the nail varnish off the floor. Maybe it was the two pints with Jim or the stress of the day, but the fact that she'd aimed it at his head when she threw it didn't really dawn on him until much, much later. And even then, it occurred to him he had been lucky, because at least it was just a tiny bottle. He suspected that if she'd had a wine bottle in her hand, she could just as easily have thrown that too, and it probably wouldn't have missed the target. Perhaps he could convince himself that was the price of passion.

Luke had been trying to ring Carrie all day. He had to thank her for dinner in Hoffa's, for a start, but there was something else too. He needed to talk to her, to somehow set things straight between them. He shouldn't have kissed her last night; it was a crass and stupid thing to do. After all, she was still getting her head straight after

Kevin, she'd told him so herself. Still, their friendship meant a lot to him, more than he'd realised before. When she didn't answer, he immediately thought he'd messed things up.

'Hey,' he was relieved when he finally got through. 'I thought you were avoiding me,' it was better to make a joke of things. 'I've been trying to call you all day...'

'Sorry, it's been a bit mad here.'

'Oh, well, I've only been ringing to say thanks...' he stopped, registering the distance in her voice. 'Is everything all right?'

'Yes, of course, well... we've had a break-in. I thought you might have seen all the activity here... it's been policemen and technical detectives all afternoon.' She laughed, a high-pitched nervous sound, very much out of character for her.

'Shall I come round? Is there anything I can do...? I mean, you're not on your own there, trying to cope with all of this, are you?'

'Ah, that's very nice of you, but no need. I'm off home for a long soak and a bit of spoiling... my mother is coming over to tuck me in for the night and settle my nerves,' she said this ruefully and Luke had a feeling that it could be a late night.

'Well, the offer stands. Does Jane know?'

'She couldn't not,' Carrie sighed. 'It might be good if you had the time to go and visit her for the evening, I'd say whatever state her nerves are normally in, they'll be well shot after seeing today's spectacle of police cars.'

'I'll do that,' Luke said softly. Of course, it was typical Carrie, thinking of the effect all of this could have on Jane. Luke thought she sounded weary. He should have checked if he could call round for coffee or asked her out tomorrow, just to take her mind off things, as a sort of payback for the superb dinner.

Jane quickly turned his thoughts on other things. The lonesomeness of the bar stretched out to him when he pushed open the door. She was sitting before a fading fire, the lights low and the silence of the deserted bar ringing loud in contrast to what this place might have once been. He sat next to her, filling time easily that might otherwise pass unnoticed.

'Brandy?' she moved towards the back of the bar and took down two glasses and the large bottle that stood ready. It didn't take long for her to tell him of her restless night and the activity at the restaurant across the road. The whole thing had taken far too much out of her and it lingered between them that she feared The Marchant Inn could be next.

The brandy was steadying, an indulgent welcome that passed through him and made him feel warmed right into his bones. They sipped slowly. Outside, a gusty wind played through Dublin's cobbled lanes; intermittently it rapped against the windows along Finch Street before running on to bother someone else.

'You know you'll have to tell Carrie,' Luke said gently. The fire was almost out, but there was a gentle glowing heat and he was reluctant to build it up again at this late stage. The hours had melted into each other easily. When the darkness of night drew in, Jane locked up the front door and told Luke about the previous evening. 'I'm not even sure that I saw anything. It feels like it was a dream now.' Jane shook her head. How could she have been so stupid not to realise that those two men were actually robbing Carrie's business blind. 'And it's not like I can even give a decent description of them.'

'And that's okay, but you'll surely be able to help in some small way. I mean, that's what the police say all the time, isn't it? They talk about even the smallest details making all the difference.'

'I suppose I could describe the van, they might pick it up somewhere on street cameras.' She shook her head. 'I've been watching too many detective programmes, haven't I?'

'It's no bad thing, although it might pay not to watch them before bedtime.' He looked at his watch and began to yawn.

'Here, one more drink before you go back to the bed and breakfast, it'll help us both sleep.' It was funny but after all the comings and goings of the day, Jane seemed as if she was wide awake. Although Luke was sure no one would be foolish enough to carry out a robbery in this area for a long time again, what with the place full of policemen all day long. A volley of sparks flew up the chimney then, as a log crackled with a concluding pirouetting flame taking off unexpectedly along its side.

'Oh,' Luke exclaimed. 'Those men...' he shook his head. 'Those foreign men, I wonder...' He sat back in his chair, closing his eyes for a moment.

'What? What is it you're thinking?' Jane sipped her brandy.

'When you were in hospital, I was here, cleaning out this chimney, two men came into the bar. There was something about them, I'm not even sure if I could properly recognise them again, but they were shifty, as if they were sizing the place up.'

'Oh, God.' Jane whispered.

'No, don't worry. They assumed I was the owner, that I was going to be here all the time. I saw them out the front door and I had no fears that they'd be back to take me on.'

'Well, that's something, I'm glad you were here.' She said relaxing a little at the idea that any danger might have been put off.

'But the thing is, they were foreign, I think they said they were South American...'

'Colombian?' Jane echoed and they looked at each other long and hard, unsure if that made things better or worse for Carrie. Instead of saying anything, they sat listening to the rain on the windows, the wind whistling all the way down those tall chimneys.

'Do you know, Jane,' Luke said, yawning, 'I wouldn't half mind taking you up on that offer of a room tonight.'

'Really?' Jane's voice sounded pleased and her expression gave away the flooding relief washing across her. 'Well, take your pick and we'll make one up for you, right after I call the police station.' Then she got up and moved to the back of the bar. Thoughtfully, she took the phone from its cradle and stood at the counter before meeting his eyes. 'I know it's late, but I think the sooner I tell the police what I saw the better.' She smiled. 'It'll be lovely to have a bit of company about the place,' she said softly as she watched the last sparks from the day's embers race up towards the blasting cold of the night sky.

At four o'clock, something woke Kevin. He lay in bed for a while, the darkness soothing, putting off getting up to see if Valentina was about. The bed was icy, for the first year in as many as he could remember, November came in freezing and already it looked as if December could be the whitest in years.

When he stood, Kevin felt the effects of his earlier can of beer and the pints with Jim. Carrie once joked that he was a cheap date and she was right. Two pints was his limit, he should have known better. He walked about the apartment in darkness. No sign of Valentina. He turned on the light in the living room and sat for a moment on a high stool he pulled from beneath the kitchen island. Tonight, catching up with the British soaps and some old American sitcoms, was the first time he'd really relaxed here since they moved in. Why was that? Perhaps it was just settling in, getting used to sharing his home with someone new. Maybe, in five years' time, things between himself and Valentina would be as easy as they were with Carrie.

He scratched his head, an odd buzzing feeling racing through his thoughts. He might as well be honest; he and Valentina would never be the same as it was with

Carrie. He'd known that from the start. He believed it was because she was somehow better than Carrie. She was younger, beautiful and exotic – he believed all of these things added up in some way to make *him* a better man. Better? He qualified the word in his mind. What did better actually mean to him. Richer? More successful? Respected in some macho way? Yes, maybe all of those things, but really, he could call it here, on his own in the middle of the night, he could put a name on why he left Carrie for Valentina, couldn't he? He wanted to feel he had something that was way beyond what everyone else had. He wanted Jim and all those other blokes who discounted what he'd done with The Sea Pear by giving the credit to Carrie to see he was better than them. He was better than any of them, because he could have a younger, sexier woman on his arm and he didn't need Carrie to make him into the man he had become. The thing was, in the silence of the apartment, with his head throbbing, he wasn't so sure about any of it anymore.

15

It seemed everyone was relieved to get back to normal except Carrie. One of the newspapers even rang to ask when The Sea Pear would open again after the burglary. Kevin greeted the news that the forensic team had finished up with great enthusiasm. They agreed to meet on Finch Street early in the morning to assess how much would need to be done before the restaurant could open to customers. Certainly, the dining room would need some sorting out and Carrie knew that the kitchen was a mess too. It seemed that The Sea Pear had lost its magic for her and Carrie wasn't sure if she could wholly blame the break-in for this. Rather, it was a heavy feeling that greeted her as she walked through the front door, as if there was deadness about the place that would drain the life from her if she stayed here much longer. Suddenly, she knew she was ready to leave it all to Kevin and Valentina – they were more than welcome to it. She tried to shake off that heavy feeling as much as possible and got on with sorting out the dining room.

The post arrived at eleven, and when she looked about, she reckoned she deserved a coffee break. Rather than going back into the kitchen to sit with Kevin, she decided she'd head out to one of those fancy coffee shops along the canal, where the music played loud and everyone was too busy studying their iPad to notice very much else. She brought the post with her to salve her conscience at leaving Kevin behind in the kitchen.

Once she was out in the fresh air, Carrie was relieved to feel her spirits lift. It could be a spring day, so dry and crisp, with the icy sunlight peeping through the clouds occasionally. She picked a table outside, it suited Teddy best, and anyway, it was a nice day and there was a huge heater blasting out warm air just next to her. A lovely young girl brought her a giant cup of coffee that she knew she'd never get to the end of.

The post was mainly junk and bills, but at the bottom of the pile, the bank statements for The Sea Pear were in for November. She scanned them quickly; really, unless she had the notebook she wrote up all the lodgements in, they meant very little, other than she had a feeling that takings looked as though they were down quite a bit on other years. Then again, most of the other restaurateurs were complaining that the Christmas season seemed to start later and later each year, so perhaps that was it. She put the pages down on the table, her eyes drawn towards the canal. It was lovely to sit here, with the buzz of people coming and going and be, for once, just another customer with no agenda other than drinking coffee and watching the world go by.

Carrie glanced at the statements again, there was something wrong. She ran her finger along the line of numbers, searching for one particular lodgement. She remembered the night quite clearly, they had a party from a golf club that had stayed late and tipped miserably, but they spent cash, and the takings were far greater than any of the lodgements listed. Perhaps there was some mistake?

Now, as she stared at the statement, it seemed all the figures were deflated, they were all much lower than she remembered cashing up. If anything, the figures here were roughly the amounts they took in from credit and debit cards. Totting up the differences as far as she could in her head, she calculated there was at least ten thousand euros missing.

Carrie sat until her enormous cup of coffee had grown a thin dark skin across its top. A sense of terrible dread had taken over from the lovely light feeling she had when she sat here first. Someone was pilfering the cash amounts from the lodgements and there were only three people who had the means to do that. Two of them had nothing to gain, not really, but the third...

Oh, God, she wasn't sure which was worse, the idea that Valentina might have stolen from them, or the notion that she couldn't leave The Sea Pear now, not until this was sorted out. Suddenly, the idea of leaving Kevin, much as she might want to put him behind her and move on – well it seemed like desertion. Kevin was a lamb to the slaughter, Valentina would clean him out and walk away – perhaps she'd already cleaned them out. God, she could pull their whole business apart and leave them with nothing after all their years of hard work. That thought sent a rattling fear right through Carrie and, suddenly, she wasn't sure what to do about any of this mess.

'You'll have to tell Kevin,' Anna said when they met up later that day at her flat. Teddy was glad of the walk and it felt as if he was leading the way for most of the journey. Carrie had to tell someone and Anna was her best bet. 'And the police, this isn't just about a lovers' tiff or sour grapes.' Anna was as shocked as Carrie. 'I mean, there's a difference of thousands of euros, Carrie... *thousands*,' she shook her head.

'I don't know if he'll even believe me, Anna. After all, I was the one sorting out all the bank stuff between us.'

'Seriously, Carrie, you're as honest as St Patrick, he'd never think you would do something like this.'

'Maybe, but he's head over heel in love with Valentina. I've never seen anyone so totally smitten, I have a feeling she could convince him night is day.'

'Then it's time for him to see her for what she really is, isn't it?'

'This is going to break his heart.' Carrie looked across at her friend who was staring at her blankly. How could she explain that even if she didn't love Kevin anymore and although he'd treated her miserably, she couldn't bear the idea of him being so badly let down. 'And it's not just that, Anna, it's been going on for months. I mean, it looks like as soon as Valentina could get her hands on the lodgement bag she had started to empty out the cash.'

Apart from being angry and upset, Carrie couldn't help feeling sorry for Kevin. 'So much for true love, eh?'

'Well, it's all there in black and white,' Anna said and there was no nastiness in her voice. Poor Kevin, he had been taken for a prize mug and whatever about all the money they'd lost, this would truly devastate him. 'I can see, it's not going to be easy.'

'I know, I'm not sure I'm even up to having the conversation with him yet,' Carrie said.

'But you have to, you can't let her just keep on emptying your pockets like that.'

'Oh, Anna, I've no intention of letting her touch another penny. She won't get near the cash register or the tips jar.' Stealing from the tips jar was probably the lowest thing Valentina could have done. 'I'll be doing the lodgements from now on and I'll be taking everything to the accountant before I speak to Kevin.' The truth was, he seemed to be so under Valentina's spell, Carrie wasn't sure she could convince him that this was real anyway.

'Well, you know best, but be careful. You've worked really hard to build up The Sea Pear, I couldn't bear it if it was all ruined because of that thieving cow.' Anna hadn't been much help in the way of advice, but still it was good to be able to tell someone and it wasn't the kind of conversation she could really have with anyone else. After all, it was bad enough to be thrown over for a younger woman, but to be thrown over for someone like Valentina? 'Make the call now, set up a time to see the accountant. I'll come along too if you'd like, but you have to get moving on this today.'

'Ah, you're very good, Anna, but no, I need to do this on my own,' Carrie said firmly.

She made an appointment to visit the accountant and ignored the text on her phone from Luke. They had something to tell her. Could she call to see Jane later? It could be urgent, it was hard to tell either way from the text. Well, she'd try, but by the time she'd finished with the accountant and made it back to The Sea Pear, she had a feeling that she'd be far too wiped out to be much in the way of company. Eventually she texted him back to say she couldn't make it this evening, but hopefully tomorrow she would pop across to The Marchant Inn.

Luke finally managed to track down a matron before he left his father for the night. The truth was, his father had never looked so unwell. This was more than a chest infection. For the first time in weeks, Luke looked at his dad and he realised he was a very sick man and he needed to be seen by a proper doctor, one who could clear up whatever had rattled the life out of him so quickly.

'Ah, Mr Gibson, it's nice to meet you at last.' The matron was a middle-aged, stout woman who peered at him over glasses that were too trendy to look good on anyone over seventeen. 'I had been hoping you'd call to see us one of the days, your father is being... well, you know him better than we do, I suppose...'

'I should hope so. What's he being, exactly?' he asked. He had searched this woman out to find out why his father was still using an oxygen mask; he had a feeling that wasn't why she wanted to talk to him though.

'Well, he doesn't listen, we are only trying to help, but...' she shook her head.

'Oh?' There was no doubt, his father had lived an interesting life, perhaps they were not used to men who had a taste for more than meat, two veg and an occasional bottle of stout, he thought. 'He certainly knows his own mind, if that's what you mean.'

'He does that.' She pinned on a smile that didn't stretch far enough to be warm. 'For now.'

'What's that supposed to mean?' Luke asked.

'Well, the drugs, they take the pain away, but they will make him tired, disoriented, you know, eventually,' her voice softened, 'they break everything down.'

'What drugs?'

'The morphine. Of course, he needs it more now, surely you've noticed that he's weaker, he's fading very quickly, I'm afraid.' Her words tapered off to a quiet end, perhaps she realised that he hadn't known. 'I'm sorry, sometimes, being here, surrounded by... well, you know, we're under fierce pressure and it can make us a little too business-like.'

'Morphine...' Luke echoed the word, it felt like he'd been torpedoed off course, suddenly, it all made appalling sense. 'He's dying?' he managed to whisper then.

'Yes.' The matron was nodding at him, realising now just how badly she had put her foot in it and, worse, that she'd broken confidentiality without realising it. 'I'm so sorry, I thought you knew.'

'My father is dying?' His words echoed, but they were too far-off to get a proper grip on their meaning.

'Let's not talk about that now,' the woman said, taking his elbow and leading him into what he supposed was a staff kitchen. 'Let's just get our heads around how we can help him for now. Okay.'

Luke stayed at Ballyglen that night, but he was completely dazed. It was as if he'd walked into a different room and the door to the life he'd known before had been firmly closed behind him. Now, whatever intention he'd had of calling Carrie, to make sure she was all right drifted from him. He meant to ask her for coffee, now it seemed like such a useless thing to fret over. In the greater scheme of things, she was probably up to her eyes in all sorts of things, from insurance to dealing with the police. Although a small part of him wondered if she wasn't just a little bit distant because of something he'd said or done wrong without realising it. He had to face it, she was probably still getting over Kevin Mulvey. Some random man she met for dinner wasn't really going to mean a lot to her in the face of everything else she had going on in her life now. It was only as he was drifting off to sleep in an uncomfortable chair at the end of his father's room that he began to wonder about why his father had chosen to come here to die. In his heart, he knew there must be a reason.

'So, you're going to the wedding?' Kevin felt like someone had pulled the air from the room for a moment. These last few days, since the break-in, Carrie was more distracted than he'd ever known her to be before. She was almost icy with him and beyond reserved with Valentina, although she managed to cover it over so no one but Kevin would notice. It was a strange thing, but now Kevin found himself forcing lightness between them when they were together. It seemed their roles had reversed and he needed to jolly her along in case some fine line would be crossed and she might just tell him exactly what was annoying her.

'Of course I'm going, Kevin. Don't be daft. I'm the maid of honour; I kind of need to be there.' Carrie rolled her eyes in a way she never used to; now she made him feel like she could see just how pathetic he was. 'Are you going?' she asked and there was a strange wistfulness to her voice, as though she half wished he would say no.

'Yeah, well, Valentina is looking forward to staying in a castle, so...' They both knew weddings were not his thing. He was roped into being best man because he was the only one of their friends who'd never been asked and, when it had been arranged, it worked well with Carrie being matron of honour.

'Oh, so you managed to get a room?' She was searching in the shelves beneath the narrow maître d' counter, but she looked at him now, interested for just a moment. 'In the castle?'

'I, well, no. I just assumed that...'

'That what?' She stood up now to her full height of less than five foot three and looked him in the eye, even though he had a good eight inches on her. 'Oh,' she smiled. 'I see, you thought that you and Valentina would stay in the room *I* booked, was that it?'

'Well, I just thought that maybe...' Kevin's voice petered off.

'Sorry, Kevin, but I'm going. As it turns out, I'm really looking forward to it. It's one of the best rooms in the castle, with a view of the lake, a double bathroom and sitting room. Actually, they've thrown in a third night for fifty quid, so I'm staying on an extra night.' She winked at him, there were no hard feelings, she had made the booking, paid for the room, it was hers to enjoy.

'No. No. Of course you must stay there, I'll book something else.'

'Will you?' She looked at him quizzically and he wasn't sure why. Then he realised he'd never booked a holiday away for them, that had always been her territory, not that they'd gone away too often. Then she smiled, 'Maybe you'll be lucky and pick up a cancellation, fingers crossed, eh?'

'Yeah, fingers crossed.' He meant it. He really didn't fancy telling Valentina she'd be staying in some dive while everyone else lived it up in the lap of luxury. Why on earth hadn't he sorted this out sooner – it wasn't as if he hadn't realised that it would be impossible to get accommodation at this late stage. Valentina. She had been in foul form since the burglary. It was as if she'd taken it all personally and could hardly look at Kevin these days without biting his nose off. 'I suppose I better get onto it.' He backed away from Carrie, but by the time he'd made it to the kitchen she was humming some tune under her breath that made him think of years earlier when she did that all the time. They were happy then – was she happy now?

He spent almost an hour on the phone and, at the end of it, he was no better off than when he started. It seemed that every hotel and guesthouse within a fifty-mile radius of the wedding venue was booked up or closed for the Christmas holidays.

When Valentina came into the kitchen, he moved away from her. He could feel sweat dripping down his back, his face blotched from the stress of it all; the last thing he wanted was to have to tell Valentina that they had nowhere to stay for the wedding. He went outside the back door of The Sea Pear to think and to breathe. In the end, the best thing was to ring Ben. Surely his friend, the groom, could pull some strings and get them a room somewhere in the castle. After all, Kevin reasoned, the best man needed a room in the same hotel as the wedding.

'Sorry, mate. The village is booked solid since last year. We sent out a list of accommodation with the invites, but most people booked straight away. Carrie booked the suite before we even sent out the invitation, that's why she got such a good room.'

'Great. Bloody great.'

'Blast, didn't mean to rub it in, it's just, you and Carrie, it doesn't feel real that you're not together. You've been a couple as long as me and Melissa. I'm sure I'll be putting my foot in it all day with this new girlfriend you're bringing along.'

'Oh, no Ben. You won't put your foot in it with

Valentina,' Kevin said with complete assurance. What he meant was, *you won't put your foot in it if she's in the kind of dark mood I've been seeing these last few days.*

'The best thing I can think of is the caravan park. It's run by the hotel, it's like glamping. Melissa's brother and his kids are staying in a converted horsebox and it has everything you need... it's all the rage apparently,' Ben enthused.

'Hm, maybe.' Kevin couldn't see Valentina being impressed with a bed in a horsebox. She'd hardly look at eggs because they were peasant food, she certainly wouldn't sleep in a trailer, not when she realised that Carrie had a suite overlooking the lake.

'Seriously, mate, it could be fun. A bit of rough and tumble in the hay... I wouldn't mind it if I had a young Colombian...'

'Yeah, well, you're getting married, so there'll be none of that for you.' Kevin tried to sound serious, but really he loved the idea of Jim or Ben or any of his friends thinking he'd scored a better looking girl than any of them were ever likely to have.

'Ah, I suppose so. Sure, over here, there's South Americans at every turn. All the older men are shacking up with them, they're looking for visas.' Ben cleared his throat quickly, 'Of course that's not to say that's the case with you and the lovely Valentina.'

'No, it's certainly not the case,' Kevin said and he tried to keep the anger from his voice. Was that what they thought of him? That he would be taken in by some money-grabber? Or that the only reason someone like

Valentina would be interested in him was because she wanted Irish citizenship? Well, he'd show them. 'You'd better give me that number, I'm not sure that Valentina's going to be very impressed with a horsebox; she's not some cheap piece like you're used to seeing over there. She has real class, but we're in love, so it won't really matter where we stay, I suppose.' Kevin could feel his blood pressure rising.

'Keveen, I can't believe you theenk I will sleep with you in a horsebox.' Valentina was livid. To be fair, it wasn't helped by the fact that she had learned about the luxury suite that Carrie booked in the castle for three nights, while she would be staying in what was basically a campsite, no matter how you glossed it over.

'But, Valentina, it will be romantic.'

'There is nothing romantic about it. I want to stay in the castle. I am not staying in a horsebox.'

'It's the only accommodation available and it's costing a bomb. It may not be as obvious as a castle, but it is very charming. We can always go back and stay at the castle again. We could go there for our honeymoon if you like.'

'Keveen, people don't go to Sligo on their honeymoons, have you not heard of the Seychelles. Really, you are the disasters, you men.' She threw her hands up in the air, and even if she couldn't get her diction quite right, he knew from her expression what she meant. She flung the magazines from the chair beside her and, for a moment, he thought she looked like a petulant child who was not getting her own way.

'Of course we'll go wherever you want on honeymoon, Valentina, but first we have to go to Ben and Melissa's wedding. I'm sorry about the room, but I'm so looking forward to showing you off.' Kevin knew that if all else failed, flattery might just work with Valentina.

'They will say you are a lucky man.' Valentina laughed throatily. 'Especially when I stand next to Carrie for the photographs, everyone knows that bridesmaid dresses are always made to help the bride shine brighter than anyone else.' She cackled at this and Kevin caught a cruelty in her eyes that he hadn't noticed before. True, compared to Valentina, Carrie was plain, but then Kevin knew that in many ways, in terms of physical attractiveness, he would rate probably behind Carrie, and so maybe that made the barb hurt a little more. 'Yes, so, I weel stay in your glamping horsebox, and we weel make them all jealous with how much you are in love with me and we can tell them all about how much better our wedding will be one day soon.'

'Maybe we should keep our own plans under wraps, just for now.'

'Why?'

'Well, with the robbery and everything. It's all been very...'

'Yes, I have felt it too, Keveen. I have felt it too.' She sighed dramatically. She hadn't wanted to talk to the police. Eventually, Kevin convinced her she'd have to answer their questions. In the end, she told him, it was not for her own sake, but rather for Simo and Reda's. 'They are illegal, here. If the police find that out, they will send them back and there is nothing for them in Colombia, only trouble and ends that are dead.' Kevin had convinced her that she didn't have to mention them and that all she had to say was that she was Kevin's fiancé. He didn't add, they couldn't but notice her ring, it was the size of the Dublin Mountains on her slender hand.

'How did you get on with the police, by the way?' Kevin asked her, as much to change the subject as anything else. He'd seen her, chatting away happily to them, all her worries about being illegal or Simo and Reda evaporated.

'Very well. I think they liked me,' she said, throwing her head back and laughing that dirty laugh that had until so recently seemed like an invitation to seduce her. Funny, but these days he wasn't sure if he was too irritated or plain worn out, but seducing her was at the bottom of his list of priorities.

Jane had a feeling that there was something Carrie wasn't saying. It felt, to her at least, that since the break-in, something was weighing heavily on her mind and whatever it was darkened her eyes far more than any troubles caused by Kevin Mulvey. 'Is everything all right?' Jane asked, reaching out to touch her arm in a silent act of solicitude.

'Oh yes, I'm probably just a little shocked, you know, don't worry, the break-in has only temporarily knocked the stuffing out of me.' She laughed, but her mirth didn't reach beyond the sound that carried across the fireside rug between them.

Carrie was as attentive and genuine as ever and when they spoke about the robbery, she tried to put Jane's mind at rest, thanking her for contacting the police. After all, any information she had would help. The details seemed to fade between them, such was the extent of Carrie's distance, Jane wondered if perhaps something had happened with Kevin. The stress of the robbery might be enough to push them back together again.

'You have something on your mind,' Jane said eventually.

'Ah, no.' Carrie was defensive, 'just this whole break-in business, you know, it's thrown me out of sorts.'

'Well, I can understand that,' Jane said sadly. 'And Luke, has he been in touch?' She didn't want to hit any raw nerves, but it was at a time like this they should all be rallying around Carrie.

'To be honest, I've hardly had time to bless myself until now.' She bent down, patted Teddy on his head. He was sitting in the soft winter sunlight that faded across the quarry tiled floor. 'He rang after, but... not a dicky bird since,' Carrie smiled sadly, 'perhaps he's ready to move on to pastures new.'

Later, when Carrie went back to the restaurant and the bar echoed heavy with memories, the only sound a struggling fire in the grate, Jane dialled Luke's number. She hadn't seen him since he'd left to visit his father in the nursing home. It rang out and for some reason, its numb tone resounded gloomily in her. She sat for a long time, thinking over the last few weeks. It seemed for a while as if there had been a glimmer of hope in her world, but today, on this grey afternoon, she could feel that flicker dying slowly.

16

'I don't expect you to understand,' Luke's father struggled for breath and he placed the oxygen mask before his face, sucking in air as hungrily as he had drawn on tobacco over the years.

'Well, we have all day.' Luke smiled, trying to keep himself away from that quarry of despair that threatened to pull him into its core.

'I didn't want you to worry,' Conn smiled sadly. 'I know, I know, it sounds stupid now…' his eyes closed as he drew from the mask again and, for a moment, Luke wondered if he hadn't fallen asleep. 'I'm not even sure if I can explain… I've always had this emptiness, I've carried it around with me; it comes from long before I met your mother. You were the only thing that managed to fill it for me, but then, when I knew I was dying, I had… questions to answer, I knew I had to put things right.'

'What kind of things?' His father had told the matron that he wanted to be buried with his mother. 'Your family? Your mother?' They never talked about Luke's grandparents. He knew that his grandmother had been widowed, that she had married a second time and shortly after that, Conn had set off on his travels. That was as much as Conn would ever say.

'My mother had a second son. I had a stepbrother, but there was over ten years between us and my stepfather did his best to make sure that I knew this new family was not mine. We never got on, maybe, looking back, it was just one of those things, but when you're young, well, your perspective is...'

'A little underdeveloped?'

'I left London with the clothes I stood in and a hunger to see the world. I decided that I'd never see any of them again, but then, when you arrived and I knew what it was to have a child, I went back to where my mother owned a pub in London and it was gone. The neighbours were still there and they told me she had moved back to Dublin.'

'She would be very old now.' Luke knew she'd be well into her hundreds. 'Is that why you came back here?'

'Don't worry, the drugs haven't completely robbed me of my mind yet,' he chuckled a throaty, chesty sound that borrowed too much oxygen and demanded that he place the mask before his mouth again. 'She is the closest thing I have to home, or she was, and I thought if I tracked her down...'

'Yes?' Luke prompted.

'Perhaps I could be buried next to her?'

'Except you have no idea if she's even buried in Dublin or she could have been cremated...' So that was his request.

'I have a feeling that she is here, in Dublin.' Conn said with conviction. 'And I thought...'

'So, let me get this straight, you were going to send me on my way, to the furthest part of the world, while you died slowly on your own and then I would come back here for a funeral that I would have to research first...' he shook his head in disbelief. 'You're something else Dad,' he laughed then and he wasn't sure why, because in all of this, the only funny thing was this whole ridiculous notion of his father's.

'I know, it sounds a bit... unconventional.'

'You can say that again.' Luke shook his head slowly, but now, it felt as though so much of their lives together was beginning to take on some new meaning. It was why his father always returned to Ireland at the end of each contract. The fact that he'd insisted on Luke going to university in Dublin and even their jaunts since he'd come here. Luke had thought it was such an odd thing to want to visit old graveyards every time they went out together, but he'd put it to the back of his mind as another of his father's unusual quirks.

'I thought you could go on having a normal life and that when I... passed,' he made a face as if the idea was farcical, 'well, I thought you might find some family to fill that vacuum when I'm not around anymore.'

'Oh, Dad.' Luke shook his head. 'No one, not a tonne of Gibsons, could replace you.'

'Well, that's the thing Luke, my brother wasn't called Gibson – he was called Marchant, just like my stepfather.'

'Marchant, you never mentioned that name before,' Luke said thoughtfully and suddenly so many wheels began to turn in his mind and he had a feeling that they had come full circle and they had ended up exactly where they were meant to be.

Christmas would be different this year. Usually, Carrie cooked a big family meal back at the restaurant, with her mother and Maureen Mulvey each at an end of the table, Penny and her family squabbling and fussing, Kevin getting quickly sloshed and Carrie serving up the dinner she had begun preparing the night before. She wasn't entirely sure how the tradition had evolved, but it had become their ritual, whether she liked it or not. Funny, but a year ago, she hadn't considered whether she did like it, nor had she ever thought about changing it. This year, though, she was actually looking forward to Christmas. She had bought a small bird, frozen, and packet stuffing. She filled her cupboards with food from the supermarket and she had absolutely no intention of making anything that didn't come from a box or a jar. This was going to be her Christmas. Her mother was in complete agreement and when she mentioned the idea of asking along Jane Marchant it seemed only fair to warn her that it was going to be an extremely relaxed day all round.

'Oh, it sounds just lovely,' Jane said. She had hung some tinsel about her little upstairs sitting room and a tragic miniature Christmas tree sat on a sideboard to mark the holidays, otherwise, you'd hardly know Christmas was approaching here. 'And you're sure you don't mind, I won't be in the way?' she said then, a little stain of worry streaking across her features.

'My mum is looking forward to meeting you,' Carrie said as she emptied out a huge bag of old decorations that had been hers and Kevin's. There were Christmas stars, angels complete with harps and gifts, and enough holly and ivy to bring Christmas right into Jane's living room.

'It would be lovely if Luke could come,' Jane said softly, as she was patting Teddy's head, hardly noticing his adoring gaze. They hadn't seen Luke in days; Carrie was convinced he'd left Dublin without telling them.

'Well, he's welcome if he's still around,' Carrie said lightly, although she did wonder if he'd fallen out with her. He hadn't come near her since Hoffa's, not that it mattered, not really in the greater scheme of things. She had enough on her plate trying to stay sane while all the time, at the back of her mind, she worried that her life's work might be slipping from her. 'Of course, he might prefer to spend it with his father...' She looked at Jane who seemed to be just a little crestfallen. 'Go on, ring him, invite them both if you'd like, the more the merrier,' she said, not really expecting to see either Luke or his father.

Now that he wasn't around, Carrie realised she liked Luke, a lot. Of course, it was hard to really see it, with everything else that was happening, but there was no denying she'd missed having him around these last few days. She might have told him about Valentina if he was. He seemed like the kind of person she could talk to; he wouldn't judge or want to rush in and put things right. When she thought about it now, in the grey light of everything else around her, she should have asked him to Melissa's wedding. Really, the room she'd booked could easily have been made up so he could have stayed in the sitting room and he certainly would have been good company. It was a funny turn of events, but now, she no longer cared about making Kevin jealous, or thwarting the pity of their friends. Rather, she knew that after the Christmas rush was over she would have to spell out the extent of Valentina's deception to Kevin and that heavy dread just made her feel sad. Kevin, for all his faults and for all he'd done to her, she knew he didn't deserve this.

'You are such a bore,' Valentina screamed at Kevin, 'you never want to have fun.'

'Don't you understand? We can't just go skiing – this week, it's our busiest time of the year... Any other time, but I can't just walk out of the restaurant and expect Carrie to keep everything going, not this week.' Kevin wasn't sure if the dread in his stomach was anguish or rage – it made no difference, he bit down on it either way.

'Well, I've promised now, you weel make me look like I am stupid or, worse, like some sad waitress who is nothing more than...' her face was thunderous, 'your... your... you know what they weel say, that you bought me from Colombia, Keveen.'

Suddenly, he filled with panic. 'Don't be daft, of course they wouldn't say that, they know we're a team, a...' There was no point, he'd never win an argument with Valentina and then he realised that the things he wanted to say would not make any difference to her. Was it so terrible to want the things he'd taken for granted every other year? A roaring fire in the grate, an advent calendar peeling off the days to Christmas and mince pies that smelled of childhood memories he wasn't even sure were his. Carrie made a big deal out of Christmas for the family, everyone got a thoughtful gift, wrapped and ribboned and receipted, although they never were returned. Carrie would have the gifts all sorted by now. Kevin had a feeling that the only present he'd see from Valentina this year was a basket of dirty clothes to be washed and a credit card bill to keep him working hard in January.

'Oh, Keveen, sometimes, you can be so naïve, you are like a child. They look at me and then they look at you.' She wrinkled her nose, as though she had only just noticed his greying hair and the dark circles that bulged beneath his eyes. 'You have everything, all the money, this place,' she waved her hand about the overpriced apartment they were leasing, 'and then they see you have this very beautiful woman and she has nothing.' She shrugged her shoulders and waved her hand about as though he really was holding all the cards in their relationship.

'Well, if I go swanning off to some flash resort at our busiest time of the year, we'll both have nothing and your friends won't be saying much about us then, will they?'

'Keveen, they are *our* friends.' She moved closer to him, some new emotion crossing her features that he couldn't read. 'Ah Keveen, it is different for you. All of this, you are happy with this, with the seeting about the apartment

277

and eating eggs for dinner, but I am young and I need excitement, otherwise...' she raised her perfect eyebrows, and even though she didn't finish that thought, he felt a tremor of fear rinse through him.

'Very well, if you want to go and stay in their chalet for a few days over the Christmas holidays...' Perhaps they could fly out after they closed up the restaurant. Actually, leaving Dublin for Christmas Day might be the best plan of all. He dreaded bringing Valentina round to his mother's where already Penny had filled the fridge with her version of traditional Christmas fayre. Kevin knew that he'd be left with the cooking, and if they expected Valentina to do the washing up, he'd be left with that also.

'Oh Keveen, I knew you'd see the senses. There is no reason for me to stay here when you are so busy in the restaurant.' She pulled out her phone and began to text furiously, 'There is just one seat left on Dean's plane and Raleigh said it is mine if I can make it.'

'So you're going to leave me here?' Kevin knew he was standing with a slackened jaw while the words fell across the marble floor between them.

'Well, of course. You said you can't take time out of the restaurant and it's not as if we have any plans for the holidays, is it?'

'But, what about the wedding?'

'Oh, I'll be back for that, Dean is bringing the plane back for a meeting here in Dublin on the day after Christmas... I'll be back before you know I'm gone.'

'But...' there was no use talking about it anymore,

with a flourish of her red talons it was all organised and she was pulling out clothes and discarding most as unsuitable for the trip. It seemed there would have to be hours spent on getting ready.

It came as a total shock. Kevin had never had a call from the bank before. Thank goodness he was here, in The Sea Pear, not at home – it felt strange to think the apartment was home, it still didn't feel like it. Tomorrow would be their busiest day of the year – although they would close early, Christmas Eve was a long, hard and joyless day in the restaurant trade when you worked in a busy kitchen. Even so, he came to the restaurant this morning, not to work, but to eat breakfast in peace. He wanted to sit alone for a while without Valentina's two bullish cousins making him feel uncomfortable in his own apartment.

It was almost Christmas and Kevin was tired. This time of year, it always felt as if the year's stresses packed up on him, so he was just going through the motions, working, sleeping, eating, until he could close the restaurant on Christmas Eve and relax. He took the call while his coffee was brewing. A bored-sounding woman telling him he was overdrawn made him cross at first. *Imbeciles* – he thought, until she reeled off the list of payments. It was all retail, fashion and accessories. Valentina had spent a fortune in the space of a couple of weeks. Kevin slumped miserably into the stool he always thought of as Carrie's. He was up to his eyeballs in debt, there wasn't enough to pay the rent, never mind the price of accommodation in Sligo for this wedding or to meet the Christmas plans that Valentina was making with her new rich friends. That had been another row, before he caved in for the peace of it. Her venom still rang in his ears. He thought she had stopped spending. He had cut his credit card in two – how was this possible? Then he convinced himself, weakly at first, that it was some terrible mistake. Perhaps his card details were stolen, that was more like it. A trickle of anxious sweat crawled down from his forehead. He explained that he had decommissioned his card, he'd cut it in half and threw it in the bin, bravely, he thought at the time, in the face of Valentina's filthy temper.

'Our records show that all of those payments were made with your new card, Mr Mulvey.'

'My new card?' he wanted to be cross, but rather all he felt was that searing sense of defeat. He felt like his father, being put back for something his mother had once more set her heart on. 'My new card?' he echoed again.

'Yes. According to your credit account here, a replacement card was sent to you after your old card was stolen.'

'I see,' Kevin said and, of course, he did.

He hung up the phone and suddenly felt trapped; he'd been backed into a corner and he had no idea how to get out. Carrie would know what to do about this, but he couldn't ask for her help, not now, not with this. He couldn't face the humiliation. After all, Carrie seemed to have come out of this with so much more than he did – he should have expected that from the start. To top off the fact that all their friends so obviously preferred her to him, she had their little house tied up neatly. She was the toast of the Dublin restaurant scene; a brilliant reviewer and she seemed to be quite happy with that little dog and the odd assortment of friends she gathered about her.

He tried to calm himself while his coffee cooled. He stared into space, trying to think of ways to make this go away. At least Valentina couldn't get her hands on the restaurant card or any of the restaurant cash. That thought was some small relief. He would slowly begin to pay off the huge mountain of debt she'd built up and he would have to talk to her when she got back from this skiing trip. She would have to take some responsibility for this – that idea sent rivulets of something that lunged between fear and panic through him. No, he had to be a man about this. He would explain that the spending was over and... Oh, God. He was dreading this, perhaps it could wait until after the wedding in Sligo? It was the coward's approach; he knew that. But then, he was also beginning to see he was more of his father's son than he'd ever have admitted to before this. That was just a truth too much. Kevin felt a terrible weight of emotion well up in his chest and before he could stop himself, tears were running down his face. He was crying like a baby, couldn't help it, how had he managed to make such a complete mess of everything? Despair leaned heavily upon him, it seemed to Kevin, at least, that there was nothing he could do – it was all so depressing and, worse, every bit of it was his own fault.

*

Luke walked up Finch Street, undecided if he should call on Jane or Carrie first. Tonight, the twinkly lights that adorned the street trees seemed to blink in time with some deep pulse that moved beneath his feet. It was almost Christmas and Luke had no plans, beyond spending as much time as he could with his father. All round him, it seemed there was a giddy excitement to people that he couldn't quite tap into; it felt as if time and he had stood still, every second counting for something more valuable than it ever had before. Shop windows, filled with gaudy Christmas cheer didn't touch him either; the holidays were going on around him, a commercial roller coaster, volleying towards its final checkout time.

Probably, Carrie was so busy these last few days before Christmas, she may not have even given him a second thought – although, he suspected there was more to Carrie than that. He needed to see her. He had a feeling she could somehow set him straight, if nothing else, to just lay out before her all he'd learned and maybe make some sense of the tangle his emotions had knotted themselves into. Time was a much too precious commodity to waste it anymore. On the other hand, he wasn't entirely sure how to go about what was surely the most important thing he needed to do to set his father's affairs straight. He stood outside the restaurant for a moment, looking across at The Marchant Inn. Of course, he could be completely wrong, although it did seem like all the cards were stacked against that.

'Well, hello stranger, I didn't think we'd ever set eyes on you again.' Carrie came from the door at his back. Then she halted, looked at him, obviously taking in his dishevelled appearance, the fact that he hadn't shaved since their night in Hoffa's, nor had he been able to force down much more than a cup of tea and a dry biscuit to keep the staff at the nursing home happy. They were delighted to see the back of him today, he was fairly sure of that, perhaps his father was too.

She pulled him into the restaurant. Luke couldn't help but feel a racketing up of his own isolation and misery when he looked about at the tables filled with people content and oblivious to his grief. The restaurant was warm, ambient and welcoming. The gentle music worked to untie his already sagging hold on his anguish, so he felt like he might collapse into an emotional heap right there.

'Come on,' she said, dragging him upstairs to the office, where only the muffled sound of the packed dining room below could be heard. They were alone here, apart from the occasional snores of Teddy, sleeping peacefully in his tidy basket. He lifted his head lazily, his bloodshot eyes taking in Luke's arrival; he managed a welcoming snort and then settled back into snoring once more. 'What happened? You look...' she guided him into a seat. She took a brightly printed Christmas gift bag from the corner, pulled open a bottle of brandy that had obviously arrived as a Christmas present. 'Here,' she said, pressing a large mug with three generous fingers of the amber liquid into his hands. She sat opposite him, a look of the deepest concern in her eyes. 'I thought you'd left, I never thought... did you have an accident, was that it?'

'No. Nothing like that,' he managed. 'No, I'm fine, I've been in the nursing home, I've been...' Then it all tumbled out. The cancer, the secrets, how only days ago he'd learned the truth of it all and the fact that he had a feeling that his father had a lot less time to live than he would admit to Luke.

'I'm so sorry, Luke. I'm just so sorry,' she managed to whisper at the end of it all.

'The thing is, I've spent the last few days out in the nursing home with him, but I've known all along that I would have to come back and say all of this to Jane...'

'And you really think that her husband and your dad were brothers?'

'Half-brothers,' he corrected, 'but yes, I mean, even the photographs would be enough to convince you, but how many Manus Marchants do you think there could be knocking about Dublin running a pub with the same name as the pub my father grew up in back in London?'

'True.' Carrie smiled. 'You know, your father is right about one thing...'

'Please, I don't, I mean, I don't think I have any room for a bright side, at the moment,' he shook his head, then he felt something that might be a smile turn his lips upwards even though the last thing he felt was happy. 'Oh, go on so...' he said then, feeling her warmth infect him whether he wanted it to or not.

'Well, you'll have some family here, you'll have something like roots and it'll be something special for Jane,' her voice was soft, 'to have family to call her own.'

'I suppose it will, I hadn't really thought about that. This would make her my aunt.' And that seemed like a strange thing, to have an aunt here in Dublin, but in other ways, when he thought of Jane Marchant, somehow it seemed to fit perfectly.

'Come on.' She pulled him from the chair.

'What the...' his mug almost tumbled from his hand. 'I can't go over there now, not at this hour of the night.'

'Oh yes you bloody can and you must. I wouldn't waste one more moment before telling her. There's so much to be done...' Carrie's voice held an unmistakable happiness and, suddenly, Luke realised, that in the time he'd known her, he'd never seen her like this. For all the time they'd spent together, she had been nursing her own broken heart, quietly and stoically, but this quality, this upbeat woman, was a completely different person to the dutiful Carrie he'd thought her to be until now.

Before he quite knew what was happening, he was following her across the road, the little dog at their heels, pushing into The Marchant Inn and Jane Marchant had her arms around him while the whole story tumbled between them like a broken, faltering, half-finished saga that needed to find its happy ending.

'I can't quite believe it,' Jane said and she took down a photograph of Manus. They studied it hard, really seeing the family resemblance that before just seemed like an odd likeness, one of those quirky coincidences that litter relationships sporadically, but commonly enough not to notice. The bar was empty now, the only customers gone home for the evening, the doors closed on the Dublin evening outside; it felt as if they were all three of them cocooned in a world so far removed from the reality of the dark December beyond. 'I'd love to visit your father; do you think that would be all right?'

'It'd be more than all right, I'd say nothing would make him happier.'

'I can't quite believe that you're Manus's nephew,' Jane squeezed his hand again. It was just the two of them here now, Carrie had gone back reluctantly to the restaurant and promised to return as soon as she had closed up for the night. 'You know, he talked about his brother, often, they assumed that he had died, eventually, when he never came back. I think their mother believed that he'd gone off somewhere and perhaps been involved in an accident and...'

'It's something that's weighed heavily on my dad for most of his life. I never realised it, but since he's told me, I can see it's always been there, colouring out all his happiest moments as though there's always been something missing.'

'Yes, I can imagine how that would be,' Jane said sadly.

They sat until the early hours, drinking tea and with Jane sharing what she knew of Manus's life before she met him. Luke hung off her every word.

'The thing is, I'm not sure that his father was all that nice to Manus either, I think that when they came back here, it was as much to leave behind whatever kind of life he'd given them as it was to be back in the old country.'

'So, he died.'

'I'm really not sure. I think he may have taken up with someone else and left them to it, but whatever happened, they arrived here, took on this place and it was only years later, Manus managed to actually buy the place.'

'Perhaps if my father had stuck around...'

'Well, who knows? The main thing is, he's come back now.' Jane smiled. 'And we'll make sure that for as long as he's here he's going to feel he's come home.'

It was like looking at Manus, Jane thought when she first set eyes on Conn Gibson. He was older, of course, probably more than twenty years older than her Manus would be now. Even if he was still here, she suspected Manus would be taller, tougher, leaner – he had a harder set to him than this man who wore the signs of a trade much softer on his frame, but it was still there, the similarity, it was unmistakable.

It seemed to Jane that time stood still while carol singers, decked out gaily in red hats and scarves, young and old, filled up the corridors with rousing choruses of hymns she had not heard in years. She smiled happily as she listened to 'Good King Wenceslas' and 'O Come, All Ye Faithful,' through the open doorway. Luke invited the group in and as they listened to 'Silent Night'. They all swayed silently to its simple words, brought closer by amity and a Christmas spirit that had for years been elusive to her. It seemed as if Christmas had been missing from her life for far too long.

'It reminds me of Christmases years ago,' Jane said as she wiped a nostalgic tear from her eyes, but she was not sad. Rather, she felt at peace, as though somehow things were finally righting themselves.

'So, you were happily married to Manus,' Conn Gibson pulled himself up in the bed, his eyes inquisitive but full of warmth and welcome. She could feel the longing in him that she'd so often felt within herself, it was a deep need for connection, for people linked to you in some meaningful way; for family.

'Indeed,' she smiled fondly, 'we were married over forty years ago.' She held his hand, it seemed like neither of them wanted to let go, she moved in closer to hear his breathy words.

'I thought about him and my mother, always, but it seemed there was no place for me...' he took the mask.

'He felt the same, his father was a cruel man, perhaps you just experienced it before he did, but all the same, he was never sorry to be away from him. His mother though...'

'Yes,' Conn's voice held affection, 'she was lovely, quiet and kind, but...'

'They came back here, both of them together. She lived in the pub with us until she died. She never forgot you...'

'Ah, I'm not sure if that makes me feel better or worse.'

'It should make you feel better, even when she was dying, she insisted that we put the notice in the Irish and the English papers, just in case. Her grave is...' Jane stopped, she wasn't sure if she should talk about this now.

'Go on.' Conn tried to pull himself a little higher on his

pillows, but then Luke bent in and straightened him so he seemed to be a bigger, stronger man than before. He was more like Luke than she had realised at first.

'Well, she's buried in a large family plot, out in Glasnevin. At the time, Manus thought she had left room in case you were ever found... she thought you had passed away, that perhaps...'

'Ah,' he said simply and smiled as though she had answered some deep lingering question.

They sat for hours, catching up the time between the missing brothers, so she garnered what she could in some way shoring it up on Manus's behalf. Funny, but somehow it made her feel better, as if in the knowing it helped settle his memory in some more peaceful way.

Orange light danced low on the walls as the dinner ladies made their rounds, an aroma of cottage pie and squeaking trolley wheels heralding their arrival in advance. Luke offered to take Jane back to The Marchant Inn.

'You'll come again, soon?' Conn asked hopefully as she leaned in to embrace him before she went.

'I'd love to,' Jane said simply and thought the only sadness was that they had all found each other so late.

Christmas morning, and snow drifted against the kitchen window as Carrie drizzled a little extra fat across the sizzling turkey. Her garden was a perfect Christmas scene, even a robin came to rest on the fence as she held her breath and inhaled the mixed aroma of cooking lunch and heavily scented mulled spice candles she'd lit throughout the house. She realised that the memory alone of the last few years was wholly depressing. It had been a round of peeling and preparing, timing, serving and then cleaning. Each year, Kevin would exclaim it was his only day off and then he would proceed to act like a spoiled child because the bird wasn't just how he liked it. Of course, anything Carrie served up would never quite make the mark for Maureen Mulvey either. Secretly, she'd thought for some time that her own mother might have cried off the day, but she saw it as a way of supporting Carrie as she worked deep in enemy trenches.

Today, on this lovely snow-covered morning, Carrie felt much lighter than she had in years on Christmas morning. She would enjoy the day ahead. She had made up the two spare rooms and she was looking forward to having her mother and Jane here in her cosy little house. Under her Christmas tree there was a thoughtful gift for each of them, even Teddy had a bow tie and waistcoat to wear for their celebrations. She had every intention of drinking too much and falling into bed when she couldn't eat or drink another drop. She'd finally conceded and made a fresh tiramisu and chocolate pudding – they would enjoy a little of both before the day was out.

In the morning, Carrie and her mother rang all the relations they could think of to wish them a happy Christmas and Carrie thought of Maureen Mulvey. She hoped that her day would be happy too. It struck her that she could only wish the old girl well, since she was missing out on what was probably one of the nicest Christmas days Carrie had in years. She wondered, at one point, what Kevin would be doing today. Quickly she put him, his mother and the dreadful Valentina out of her mind; really, she was much too content to think about them today.

At around eight, with darkness enveloping the little house and all the curtains pulled tight against the snowy streets, her doorbell rang and she went to open it, not sure who to expect.

'Hey,' Luke Gibson stood, a little awkward, picked out in the narrow glow of the porch light. 'Now, I'm here... I...' and Carrie could see that suddenly he was a little shy. 'I just thought I'd wish you a happy Christmas.' He stood on her doorstep; unsure if he should have come at all.

'Oh, I thought you did that yesterday,' she laughed, the wine and Bailey's coffee had loosened her humour so she didn't feel the kind of fear that maybe she could say or do the wrong thing with him.

'Well, I suppose I did,' he laughed too, but he didn't sound as if he'd been helping himself to the drinks cabinet. 'I have something for you and...' he leaned forward and gently kissed her on her lips. He pulled a large shopper from the doorstep and looked apologetically, as though his gifts were some sort of guilty secret that he'd much prefer to hide. 'They're just tokens,' he dug out a parcel, wrapped in paper from the Dublin woollen mills, and handed it to her, 'a hat and scarf to keep you warm.'

'Aww, that's so nice…' Carrie said, touched by his thoughtfulness, because suddenly, it dawned on her, she couldn't remember the last time she'd got a gift from Kevin.

'Who is it?' her mother called from the sitting room, intrigued by her daughter's mysterious caller.

'It's…' Carrie shook her head. From the sitting room behind her came the unmistakable sound of laughter, both Pamela's and Janes'. 'You'd better come in or my mother will think I'm hiding you.'

'I heard that,' Pamela, two sheets to the wind, laughed. 'Ah, Carrie, bring him in here, he can have an Irish coffee to warm him up.' Her mother leaned ever closer to the end of the couch, craning her neck to get a look at Luke.

'Oh, God.' Carrie breathed. 'I suppose, you'd better come in and see the absolute pigs we've made of ourselves?' She laughed and Teddy yapped, happily delighted to welcome Luke.

'I've missed you too, buddy,' he said as he stood to shake out of his snow-covered jacket. 'I feel a bit underdressed,' Luke bent down to admire the little dog's dapper bow tie, fussing over him, Teddy was delighted.

'Don't, we're all a little the worse for wear, but it's been a lovely day,' Carrie said as she took his coat and hung it on the hall stand. She couldn't help but feel it's chunky softness and suddenly wondered what it would feel like to have his arms about her. 'How's Conn? Did he manage Christmas dinner?'

'We made the best of it. We even managed to get down

to the day room and pull a cracker or two.' Luke smiled at a memory made more precious because there was so little time to make many more.

Carrie placed a hand on his arm gently. 'I have a feeling we've already pulled most of our crackers, but there's plenty of food and drink, so…' She stopped, caught her breath while he held her hand and their eyes met, for one long lingering second that seemed to go on for much longer than it should. Carrie felt as if she'd tumbled into an unexpected place. She giggled nervously, saw the same apprehension in Luke's eyes, and pushed open the door to the sitting room.

They were a contented foursome, gathered around the little Victorian grate, sipping their drinks as, all around Dublin, families settled into their Christmas night films or games of charades. In Carrie's little house, it was a night for new beginnings and she very much liked the look of the chapter that was opening up before her eyes.

'So,' Luke said at almost midnight, 'I really should be getting back, any more of your hospitality and I'll be well over the limit,' he said, yawning as he pushed his way to the end of the chair.

'I'd say you already are?' Pamela was interested in everything about this new man in her daughter's life. 'Where is home?'

'I'm staying in a bed and breakfast at the moment, just until I figure out what I'm going to do next.' He smiled at Carrie.

'That sounds as if there are choices to make,' Pamela said.

'You could say that all right,' he sighed now, leaned back in the chair again; suddenly he looked tired, perhaps the exhaustion of the last few weeks finally catching up with him.

'His dad's really ill, Mum,' Carrie said softly, 'I don't think his choices are the kind you think.'

'Today he looked much brighter than he has in ages, I'm putting it down to Jane,' Luke said softly smiling at Jane who was sitting next to him. 'Actually, he was talking about you too,' he nodded over at Carrie.

'Oh?' Carrie was surprised.

'Yes, it seems that my *aunt*,' he emphasised the word, it was one he used carefully, as though he was trying it on for size and liking how it felt, 'my aunt mentioned that there might be a spare invite going for this posh wedding down in Sligo?'

'Oh, Jane,' Carrie covered her face, a mixture of embarrassment and amusement. 'Honestly, you'd think I was an old maid in need of fixing up.'

'Oh, no,' Luke said very slowly, catching her eye so there could be no mistaking his sincerity. 'No one is going to think you need anyone to get you a date, but I think she felt it might be nice to get my father to herself for a few days,' he shook his head fondly.

'Oh yes, and Teddy – I am hoping Teddy will stay with me,' Jane smiled as if she had accomplished something she'd set her heart on ages ago and Carrie suspected it had very little to do with Teddy.

'So,' Luke exhaled a long breath, sweeping aside any jokiness that went before. 'What about this wedding in

Sligo – have you asked anyone along yet?' He looked over at Pamela who held up her hands in the air, it was entirely up to Carrie.

'Would you really like to come along?' Carrie asked, trying to read the sincerity in his eyes.

'There's nothing I'd like more,' Luke said.

It was the right thing to do, Carrie knew that to insist on Luke staying with them for the night. How could she let him go back to a soulless bed and breakfast? He was happy to camp out on the sofa. Even so, when Teddy woke her early, she was surprised to see him standing in her kitchen, in his jeans and T-shirt, hair ruffled from sleep.

'I was just going to make some coffee and slip out for a walk before heading over to see Dad,' he said, handing her a cup. 'I can take Teddy as far as the park, if you'd like.' He smiled at her lazily.

'That would do him the world of good, walk off some of yesterday's dinner.' She smiled as she watched the little dog make his way around the garden, hoping to find an unsuspecting cat to pounce on. 'Actually,' she spotted the empty tiramisu dish and groaned, 'it probably wouldn't do me any harm to join you either.'

It was a crisp, fresh start to Boxing Day as Teddy ran excitedly ahead of them towards the nearby park. The only prints in the freshly fallen snow belonged to stray birds, who had landed fleetingly in search of crumbs and grubs before taking off again.

'Are you sure about coming to this wedding with me?' Carrie asked as they crunched along the path.

'Yes, I'm sure. I think Dad really wants to see the back of me, for a day or two. I've virtually moved into his room these last few days, so...' he shrugged. 'I think he wants to spend time with Jane, there are things he needs to say and I suspect he wants to learn as much as he can about her before it's too late.'

'Of course. Well, Coole Castle will be very different to Ballyglen,' Carrie laughed. Luke had admitted that even her couch had been more comfortable than the chair he'd slept in for the last few nights at the nursing home. 'You won't know yourself, living like a lord for a few days.'

'Carrie, I have a sense that as long as I'm with you, I'd be happy to dock down anywhere,' he said softly and he waited, just a beat, as if she might say something more, before turning her towards him and pulling her close to kiss her long and passionately on her lips.

'I...' she managed when they pulled apart.

'I'm sorry, I shouldn't have...' Luke said.

'No, it's me... it's okay, I...' Carrie was flustered; she wasn't sure what she felt. She really liked Luke, she wanted to kiss him, she knew that, but it was all so very soon. Or was it? 'I...' she reached out, wanted to kick herself when she saw the hurt and confusion in his eyes. 'It's early days, that's all, I'm a bit...' then she smiled and wrapped her arms around him. 'I'm out of practice, that's all,' she said and she reached up to his face, bringing his mouth close to hers once more. She kissed him back, slowly and it felt as if she was losing herself in the connection between them. For the first time in her life, something pulled within her, like a magnet drawing her to him. When she drew away, she looked into his eyes and she was glad she had kissed him. It was even sweeter, on this snowy morning that felt as if they were the only two people in this silent city.

Kevin didn't want to complain in front of Valentina, he knew it would only make things worse. She had arrived back from the skiing holiday in foul form. It was a bit rich, really since he'd been the one who'd been left behind. Christmas at his mother's house, just the two of them, talking about her gout over a too big turkey that he'd had to prepare and serve by himself was hardly his best Christmas ever. At the end of it all, his mother had sighed and said it was probably her imagination, but she could have sworn that Carrie made a better job of the turkey after all. Penny and her gang had mercifully cried off and headed to Italy, for a warm Christmas with the in-laws. The whole day, because that was all it was, just one day, had been among the most draining and miserable of his whole life or at least, his life since he'd met up with Carrie all those years ago.

He felt as though this wedding, this trip across the country was more a sufferance on Valentina's behalf than what he had hoped. God, he had intended this as a moment of triumph when they would be the perfect glittering couple to make his friends pea green with envy. Valentina had insisted on having several expensive beauty treatments before they left Dublin. He couldn't help but fret about the cost of all that pampering, but he bit his tongue as they hit the evening traffic at its busiest. They arrived later than he would have hoped on the evening before the wedding. The glamping site turned out to be a swampy caravan park in mid construction with a couple of glorified horse trailers with patchwork windows and circular doors on the end. Inside, they were twee and uncomfortable. Kevin had managed to get a single berth, so they would have to sleep toe to head just to fit in the narrow bunk.

'Eet is sheet,' Valentina said when they arrived. True enough it was a rough-and-ready destination and kids swarmed around the other trailer nearby. 'Glamping, pah! There is nothing glamorous about eet.' Kevin knew that passing by the castle on the way to the site had only made matters worse.

'Maybe tomorrow morning, we can go out for breakfast?' Kevin said in an attempt to mollify her. 'Somewhere nice, we could have the works, champagne...'

'Keveen, you know I don't eat breakfast. I can't face anything first thing in the morning.' She dug deep into her bag and pulled out a packet of French cigarettes, lighting up one she examined her expensive manicure. 'Anyway, I weell have too much to do if we are going to this wedding by one o'clock.' She sighed as if there was still a chance they may not actually bother going at all.

'You're beautiful without doing another thing with yourself.' *Or*, Kevin thought, *you would be, if only you'd smile like you did when I met you first.* But, he knew, that was unfair. Valentina would be the most beautiful woman at the wedding, he only hoped she'd also be the most gracious. 'I'll have to head off up for a little while, Ben asked if we could go through our paces beforehand and, to be fair, I don't even know where the church is.'

'Eet is in the castle.'

'Yes, but...' It was true, the church was tucked into the underground belly of the castle, but Ben was nervous, Kevin had heard it in his voice. Ben was one of those guys who'd always panicked unless he knew everything was doubled and triple-checked. He had insisted on hearing Kevin's speech a week earlier – so Kevin had read each word slowly over the phone, including thanks and jokes that Ben suggested. 'Anyway, he wants to run through my speech and all that as well, so...' Kevin would be glad to get out of the trailer for an hour. He couldn't face meeting anyone with Valentina in the kind of humour she was in now. The more he thought about it, he had no intention of going anywhere near the castle. He just needed to get out of her way. A little time away from Valentina; it would settle his nerves, it seemed now all they did was pick at each other.

He walked with a sense of limited freedom towards the castle, knowing that for an hour at least there would be no pressure, no one looking to take from him.

The route for the most part was through a sparse forest, the way signposted as a shortcut. Occasionally, in the darkness, through the trees he caught glimpses of twinkling lights shining out of mullion windows from the great looming castle in the distance. He'd never been a man for old buildings, never been sentimental about heritage and, certainly, any romantic notions of castles or weddings had never burdened his imagination. Tonight, here in the stillness of the woods with the snowy path picked out in the moonlight he thought he'd never felt such peace. This place, well, it was different. He could sense it, walking through the snow-carpeted woods alone. Passing by trees he could not name, he heard occasional falling leaves and picked up the scent of childhood he remembered from a time before he became the man he is today. Was he a better person then? Probably not, he had not changed that much, but he'd had time to hear the rustle of the world about him and, more importantly, he'd had time to appreciate it. What had happened, he wondered to change that? Maybe it was just getting older? Getting wiser.

He scratched his chin where unfamiliar stubble itched him slightly. He was getting maudlin; perhaps it was just this place, this day. When they'd talked about coming here, he and Carrie, it had seemed lifetimes away. Closing the restaurant, booking the room, the idea of spending two nights in the country away from the restaurant had somehow seemed like a remote possibility back then. Perhaps that's what it had remained. They'd never actually made it, him and Carrie. He hadn't imagined for a moment things would turn out like this.

Then, something else struck him. This day, this weekend, it would have been the ideal time to propose to her – not that he'd ever have gotten around to it. But now, he stood, looking at the strong turrets that had cast long fingery shadows upon this place for over four hundred years, and he knew for certain, that this would have been the time. All of their friends were married, they were literally the last pair standing, this would have been the time to take that final step. Kevin felt something stab at him, like a searing pain through his core. He knew what it was, even if he didn't want to put a name on it. Inside, deep inside, he knew that he was filled with emptiness and it wasn't just because he didn't love Valentina – he knew that, in this instant, he didn't love her, maybe he never had.

He loved Carrie. There. He said it. He knew it. He'd always known it. What had happened to them? No, that wasn't the question he needed to ask himself. The question was, what had he done to them? And it wasn't just how despicably he'd treated her with Valentina, it went back way further than that. He'd been a shit. He'd been a grade-A shit to Carrie from the start and she'd taken it. She'd let him take the credit for the success of the restaurant. She'd cleaned up after him, held his hand when he needed it and generally taken care of him, while he'd... What? What had he done for her in their years together? He'd loaded every single responsibility he had onto her, from looking after his mother to buying his socks. That's what he'd contributed to their relationship. On the few occasions they'd gone away, he'd left everything up to her. For Christmas, she cooked dinner for their families and made sure that each and every one had a gift that was special and thoughtful and wrapped beautifully. Carrie was the glue that held his world together, she made sure they kept up with friends, she remembered every birthday, every anniversary and every card she sent was from both of them. Kevin knew his contribution had been little more than a paid employee in their restaurant and an exacting spoiled guest in their home.

That was it. It pulled him up short when it hit him. He'd been a complete prat and, worse, he'd thrown away the best thing he had in life, maybe the best thing he'd ever have in life. And then he felt his legs almost go from under him. He stumbled back, two, three, four steps, until he stopped full and hard against a great mossy damp oak. Penny's words came back to him. All she'd said about his mother and father and Thelma Jones. He was making the exact mistake his father had made all those years ago. When she'd gone on and on about it, he knew she was telling him something, but of course Kevin was much too pompous to think that Penny might have something important to tell him. How could he not have seen it at the time, when now it became blindingly obvious as he leaned back, his head raised towards the treetops? He'd swapped Carrie, truly the love of his life, for Valentina, who would never make him happy. He had taken on a woman like his own mother, for whom nothing would ever be good enough and in that moment he swore, sick bile creeping up through him. What had he done?

Kevin Mulvey didn't know how long he leaned against that tree, but when he heard Carrie's voice travel through the forest he knew he smelled of sweat and his five o'clock shadow made him look as if he'd spent the night on the tear. He stepped behind a great oak and watched her walk along with a man he'd seen around Finch Street once or twice before. For a moment, he wondered if he was dreaming, as he watched them walk hand in hand talking and laughing happily. Carrie looked completely different. He knew it was a measure of how much she was no longer his. Only feet from them, he felt like a voyeur. His heart thundered fast in his chest, the terrible commotion in his stomach fought against his breath. They stopped to kiss before a flurry of glistening berried holly trees. Kevin held his breath, half-afraid that if he exhaled, the very sound might shatter their private bliss. This place had done something to him. The fact was, he had never felt clearer-headed in his life. The only words coursing through his brain as he had moved through the forest were; *please, let it not be too late.*

17

Truly, the view from her room was magnificent. Carrie always loved castles. She loved the history of this place, the idea that so many stories studded its walls, lifetimes, loves and losses all spun through its every fibre. It was the perfect place to capture the romance of a fairy tale wedding. If she'd wished for anything as a girl, it would have been a wedding like Melissa's. All of those dreams had vanished during the years she'd spent with Kevin. None of this was his scene; actually, she was a little surprised he was still willing to be best man and hadn't decided to open the restaurant for the two days instead.

Valentina, of course Valentina would have wanted to come here. Perhaps they would make it special for themselves. Carrie felt that familiar wrench of betrayal gnaw at her once more. It shouldn't come as a huge surprise if they announced their wedding date this weekend. Things had moved very fast between them already. Valentina was wearing a vulgar engagement ring the size of a muffin and it seemed Kevin was completely smitten. The night they told her, he just said, 'when you know, you know,' as if that covered everything and made it all right. Of course, it had devastated Carrie, but she wasn't going to think about that now. She would have to tell him about the accounts, the missing money and God... she shivered as she thought about it. She'd have to tell him she suspected Valentina was somehow involved and all of this as soon as they arrived back in Dublin, but that didn't mean it had to consume her for the next three days.

She pulled herself out of the drifting melancholy that still netted her when she was least expecting it. She was in the most romantic location she could imagine with one of the most handsome men she'd ever laid eyes on. Even if it was early days and she didn't know what lay ahead, she knew there was much to be thankful for. This was going to be a great weekend, Carrie decided, she would make sure it was and not let it slip by with some overemotional thoughts. She was going to make the absolute most of it.

She walked through to the grand sitting room where Luke stood lost in thought. He was standing inside the window, drinking in the view. She stood next to him, just a little closer than she would have before.

'Any complaints?' he was kidding, of course, everything was just perfect. He turned to her and took her in his arms, then lowered his voice, 'Could we ask for a more perfect setting for our first time?'

'Our first time?' she asked, an unfamiliar tingling feeling running through her.

'It could be...' Luke bent down to kiss her; she was still getting used to it – kissing someone who was not Kevin.

Luke's kiss was warm, searching, his arms pulling her towards him so she could feel the longing in him as much as she felt in herself.

'Would you think less of me if I...' now she was joking, but she reached up and traced her finger around that increasingly familiar mouth and knew that this was something they both wanted.

She wasn't sure later who wanted it more, but he pulled her close, carried her to the huge four-poster bed and when they'd finished making love, she knew that she'd never experienced anything close to such sublime happiness in her whole life.

'Let's take things at our own pace,' he said when they lay in each other's arms. Soon they would have to get dressed and go down to dinner with the friends Carrie had shared for years with Kevin. Part of her was dreading it. It would all be so different, but then she looked into Luke's eyes and she had a feeling that his easy manner would win them all over.

She needn't have worried. Everything about the place and the evening was lovely, an orange sun setting deep over the distant Atlantic; it bathed the restaurant in an amber glow and made the glasses and cutlery shine even more. Beneath them, the lawns, perfectly margined out between various gardens, swept towards the lake in a pristine snow-white carpet. Melissa was radiant and Carrie was so happy for her friend, she hugged her tight and knew with certainty that she and Ben would have the happiness they both deserved.

'This place, it's inspiring, don't you think, it feels like

anything could be possible here.' They had stepped out for a breath of icy air in the moonlit gardens. Luke ran his arms about her shoulders and held her close to him. 'It's not just that it's like a winter wonderland, it's something else...' he sighed contentedly. 'Mind you, we do have a lot to thank the weather for,' he said lazily.

'The weather?'

'Well, that night, if it wasn't for the snow, we might never have met.' He laughed then at that. It seemed so long ago, Carrie had almost put it from her mind.

'No, if it wasn't for Kevin, you wouldn't have met me!' She smiled and shook her head, it was good to laugh about it now, not that it didn't still hurt, but she knew that things were as they were meant to be. She had finally told him, when she lay in his arms earlier, what had driven her out to that doorstep, to smoke a cigarette in the driving rain and sleet. Now, she realised, it was no wonder her nerves had been rattled.

Dinner was lovely, not only was the food excellent, but it was nice to catch up with her friends. Best of all, they all liked Luke and he seemed to fit in from the moment he met them.

'Who's the dish?' Melissa whispered while they waited for their table.

'Oh, Luke?'

'Yes, I got his name, but where on earth did you meet him?'

'Through a mutual friend,' Luke butted in. 'We met through a mutual friend,' he smiled at Carrie and she knew she could elaborate or not after that. Of course, their mutual friend was Teddy – but that was something they could keep between themselves for now.

'So, this is your mystery man?' Jim said as he shook Luke's hand firmly. Soon they were talking about horse racing and who would win the big races the following day and both were in their element.

'No word from Kevin?' Anna asked as they sipped Irish coffees at the end of their meal.

'No, but they're here. We saw them earlier, probably just after arriving at the campsite.'

'The campsite?' Anna couldn't help laughing, she knew Kevin long enough to know that he would not like camping.

'Well, actually, they're glamping,' Carrie cut in, 'but when you meet Valentina, you'll probably laugh more, because it's even less up her street than it is Kevin's.'

'Wonder why they didn't come up for dinner?' Anna said.

'Maybe they're getting an early night, keeping the neighbours awake with their hot love-making?' They giggled at the notion of Kevin being in any way hot. Almost automatically, their gaze travelled to Luke.

'Now, there's hot.' Anna winked.

'Mmm...' Carrie said, but she couldn't help smiling when he met her eyes.

'You're a dark horse, I'll give you that,' Anna snorted.

'Seriously, Anna? He's way out of my league, that's if I'm even in a league anymore. And I have a feeling that he'll never settle in a place long enough to put down any real roots.'

'Maybe, but he's here, you're here, you're both adults. At least you can enjoy this weekend and you know...' she smiled then, one of those expressions on her face that had always irritated Carrie, as though she somehow knew more than everyone else. 'I have a feeling he's more ready to put down roots than you think.'

After dinner, they all walked down through the castle to the little church where the ceremony would take place the following day.

'It's really beautiful,' Carrie heard herself whisper to Melissa. And it was. The little chapel was just a simple room stretching beneath the castle's belly, with walls of bare stone and oak pews. It ran long enough for eight lines of pews, and a train of maroon red carpet swept up the centre aisle.

'You don't have to whisper, it's not a real church anymore, but it is beautiful,' Melissa agreed as they stood looking about. It was true, there were no religious pictures or crosses and the stained-glass windows high above them were elaborate but abstract in design. The only adornments were candles and flowers. The dais was a simple affair with ornate chairs for the bridal party, an altar for the ceremony and, off to the right, a pulpit hung loftily above the seats with steps carpeted and much less worn than the centre aisle. 'It's perfect, just what I've always dreamed of.'

'I'm so happy for you,' Carrie hugged Melissa with the warmth of best wishes, knowing that things were really falling into place for her friend.

'I wish…'

'What?' Carrie asked.

'I wish you were getting this chance at happiness too. I wish Kevin hadn't been such a prat,' Melissa said. 'It just didn't seem real before, you know, but you being here with Luke, well… he's lovely, but it all seems so strange.'

'Honestly, being this side of things, Melissa, I think Kevin did me a big favour.' Carrie knew that as she said the words, she actually meant them. 'And Luke, well, he is lovely, but nothing is set in stone, you know?'

'Really, you're glad it's over with Kevin?' Melissa had only ever known them as a couple and Carrie could understand why it was hard to take it all in. Although they were great friends, they had met through Kevin and Ben who had been friends since school. When Melissa and Ben had moved to Scotland, it was Carrie who kept in touch.

'Yes, and I know this is hard to believe, but I'm actually glad he has Valentina. I'm glad he's fallen in love.'

'I didn't think you liked her.'

'Well, that's true.' Carrie couldn't lie, what was the point? 'But I'm not engaged to her. Kevin is and he's completely smitten. It's changed him; I don't think he's as…' She searched for the word. 'As dependent anymore, that's it. Somehow, she's made him into more of a man, if that makes sense.'

'Absolutely, sure you had him spoiled rotten. You were all but putting him in a nappy going to bed to save him having to get up in the middle of the night.' Anna stuck her head in between them. 'Now he has to look after his own mother, at least.'

'You're probably right.' Carrie giggled, it was good to laugh now at her foolishness.

'Well, don't go doing the same with this one,' Melissa said.

'No, Luke isn't like that. It's never going to be like that with him.' Carrie fought hard to keep the wistfulness from her own voice.

'She's only with him for the sex, that's what she's saying,' Anna piped up. She really was incorrigible.

'Stop it, you're an awful woman, really,' Melissa said. 'Anyway, I think he's great.' They all looked across at him now, and as if he knew they were talking about him, Luke caught Carrie's eye for a moment too long.

'Christ, but if you let him slip through your fingers you're an awful fool,' Anna said before gulping back her drink.

The ceremony was due to start at one, but guests would be arriving from twelve onwards. Valentina could take hours to get ready, so Kevin tiptoed about her, handing her what she needed and making sure that she didn't get upset, that could add an extra hour to the time it would take to get to the castle. The stress of just being on time felt like he'd done a mini marathon before they even left the campsite. They just managed to make it on time for the first guests arriving.

'Eet is freezing here, Keveen, can't you ask them to turn

on the heating,' Valentina whined as she stood behind him while he welcomed friends he hadn't seen in years. 'Why don't you get a seat, it's bound to be warmer in the chapel.'

'No, I am not seeting there, I don't know these people, you can't expect me to seet there with these strangers.'

'Well, if we'd come up for dinner last night, then they wouldn't be strangers, would they?' He smiled at Ben who was standing opposite them. 'Maybe you should have worn some sort of coat?' It was true, she was hardly wearing any clothes at all. The dress she'd paid an obscene amount for was off the shoulder and dangerously low across her boobs. It slit sideward up most of her leg and had a slapper window across her tummy, showing her piercings as well as her washboard stomach. A couple of months ago, Kevin would have considered himself lucky to have her on his arm, now he felt that maybe she was just too obvious, trying a little too hard and missing by a mile. Her normally luscious hair was scraped up into an elaborate knot that ran over the back of her head and gleamed as though someone had dipped her in dark ink. He didn't like it. He thought, looking at her, that once she was done up with her elaborate make-up, she wouldn't look out of place on a carnival float in the Mardi Gras.

'Ah Luke, there you are, and Anna, you look just beautiful,' Ben said and then he turned towards Kevin, painfully aware that Valentina was hanging about them like a sore thumb. 'Maybe you'll bring Valentina in with you and you can sit together.' He pointed across at the sullen Valentina.

'Anna,' Kevin greeted Carrie's friend. He hadn't seen Anna in months and, if he was truthful, he wasn't sure how Anna would react to him today.

'Kevin.' She nodded towards him and then looked at Valentina. Kevin noticed how her eyes travelled over the woman he'd dumped her best friend for, but they didn't hold any anger or malice, instead he saw in them something close to triumph. Surely that couldn't be right, but perhaps it was; Anna was a very astute woman. People who underestimated her did so at their peril, far too often she had told Kevin exactly what was what and in so doing had knocked him off his comfortable pejorative little perch. 'So, this is the lovely Valentina,' Anna said neutrally and put her hand out to take her with them towards their seats. Then she looked back at Kevin, 'Honestly, Kevin, the least you could have done was forked out enough for a jacket for the poor girl, she's in real danger of a kidney infection in a dress like this.'

Kevin turned away, knowing Anna well enough that she would enjoy whatever his reaction was and he had no intention of biting at her bait today. Kevin didn't want to think about what they might be saying to each other in the quiet of the church. The last thing he wanted was for anyone to upset Valentina or he'd surely find himself driving her home before he even managed to make his speech.

'Where did he spring from?' Kevin asked Ben as they watched Luke walk towards their seat. Of course he recognised him from the previous evening, but all the same, actually seeing him here was a bit of a jolt. He had managed to convince himself that perhaps the man in the woods with Carrie wasn't quite so...

'Oh, that's Carrie's date, Luke.' Ben smiled, 'sound bloke, met him last night. You'll like him. They seem to be very content together.' He was still watching Luke, like an awestruck puppy. 'Everyone really liked him, he's not what you expect, at all.'

'How do you mean?' Kevin narrowed his eyes. Here, head on – well, he was just a little more... Kevin didn't want to put a word on it, but he knew, what it was, it was that feeling that Luke was in some way *more* than him.

'Oh, come on, Kevin, look at him. He's like he walked off a movie set, the kind of bloke you'd expect to be hanging about with all the beautiful people... but, like I say, he's just a sound bloke.'

'So, Kevin, you made it,' Jim strode up to them.

'Of course I made it,' Kevin said.

'Just saying, mate, Luke...' Ben cut in between them, perhaps sensing that Jim was trying to annoy Kevin.

'Oh, yeah. A good guy, not at all what you'd expect Carrie to pull out of the hat.'

'Why's that?' Kevin felt like this conversation was happening around him. He was an outsider while they admired the Adonis before them; even Valentina seemed to be hanging off his every breath. Kevin noticed her looking up into his eyes as though mesmerised.

'Well, he's just...' Ben had the good manners to look embarrassed.

'He's nothing like you, that's what he's trying to say,' Jim cut in with his usual lack of diplomacy. 'Look at him, sure he's a bloody…' he kept his voice low, 'I'd nearly fancy him myself, and you know how I feel about all that malarkey.' Jim was the most heterosexual male any of them knew. 'Sandra said all the women are in love with him. Seriously, it's not just that he's good-looking, he's on the level.' Jim shook his head, as though to distance himself from any possibility of being considered anything less of the kind of man he believed himself to be. 'Sure, the women love those clever types – doctors, engineers and archaeologists – they're the big winners on Tinder,' he coughed, 'or so they say.' Kevin didn't have to be the most perceptive to see that if it came to a beauty contest, Luke would beat him hands down, and he didn't want to hear that Jim thought he was a decent bloke. They both knew what Jim thought of Kevin – he could see clear through him.

From then on, Kevin tried hard not to stare at Luke. God knows, he said to himself, Valentina was doing enough of that for both of them. Somehow, Luke fascinated him. Kevin felt drawn to the man, as if there was something familiar about him, like they'd met before, not just here, but before, somewhere else, perhaps in the restaurant or in the street? Maybe it was because he was the new man in Carrie's life. Kevin wondered if Luke was responsible for the contentment that had washed through her of late. It was making her seem so much more confident, yes, much more desirable, these days.

The ceremony went off without a hitch. Kevin did what

he was meant to do. He stood like a prat at Ben's side and then passed on the rings when they were called for. Behind his back, he could hear an occasional muffled sob, but Kevin focussed on the job in hand. Everyone said the bride was beautiful, but Kevin only had eyes for Carrie. Across from him, Carrie looked amazing. It wasn't just the dress that seemed to shimmer like the night sky filled with stars, it was something more than just her trimmer figure and easy confidence. When she smiled across at him, it felt like he had a glimpse of heaven. His nerves were gone as long as she was here; his discomfort didn't matter to him anymore. Had she always made him feel like this? There was so much he'd taken for granted over the years and now he wondered if he'd ever really loved her when they were together, or indeed if he'd ever really seen her. He could see her now and he knew she was more beautiful than he'd ever realised.

As they stood there, on opposite sides of the altar, another thought struck him – it was one that came from nowhere and it unsettled him more than he'd have thought possible. He realised that standing here today, before their friends, this might have been them. They might have married in a ceremony just like this and made a day to remember for everyone and embarked on the happy future that until so recently seemed a sure bet. God, when he caught her eye, he felt like such a loser – and that wasn't at all how he'd expected to feel today.

The day whizzed by in a blur of photographs and smiles and, for the first time in years, Kevin's smile was genuine. Normally he hated weddings; with this one, he didn't want it to end. They travelled deep through the woods for the perfect photo album backdrop and posed for ages in the cold afternoon air, but it seemed like only a heartbeat to Kevin. Making their way back to the castle again, he sat beside Carrie, he could feel her arms icy beside him and went to reach around her to pull her close, forgetting for a moment that she wasn't his anymore.

'You're freezing, here,' he said, taking off his jacket. He'd never done that for her before and it seemed a little strange to do it now, but perhaps better late than never. Later, when he put it back on, he could smell the familiar scent of her perfume. It was funny, but he didn't even know the name of it, though she must have been wearing it for the last ten years.

When he went looking for Valentina he found her hanging off Luke. 'Well,' he said to the man he so wanted to dislike.

'Ah, you're back, is Carrie here too?' Luke asked in his deep gentle voice, then he smiled the kind of smile that told Kevin this man adored Carrie. He wouldn't be fool enough to fall for the likes of Valentina with her cheap shallow charm and throw aside a treasure like Carrie.

'Yeah, she's just nipped upstairs to fix up the bride,' Kevin said. He was in two minds as to whether he should stand and talk to Luke and Valentina or not. After all, there were plenty of people here he knew and he should be doing the rounds. He had a feeling that Valentina wouldn't mind being left on her own with Luke anyway. Kevin decided against leaving, but only because Valentina seemed to have had a glass of champagne too many and there was no knowing what she'd do or say. 'So, what do you do for a living Luke?' Perhaps he could trump him in terms of career success.

'I'm... well, I'm a historian,' Luke said. Kevin thought there was something shifty in the way he answered. He was surprised at how much he wanted to pick out a chink in this seemingly perfect man's armour.

'Luke has worked all over the world. It's a veery good job,' Valentina supplied sultrily while her eyes drilled into Luke. 'He has worked everywhere, in Paris...' she said dreamily. Kevin had a feeling that she harboured dreams of the Paris catwalks. She certainly spent enough time poring over them in her expensive magazines. 'Keveen, why can't we go to Paris, it sounds so romantic.' She touched Luke's arm, rubbed it gently, as though she was stroking a coveted coat.

'It's not at all romantic. The last time I was there it was dirty and...'

'That was twenty years ago, Kevin.' Carrie appeared at his elbow. 'It's very different now. You should take her, Kevin, Valentina would love it.'

'And so, you would live there now, would you?' Kevin asked Luke, suddenly the day had brightened up quite a bit. 'Permanently?'

'Maybe, if it suited everyone, but...'

'Are you okay Luke, not feeling too abandoned, I hope?' Carrie smiled at him.

'No, I'm fine. Valentina and Kevin are looking after me. Go do your thing and enjoy your day.' He smiled at her and Kevin envied him the genuine warmth he shared with Carrie.

They watched as she made her way around the room. Kevin could not take his eyes off her, and he knew, by comparison, Valentina was the booby prize. How could he have been so stupid?

When the drinks waiter came round again, Valentina took two glasses and Kevin commandeered one of them. 'Loads of time for that, Valentina,' he said with an unusual authority.

'Ah, Keveen, you are so stuffy, eetees a party,' she scowled at him, but smiled at Luke as though to include him in a game of pick on Kevin.

'No, it is a wedding and I have speeches to make and later, perhaps, you would like to dance with me.' He didn't add that it would be hard to do that, if he was picking her up off the floor.

It really was the most perfect day, Carrie thought as she stood sipping from her glass, looking out across the grand dance floor. The bride was radiant in a creamy lace creation that stretched across her pencil frame and covered her modestly from her neck right down to her ankles.

'You look like a character from *Downton Abbey*,' Anna giggled. 'One of the good ones – Lady Mary, or maybe even one of the princesses after the First World War.'

'You see… I told you so,' Carrie said triumphantly. She had been the one to suggest the bride go for accessories and hair that suited that post-war era. Melissa had a tiny frame and features that might look lost on a porcelain figurine. Everything about her was dainty and ladylike. 'Ben is the luckiest man in the world today.' She hugged her friend affectionately.

'Well, if he is, I'm certainly the luckiest girl in the world to have friends like you lot,' Melissa said. They looked down over the balcony to where Kevin sat examining his drink. Valentina had been carted off earlier, too drunk to stand much longer. 'He looks glum.' Melissa said.

'Funny, but this wedding hasn't turned out at all as I had thought it would,' Carrie said then, feeling just a little sorry for Kevin.

'No, I suspect it hasn't turned out as Kevin thought it would either.' Melissa said softly and Carrie wondered if perhaps he was finally beginning to see a different side to Valentina.

'Your speech went well,' Carrie said as they sat in deep velvet chairs in the private bar. The dancing had finished up at one and it took another hour for most of the guests to leave. The wedding couple and their friends had agreed to have a nightcap after the day was over and now, on their second, they were sprawled across the sofas regaling each other with stories and reliving some of the best moments of the day.

'Do you think? I was really nervous,' Kevin said.

'How is Valentina, shouldn't you go to her?' Carrie sipped the brandy that Luke put in front of her. It had been a fabulous day, they'd eaten lean and rare Irish venison, drank probably too much champagne and danced until Carrie's shoes had to be abandoned at the side of the grand dance floor.

'No, I'd say she's flat out. The fresh air on the walk back down to the campsite was the final straw,' he shook his head. He was beyond being embarrassed now, after all it was one thing to see your fiancé chasing round after your ex's boyfriend, it was quite another when she decided to impress him by doing a lap dance in front of all your friends.

'I'm sorry, Kevin.' Carrie meant it, even when she was at her lowest, she never wished anything bad on Kevin. Well, nothing worse than cold feet, erectile dysfunction or a good old-fashioned dose of the crabs!

'For what? You certainly didn't do anything wrong.' He sighed. 'No, this is my mess. From start to finish, it's all my own doing. I should never...' Kevin stopped himself as Luke squeezed in beside Carrie on the sofa. 'Anyway, it's water under the bridge now, too late to be thinking about...'

'It is never too late,' Luke said gently. 'You're not married to her yet, you can still...' he said misinterpreting the way Kevin's thoughts were running.

'I'm afraid, Luke, it's too late to do the right thing, for me at least.' Kevin looked meaningfully at Carrie and she caught a look of regret in his eyes.

'I think it's time I was off to bed. I don't work well on late nights.' Luke said and he kissed the top of her head lightly before he left them. Carrie knew he was trying to help her. He was giving her an opportunity to talk things through with Kevin.

'I'll be up soon, Luke.' She smiled at him. It felt strange, this act of verging on being a couple, and still it felt normal, perhaps because in some ways she felt closer to him than she ever did to Kevin. There was no sense that she had to walk on eggshells around him, instead there was a mutual loyalty and understanding that went much further than the old staid rhythm that she'd fallen into with Kevin.

'He knows, doesn't he?' Kevin said quietly when Luke made his way towards their room.

'What's that?'

'He knows how I still feel about you,' Kevin said in an unsteady voice that she'd never heard him use before. 'He knows that I made a mistake and that I'm more in love with you now than I've ever been before.'

'Don't be daft Kevin.' Carrie wasn't sure what to say. Kevin had never been one for throwing his emotions around too easily; certainly telling her he loved her was not a frequent event. 'You've had too much to drink.'

'Don't.' He closed his eyes. 'I've said it now, I'm more in love with you tonight than I ever realised I was when we were together. That's it. All our friends can see it and maybe now even Valentina knows it. Certainly, Luke knows it, but then he's already fallen in love with you, so it's not going to be anything strange to him.'

'And it is to you?' Carrie was interested, she thought they were in love for the decade together, but then these last few weeks, she had begun to learn that love was not all about giving, that sometimes love was so much more than that.

'I'm sorry, Carrie. I'm sorry for everything.' Tears filled his eyes and puffed up his face. Carrie could feel their friends watching them, but there was no stopping him now. Kevin seemed to be oblivious to the people around them. 'I'm sorry for how I treated you when we were together, for not appreciating you and not spoiling you. I'm sorry for all the times I took you for granted, but this weekend, the biggest thing I'm sorry for is not asking you to marry me.' He opened his eyes now and his gaze was steady and piercing. 'It dawned on me today, making my way through the woods, if I had anything to me at all, this is the weekend I should have proposed to you. Instead, you're here with someone else, and I've messed up so badly.' The tears were rolling down his face now, but he was not crying, his voice was low and empty, as though all hope was gone.

'Hey, mate, come on, get a grip on yourself.' Jim gave him an elbow in the ribs. 'If you want her back, that's not the way to go about it.' He smiled at Carrie and raised his eyes to heaven. Jim was too used to seeing Kevin drunk after just a pint or two.

'I should really be getting to bed,' Carrie said and caught Anna's eye on her way towards the stairs. She had to get out of here; it was all too much to take in. Kevin babbling like a baby, Valentina carted off to bed like a drunk. She didn't want to hurt Kevin and it was the knowledge of what lay ahead when they got back to the restaurant that was to blame for that leaden feeling within her. It weighed too heavily on her, even sharing it with Luke seemed like too much of a burden now that he had learned the truth of his father's condition. They were being robbed blind in the restaurant and even if she wanted to, Carrie couldn't bury her head in the sand – it would have to be met head on when they returned to Dublin.

Snow was falling heavily as Kevin made his way back to his bed that night. He hardly noticed. He was too depressed to care, too humiliated to feel anything much beyond numb emptiness. Instead, he trudged back along the damp path, made his way in as quietly as possible and drank the remainder of the milk from the carton in the fridge. Valentina never drank milk in her coffee, so it didn't matter, not that Kevin thought of that until after he'd put the empty carton back in the fridge.

He peeled off the monkey suit, hired for the weekend, and flung it over the back of a kitchen chair. Drained after the long and emotive day, he flopped into the bed beside the snoring Valentina. His sleep was deep and filled with uncertain dreams. In the morning, he would remember images of Carrie and Luke dancing together, making love, living the life he'd always thought would be his. These images hurtled through his dreams with a ferocity that he could hardly bear to contemplate the next day.

When he woke, his head hurt, but the emptiness inside him had nothing to do with drink and everything to do with the surety that he had chosen the same path as his father before him. He couldn't bear to look at Valentina now. She represented more than just his weakness. She represented his stupidity, his shallowness and, worse, the complete hollowness of the future stretching before him. He drank coffee, black and bitter, instant and hot enough to make him feel like it was burning into his very soul. It was hopeless; he knew that in the dewy early greyness of the morning. It was hopeless, he had chosen Valentina and let go of Carrie and now she had Luke.

Kevin went outside, cared little for the damp about him, the odour of the forest waking from its frosty sleep. He sat for almost an hour, oblivious to the time, until he heard the rustle of leaves in the trees above his head. The birds had woken early and now they welcomed this day the same as any other, and that was it, just another day to everyone else. He knew then he would have to get on with things. Would his life be a case of just going through the motions forever more? Is that what his father had done before him? Trundled along, propelled by his love for Thelma, surviving between their times together on the anticipation of their next meeting. It wasn't enough for Kevin, just meeting Carrie at work, watching her from afar. He couldn't live as a spectator while her life went on without him.

He went back inside the trailer. He would make another cup of coffee; it was reviving him at least. Maybe if he had a shower, things would look better. He checked his watch. In three hours, he would have to head to the castle for brunch before everyone set off back to normal life once more. Three hours would be enough to pull himself together, surely?

There was no getting away from it, Ballyglen would never be somewhere that Jane would want to call home. It was well run, clean and bright – it was obvious that there had been much thought put into making the rooms cheerful and festive, but it all came off as a covering over for the real business of the place. No, Jane was quite sure; she would not want to spend her final years in a place like this. She had been silly to be nervous on her first time to visit here with Luke, but it felt as if she was crossing some bridge that had long been closed off from her. She was reaching out, unexpectedly into the past and at the same time; it felt as if she was reaching towards her future. Her steps, taken tentatively along corridors that ran endlessly past matching, firmly closed doors, seemed to measure out her trepidation. The afternoon grey winter light did not penetrate these halls; it was the smell too, not a bad smell exactly. It wasn't like food past it's sell by date, or worse, rather, it was the heavy aroma of flowers that belonged to seasons past, forcing its way above the scent of living and dying.

In saying that, she wouldn't swap coming here to visit Conn for all the world. Her first visit, far from being awkward, had left her with a sense that she had found a touchstone. It resounded within her even when she returned to the pub, late into the night. Now, when she lay awake, she was not listening for out of kilter noises, but rather, her memory filled with every word that passed between them. Conn Gibson was, perhaps because he'd never settled anywhere for long, one of those people who carried within him a sense that he was already home. Jane felt it, as they spent time together, that she was returning to some place within her that was home too. It was unspoken, but she suspected that Conn felt the very same.

'I'm glad you convinced Luke to go to that wedding,' he confided in her. 'It gives us a chance to...' he pulled his breath in and she was grateful for every time he managed to inhale. Luke, when he was here, spent his time flapping about his father, not wanting him to waste a precious breath of life.

'To be honest, it didn't take very much convincing on my part. I have a feeling that he and Carrie are more fond of each other than either of them realises.'

'Still, it's nice, isn't it?'

'It is,' she agreed gently.

'I'd love to think that he found somewhere to call home and people to call his own, before I...' Conn said hoarsely and a flicker passed across his eyes. 'I have no right, I know to look for anything more now...' he shook his head smiling bravely. 'A year ago, all I'd wanted was to find my brother or his family and now here I am hoping for...'

'It's only natural,' Jane hushed him, 'to want the best for your children, I suppose.' She thought about Luke and Carrie. In an ideal world they'd fall in love and live happily ever after, but she wasn't sure that either of them was ready to see what was best for them. 'Well, you never know what's around the corner. If you wait around long enough, you might get the chance to match-make a little more,' she said smiling and they both laughed softly then.

In some ways, Jane felt that visiting Conn, was like being given a chance to spend a little extra time with Manus. He spoke with the same soft inflection. Although his accent was less local, there was no missing that same hint of diluted London, with a dash of everywhere but a body of Irish. It marked out not just his voice, but his words too, so Jane found herself picking out phrases that she hadn't heard in years.

'You're smiling,' he said when he'd finished telling her a story about his time spent in Northern France.

'It's just I'm so glad that we managed to find each other, it feels like a chance to make some more connection with Manus.'

'Are we really that alike?'

'More than I can put into words.' Then she thought for a moment, 'I think that's what struck me about Luke, even though I couldn't have explained it at first if I tried. I just saw him in the distance. Actually, when I think back, I could hardly make him out, but I felt as if he was rooting for me. I was being carried off on that stretcher and, in some funny way, it seemed as if we had connected and I wasn't quite so alone as before.'

It was still early in the afternoon when the taxi collected her to bring her back to The Marchant Inn and Teddy. Were it not for the little dog, she might have stayed in the nursing home all evening. But she could see that Conn was tired, no matter how much he wanted her to stay, she had a feeling that the nurses were glad to see her to the door so they could get on with the business of readying him for the night. Teddy had a warm welcome for her at least, even if Finch Street felt emptier now, with the restaurant opposite closed up while Carrie was down in Sligo.

Jane made her way through the bar, she hadn't opened for business after dinnertime in a decade – her trade was afternoon, accidental customers who called more for a chat than anything else. Pamela Nolan promised to call in the following evening, but for tonight, Jane would have to make do with Teddy and the television for company.

18

Luke and Carrie were walking back through the woods, the light fading fast, making the trees appear velvety, as if they'd been drawn by shaky hands on a perfect stage set. Ben and Melissa had headed off an hour earlier, in a flurry of excitement for a honeymoon that would only last a week but cost a fortune. They were madly in love and Luke wondered if perhaps there was something catching in the air as he held Carrie's eye when they waved them off.

'It's been the most amazing place to stay, hasn't it?' Carrie said, still drinking in the beauty of the snowy woods around them.

'Thanks for bringing me along,' Luke said, pocketing his hands deeper into his jacket. 'We probably should have brought more clothes though,' he laughed then and wrapped his arm about Carrie's shoulder. It felt good to draw her near. Everything about being with her was good and Luke knew that this was influencing his future plans far more than he'd ever have expected. There had been women before Carrie, those who'd filled months at a time and one who'd taken up almost two years, but nothing had ever felt like this. Carrie was like coming home – it was that simple and yet, for Luke, it was that profound. The buzz of his mobile sounded tinny and unwelcome in his pocket. He looked at Carrie, it seemed a shame to break up this peacefulness by taking a call, but since only a handful of people had this mobile number, there really wasn't much of a choice.

'Hello, it's Breege Daly here, I'm the matron at...'

'Of course,' Luke remembered the woman who had inadvertently broken the most terrible news to him only a short time ago. 'How are you, Matron? Is everything all right with my father?'

'I'm sorry, but I think you should come, straight away, he's had a turn...' she faltered in that way that people do when there is bad news but they hope you'll stitch together their silences, saving the work of putting your worst fears into words. 'He was fine earlier, sitting up in bed, chatting away to his friend... Of course, it can happen like that... a real brightness and then...'

'He's dying?' Luke said in an automatic way that didn't really register with him.

'I'm sorry, but yes, I think he might be. Can you come quickly?'

'I'm in Sligo...' he said, but, of course, he knew the business-like matron couldn't postpone things at her end just because he found himself at the furthest corner of the country.

'Well, can you make your way here as fast as possible?' Urgency stretched out the silence between them cruelly.

'Of course, we'll set off straight away.' Luke said and

next to him, Carrie was already picking up their walking pace so they could pack up and get on the road without wasting any time.

Luke wasn't really aware of the journey back to Dublin. It was a two-hour blur of green darkening into ephemeral navy and then, too soon, to dismal grey-black. He hardly noticed driving through the tall pillars of Ballyglen or up the long narrow drive that usually irritated him with its promise of expanse that most of the residents only saw as they made their way in to the place.

Carrie pulled her car into a parking spot reserved for staff and Luke had a feeling that no one was going to tackle either of them. The corridors, normally deeply burdened with a heavy scent of something that might masquerade as lavender or vanilla on the label, tonight just smelled of frigid dread. Luke had a feeling that this was always here, kept neatly at the edges, like turned-in sheets that dare not break their ironed configuration. His father's room was at the end of one of those many endless corridors – whose attempt at homeliness stretched to gaudy watercolours but fell far short of anything beyond functional relief. Pushing the door open, Luke felt the kind of trepidation he remembered from somewhere in his childhood, although he couldn't put a finger on what could have brought up such a mixture of love, fear and grief in him before.

'Ah, you made it...' the matron turned to look at him from taking his father's pulse. She lay Conn's hand gently over the bedcovers and needlessly tucked the blankets close about him.

'Dad...' Luke whispered and he realised that if he didn't know that this was his father, he would have questioned if it wasn't some cruel joke and someone hadn't replaced his dad with a shell that might vaguely resemble the man he'd known all his life. 'Dad, can you hear me?' he asked softly.

'He's had a lot of medication, the pain, you see...' the matron was whispering to Carrie, 'he may hear you, but it's unlikely he'll be able to speak to you. Earlier, he raised a smile, so...'

'He's not in any pain now?' Luke asked.

'No. He's just sleeping peacefully, but... without the medication, well, it would be unbearable, so...' She nodded towards a drip that stood to attention over his father, like a drill sergeant. 'If you weren't here, I'd stay with him all night, but...'

'We'll stay...' Carrie said softly, sitting on a chair in a darkened corner of the room where the light could not reach to pick out the shadows or the heavy overhanging grief that pushed in uninvited.

'Can I get you something? Tea or maybe something light to eat, if you've driven all the way from Sligo...' the matron was saying, but this was not a time for food or drink.

'Maybe I could use a bathroom,' Carrie asked and she followed the matron out of the room, as much, Luke figured, to give him time alone as for any other reason. In the hallway he heard the matron say it would not be long, Mr Gibson had no more than hours, it was a miracle that he'd held on this long.

Luke dropped down beside his father, rested his head across that shrunken chest, he listened for that faintest heartbeat moving featherlike within; precious, brief and inadequate.

'Oh, Dad,' he whispered, there was so very much to say, but Luke had a feeling that he was drifting away, a diaphanous sheet upon a timeless plain. He imagined him wandering across the Phoenix Park, watching the herds of deer and then drifting out into the ether – content and happy that his life had somehow brought him back so he could repose with the family that he'd always felt he missed.

By the time Carrie arrived back, he was gone, it was one long contented sigh and then his quivering heart was at rest. She put her arms around Luke and rather than feeling overwhelmed with grief, the inevitable sadness that he felt was textured with something else, and when he looked down at his father's face, he had a feeling that the old man was smiling at him. He had brought him here, to Dublin, to The Marchant Inn, to Jane, and maybe even to Carrie.

It was after eleven when Jane heard an almighty crash downstairs in the bar. There was no mistaking it, someone was moving about, grubbing, searching, emptying. Teddy, at her feet, began to growl, low and constant, as if he was content to lie in wait but wouldn't leave her side, no matter what. Jane placed a hand on his head and shushed him, she was glad he was staying with her tonight, but, she thought, better to keep as still as possible. All the same, Jane thought her heart might explode in her chest from fear. It battered firm and fast as though it might break out if it got a chance. She placed her hand on it to feel it thunder beneath her clothes, then she realised her fingers wrapped around the cool chain on her alarm. She pressed it hard, kept her fingers on it, so she wondered if she mightn't have broken it. She took a deep breath, she couldn't think like that. They would send an ambulance, but it didn't matter. She didn't care who they sent, so long as someone knocked at the front door and broke it down if they had to, to get to her.

Now, it felt like the whole city had fallen into an incubated silence, as if Dublin was holding its breath with her, even the noises downstairs stopped. Jane could almost convince herself that it had been her imagination; that her mind, vivid and normally on edge once darkness fell, had finally fooled her into believing that they'd come back. That was silly, of course, the men who'd broken in here fifteen years earlier were well gone. The police told her at the time that they'd taken off to England and that was the last anyone would see of them. They had done the unspeakable and they would never come back here, even Jane knew that.

Mentally, Jane began to go through what the men might take from the bar, it seemed to her that the more they could take, the longer it would keep them downstairs and that gave her more time. There were a few unopened bottles of spirits, a pittance in the till and, of course, the old-fashioned cabinet where she kept tobacco and cigarettes. That was something that would take time to empty and its contents would be worth stealing. Even if they sold it all on for half price, there was still a couple of thousand euro of stock there.

She wondered if she should hide, but apart from the fact that she wasn't confident she had the courage to move, there was also the risk that if she made a noise, they might come bounding up the stairs all the sooner. The only thing she could do was to place the pendant underneath her, then at least if they did find her, they would not know that she had already called for help.

Then she heard it, an ominous, creaking noise that sounded too loud to be real. It was unmistakable though, the door that led from the bar to the bottom of the stairs. It opened with a ferocious creaking slowness, as if a child had pulled the handle back to reveal a fairyland beyond. The heavy steps that loped two or three at a time towards her told Jane these were no children. Teddy, at her feet, snarled more viciously with each tread on the stairs. Jane pulled his head closer to her; she couldn't bear it if they hurt him just to keep him quiet. The sitting room door heaved open with a sigh of relief, as though it expected more. And then, Jane felt the blood drop from her head, right down to the soles of her feet. Two men, both obscenely big and brutish, it seemed to her at least, stood at the doorway. They filled it up, as though their very intentions were too malicious to be held within their frames. The first, stalking into the room, cast narrow eyes about, taking in what might be valuable to him. Of course, he didn't count her or the years of memories that filled this room as having any real value in the terms he measured it. The second, it seemed to Jane, even bigger, thuggish, didn't have such an assessing stare, but he had a rough blankness about him, so she had a feeling her life would not weigh heavily on his conscience.

'You, old lady, where is the safe?' the broader of the two was foreign, hard, and his black eyes were unforgiving. Even his tattoos made her scared, but then she thought about Luke and the men who called here one day while she was still in hospital – these two fitted everything Luke had told her about them.

'There's nothing here, but look...' On any given day, the takings were small, but Jane hadn't opened the bar in days, so there was nothing. She moved towards the old safe that stood beneath a fringed cloth and acted more as a side table than anything else. She kept it open, afraid now that if she locked it, there was always the chance that she'd forget where she'd left the old-fashioned key. 'Here, this is where I used to keep any takings, but there is nothing here, the bar's been closed since before Christmas,' she said. But they weren't listening to her, instead, the slighter of the two was reaching into the back of the safe, pulling out certificates and deeds that had been left there.

'Pah, there is nothing here,' he said, stretching over her.

'My purse,' Jane said, pointing towards her bag on the door hook behind them. One of them pulled it down while the other began to pull apart the contents of the old sideboard. Jane fell back in the chair. Teddy's collar slipped from her hands, but he stood resolutely at her feet, a line of defence shielding her from harm. She should make her way towards the door, she knew that, she should try to get out of here, but she had a feeling there was no point. These men would not just let her walk away. In the distance, she thought she heard the wail of a siren, but the two men were far too busy to notice. She put it from her mind, she needed to stay calm.

'There must be more here than just this,' the stockier man said now. 'Old lady, it would not be smart to hide or make the fools of us,' the man laughed, but there was nothing funny about his eyes.

'No. No, I haven't anything more, really. You can pull the place apart all you want, but you won't find anything more.' She shook her head and hated that her voice sounded so frail.

'Come on, Simo,' the thinner man said, making his way towards the narrow stairs that led to the top floor and rooms that Jane never used anymore.

She heard them thunder upwards, knew that now was her chance to make her way towards the front door. She slipped silently from her chair, moved softly towards the door and pulled it gently behind her, turning over the lock with a whispery click. At her side, Teddy moved silently too and, for a moment, they might have been in cahoots in some childish game, apart from the devouring fear tightening within her chest. She held on to the stair rail steadfastly and she made her way as quickly as she could down the stairs. As she crossed through the bar, she thought her heart pounding so hard in her chest felt as if it was loud enough to alert the whole city, never mind the two upstairs. Shattered glass lay beneath the door that had been their entry, she realised it had been easy, she had just left the key in the lock, an invitation sitting there all this time.

She pulled at the locks on the door, realising too late that they'd thrown them over and taken the keys with them. She was locked inside, part of her wanted to run to a corner and fall into a crying heap, cover her eyes and wait until this was all over, but she knew that would do no good. She would have to go back upstairs again. The two men would quickly break through the locked door upstairs and then she had a feeling that they would be even nastier. Too late, she heard them push against the door; it was as though they were throwing their huge weights at it.

Outside, not so far off, she heard the wail of sirens in the distance; help was coming, if it would only get here before they made it down the stairs. She rattled the front doors once more, knew it was useless. Perhaps if she went around the back, but it was just a closed-in yard, there was no way out of there. Still, if she was out of their way, the men might just decide to head out into the night. She opened the back door to a blast of icy air, but it did not matter. Out here, it sounded like the silent Dublin she remembered as a child. Now, surely, all she had to do was wait...

★

Luke was adamant, he needed to go and tell Jane. It did not matter that it was the middle of the night, he told Carrie, she would want to know. They spent what must have been hours at the nursing home, but it seemed to Carrie it was a timeless spell; such was the unreal quality of it all. It was hard to believe, only three short days ago, they'd spent Christmas night in her little sitting room, sipping drinks before a roaring fire. The funeral would be sorted out the next day, or even the day after, but the formalities of death and, more importantly, the formalities of death in Ballyglen could not be put off. Forms were signed, condolences given and the doctor arrived to call what they already knew and sign it off without delay.

'Anyway, I have nowhere to stay, remember. I've checked out of the bed and breakfast until tomorrow.' He smiled at Carrie and she knew Jane would not mind what time they called, especially with news of Conn having passed away.

'Well, we wouldn't see you without a bed,' Carrie said gently and he squeezed her hand, an unspoken sentiment passing between them. She wasn't sure if it was gratitude or fondness, but at this moment, it didn't matter either way.

Carrie had an ominous feeling as she was about to turn onto Finch Street. They'd heard the sirens in the distance, but everything about tonight was unreal, so it never registered that they might be here. Finch Street was a sea of wavering blue lights, two fire brigades lit up the buildings with their blue hue, intermittently meeting each other on the familiar buildings either side.

'It's Jane's – The Marchant Inn is on fire,' Luke breathed and Carrie pulled the car in where she could. The road was blocked off with police tape; an eager-looking youngster in uniform stood on high alert for nosey parkers who turned out no matter what the time. 'That's my aunt's pub, is she there? Is she...' Carrie heard the panic in Luke's voice.

'Your aunt?' the guard shouted above the din of sirens and then registered the worry on their faces. He pulled back the barrier and led them closer to the bar.

'What happened?' Carrie asked.

'We're not sure,' an older man turned to her. 'We got a call from a private alarm company, they had an alert, but by the time we arrived, the fire had already started and...'

'Could it have been a burglary?' Carrie asked.

'It's possible, even from here, you see one of the doors has been shattered, but we couldn't get close until the fire brigade arrived. Why?'

'We were broken into too... a while back, but...' Carrie said and then she pointed towards The Sea Pear, 'I own the restaurant across the road.'

'Right,' the detective said and he wrote something in his notebook. 'Anyway, we arrived and we were going to carry out a search of the building, but then one of the locals said that the old lady who lives there had closed up for Christmas and gone away for the holiday...'

'Oh, no.' Luke groaned, a low visceral sound that resonated with dread and terror in equal measure.

'She could still be in there?' the officer whispered

emptily and Carrie could read a million different stories fade across his eyes as he cast them towards The Marchant Inn. 'The fire-fighters took a quick look round, but they didn't see anyone... the doors had been left open, so it's possible that whoever was in left before the flames took off,' he shook his head. 'There's no other way out, only...'

'There's a rear door, it goes out to an enclosed courtyard,' Luke said. 'My aunt, she's still in there?' his voice was a reedy echo.

'Oh dear God...' Carrie had the most terrible thought. 'Do you think that she's trapped?'

'No,' Luke said, but his voice was steel and the next thing Carrie knew, he was running towards The Marchant Inn, breaking past the fire-fighters, hurtling through the open doors and disappearing inside. Carrie felt her whole body dilute, as if some measure of herself had been watered down and stripped away. It was too much to take in, Conn passing away, The Marchant Inn in flames, perhaps Jane still in there and Teddy...

She couldn't think about what was happening, then she felt the strong arms of a policeman beside her, holding her back, making sure she didn't leave the path. It seemed that the flames were licking harder against the upstairs windows, inside the bar itself, an occasional crash of fracturing glass, but the fire was only just rooting its way down, rather it seemed to prefer to dance about the upper rooms.

'Can it hold?' she whispered, thinking of the ancient beams that ran across the bar ceilings.

'It's not the fire that's the danger at this stage...'

the officer breathed the words into her hair and, of course, she knew, that once that back door was opened, the air would only act as a fan, feeding the flames to make them fatter and greedier than before. Surely Luke would know that, surely he'd remember the basics of keeping safe. But then, Carrie realised, he'd just run into a burning building without so much as thinking of his own safety.

It seemed the seconds drew out like some extended terrible symphony, playing an opus that would only end in tragedy. Carrie covered her eyes; she couldn't watch the fire anymore. She couldn't witness the thwarted efforts of the hoses, like futile fingers on a burning pyre. And then she heard a roar from the scene before her, it was louder than she would have believed possible among the other emergency sounds. Surely it was too late, but she felt herself propelled along the path, the officer behind her, half carrying her, half pulling her along until they drew up to a stop and she felt her hands being lifted from her eyes. In the distance she saw him stumble, run and falter, he'd cleared the door and made it to the path, and in his arms a tiny, balled-up bundle, at his feet, running, yapping, smoky, Teddy looked worse than he did on that first night. When he dropped to the path, it felt to Carrie as though the city shook like thunder and she ran towards them, half-afraid to reach their sides.

'Oh thank God,' she heard herself say over and over.

'We're okay, we're okay,' was all Luke managed to say, but when he found her eyes amongst the earnest faces, something in them connected and they both knew that there was a lot more saved tonight than just two people and a dog from a burning building.

Kevin woke the following morning to the sound of Valentina's quickened shouts on the phone in Colombian. He knew, even before she mentioned it, that something was up with Simo and Reda.

'They have nowhere else to go, Keveen, do you want my cousins sleeping on the streets.' Valentina was pleading and it was hard to say no to her like this, but Kevin didn't want his lovely apartment turned into a doss house.

'Valentina, there's an agreement in the lease I signed. We can't have them here for—'

'You, you have no humanity, Keveen. You know what their landlord is like, they should sue him, probably, but in this country only rich people can get any justice.' Valentina threw her hands up in the air and Kevin thought she looked like a fishwife in a dress too expensive to allow her a position on the socialist side of any argument.

'Maybe, but the same applies to Simo and Reda; if they broke their tenancy agreement, then the landlord has every right to turf them out.'

'They are my cousins, Keveen. If they are sleeping on the street, how can I sleep in the comfortable bed here with you?' she pouted at him and he knew he'd have to give in, a little anyway.

'Tell them they can stay for two nights, then they need to move on, because, Valentina, I'm serious when I say they can't move in here.' Even as he said the words, Kevin was regretting it. He couldn't live with Simo and Reda. If he was honest, it wasn't just that they made him feel like an outsider in his own home, it was more that they scared him. There was no particular reason. They never actually threatened him, he never saw them lash out or even lose their tempers. It was more than that, something deeper, something feral. They were dangerous men, and no matter that they didn't flaunt it, they could never truly hide it either.

'They will be so happy. Can I tell them a week?' Valentina wheedled and he knew he might as well be hung for a sheep as a lamb. For the next week, he would be at work more than at home anyway; these days he virtually lived in The Sea Pear. He'd hardly see them if he left early and returned late. Simo and Reda had a habit of playing Xbox games until the early hours of the morning, but the truth was, he could let a bomb off in the kitchen behind them and the only thing they were likely to say was 'pass us a beer, Kevin'.

Still, he hated having them around. He wasn't sure which was worse, Valentina being in a strop with him because he wouldn't let them stay or feeling like an unwanted guest in his own home, such was their formidable presence.

Far from providing solace, as he made his way to Finch Street later in the morning, Kevin had a feeling The Sea Pear would just feel empty without Carrie. Once, she spent every spare moment between the restaurant, the house or his mother's. These days it seemed her life was too hectic to turn up for much more than her shift, and then Kevin was too busy working in the kitchen to see much of her at all. With the place closed during the day, being here without her felt as if he was missing something from himself. It wasn't that they even spoke to each other properly anymore. They hadn't done that for a very long time. It was both more intangible and perversely profound than that. True, their relationship had for quite some time faded into something that was no longer passionate or vibrant, but it had matured into a penetrating embrace that fed both Kevin's creative soul and shallow neediness. Carrie was more than a partner. She had become a nurturer, a protector. He could count on her for everything and he missed her. There, he could admit it, silently to himself; he needed her. He longed for their lovely little house and how she would talk to him; she had always encouraged and empowered him. He craved the safety of having her in his life and he ached when he remembered her familiar reassuring smile.

As if she knew that he was thinking of her, his phone rang just as he was driving past the canal on his way to Finch Street. He answered with an unfamiliar optimism, glad to hear her voice, no matter why she rang. *A fire, Luke, the old dear across the road*, the words ran into each other and then he caught the last few sentences. *A break-in, lucky Jane Marchant wasn't killed,* and somehow, for no reason he could name, Kevin knew his foolishness was coming back to eat him whole.

'Do they know who broke in? Is it connected to The

Sea Pear?' Kevin felt like a penny was dropping through a complex slot system in his brain and it made him cold in a way he couldn't describe. He turned onto Finch Street, slowly, taking in the damage to The Marchant Inn.

'Well, they don't know yet, it's a bit of a coincidence, isn't it, but...' she laughed then, a hollow empty sound to his ears. 'We were probably lucky that they broke in to The Sea Pear when we weren't about. The police have descriptions, so it's only a matter of the police tracking them down now,' Carrie said.

He was sitting in his car in front of the restaurant and looked across at the charred remains of the bar opposite – is this what they had come to? Him, feeling like he was outside the action of his own life and Carrie dating Superman?

'And?' Kevin heard the word, buried silently in that nervous sentence, but it was the only word that cut through all he saw before him. There was something she wasn't telling him, he knew it and it wasn't good.

'Oh, Kevin, there is something else, but not on the phone, it's not the time to tell you.' Carrie's voice had dipped to somewhere he had never heard it go before.

'It's about Valentina, isn't it?' Of course he knew it, how could he not.

'I think – that is, I know, she's robbing us blind, Kevin.' It sounded as if she pushed the words out. She had every right to scream and shout and hate him, but somehow, it felt even worse that all he could hear was her pity for him. 'For weeks, she has been taking money from the nightly cash-up, it's why...'

'It's why you've insisted on staying on or turning up last thing at night,' he could see it all now so clearly. Valentina hadn't just taken him for a fool, she'd been stealing from the restaurant too. It was funny, but hearing it, this sounded far more personal than just running up bills on his credit card. 'How much?'

'It's hard to say, obviously she couldn't take any credit card payments and they make up a big part of the takings, but it could be thousands.' She sighed, 'The accountants are working their way through it. We'll have a better idea in a few days' time. Kevin, we're going to have to do something about it…'

'The police?' It was the only way. Things with Valentina had got out of hand long before this; today was just about facing up to it.

'I'm so sorry, Kevin.' The words echoed in his mind long after he hung up the phone. 'We'll talk later, I'll make an appointment with the accountants, we can go through it all there and then we'll figure what's best to do next.'

Kevin pushed open the door of The Sea Pear, knowing he must shake these thoughts from his mind. He would have a cup of coffee; get things straight in his head. He must have been sitting there for an hour. He needed to brace himself for the storm ahead. Then something occurred to him, he had not asked if Jane Marchant was okay. It was like the opening of a dam, because suddenly he realised just how wrapped up he'd always been and how great the gulf had spread between himself and Carrie. The tears that flowed from his eyes were the first genuine outpouring of regret he'd experienced in years.

19

There was a funeral to be organised, but it would be a simple affair. A few brief words, non-religious, perhaps a piece of music from Chopin and then Conn would be buried alongside his mother. It would be a homecoming and so it felt as if, when they were making the arrangements, they were making things right, rather than saying goodbye. Luke knew his father wanted him to take care of Jane. Her hospital room was not unpleasant, they'd given her a private room and the nurses came and went quietly, so Luke managed to fall asleep for an hour or two.

'We were lucky,' Luke said when Jane woke, and of course, they were. They'd escaped without a scratch, apart from smoke inhalation and shock. They were lucky, the paramedics had brought Jane to the hospital for assessment because of her age as much as any fear of injury.

'You're very humble. I wouldn't be here if it wasn't for you. They'd never have realised that I was locked outside.' She smiled at Carrie, 'I think luck didn't have half as much to do with it as your mad-hat bravery, Luke.'

'You were amazing, I still can't believe you ran into a burning building.' Carrie shook her head, 'Even if I wanted to murder you for being so daft,' she nudged him affectionately.

'I didn't really think about it, I was in there, rattling at the lock, before I'd realised what I'd done,' he said modestly. 'Teddy was the one who kept you safe, barking away like a distress signal; I couldn't have missed you if I tried.' The little dog was a hero, but he was just happy to get back to his comfortable bed in Carrie's kitchen and sleep off the drama of the night.

'Well, it was very brave, all the same, and if it weren't for you and Teddy...' Jane whispered and it was only in her voice that there was really a residue of the night before.

'I can't believe that they'd do that,' Carrie said, fixing a stray strand of Jane's hair that was intent on falling forward. 'I mean, surely it was enough to break into the place, setting a fire and leaving you there, they must have realised...' she shivered, although the room was not cold.

'Anyway, it doesn't matter, the important thing now is that we're all okay and they'll be sending you home before you know it,' Luke said brightly.

'Home,' Jane smiled sadly. 'I don't suppose The Marchant Inn will ever be home again.'

'It's really not so bad,' Carrie said gently. For all the flames, the bar was hardly damaged at all. 'Upstairs is a bit of a mess all right, but...' Everything would smell of smoke, probably all her clothes and any soft furnishings were for the dump, but there would be insurance, these things were not the end of the world.

'We'll have it right as rain before you know it,' Luke said.

'We will?' Jane asked.

'Of course we will,' Luke said softly. 'I'm staying in Dublin, after Dad is... well, you know, after the funeral, I'm settling here and...' he smiled across at Carrie and then held Jane's eyes for a long moment, 'if either of you will have me, I'm looking for a room...'

'Well, I have two rooms going spare at the moment, so perhaps while The Marchant Inn is being put to rights, I'll go into the bed and breakfast business,' Carrie wrapped her hand around Jane's. 'Not that I'm promising a fry-up every morning, mind...' she pushed Luke fondly when he made a face.

'Really?' huge tears faltered in Jane's eyes, and she rubbed them out as though they had no place there anymore. 'I could stay with you until...' She knew Ballyglen would never be a home to her, that much she'd figured when she'd visited Conn. Luke had been relieved to hear it. 'I don't know what to say...'

'Just say you'll stay for as long as you need to and when the pub is put to rights you can make your mind up then about what happens next,' Carrie said softly.

'You know, I was thinking, last night...' Luke said.

'Yes?' Carrie smiled, she had a feeling she was going to like this idea.

'Well, The Marchant Inn, it's very old, isn't it? I mean, that whole area, it's built over a Viking settlement, right?'

He set his head at a slight angle, 'I could research its history. You never know, there might be a book in it?'

'And even if there's not, it'll certainly enhance whatever happens with the place going forward,' Carrie said.

'Let's take things one step at a time,' Jane said. 'You know, if the competition across the road could stand it, I might just look at getting in someone to run the place properly...' she looked from Carrie to Luke. 'A lunchtime food trade, all those office workers, maybe we could get a fancy coffee maker in...' she smiled, it was make-believe stuff, but it was nice to dream, all the same. She had a feeling she'd have lots of help to breathe new life into The Marchant Inn. That was all she had to think about for now, certainly she wasn't thinking beyond getting the business up and running.

New Year's Eve dawned sunny, a watery thaw was setting in and there was a sense, even in the city streets that they were teetering on a new start. Between Conn's passing and then the fire at The Marchant Inn, it seemed that time had disappeared like a fox into his den and no matter how Carrie reached for it, there was no pulling any of it back. Now, mostly it seemed unreal as she sat on the couch, wrapped up in a Foxford blanket, listening to the familiar silence of her home.

Today, for all of that, Carrie had to do the one thing that she'd been putting off for too long. She knew it was time and so she showered and scraped back her disobedient curls. It was a day for comfort and ease, she pulled out her windcheater and jeans and set off after a cup of tea. She had made an appointment for herself and Kevin with the accountant; it was time to face up to things, for both of them. They needed to know the extent of Valentina's pilfering. She couldn't go on convincing herself that things would sort themselves out so long as she kept a tight rein on the finances at The Sea Pear. She had made sure that Valentina had not cashed up since she'd spotted the discrepancies, but this had to be sorted. The last few months had opened up, however brutally at first, a conversation within herself. She had outgrown The Sea Pear and perhaps she had outgrown Kevin too, long before he'd cast her off. Even so, she couldn't just walk away from him, knowing that he was being robbed blind.

'It's worse than we thought at first. The daily takings certainly, until you noticed it, are well down on previous years. There have been quite a number of days here when the only amounts lodged to the bank are in cheque or card. There was not a penny of cash for a whole week here,' Don Hemming, the accountant, pointed to the week she'd taken off to sort things out. His carroty red hair had turned to silver over the last five years. Carrie always thought it made him look more severe. Today, it added mild constancy, maybe even a touch of wisdom to him. He had been in college with them, before he'd had a road to Damascus calling to chartered accountancy and she was glad he was the one sorting out this mess for them.

'Oh, dear God,' Kevin said, scanning through the

figures. 'We should be making twice this…' and then he caught a look that passed between Carrie and Don and maybe they didn't need to spell it out for him. 'How long has it been going on?'

'I'm so sorry, Kevin,' Carrie said gently. 'It's been going on a while, she's taken anything she could get her hands on, from the tips jar to… well, now I'd put my money on her being involved in the break-in.'

'She will have to find another job…' but his words petered off, perhaps he already knew.

'Kevin,' Carrie said gently, 'this is much bigger than just dismissing her, we have to tell the police. She's stolen from us; that means she's stolen from our creditors and the tax due to the revenue commissioners also.'

'Are we sure, we need to be sure,' his normally high colour had washed out to a faded grey and Carrie knew it was better to let the news sink in.

'And so, have we managed to break even in the run up to Christmas?' Carrie looked down through the figures before her. Margins were tight, profit came only after other overheads were covered, and even if Dublin was booming, so too were wages, insurance and every other cost that had to be paid out first.

Don took his glasses off, held them over the sheets before him. 'I'm afraid, it's worse than not making a profit.' He pulled out a sheet that looked like an official report. He handed it over to her.

Carrie sighed, 'How on earth can this have happened?'

'She's been taking at every turn and your margins are so tight…'

'Valentina?' Kevin whispered as if he might cling on to the woman he had believed her to be and then he covered his face with his hands. Carrie was not sure if he cried or if he still couldn't quite believe that this was where they'd ended up.

'But why didn't the bank contact us, I mean...' Carrie was shocked, even she hadn't expected it to be this bad.

'She's very clever. She's seen them off before they got a chance to become too suspicious. She must have all your codes and account numbers.' Don shook his head sadly.

'Probably she has Kevin's. I changed around our accounts, but I left all of his the same... you know what he's like,' Carrie said softly, her words held fondness; there was no trace of reproach. At this stage she pitied Kevin, getting angry wasn't going to make things better.

'Well, at least she won't have managed to clear out your accounts too.' Don stared at the sheets littering the table between them. 'I dread to think what state Kevin's accounts are in now,' he said sadly.

'What does it all mean? Are we finished, has she managed to bankrupt us under our very noses?' None of this gave Carrie any pleasure. After all, apart from the fact that Kevin would be devastated, it meant a pulling apart and maybe even the loss of everything they'd worked so hard for.

'Honestly, it's hard to say. The restaurant has bled a lot of vital cash. Really, at this point, or at least from what I can tell, you're starting back where you began. You'll be working off cash flow and doing your best to keep on top of paying creditors,' Don explained sombrely.

'So, what's next?' There was no point thinking about the long-term plan for the restaurant, not really. That was something she'd have to agree with Kevin, and even now it seemed that their options were far more limited than she'd have ever imagined. 'Surely there are things we should be doing to…'

'I'm afraid this is a criminal matter, we have to call the police and we need to do it before Valentina gets the chance to enter The Sea Pear again. She has emptied your business of thousands of euro, it isn't something that you can just gloss over. Fingers crossed the end of year tax cheque doesn't bounce.'

'I don't think I can face all of this,' Kevin said, staring blankly at the floor.

'I'll contact the police, but you're going to have to confront Valentina at some point,' Don said evenly.

'We'll talk to Valentina together, about the business, but the rest, what she's taken from you, you'll have to tell the police too, Kevin. You can't let her get away with this.'

'They'll send her away,' he wasn't sure how that made him feel. 'Back to Colombia, she won't want to go back there.'

'In my hat, she belongs in prison and if she thinks she's going to wriggle out of this she can think again,' Carrie said flatly.

'And as to The Sea Pear,' Don said, 'you could just fold, liquidate and start again, it might… be less messy.'

'Close up shop?' Kevin's voice was high-pitched; it was obviously the last thing he wanted. Carrie felt for him, bad enough to learn his girlfriend was stealing from him, but to see his business brought almost to its knees was too much to take in.

'I can't think about that yet, but of course you're right. We'll have to make some sort of agreement about the future of The Sea Pear. Can you draw up something so we can see what's best for all of us,' Carrie said, gathering up her coat and scarf.

'We could start over...' Kevin said through tear-filled eyes. 'We could start again, I mean, even if The Sea Pear is finished, we're a great team, Carrie, you know that...' He was pleading now.

'I'm sorry, Kevin. We *were* a great team, but I'm ready to move on now.' She could hardly look at him, the pain that weaved across his face was too much. 'I'm so sorry, if there was any other way...' she said shaking her head.

'You can't just leave me?'

'Oh, Kevin,' Carrie shook her head sadly, 'I won't leave until everything is tidied up, but I'm not going to spend the rest of my life at The Sea Pear. It's time for something new.' Carrie hadn't a clue what that might be, but her future wasn't with Kevin or The Sea Pear. It surprised her that mixed with the relief of letting go was a real sense of sadness, as if grief might be a part of walking away from this business that had become so much to her over the years.

'I see,' Kevin said and pulled himself up out of his chair so it seemed to Carrie that suddenly he was less than he'd ever been before and that just made her sad. She was glad to get out onto the street again.

'Okay?' Luke was waiting for her, they'd agreed to go for lunch and she was pleased to feel his arm about her.

'All right, Kevin, mate?' his expression full of concern.

'Well, I've had better days,' Kevin said flatly.

'Could be worse,' Luke said. 'I've just left the hospital, Jane Marchant is doing much better.'

'What? Well, that's good?' Kevin said distracted.

'She's lucky to be alive,' Carrie said.

'Those two men who broke into the pub, they torched the place and left her for dead. We're only lucky that Teddy was with her and we got her out before it was too late,' Luke said softly.

'Lucky, indeed. Luke was a true hero, he ran into the pub while the fire was raging and pulled her out.' Carrie looked up at Luke and she couldn't hide the love and pride in her eyes.

'Do they know who...?' Kevin asked.

'They were Colombian, two really nasty types, they've been hanging about Finch Street for months, one way or another. Seriously, they should be thrown in jail for attempted murder, the pair of them, if they're ever caught,' Carrie said.

'Colombian...' Kevin's voice seemed to filter in the morning air, as if something had knocked the clout from it. 'Colombian, dear God...' he said and he turned from them and headed in the direction of Finch Street.

Carrie felt a yawning sadness as they walked away from Kevin and the life they had built up together. Today, this meeting with the accountant was the beginning of the end; on her terms. Then Luke's arm around her brought her back to the present, it was time to start again and it felt as if she was starting on the right path, even if she wasn't quite sure where it was going to lead.

They couldn't put it off forever, and Carrie for one wanted it over sooner rather than later. She called to the apartment after she organised someone to drop by and change all the locks on The Sea Pear. Valentina would never set foot in the restaurant again. It was Carrie's first time here and she couldn't help but take in the opulence of the place. It really was like stepping into another world. In the elevator, she'd bumped into a couple of models that she recognised from the gossip columns. The apartment was even more impressive than she expected, with breath-taking views out across the Dublin skyline. Yet for all its opulence, it had an empty feel to it, as if it was fully furnished, but there was no ambience. Someone had forgotten to add in a vital ingredient – it was the antithesis of her lovely, homely little house.

'What is she doing here?' Valentina hardly lifted her head from the important job of painting her toenails. It was obvious that Kevin had shied away from any of the conversations he needed to have with her.

'I'm here to talk to you, actually,' Carrie said and she knew that it must have been something in her voice, because Valentina's head jerked up sharply as though alerted to some clear danger about to present itself.

'Kevin, what ees thees all about?' She dropped the nail polish and was on her feet in a turn.

'Valentina, we need to talk.'

'Oh, I see it now, she ees putting the poison in your ear about me, she ees jealous, Kevin, she always has been.'

'Oh, dear,' Carrie shook her head. 'No, Valentina, I am not jealous, but I am annoyed. I'm angry that you stole from me.'

'I didn't *steal* Kevin from you, he wanted to be with me, because I am more beautiful.'

'Actually, Valentina, I'm not even sure that you are that anymore,' Kevin said from behind her and Carrie watched as something close to madness flashed across Valentina's face.

'Oh, so now we see the truth of eet. You have no backbone, I always knew that...'

'Valentina, we know that you stole money from the restaurant,' Carrie said calmly.

'I stole money? No, now you really have lost your minds.' Valentina threw her head back and laughed hysterically, as if nothing could be further from the truth.

'We know that you stole and we know exactly how much.'

'Really? You come here, with your beeg hair and your broken heart and you think you can accuse me. Just because I am from a poor country, does not mean I steal your money.'

'We have proof, Valentina,' Kevin said firmly.

'So you are een thees too. How deed she turn you against me?' She was appealing to him now, pouring every ounce of charm she could conjure into the space between them.

'I'm not in anything. We are telling you now, because earlier today our accountant reported the theft to the police.'

'You... you, you...' and then a torrent of Colombian words filled the room and Valentina was moving in a frenzy towards Carrie. Suddenly, she was upon her, shaking her with venom that could only come from hatred. Carrie heard her jacket rip, a distant unreal sound so quietly insistent amidst the manic screaming of her attacker.

'No, Valentina, no.' Kevin was pulling her off, dragging her away from Carrie.

'It doesn't matter,' Carrie said and she straightened out her clothes, looking at Valentina now; she was only showing her true colours. 'It doesn't matter, the police will come and you can try and wheedle them, but the facts speak for themselves, Valentina. You are never to cross the threshold of The Sea Pear again because, if you do, I won't be responsible for my actions.' Carrie turned on her heels, a nervous wobbly feeling in her legs. She wasn't used to this kind of confrontation, she didn't like it, but she knew she had to face Valentina and show her that she was no fool.

'You, with your beeg bum and your bad shoes... you can't prove one theeng, not one theeng, and just wait and see. You haven't heard the last of this yet,' Valentina was shouting as Carrie made her way to the door.

Outside, Kevin walked her towards the elevator.

'I'm so sorry,' he said and she could see he was distressed at what had happened.

'I'm okay, really, she's all bark. Will you be all right?' For all of that, Carrie was glad to be getting away from Valentina; she was a very angry woman.

'I'll just go for a walk, around the courtyard. Actually, I think I'll stay outside until the police arrive.'

'Well, they should be here soon, I just spoke to them on the way over and they're going to take her in for questioning, so you'll have the place to yourself for a few hours.' Carrie wasn't sure if that was what he wanted, but she figured it was better than sharing the apartment with Valentina at this point.

Then Kevin cleared his throat. 'There's something else,' he said, his eyes digging deep into the wall behind her as if he would bury his way through it if he could get away from what was coming next. 'You should know,' Kevin's voice was leaden with news that couldn't be good, 'the two men the police were looking for in connection with the break-in?'

'Yes? They were Colombian?' Carrie had a feeling there had to be a connection to Valentina – it was just too coincidental, especially when you saw what kind of a person she really was beneath the gloss and glamour.

'It was...' he sighed, a long weary sound as if he was going through the details for the umpteenth time. 'They were arrested earlier today and...' He sighed again. 'You're going to find out anyway, they're all going to know about it in the restaurant soon enough.'

There was silence for a moment, but it didn't frighten Carrie, she had a feeling that it was just Kevin being theatrical. God how hard she'd worked over the years to keep life on an even keel so she didn't have to endure those long drawn out pauses.

'For heaven's sake, Kevin, just say it, will you?'

'Okay, they were cousins of Valentina's – the men who broke in to the restaurant, were Valentina's cousins. I had a feeling when you told me about Jane Marchant. I knew it had to be them, so I told that grumpy detective Coleman and I gave him an address to pick them up for questioning.'

'You knew where they were staying?'

'They were staying with us after they left their flat.'

'They were staying with you when the police were looking for them?' Carrie knew she sounded like a parrot, but really it was too much to take in. Kevin Mulvey, harbouring criminals – wonders would never cease, she had a feeling that one day she and Anna would laugh at this, but not yet. Not for some time to come, perhaps.

'Yes. But, I had no idea then that they were involved. Valentina said they were thrown out of their own place. I assumed they hadn't paid up the rent, or maybe had a run-in with the landlord or something like that.' Silence again.

'If they can prove it was them, the police will charge them with attempted murder, you know that?' Both Luke and Jane could identify the men they had seen in the bar. She wasn't sure if fingerprints could survive the smoke and fumes of the fire, but there was CCTV on the street and enough compassion among the detectives to make sure they got the men who left Jane to die in her own home.

'Honestly, Carrie, I had no idea.' He sounded like he might cry. 'I'm so sorry.' There was another pause. 'For everything.'

'Heaven's sake, but it's been one heck of a day for both of us,' Carrie smiled. She was looking forward to getting home, putting her feet up and having a good strong cup of tea with Teddy sitting on the hearth rug. 'At least you did the right thing, turning them in to the police. I mean, for Jane, knowing that they are behind bars, it'll give her peace of mind.' She was about to reach out, put her hand on his shoulder, when the arrival of a police car, siren raging, broke the silence between them. Just as well, perhaps, she thought, just as well.

'Hello,' Kevin moved towards the car. 'You're here for Valentina?' he said and they led the way back up to the apartment where Valentina waited in her highest heels, her lowest cut dress and probably the biggest sob story she could concoct in such little time.

It actually was not as bad as Jane expected, it was a New Year and perhaps the optimism of that helped, but really, considering what might have been, she knew it could have been much worse. The fire officer had already signed off on the structure and it was safe to walk from the cellar right to the top of The Marchant Inn.

'The smoke is probably the worst,' she confided to Carrie as they made their way through the flat she called home. 'There's not a lot we can do with so much of it. I suppose a huge skip...' Teddy barked at that, perhaps he liked the idea of a skip and clearing out the place as much as the notion appealed to Jane.

'Well, it's never a bad thing to let things go,' Carrie said softly. 'It makes room for more good stuff to come into your life.'

'That's a lovely way of putting it,' Jane said, although she had a feeling Carrie was only saying it to make her feel better.

'Why don't we take a few bits with us now?' Carrie picked up a Toby jug that had been in the pub for years. 'Just photos and little bits that are sentimental,' she said. They walked through each of the rooms, selecting knick-knacks that were precious memories in themselves. In the bedroom, Carrie wrapped Jane's few pieces of jewellery in tissue and placed them carefully in a bag. There wasn't much, not really, a photo album and her mother-in-law's recipe book, Manus's tie pin and a scarf that had long lost his scent but Jane could still conjure him up in her imagination when she held it close.

'This is probably the most precious thing I have,' Jane picked up a silver frame with herself and Manus on a day out many years earlier. They were captured in a happy moment, smiling and in love, and even now, when she looked into those eyes, it made her feel he was still close beside her. Teddy nuzzled into her knees, as if he knew exactly what was going through her mind.

They had almost filled a laundry basket with little bits and pieces that each had some sentimental value and Carrie struggled to get it down the stairs.

'We'll come back for more, but if we bring these home

and clean the smoke from them, it'll make you feel as if you've saved something from the wreckage.' Carrie loaded the basket into the back seat of her car.

'It's a strange thing, Carrie, but even with the place burned out, I don't feel as if I've lost all that much,' Jane said and the realisation had surprised her at first.

'Well, I suppose, the insurance will cover any damage, so really it's just the inconvenience,' Carrie was concentrating on pulling the car out into traffic.

'I'm not sure that's even it. Really, it's the way it's all happened. You know I could have been left for dead, but it's the idea that Luke thought enough of me to risk his own life to get me out.'

'He was very brave,' Carrie smiled wistfully.

'And not just that, but now, look at you, letting me stay in your house. I don't know when I felt more cared about.'

'So, out of the ashes…' Carrie said. They had pulled up at the traffic lights and for a moment, there was complete silence in the car.

'I want to do something for both of you,' Jane had already made up her mind. It had occurred to her in the hospital, it was something she could do easily and it was the right thing. 'I want to make you partners in The Marchant Inn, both of you.' It would give Luke another reason to stay in Dublin and she had a feeling it would be good for Carrie.

'You're not serious?' Carrie said, and then an irate driver honking behind them reminded her that the traffic lights had turned green. 'You can't just…'

'Oh, but I can.' Jane smiled. 'It would be good for all of us and I have a feeling that with the success you made of The Sea Pear, it would be good for The Marchant Inn too.' Her mind was made up and with it Jane had a feeling that it was the right thing to do for everyone, and maybe especially for herself.

Carrie rang Kevin first thing. She asked him to meet her at The Sea Pear for lunch, it was as middle ground as they had and she knew that her news would come as something of a blow.

'This is nice,' he said and she realised he'd never been so polite or appreciative when they were together. It was as if their separation had given him an odd unfamiliar respect for her. Sometimes, although she knew it was crazy, she thought she caught admiration in his eyes. But then she convinced herself, she was probably mixing up his signals. 'We should do this more often,' his voice was gentle and she sensed their purposes were very different.

'Well, neutral territory,' she said lightly. She'd cooked for him, pasta with fish and cheese and chive sauce.

'Oh?' He was wearing a musky scent, too much aftershave, as though his mother told him not to spare it.

'Sit down and eat, then we'll talk.' She took a deep breath. Her appetite was not what it had once been, but she knew she had to get this over with. Now with Kevin before her, resembling an abandoned puppy at the refuge, she wasn't sure she had the heart to go through with this.

'Carrie, can I say something?' He put down his fork,

but he'd only moved the food about his plate, like her perhaps he was too nervous to talk. 'These last few weeks, they've been…'

'Hell?' she smiled at him and they both laughed at the irony of it all.

'No, since Valentina left, actually, they've been good. They've been surprisingly good, because you've made them good. You've been here, like you've always been here, but before, I suppose I didn't really see you. Does that make sense?' It was funny, but knowing Valentina was going to get her comeuppance hadn't really given Carrie as much satisfaction as it had Kevin.

'I have a feeling that it does to you.' Carrie knew she should stop him, but she knew too that what he was going to say was long overdue. These were the things she should have been told years ago and maybe some small part of her needed to know that at some point in their relationship Kevin Mulvey had actually loved her.

'Well, there's something else too, Carrie. These last few weeks, they've made me see that I made a terrible mistake. I thought I was in love with Valentina but the truth is, I'm not sure I knew what love was. I think it wasn't until I saw you with Luke at the wedding that I realised I was in love with you. I thought the jealousy would eat me up at the wedding. I mean, I was in denial, I think, but looking back, I spent all my time trying to convince myself I was in love with Valentina and even more convincing myself that I wasn't in love with you.'

'Kevin, I don't know what to say.'

'Say you feel the same. Say you forgive me, that you

want to give things another go?' Kevin was looking at her now, expectantly, as if this might be a real possibility. Of course, the last few weeks, they'd slipped into something that might seem normal to him. She came into work each day, carried on so they could at least balance the books and make sure that all of their creditors were paid. They had been polite, friendly, kind to each other, but each evening she left him to return to Luke and Jane while he... well, she assumed he was staying in the luxurious vacuum of that apartment that had probably seemed like heaven only months ago.

'Of course I forgive you, Kevin. At this stage, there's nothing to forgive. I felt, months ago...' Carrie tried hard to find the words. She didn't want to crush him, she wouldn't want anyone to feel as she had felt that night in the rain when Luke had walked into her life. 'I felt that what you did, breaking up with me, that it was the best for both of us.' She caught his eye, could see the fear there, but she didn't love him anymore and, unlike Kevin, she couldn't pretend. 'What I mean is that when you finished with me, Kevin, we weren't in love then. We probably hadn't been for a long time, we were just going through the motions, but I didn't realise it. Then you had a taste of what it was like to fall for someone, and I...' she thought of Luke for a moment, she had learned with him what it was to be in love. Carrie smiled, 'I fell in love too. It's a love like I've never experienced before and, Kevin, now that I've tasted that, I'm sorry, but I just can't settle for anything less.' She wanted a man like Luke Gibson, who would stick by her through thick and thin. She wanted someone who was strong and stable, who had more than just good looks or a fat wallet. She wanted something that she had a feeling Kevin couldn't even begin to grasp.

'Oh. I see.' Kevin studied the table hard for a moment. Carrie felt compassion far greater than she'd ever have expected to feel for him.

'The thing is, Kevin – I wanted to talk to you today, not because of our relationship, but because I've been offered a job, well an opportunity...'

'Oh?' He raised his head slowly, his eyes darkened with a sadness she'd never seen so heavy in them before. 'The reviewing?'

'No, I'm giving that up, it really was only something to distract me, when I needed... more.' She smiled, that was the truth of it, really. It was not a job, not something she wanted to do forever.

'So, something else?'

'Yes, it's The Marchant Inn, once the work is complete, I'm going to run it for Jane.' It was all agreed, Luke had managed to secure a post in the university and they were both happy to let Carrie have the run of the place. They would be partners, even and square, but Carrie would be in charge.

'So how will it work, I mean, you can't just be giving up this place to take a job somewhere else. You're a business owner here, Carrie, even if we're just clearing our debts, we'll work our way back into healthy profits very soon.'

'No.' Carrie stopped for a moment, considered her next words carefully, then realised there was no easy way of saying them. He was already bruised, in shock perhaps, she would have to be direct, but kind. 'Jane is making me a partner, Kevin. I'm leaving The Sea Pear and starting up a new business with Luke as a silent partner. That's the reason I wanted to talk to you today, here...' she put her hands out, indicating the restaurant they'd built up together.

'Neutral ground?' he said, an echo of her earlier words, now they made sense.

'Yes. The thing is, I still have my stake in this place and I'd like to sell it to you, if you're interested, but if not, then I'll put it out for sale openly.' She tried to keep her voice as gentle as possible, but she knew that even without their earlier conversation it was a lot to take in.

'So, you're leaving me? I mean, you're leaving The Sea Pear? All that we've built up, it's all just being left behind.' His voice wobbled, the despair in it pulled at her, but she knew this was for the best, for both of them. They couldn't go back to how things were.

'It's time,' Carrie said simply and it was just that. 'This is a great opportunity, I'd be mad to pass up on it. Dublin is a small town, Kevin, and I know I can make The Marchant Inn every bit as successful as The Sea Pear.' She smiled, hoped that he didn't feel anything near the emptiness she'd felt all those months ago.

'I see.' He got up from the table. 'I'll need to think about this. I'll need to let it settle. You don't want an answer now, do you? I mean there's no rush, is there?'

'Well,' she bit her lip, just for a second, this was the hard part. 'I need to start as soon as. I want to oversee the work as the pub is being rebuilt, I can pop over and back here for the first month at least, but after that...' He needed to know that this was a final split, she would not be holding his hands once she left, he would be on his own.

'But...' Kevin said the word, seemed to stumble over what would come next. When he turned to face her, she saw he was crying. 'But, Carrie, what will I do without you?'

'I'll talk to Andrew, see if he'll take over for a couple of weeks. He's good with the rosters and all that stuff.' She was clearing off their plates; neither of them had touched their lunch. 'We'll give it a couple of weeks, but then you'll have to make a decision, Kevin. I'm not coming back to The Sea Pear. You need to know that, the question for you now is if you want to run it on your own or if you'd prefer to take on a new partner.' She was standing squarely before him. They were equals; however, it was only now, as she was about to leave, that he was ready or able to admit it. 'I'm sorry, it's just business, Kevin, you know, it's not that I'm leaving you personally, that was all done and dusted months ago, right?'

They sat for a while in silence, perhaps just taking in all that they'd built up between them. It was a little strange to think she'd be leaving this place behind soon, but also, strangely liberating.

He hated the apartment now that Valentina had left. Strictly speaking, he had asked her to leave, but it had taken time, terrible, awful days when she had been in and out of the local police station and when she was here, she screamed at him and made him feel as if he was in the wrong. By the time he eventually got his key back, he hardly knew why he wanted her in the first place. It seemed that from the very beginning things had started to disintegrate between them.

'Where is the ring I bought you?' Because the rest of it, the clothes and shoes and bags, they were worthless now, not that she had left them lying around, they had been packed up and moved to somewhere new.

'I sold eet. Eet was mine to sell or are you going to say I stole that too?' She was still claiming her innocence, even here. 'It was only worth ten thousand euro, in the end.'

'Ten thousand euros?' he felt himself fall back into the sofa, he was lucky to be able say the words. 'But, Valentina, that cost...' he couldn't even think about the cost of it, knew this too was a lie, it had been worth far more than that. Later he wondered how he hadn't had a stroke there and then.

'You should be paying me to finish our engagement,' she'd said, twirling her long dark hair through red talons that had begun to revolt him more every day. Occasionally, he wondered how they had at one time been so attractive. 'You have put my friends in jail and eet looks like you will do the same to me, if you get the chance. I theenk, for all I have put up weeth from you, that this money is the least I should have.' She was as cool as a breeze and there wasn't a thing he could do about it.

373

Her bags were packed, thousands of euro in clothes and shoes were gone, her wardrobe yawned wide, with just a few straggling hangers left and old clothes that she no longer wanted.

'It's only fair if we agree it. You can't just sell it on, you've taken too much already.' He still shivered at his own stupidity. Would he have known? When would he have realised, had it not been for Carrie. Carrie had been contrite, she'd wanted to break it to him gently, but what with Luke's father passing away so suddenly and then the fire at The Marchant Inn, it seemed that Kevin had fallen even further down her list of responsibilities. He had a feeling that she'd put it off as much to spare his feelings as anything else and that only made him feel even worse. 'It's daylight robbery.'

'I theenk, Keveen, that if you decide to challenge me on this, you will find it very hard to prove that you didn't pay me for my services,' she'd smiled at him. 'I wonder, would your mother enjoy hearing what you liked me to do for you een the bedroom? Or some of your fancy customers? How would they feel if they realised you took advantage of a poor girl from Colombia?' They were pressing charges for the theft at the restaurant, but Valentina would go and do the same thing to the next unsuspecting man she met if something wasn't done to stop her.

'That's blackmail, pure and simple, Valentina,' he'd said.

'You can call eet that, but if you try to tell the police that I have taken anything from you, I will make sure that you are a laughing stock in Dublin. You weell never be able to face your friends or your customers again.'

'Well, now we know.' She was right, of course, he didn't really want a court case, but on the other hand, he couldn't face Carrie if he let Valentina get away with this. For her part, Valentina guessed he couldn't face the indignity of having her suggest that he paid to have her pretend to be his girlfriend. Maybe it was worse, because he'd always known that if he didn't own The Sea Pear and drive a nice car, Valentina wouldn't have given him a second glance. Yes. That was true, he'd known it all along. Funny, because he hadn't quite thought about it like that before. 'What will you do now?' he asked, because he had a sense that she had already made plans.

'I will be helping the band weeth their costumes,' she'd said, a little imperiously, considering when she arrived in Dublin she was hardly qualified to clear tables. 'They are going on tour in a week, so you won't be seeing me around Dublin again.'

Instead of being heartbroken, Kevin had felt an odd sense of liberation, as if she'd let him off the hook. It was absurd, he knew, to be such a coward, but he couldn't change now. She was walking out the door with thousands of euro's worth of clothes and jewellery and he'd felt nothing but relief. When the door closed, Kevin had picked up his phone.

'Hello, Detective Sergeant Coleman?' he'd asked for the older, cynical policeman who had seen straight through him that day in the restaurant. There was no hiding the truth from this man, he could see Kevin for the spineless man he was. 'I've just had a conversation with Valentina and, strangely enough, I must have pressed record on my phone... you might like to hear it, there's an admission of blackmail on there, at the very least.'

'Well, now, that's very convenient,' the detective had murmured.

'I think Valentina plans to leave the country,' Kevin said into the phone. On this occasion, he was going to make sure she got what was coming to her. He gave the detective all the information he had about the bands' plans to tour, or as much as he could.

'Well, that lady is going nowhere,' the grumpy old police officer said with a wheeze. 'We'll be taking her in right away.' Kevin put down the phone with a degree of satisfaction he hadn't known before. Valentina, Simo and Reda would spend years in prison, and in Kevin's opinion, if they threw away the key, the world would probably be a better place without any of them.

'They saw you coming, mate,' Jim said when he told him about Simo and Reda.

'What do you mean by that?' They hadn't met for a pint since the wedding. Jim just hadn't shown up and, in the end, Kevin rang to see if they were okay. So, Jim turned up a week later, his same disgruntled, philosophical self.

'Sure, there you are, sitting on a nice business, falling for the questionable charms of Valentina for a start.'

'That hardly makes me a target for burglary?' Kevin

said, wondering for a moment if this friendship would have gone south had he not rung up Jim.

'You said yourself they were always looking to do "security" for the restaurant. They bullied their way into your home.'

'Ah, now, hang on a minute; they were only staying as a favour to Valentina...' It turned out they weren't even related to her. Rather, like rats, they had banded together, but now, in custody, they were each happily blaming one another in an effort to get off more lightly themselves.

'Exactly, but, can't you see what a tyrant Valentina was? We all saw it at the wedding, mate. A few of us had a bit of a book going that you'd probably be a victim of domestic violence. She is a very angry woman.'

'She was.' Kevin had to concede on that, but of course, he'd never tell his friend that she threw things at him and had hit him twice. He couldn't face telling anyone that, especially not when he'd crowed so loud about how lucky he was to have such a beautiful woman on his arm.

'All kinds of beautiful, mate, and it's only skin deep, but that kind of ugliness goes to the bone,' Jim said as though he'd read his mind. 'So, you've kicked her out.' It was a statement of fact, rather than a question.

'Well, she's gone now, yes.'

'And you finished it?' Jim hadn't liked her even before he heard about Simo and Reda. 'Tell me you had enough backbone to finish it.'

'Yes, I finished it. But she didn't leave until she was ready to go,' Kevin said. There was no point lying. 'She waited until she found...'

'Another mug? Someone else to go to, you mean?'

'Remember the boy band? Well, she planned on moving on with them when they went on tour.' Then a sliver of a smile made its way onto Kevin's lips, 'Only, I contacted the police and now she's locked up safe and sound.'

'Good, I'd hate to think of her moving on to some other sap, where would be the justice in that.'

'To tell you the truth, by the time she left, I didn't think it mattered where she went, still it's nice to think she's behind bars and she's not under my roof anymore.' Technically, it wouldn't be his roof for much longer. He knew he had to tell Jim about his house-moving plans. 'She cleaned me out Jim, weeks ago. It's all gone. She even flogged the engagement ring.'

'You can press charges?'

'Oh, yes, I think that will be just an afternoon in court, she will plead guilty and...' It had all backfired on Valentina, the police had only played a little of the recording he'd made, and in the words of Detective Sergeant Coleman, she'd sung like a canary. Kevin didn't want to go to court over it, but now it would be a case of a guilty plea and a verdict handed down. It would hardly make the papers; still, his mother would probably have a conniption, if she didn't have a heart attack with the shame of it.

'Seems like she was a bad lot from the start, mate,' Jim sighed, sank his pint in one long swallow. 'Another?' he pointed towards Kevin's glass, his eyebrows rose slightly.

'Why not? I deserve a night off,' he said. He knew he would end up sliding off this bar stool after three pints and slinking home to face the mother of all hangovers tomorrow. Truth was, he needed to suffer and he needed to forget. It'd be his last hangover for a while. He would be moving in with his mother next month, or sooner if he could get a new tenant to sub-lease the apartment. There was time enough to tell Jim that. After all, there was only so much humiliation a man could face in one day.

Epilogue

Six Months Later

Carrie stood in the centre of The Marchant Inn. There was a lingering smell of new paint and polished brasses, they managed to save the best of what had been here for years and match it with a modern, elegant finish. Gone were the built-in brocade seating, Formica-topped tables and heavy bar stools. Carrie had retained and restored the bar counter, the ornate ceiling and what had survived of the stained glass, but everything else had an upstate New York cool sophistication to it. It was almost hard to believe that it could have turned out so well. She had mixed simplicity with antiquity and managed to come up with a chic style that fitted well with who she was and what she wanted to project to customers. Each table was set, generously, but simply, a theme of white with a simple chrome ring, mirrored in the graceful centrepiece – a single camellia on each.

'Opening night,' Luke said and he handed her a glass of champagne. They would have a full house soon, surrounded by well-wishers. She had even invited Kevin, although she doubted he'd show up. Her own mother was making up for him, Pamela rang earlier to say she was bringing along that nice detective who was taking care of the case against Valentina. Carrie smiled, thinking of the gruff Coleman, and wondered if perhaps he could remain so stony-faced with her mother at his side. She hadn't extended an invitation to Maureen Mulvey, maybe she'd invite her over at some stage, but not tonight. This evening was about friends and family and Carrie had enough of both to fill this place ten times over.

'I shouldn't really,' she said, smiling. It wasn't nerves that made her insides flip when she caught the light aroma of bubbles, but she'd only figured out today what made her feel as if she was just a little more of everything she'd been before.

'Everything is perfect, you can afford a sip or two before we kick off.'

'Yes, Luke,' Carrie said, feeling a new-found weight-lessness bubble up inside her, 'everything is perfect.' And it was, they had settled into a new life together. It turned out that the upstairs flat, like the bar – a warren of darkened closed-up rooms – was far bigger when they opened it up than Carrie's little house. So, they'd moved in and made a home of it, leaving Jane in the cosy house she adored. Luke had fallen into a job he loved. The university was just a stone's throw away and life had taken on a new but contented rhythm. It turned out they wanted the same things – but then, doesn't everyone? To be loved, to be cherished and to belong – they had found that in each other. The worst events may have thrown them together, but the future looked brighter than either of them could have ever dared to dream.

Against her leg, Teddy looked up, his expression filled with curiosity; she bent down and patted him gently on his silky head. Carrie knew that The Marchant Inn would be a huge success, already they had bookings taken into the following year and they hadn't even opened their doors yet. 'It's more perfect than I could have hoped for,' she clinked his glass, then put down her own. 'I don't think that the champagne would put me too much off course for one night, it's just…' she smiled then and if he knew what she was going to say next, he waited until she had the chance to tell him. 'We're having a baby,' she said and when he wrapped his arms around her, she knew this happiness was real and she had a feeling that none of them would ever be lonely again.

Thank you

Thank you, lovely reader,

For picking my story out of the endless sea of books, you might have chosen. When I write a book, I hope it's a story that touches readers. I love the idea that the time spent within these covers might lift your spirits and, in some way, give you a sense that there is always time for another chance. I believe that life, in its own way, has a habit of putting what you need in your path and, with a little luck, things can turn out well in the end.

There's nothing nicer than hearing back from readers. I'd love to hear your thoughts on this story, so if you have time, please do post a short review or share it on social media – on Twitter or find me on Facebook there's something very moving about reading a review that really 'gets' the book!

If you enjoyed this book and you want to keep an eye on what I'm up to next, you could pop over to my website and sign up for my newsletter www.faithhogan. com and I'll do my very best to keep you amused.

Finally, if you follow me on BookBub you can find out all about new releases and when my books are on promotion.

Till next time,

Faith xx

Acknowledgements

It seems unreal that I'm at the end of another story, saying goodbye to Carrie, Jane, Luke, and even Kevin – I will miss them all, especially Teddy. This book came to an end at one of those times when it seemed that life had every intention of stepping in the way, but here we are…

Now, all that remains is to thank the people who have helped to bring it out into the world.

I've dedicated this book to the Aria Girls, it is my way of saying thank you for so many things that I can't even begin to put into words. Caroline Ridding, for your loyalty, hard work, kindness and infectious good humour. You have given me the best opportunity and I am still so very grateful to you. Honestly, I'm still pinching myself that I get to call you my publisher. Thank you also to Sarah Ritherdon, Lucy Gilmour, Melanie Price, Nikky Ward, Jade Craddock, Geo Willis, Sue Lamprell, Michelle Jones and new girls – Vicky Joss and Hannah Smith, who between you all will shape and shift this manuscript as only you can on its way into the world! Thank you all so much for your continued support and good humour – it's a joy to work with you.

With this book, as with all writerly, reading, film watching and publishing questions, I have to give sincere thanks to Judith Murdoch, my wise and witty agent – I am lucky to have you, I do love our chats!

To my early readers – Eilish Munnelly, Anne-Marie McLoughlin, Marcella Hogan, Anne-Marie Gilvarry, Fiona Brady, Teresa Canavan, Mabel Snee, Orla Holmes, Mary Mermet and Mary Devaney-Doherty. Thank you to Silke Kauther-Ginty and Michelle McGovern, for reading and putting up with me – it's very much appreciated!

Thanks to Bernadine Cafferkey for reading the early drafts – your opinion means everything. Thank you too for stepping in as my glamorous publicist at book signings and generally minding me and encouraging me all the way through xx

To Christine Cafferkey, thank you for keeping us all on the road, for lighting candles and doing far more than your share of the worrying – you know you're the best xx

To Seán, Roisín, Tomás and Cristín, each year just gets better with you lot, thanks for being just lovely xx

To James, you know that I loved writing this story, but books don't just happen. I'm not sure if the title of this book is settled yet – but you know, that all those years ago, you were the one that changed everything xx

Finally, thanks to you, the reader, for choosing my book, I hope you've enjoyed reading it as much I've enjoyed writing it!

ABOUT THE AUTHOR

FAITH HOGAN lives in the west of
Ireland with her husband, four
children and two very fussy cats.
She has an Hons Degree in
English Literature and Psychology,
has worked as a fashion model
and in the intellectual disability
and mental health sector.

Hello from Aria

We hope you enjoyed this book! If you did, let us know, we'd love to hear from you.

We are Aria, a dynamic digital-first fiction imprint from award-winning independent publishers Head of Zeus. At heart, we're committed to publishing fantastic commercial fiction – from romance and sagas to crime, thrillers and historical fiction. Visit us online and discover a community of like-minded fiction fans!

We're also on the look out for tomorrow's superstar authors. So, if you're a budding writer looking for a publisher, we'd love to hear from you. You can submit your book online at ariafiction.com/ we-want-read-your-book

You can find us at:
Email: aria@headofzeus.com
Website: www.ariafiction.com
Submissions: www.ariafiction.com/ we-want-read-your-book

🅕 @ariafiction
🐦 @Aria_Fiction
📷 @ariafiction